Antique Trader®
COLLECTIBLE
PAPERBACK

PRICE GUIDE

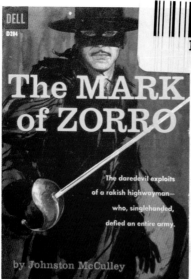

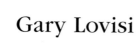

Gary Lovisi

©2008 Gary Lovisi

Published by

kp **krause publications**

An Imprint of F+W Publications

700 East State Street • Iola, WI 54990-0001
715-445-2214 • 888-457-2873
www.krausebooks.com

Our toll-free number to place an order or obtain a free catalog is (800) 258-0929.

Library of Congress Control Number: 2007934358

ISBN-13: 978-0-89689-634-5
ISBN-10: 0-89689-634-X

Designed by Donna Mummery
Edited by Mary Sieber

Printed in China

DEDICATION

This book is dedicated to the many friends who have left us far too soon: Lance Casebeer, John Garbarino, Kevin Hancer, Richard Lieberson, Bill Lyles, Wayne Mullins, Al Newgarten, Paul Payne, Tony Scibella, Blake Shira, Bill Wegerer, Jon White and Jaye Zimet.

I also want to recognize a special group of writers and artists who have passed away. They were always helpful and giving of themselves to fans and researchers and will never be forgotten: Michael Avallone, James Avati, Robert Bloch, A. I. Bezzerides, Howard Browne, Bruce Cassidy, Julie Ellis, Bruno Fischer, Kelly Freas, Ted Gottfried, Charles N. Heckelmann, Robert Jonas, Robert Maguire, Denis McLoughlin, Stanley Meltzoff, Paul S. Meskil, Walter Popp, Richard S. Prather, Howard Schoenfeld, Gordon D. Shirreffs, Henry Slesar, Dan Sontup, George H. Smith, Mickey Spillane, A. E. van Vogt, and Walter Wager.

TABLE OF CONTENTS

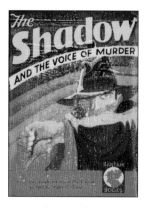

INTRODUCTION

Paperback books are to be found everywhere. These ubiquitous softcovers turn up at flea markets, yard sales, estate sales, book shows, and just about every place people gather to buy and sell collectibles and antiques. However, can you tell collectible and valuable editions from the many common ones of little value?

This book features listings with up-to-date price values for thousands of the most collectible American mass-market paperbacks in three grades of condition. It includes more than 1,000 full-color photos of editions prized by collectors worldwide. There's never been a book that covers the valuable high points so well and shows so many gorgeous full-color cover reproductions. The aim of this book is to offer useful information to collectors and dealers, and expand awareness of these wonderful books among antiques collectors and the general public, all of whom should be seeking them out.

So how do you tell the difference between a $1 book and one worth $100? The information herein will give you the tools you need to identify valuable collectible editions. Paperback treasure is literally out there waiting to be discovered, if you know where to look and what to look for. This book contains everything you need to know about finding, collecting, valuing, buying, and selling collectible paperback books. It includes information on key authors, important artists, hot series, a glossary of terms, author pseudonyms, recommended dealers, and book shows. It is your one-stop essential guide to this exciting and growing hobby. Individual book listings also note many curious items of collector interest, such as scarce or low print run editions, books recalled because of copyright problems, cover art errors, and more.

Paperbacks have been with us since the 1940s, so most of us have grown up with them. Today, they mirror our youth, our culture – the way we were. Vintage era paperbacks from the 1940s to the 1960s, and even more current editions, offer some of the most fascinating areas of popular culture for fans and collectors as well as much fun and enjoyment. There's something here for every taste – every interest or style – literally something for everyone.

I have chosen some of the most important covers, as well as ones featuring interesting, exploitative, campy or sexy art, to display in this book. I have also included some humorous or provocative cover blurbs that show how these books were marketed to the reading public at the time. However, it is the cover art that has always sold these books. The covers are wonderful advertisements for the books, like miniature movie posters, and they evoke the times in which they were created and should be looked at and appreciated in those terms.

Because of the lack of knowledge about the value of many paperback editions – even by some booksellers – it is still possible to find some for inexpensive prices. You can find them at book shows and on Internet sites, but you can still find them much cheaper – sometimes for as little as a quarter – at flea markets, yard sales, and estate sales. Paperbacks are everywhere, all you have to do is look, and now you'll know what to look for. And while the older vintage era editions are not seen as often these days, there is still much to find that is worthwhile and collectible.

This book is a celebration of the paperback book and all the wonderful cover art, a homage to all the writers, artists, editors, and publishers, who without knowing it – and without even trying sometimes – created little masterpieces that have stood the test of time. They made these books beautiful, sexy, passionate, and sometimes provocative or exploitative – but never dull or boring! Many people bought these books just because of the cover art. Publishers understood this. Often the covers are simply gorgeous, full of action or passion, sometimes having little or nothing to do with the story inside. None of that matters to collectors who eagerly acquire them for their cover art. This book showcases some of the most interesting of these covers. Regardless of your interest, paperbacks are fun to collect and are fascinating cultural icons. I am sure this book will open up a new and wonderful world for you.

Lastly, a book like this could not have been written without the help and support of many fine people. I'd like to acknowledge the vision of Paul Kennedy and the editorial team at Krause Publications for seeing the need for such a book in the collectibles field and allowing me to create it. I'd also like to thank my editor, Mary Sieber,

who was always helpful with the many questions and problems that crop up on a project as large and complicated as this one. I'd also like to thank the many fine collectors and book dealers who helped me: Tom Lesser, Bruce Edwards, Rose Idlet of Black Ace Books, Mark Goodman of Green Lion Books, Rahn Kollander, David Cochrane of D.C.'s Collectible Book Auctions, Chris Eckhoff, Lynn Munroe, Tim Murphy, Steve Santi, and Dan Roberts. Their help and support has been essential. I would also like to thank the following authors for their help in answering questions about themselves and their work: Victor J. Banis, Ed Hoch, James Reasoner, Ann Bannon, Marijane Meaker, and Ron Goulart. And lastly, I would like to thank my wife, the young and lovely Lucille.

Gary Lovisi
Brooklyn, New York
August 2007

10¢

DELL BOOK 21

REX STOUT

door to death

A NERO WOLFE MYSTERY

An unusual role for Nero Wolfe — he personally trails a killer.

COMPLETE AND UNABRIDGED

THE VINTAGE-ERA MASS-MARKET PAPERBACK

It was called "the paperback revolution" and it really was a revolution and evolution in the way books were published and sold. It offered inexpensive paperback books to the public for the first time in thousands of non-traditional book outlets that reached the masses. Beginning in the 1940s, nearly every retail establishment, from corner cigar store or magazine stand to supermarket, drug store, train station, and airport, offered the latest paperbacks for sale. People who had never been in a bookstore were now exposed to the best in books – and sometimes *not* the best – in these inexpensive paperback editions.

Paperback publishers were able to do this because of what became known as the "mass-market" system of distribution. By offering "returns" on all unsold books distributed to retail outlets – what was, in effect, books on consignment – sellers encountered no risk and were very predisposed to allow jobbers and route men to set up paperback racks in their stores. Books had never been marketed this way before, and the result was a huge success. It wasn't long before mass-market paperbacks were being sold everywhere, and they sold like crazy. The public couldn't get enough of them.

The mass-market paperback was first introduced by Robert de Graff in 1938 with a 2,000 copy no-numbered Pocket Book edition of *The Good Earth* by Pearl Buck. It was a special trial edition only distributed in New York City. Since that success, a hoard of publishers churned them out in every imaginable genre and topic, from romance to science fiction, JD books (juvenile delinquency) to sleaze (early 1960s soft-core adult novels), as well as more traditional westerns, mysteries, historical novels, bestsellers, cartoon books, game books, and a lot more – even classics and

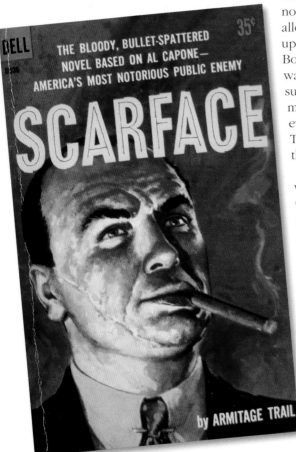

DELL

D336

35¢

THE BLOODY, BULLET-SPATTERED NOVEL BASED ON AL CAPONE— AMERICA'S MOST NOTORIOUS PUBLIC ENEMY

SCARFACE

by ARMITAGE TRAIL

quality literature. It was a glorious time of experimentation, with fly-by-the-seat-of-your-pants publishing, super creativity, and fierce competition that spawned some wonderful and quirky books, many graced by magnificent cover art.

My own theory is that in the early days of the 1940s there were basically two modes of philosophy in paperback publishing, what I call "top-down" and "bottom-up" publishing.

Top-down publishers had lofty goals; they espoused them in their marketing and advertising. Outfits such as Signet Books (New American Library) with its motto, "Good Books for the Millions," was an Americanization of the more proletarian "good books for the masses." Other publishers with similar outlooks included Pocket Books and Bantam Books, all founded and run by strong traditional book men.

What I call "bottom-up" publishers were different. These were first and foremost businessmen who wanted to make money. Most were successful publishers in the pulp and comic book areas who went into paperbacks because it was the new "in thing," and they saw they could make a profit. And they did. Entrepreneurial businessmen and publishers such as A. A. Wyn (Ace Books), Ned Pines (Popular Library), Martin Goodman (Lion Books), and Joseph Myers (Avon Books) each gave the field books that showed their pulp magazine influences and origins, and with it, excitement and passion in design and cover art that sold these books by the truckloads. A melding of these two basic philosophies created a dynamic marketplace and exciting paperback editions that the public loved during the era of the 1940s to the 1960s, and still love today.

HOW TO START A COLLECTION AND WHAT TO COLLECT

People invariably ask me how I obtained so many paperback books. I have a collection of tens of thousands of paperbacks of all kinds, which make up the bulk of the listings and images found throughout this book. I tell them while Rome wasn't built in a day, neither is a serious collection. Mine is a collection built like most collections, over many years. In my case, ever since I was a 12-year-old boy growing up in the 1960s reading Ace and Ballantine science fiction and the adventure

novels of Edgar Rice Burroughs. The collecting bug bit me early when I began to save the books I liked best, planning to reread them another day so as to relive the adventures and thrills. As I saved these books, I couldn't help looking through them, noticing the various editions, different publishers, wonderful cover art, and mooning over all those mysterious ads in the backs of the books for other paperbacks offered for sale by that publisher. It was a magic time for a 12-year-old boy. I

know many readers, fans, collectors, and authors who have felt that very same magic.

Over the years my reading tastes evolved, with more and different authors and more books of all types, into what has become an innate appreciation and understanding of the importance of all written works. I like them all, classics to sleaze, literature to the so-called hacks. It all has its special place, purpose, and value.

However, my advice to anyone contemplating collecting these books is simple: Collect what you like, what interests you, what you enjoy. Collect what turns you on. Listen to your heart, listen to your passion. Then you'll always be happy with your collection and cherish the books you have.

Paperback collectors are an eclectic group; lawyers, academics, and authors mingle with mailmen, homemakers, students, and more. They collect everything – favorite authors certainly, and by genre (science fiction or mysteries), but also sub-genres (hard-boiled crime, drug books, or science fiction romance) and just about everything in between.

One male collector whose then-current girlfriend was a blonde collected paperbacks with the word "blonde" in the title (of which there are a surprising number); another collected "bodies in bathtubs," a popular art motif for murder mysteries. Still another collector had a thing for gorilla covers, while a young woman I know well who is not a blonde likes covers that show upside-down dead girls – *especially* blondes! I like them all, and then some!

You can always go to shows and find books, but when you do that expect to pay show prices. After looking through this book, you will have an awareness of the wonderful variety and diversity available with collectible paperbacks and undoubtedly begin to seek out some of these books for yourself. The dealers and shows listed in this book will be an invaluable source for your search. You may also find paperbacks at flea markets, thrift stores, and estate sales – where the bargains are. There is nothing like the thrill of the hunt and the feeling of satisfaction when you make a great find. With such a variety of paperback material out there, you should be limited only by your budget and imagination. Half the fun is in the finding – so good hunting!

CONDITION AND VALUES

It is important to note that all the paperbacks listed in this book are *first printings for that publisher only* unless otherwise noted. Some editions will further be described as "paperback originals," "first book editions," or "first paperback printings." See the glossary for detailed definitions of these terms. Where there is no notation, the book will always be a first paperback printing for that particular publisher only.

With that understood, we can now look at the most important thing to remember when dealing with the value of collectible paperbacks. That is the importance of condition.

Collectors and dealers are sticklers for condition. It is a trend that is important across the board with all collectibles, and with collectible paperbacks as well. Condition, condition, condition should be your three bywords.

The prices listed in this book reflect current market trends, sales, and the consensus of various experts. Books in "Good" condition are valued at substantially lower prices, while books in strict "Fine" condition are valued at a premium.

I cannot stress enough the importance condition plays in the value and prices of these books. And the most important aspect about the condition of a collectible paperback is being able to grade it properly.

While this book shows values for each book listed in three condition grades, books can, and do, often sell for prices substantially higher or lower. Every effort has been taken to ensure the prices here are up-to-date as to value, but nothing is written in stone with collectibles, and that includes paperback books. And many collectors and dealers like it that way just fine. It offers them room to maneuver, to negotiate, and to deal. You can still find a $100 book for $1 at a flea market. You can still buy single books or lots from fellow collectors or dealers for substantially less than the prices in this book. You can also pay heavily in auctions for many books, sometimes in excess of the value listed herein. However, it all seems to balance out in the end if you are a collector.

The three grades of condition for paperbacks

It is crucial to grade paperbacks properly and accurately. Most dealers and longtime collectors have been grading books for decades and do it well. It can be part science, part art, and a lot of careful observation. Collectors and dealers with experience are often very strict in their grading and often bend over backwards to ensure that books are described properly and accurately. All defects should always be noted. It is a matter of professional pride and honor with them, as well as just keen business sense to make sure that their buyers are happy and never disappointed with a book because of inaccurate grading. This book includes values for the following three grades:

Fine (F):

"Fine" is the highest grade for a collectible paperback and has been acknowledged so by most collectors and dealers in the hobby for decades. A "Fine" condition book is essentially an "as new" book. Such a book will have white pages, no spine roll, no cover creases, no cover fading or tears. It will have a strong, tight binding with no loose pages, loose cover, or peeling lamination. There will be no cover markings or writing of any kind. There should not even be the normal, general wear seen on most paperbacks of the 1940s and 1950s, and color registration should be sharp and accurate.

A "Fine" paperback may be one that has never been read, or read once very carefully. There will be no condition defects on a book in this grade; the cover and cover art will be bright and sharp.

This condition is not common in the paperbacks of the vintage era (1939-1969). Collectors of books from this era must often accept books in a lesser grade. This is because the supply of truly "Fine" copies is so limited, and the price of these copies is at a premium. True "Fine" copies of vintage paperbacks can best be described as somewhat comparable to "Mile High" comic books in the quality of condition. Paperbacks from the 1970s and onward, because of their relative recent publication, often higher print runs, and better distribution are required by most collectors to be in a minimum of "Fine" or at least "VG+." Most of the books from this recent era are more easily available in higher grades of condition.

Nevertheless, a book must be in strict "Fine" condition to warrant the "Fine" condition value. While a number of books are rare or scarce in any condition, it should be noted a large number, while common in "Good" or "Very Good" condition, are scarce in "Fine" only – a term also known as "scarce in condition." Some paperbacks are rarely ever seen in this pristine state, hence the high value.

Very Good (VG):

This condition has many gradations. Books can be and often are described on dealer's lists and on auctions as simply VG; but also SVG (solid "Very Good"). However, there is also VG+, VG-, and even "about VG," so you see there can be a lot of give and take in this area. The main thing to remember here is that "Very Good" is usually the minimum condition acceptable for any collectible paperback by most collectors and dealers.

The only exception to this may be on some of the high-priced "key" editions. Those books in lesser condition grades are often used as "fillers" until a better condition copy comes along, or as a "reading copy." Dealers usually stay away from buying for resale most paperbacks in anything in less than a solid VG condition.

"Very Good" condition books often have a variety of minor defects or even one fairly major defect. These can include almost everything not allowed as a defect in a "Fine" condition book. However, paperbacks in VG will always be complete books, there will never be a missing cover (or missing back cover), no loose cover or pages, and never a missing interior page. The book will be complete and readable.

There are a variety of defects allowed in VG condition books. These should be relatively minor flaws, but there may be up to three or four of them. Taken as a whole, the defects should in no way equal more than any one major defect. Some of these more common defects include: overall general wear, light scuffing to the spine or edges, but much less so to the cover and never seriously affecting the art. A minor cover crease or two, or a group of very tiny cover creases known as "spiderweb creasing" is allowed. Pages and paper on vintage era books often turn yellow with age, some have very light browning. That is normal for the paper and age for a VG book, but the paper or pages should never be brown, never brittle. There may be one moderate to large cover crease that may be the only major defect allowed, or a sticker on the cover that can be carefully removed. No tape is allowed. There may be the beginnings of some lamination peel to the edges. It can include a bookstore stamp inside, or a previous owner's bookplate or stamp inside, which should also be noted in any description. There can be one or two of the following problems: a slight spine roll, a remainder saw cut, a small tear or two (if not on the front cover), a tiny tear on an interior page, a small reading crease parallel to the spine, very light warping, or a small back cover stain. A front cover stain could mar the cover art and might bring the book down to a VG- or even a G+. One or two of the above defects in a major way could also bring the book down to a VG-, while more severe wear or damage may cause it to drop down even lower in condition. In many cases, since the art is so often important to the collectibility of many of these books, anything that mars or damages the cover or cover art (even a minor defect) can often seriously affect the collectibility and value of

that book and drop it down in grade and, hence, value.

Good (G):

While the collector's term is called "Good," that does not mean these are good books for collectors. They are not, generally. Books in this grade, while always complete, are often too heavily worn or have considerable damage for most serious collectors (or investors/collectors) to include as a permanent part of their collections. Some collectors do keep select "Good" condition copies as fillers (mostly for key expensive books that are hard to find) or as reading copies.

"Good" condition books will have all of the condition problems described above for VG books, but more severe than VG, with often extensive damage. Sometimes "Good" books will have multiples of various problems listed in VG. For instance, while two or three minor problems might make the book a VG, five or more minor problems could put the book in "Good" only. Usually, though, there are one or two major defects that are so serious they destroy the collectibility of the book and place it clearly in the "Good" category. These "Good" copies are generally heavily worn or damaged so badly that most collectors will not include them in their collections. Dealers generally shun them.

"Good" condition copies will have major wear, serious damage, multiple tears, tape, cover creases, stains, warps, brown pages, loose pages, loose cover, binding problems, heavy lamination peel, or the lamination is entirely gone. There can be significant insect damage, whole punches, markings on the cover or insides, sticker pull affecting the cover, severe spine roll, spine tears, and sometimes all of these defects together! Nevertheless, they are always complete books. Paperbacks without front covers, or not complete, are not collectible and have no value.

However, for some collectors who do not care about condition (and there are plenty of these, too), "Good" condition copies offer an inexpensive way to obtain copies of books that may be otherwise unattainable to them on their budget. Many people on limited book budgets or fixed incomes collect "Good" condition copies and get just as much enjoyment from the books and the hobby as a collector with all "Fine" copies. These fans often care more about what is inside the book than the way it looks. However, when or if you decide to sell your books, you will have a lot easier time of it and be able to make a more lucrative deal if you're selling a VG or VG+ collection versus a merely "Good" condition collection. The harsh truth is that you may have trouble selling a collection of merely "Good" condition copies to a dealer or getting your asking price. Such a "Good"-only collection would amount to a grouping of "fillers" or "reading copies." However, since you will have paid very little for the books in the first place, and you've read and enjoyed the books along with having the pleasure of owning them for a time, that is a considerable plus for any reader and book lover. However, some people do pay from $10-$30 for reading copies of PBOs that have never been reprinted, so certain editions (listed in this book) in only "Good" condition do have value.

About the covers shown in this book

My aim is to showcase what I consider the best variety of paperback covers with the best art. That does not necessarily mean only key or high-value editions. LA Bantams with non-illustrative covers have only text, every cover has the exact same design, so I've included only one of them here; even though all are rare, they all look the same. (I *have* included some of the illustrated cover versions). Armed Service Editions likewise all have a similar cover design so I have not shown many of these. The color cover reproductions herein feature many of the best covers on collectible paperbacks of all kinds. These are the most colorful, fantastic, outrageous, sexy, violent, weird, lurid, perhaps exploitative, and sometimes even politically incorrect images – within the bounds of acceptable taste and scholarly interest. With that in mind, about half the covers pictured show key books while the rest are just interesting for one reason or another.

About the paperbacks listed in this book

Of the thousands of paperbacks listed in this book, I have included as many high-value editions as possible. This is the cream of the crop of collectible paperbacks. However, representative samples by important artists, authors, genres, cover art motifs, items of historical interest, pseudonymous works, plagiaries, errors, and anything else I feel might be of interest or importance to the collector of paperback books also appear.

About the price structure in this book

This is always the most controversial part of any such book. To begin with, you should note that prices listed here are only to be used as a general guide. They are based on my many years of experience in the hobby and determined through my collecting experience, as well as writing about paperbacks, buying and selling paperbacks, publishing *Paperback Parade*, the leading magazine in the field, and sponsoring the New York paperback show for 20 years. For years I have been deeply involved in all aspects of this hobby, interacting closely with collectors and dealers, sometimes on a daily basis. I keenly follow dealer listings, sales news, and auction results of key books to spot market trends and collector interests. My collecting and knowledge of hardcover books, pulps, and comics also help me understand the crossover interest paperbacks have in other collecting areas and their vast potential.

Since dealers and collectors put a premium on condition, I believe premium condition books deserve premium price values. With many of these books more than 50 years old, they are beginning to disappear and are not often seen in pristine condition. That means that somebody other than a major collector had to save them in new condition for almost 50 years for them to come onto the market in that condition today. That doesn't happen very often – Grandpa's paperbacks in the attic aren't there like they used to be. Collectors themselves often put a premium on

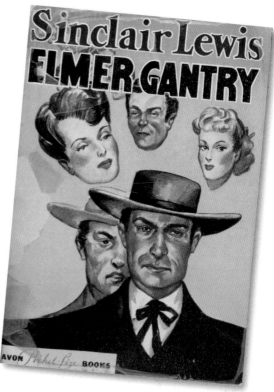

best condition books and gladly pay premium prices for truly "Fine" as-new copies of books they must have.

Older collectors will invariably notice the prices I have listed here for paperbacks that they have in their possession, and some may scoff at the values I have listed. While sales lists and auction records give us a good idea of actual prices paid, there is also a certain measure of subjective opinion in pricing. Certain collectors just value certain books more highly than other books. This also applies to dealers. Individual preferences dictate interest. One dealer might value a book at $200 because he sold a copy for that price; another may not be able to sell a similar copy for $100. There are many factors involved in any sale. Many older collectors also obtained their copies years ago – in some cases decades ago – back in the days of less expensive prices, low demand, more supply.

When considering the prices realized today in auctions on key paperbacks, most have kept consistent over the years. However, the condition of the books via mail and Internet auctions, overall, seems to have diminished. Demand has increased while supply has decreased. Whereas years ago "Fine" or even strong VG+ books were the mainstay of all auctions, increasingly we see too many merely VG books, or at best VG+ books today, yet the prices realized are the same as the higher grade copies of years ago – sometimes higher. There are also books in auctions today that years ago would never have appeared because they were thought to be too common for an auction. What does this tell us? I believe these trends show market forces of supply and demand clearly working in the areas of condition and the prices people are actually paying for these books. It means premium condition copies should have premium price values. It means many books once thought common have now become uncommon. It further means even some common editions, in condition, have become auction quality books.

With all this and more in mind, I have assembled a group of dedicated collector and dealer experts to vet this book and the price values therein. Each of these experts has dozens of years of experience in specific areas of the collectible paperback field, and each has given me their input, which has been considered for this book. In some cases I have heeded their sage advice, in others not. In some cases

advice was contradictory, attesting to market volatility, regional differences, dealer specialties, and clientele.

No price guide can ever be totally accurate, and no prices should ever be set in stone. If you buy a $100 book for $1, does that mean that book is worth $1? Of course not; it just means you got a great deal or made a great find. Generally, collectors want to see low values because they want to see low prices on books that they want to buy; generally dealers want to see higher values so they can justify selling their books for higher prices. I believe that the truth of the value of most collectible paperbacks lies somewhere in between, and I have tried to ensure that the prices listed in this book reflect that reality with up-to-date values on books in the very best condition.

Prices in the Internet Age

It's not price guides that set the prices of books today, it's auctions and the Internet. Price guides merely reflect that reality. When you get two or more bidders competing for a book in an auction, the effect of that sale is like a ripple in a pond. Many times this occurs because that book might never have been seen before by that particular buyer.

In the final analysis, the value of any collectible book is what a person is willing to pay for it, and the Internet proves that anyone, anywhere, is often willing to pay a premium price for a premium condition copy of a scarce paperback edition. The Internet also brings into the market editions that many people have never seen before, and once they see them, they want them. A collector who doesn't live in New York, Los Angeles, Chicago, or

London may never have been to an all-paperback book show and may never see most of these books but for the Internet or a book such as this one. And while antiquarian book shows are more common, they usually feature a limited selection of collectible paperbacks, usually in lesser condition and at high prices. Those prices reflect previous sales – the ripple-in-the-pond-effect come full circle. The Internet has opened up the hobby for better or worse. It has brought in many new collectors and brought many scarce books onto the market. The worldwide effect in the book world has been monumental.

Volatile areas of paperback collectibles

There are some volatile areas in the hobby. In general these include all digest-size editions. This includes the sexy pin-up cover editions to be sure, but also crime and westerns are gaining in desirability, and some collectors avidly seek out all digests. Sleaze paperbacks from the 1960s are also a volatile area, where some famous authors refuse to reveal their pseudonyms and house names. More research needs to be done in this area, and authors need to be more forthcoming. Romance paperbacks are another unmined opportunity; some best-selling authors lay hidden behind pseudonyms here, where they got their start with paperback originals. Sports paperbacks are undervalued, and since there is such a huge sports market, there are many fans and collectors who would be interested in these books *if* they knew they existed and where they could get them. Nostalgia, retro, counter-culture, TV, and movie star-related paperbacks

are always of interest, and there is volatility on the very best condition copies of key books with hot stars in these areas. However, the most volatile area is prices for the top tier of key collectible paperbacks in pristine condition and editions scarce or rare in condition.

About the paperbacks not listed in this book

While this book lists thousands of the most collectible paperbacks published in the United States, it does not list every paperback ever published. That would entail a tome the size of two phone books. That was never intended to be the scope of this book. It should be noted that there are literally thousands more paperbacks that are interesting books and also collectible. There have been, perhaps, more than 100,000 paperbacks published in the United States since 1939, and while most of them are good books that are interesting and worth reading, these more common editions are not presently valued highly in the collectible market. So knowing what is collectible and valuable and what is not is a crucial factor. But, again, you cannot go wrong if you collect what you like.

HOW TO BUDGET A COLLECTION

As with anything else, unless you have unlimited funds, it's a good idea for collectors to have a budget for their collecting purchases and to adhere to that budget.

The best advice I can offer you is to consider your purchases with care and intelligence. That often means buying with an eye toward future resale value, when you may want to sell that particular item some day. It also means being able to walk away, hoping you'll find the book at a lower price at a later date.

One of the best ways to budget a collection is to give yourself a monthly allowance to help keep spending under control. Overspending – or spending too much on one particular item – can be a problem with book auctions via mail or the Internet. Sometimes book gluttony can be a problem, also. You will at times come across great deals that are difficult to pass up.

Auctions, while offering the opportunity to acquire scarce and highly desirable books, can fuel the feeding frenzy and blow a budget right out of the water.

The hobby of collecting paperbacks offers one of the best ways to feed your book collecting interests while you maintain and expand your collection with a minimum of cash outlay, and that is to *trade* among fellow collectors. Find collectors in your area and cultivate them. They make good friends and understanding companions and are an added source of news, information, enjoyment, *and* inexpensive books.

The best way to do this is to trade duplicate copies. If you're a science fiction collector and are trading with another SF collector, you'll probably both have something the other would like to add to his collection. This can sometimes save you a considerable amount of money compared to purchasing that same book from a dealer. It's also good to have a collector friend who shares your own interests. It can be the best of all worlds.

You can also trade with collectors who do *not* share your interests. A mystery or western collector may have some choice science fiction or fantasy books to sell or trade to the SF collector. Some great trades can be made this way. Sometimes you can do a "straight-up" trade with no money involved. For a collector on a budget, what could be better?

However, even if you don't do trades and just buy books outright from a fellow collector, you'll still probably pay less than dealer prices. The book collecting hobby has operated in just this way for decades. However, with key books in the better grades getting scarce and more people coming into the hobby, the supply of good books (i.e., collectible books in collectible condition) has decreased and the demand has increased. Dealers have taken a bigger hand as middlemen and distributors. By and large they've done a good job, and while they take their cut of the price for their work (as it should be), book dealers in this hobby are a group of dedicated people who love books and know their stuff. After all, most dealers started out as collectors, just buying, selling, and trading books to add to their collections! And they do not mind sharing their knowledge with fellow collectors and fans.

Another good place to buy collectible paperbacks is at the various conventions and at specialist paperback book shows. There are many science fiction, fantasy, and horror conventions (cons) that take place all across the country. Some offer better material than others. Obviously a con that stresses print media (books) will offer a better opportunity to find good books than a Star Trek only media-related con. Nevertheless, I wouldn't dismiss any event without checking into it first. You'd be surprised what you can find in the most unlikely places. Sometimes a non-book con or show will have good books at reasonable prices simply because the dealers don't specialize in these items, or they may want to move them quickly. In either case, you're the winner, and you could end up with some good books on the cheap.

Specialist collectible paperback book shows have also existed for decades and are hardcore book-related conventions for collectors. My own Collectible Paperback & Pulp Fiction Expo is an annual New York City trade show now in its 20th year, held in early October. Similar shows in Los Angles in March, Chicago in April, and London in November offer excellent venues for collectors to gather with each other and with book dealers. The Los Angeles show, conducted by veteran collector Tom Lesser and Rose Idlet of Black Ace Books, is the biggest and has been in existence for over 30 years.

Tens of thousands of key collectible paperbacks and related items are displayed at these shows. Special guest authors and artists are also available for book signings. It's really special when you can meet the author or the artist of a favorite book and have him or her sign that book.

From a book collector's and book-buyer's viewpoint, these shows are a must because they present a large group of major dealers selling books there. Each dealer will have different stock, selling in all genres. The main thing to remember is that these dealers are competing with each other for *your* money. This is the best place for a serious collector or buyer to make a deal. In an auction, buyers compete with each other for a particular book, driving up the price. At shows, dealers compete against each other to sell to you, so there can be great bargains to be had!

Furthermore, the information and contacts picked up at these shows are invaluable, and the shows themselves are just plain fun. Careful and intelligent buying at shows can actually stretch your budget. Buying unwisely in auctions, where the reverse market forces hold true, can bust a budget. Frenzied bidding in auctions can also cause higher or inflated prices.

Book dealers, collector friends, paperback shows, and auctions are all good sources for collectors and can be a joy for fans joining in with others who share their collecting interests. You will always find something wonderful and cool for every budget and interest.

THE IMPORTANCE OF COVER ART

Perhaps the main reason most vintage era paperbacks are so avidly collected today, 40 to 60 years after they were first published, is because of the covers. Many of the artists who rendered cover art were classically trained as painters, and they created mini-masterpieces of action, passion, and danger showing beautiful women and stalwart male heroes that thrilled book buyers and compelled the public to purchase these books by the millions.

While many collectors seek out and collect books by a favorite or key author or in a favorite genre, a large group of collectors also seek paperbacks with cover art by favorite artists. These giants in the illustration field include Robert McGinnis, Robert Maguire, Frank Frazetta, Virgil Finlay, Wallace Wood, Walter Baumhoffer, Frank McCarthy, James Avati, Roy Krenkel, Rudy Nappi, Kelly Freas, Peter Driben, Paul Rader, Fred Claude Rodewald, L. B. Cole, Earle Bergey, Rafael DeSoto, Reginald Heade, Robert Bonfils, Walter Popp, Bill Ward, Doug Weaver, Bill Edwards, Eric Stanton, Norman Saunders, and Gene Bilbrew. Each has his own special group of dedicated fans and collectors. Condition also plays an important part in the desirability of these books and their values.

Other famous cover artists are also very popular, and these illustrators created fine and lasting work. They include: Verne Tossey, Julian Paul, John Floherty Jr., George Gross, Richard Powers, John Leone, Jim Steranko, Harry Schaare, Robert Stanley, Peter Caras, Louis S. Glanzman, Paul Lehr, Sandy Kossin, George Ziel, Bob Abbett, Charles Binger, Stanley Borak, Ralph Brillhart, Sam Cherry, Charles Copeland, Tom Dunn, Ray Johnson, Mort Kunsler, Lou Marchetti, Tom Miller, William Rose, Bill George, Tom Ryan, Stanley Zuckerberg, Paul Stahr, Ed Emsh, Lu Kimmel, Victor Kalin, Victor Olson, Harry Barton, Harry Bennett, Herb Tauss, James Meese, Vincent DiFate, Barye Phillips, Robert Schulz, Mitchell Hooks, Jack Gaughan, Gerald Gregg, H. Lawrence Hoffman, and many more.

There are also many cases where

THE DINO DE LAURENTIIS PRODUCTION OF KING KONG

ACE 44472/5-$1.95

With an author's preface
THE COMPLETE SCRIPT
BY LORENZO SEMPLE, JR.

the cover art by one of these artists ensured that a book (or series) was successful. Classic pairings of the right cover artist with the right author are legend. These include the Conan books by Robert E. Howard with covers by Frank Frazetta; the Mike Shayne and Carter Brown mysteries with covers by Robert McGinnis; and the steamy novels of Erskine Caldwell with covers by James Avati.

Then there are certain artists known for special talents or unique styles. There are the beautiful and classy women of Robert McGinnis; the beautiful but deadly femme fatales of Robert Maguire; the stunning western imagery of Frank McCarthy; the fantastic alienscapes and women of Frank Frazetta; and the very well-developed ladies of Bill Ward.

Cover variants offer the collector another interesting aspect to this hobby and sometimes a unique challenge. Paperbacks were often reprinted with new and different cover art. Popular and collectible cover artists often painted a cover for a later printing of a book, making that book collectible in and of itself. To further complicate things, some reprint editions have changes in cover art and design during the print run with the books having the same publication date and book number. These variants are fascinating and very desirable. The differences can be significant or minor, but they are always interesting, and sometimes crucial to the value or collectibility of the book. For instance, one cover variant of a book may be common, the other rare – that could be because the new cover was used at the tail end of the press run. Some reprints were not distributed well, so they appear to be scarce, while others

may have been printed in such low numbers that they actually are scarcer than the first printing. This is because in some cases first printings by major publishers (such as Avon Books, where I viewed original contracts) were a standard 100,000 copies, other publishers 200,000, while reprints could be as little as 5,000 copies – sometimes even 1,000!

Today, scarce, one-of-a-kind original paperback art often sells for thousands of dollars, but you can still own outstanding examples of this wonderful art on the covers of many of the best collectible paperback books for just a fraction of the price.

PAPERBACK ORIGINALS, FIRST EDITIONS, AND RARITIES

Many vintage-era paperbacks were also paperback originals (PBOs); that is, the first time a particular book ever appeared in print. Hence, some demand high prices not only in the paperback collecting hobby but in the overall and worldwide first edition and antiquarian book markets.

The collectibility of such paperback original works by Jim Thompson, David Goodis, and Charles Willeford is well known by most book collectors. Many more authors also have key or significant editions that first appeared as paperback originals. For many of today's hottest and most collectible authors, their first book, an important keystone in any collection of their work, was a paperback original! These books are avidly sought after and some command hefty prices. One example is Ed Hoch's first book, *The Shattered Raven*, a scarce Lancer Books paperback original from 1969. Other examples include mystery author Joseph Hansen's first book, *Lost on Twilight Road*, written as James Colton (National Library, 1964); James Ellroy's first book, *Brown's Requiem* (Avon Books, 1981); Harry Turtledove's first book, *Wereblood*, written as Eric Iverson (Belmont Books, 1970); and Martin Cruz Smith's first book, *The Indians Won*, written as Martin Smith (Belmont Books, 1970). All are scarce paperback originals and all are valuable editions.

Many more paperback originals by collectible authors (not necessarily just the "hot" authors) are too often undervalued in the antiquarian book market and deserve a closer look. There is much of merit here, treasure awaiting a keen eye to realize undervalued PBOs of collectible authors and classic, or soon-to-be classic works. Some of these paperbacks are just coming into their own as the collectible books of the future as their authors become better known, and you'll find many of them listed in this book.

Then there are paperbacks written under pseudonyms and house names, recalled books, plagiarized editions, and even some paperback curiosities such as the two Pocket Book versions of *Halfway House* by Ellery Queen – one bound vertically, the other bound horizontally with the latter very scarce and valuable. Some genuine rarities also exist among all of these. Prominent editions listed in this book include:

- the first 16 Avon Books (not numbered) but with "globe endpapers" (see illustration, right)

- all paperbacks with dust jackets, especially the toughest book in a dust jacket, Bantam Book #350, *Your Red Wagon*

- all of the LA Bantam Books

- scarce short run mystery digest series such as Yogi Books and Banner Mysteries

- Dashiell Hammett and Raymond Chandler digests that are true first editions

- early Avon and Dell crossword puzzle books (unworked)

- select sleaze written by famous authors under pseudonyms

- select sexy or mystery digests, which are also paperback originals

- various Artful and Kirby comics in digest format

It's great fun when you find an interesting paperback and discover that a seemingly innocuous or common book is, in fact, a collectible and valuable edition.

HOW TO USE THIS BOOK

Antique Trader Collectible Paperback Price Guide is divided into seven main sections—fantasy books, mysteries, westerns, sports books, media-related books, social issue books, and miscellaneous—with listings arranged alphabetically by the author's name and book title. A short description follows each book title. Prices are listed for books in Good, Very Good, and Fine conditions.

Book listings illustrated with a camera icon 📷 indicate an accompanying photograph of the book's cover.

An index at the back of the book lists authors' names in alphabetical order for your convenience.

FANTASTIC LITERATURE:
Science Fiction, Fantasy, Horror, and the Hero Pulps

In the beginning science fiction, fantasy, and horror were not the popular, lucrative, and separate book publishing categories they have become today. This was true even though many fantasy-oriented titles were included in that first crop of the original 10 Pocket Books published in 1939.

Science fiction (SF), while published for decades in the pulp magazines, was scorned by many people as "that Buck Rogers stuff" and had been relegated to the pulp "ghetto" by the book publishers of that era. Other than a few small or specialty presses, SF would have to wait for paperbacks to come into vogue, where reprints of novels and collections of classic stories would be offered to the public as first book editions, or paperback originals would appear by famous authors and new stars.

The first book to use the term "science fiction" in the title was a paperback, and that was *The Pocket Book of Science Fiction* edited by

The realm of fantastic fiction encompasses the wild, the wonderful, and often the quite bizarre. This section includes not only the standard genres of science fiction, fantasy, and horror, but also the weird pulp heroes who often had fantastic adventures, and some soft-core adult books that cross clearly over into the fantastic realms.

Donald A. Wollheim (Pocket Book #214) from 1943.

Meanwhile, fantasy and horror had been important and popular genres since the days of Edgar Allen Poe and Jonathan Swift (*Gulliver's Travels*), and many of the classics of these genres appeared in paperback editions for the first time in the 1940s where they were made available to the public and a new group of eager readers for the first time.

Ace Books and Ballantine Books began publishing science fiction as a genre in 1953, with some horror and fantasy titles in the mix. Gold Medal Books, while never a mainstay in the fantastic fiction field, began the paperback original in 1950 as a publishing program. Ace, Ballantine, and others soon followed. Soon they not only published reprints but began publishing original books, what are called paperback originals (PBOs). From then on these genres exploded in popularity with the public and among collectors.

Also included in this category are many of the pulp magazine heroes whose exploits often were science fictional or fantastic in nature. Many of these stories were reprinted in paperback from the original pulp magazine publications of the 1930s, and these paperback reprints in many cases are actually first book editions. These include: *The Shadow* by Maxwell Grant, *Doc Savage* by Kenneth Robeson, *G-8 and His Battle Aces* by Robert Hogan, *The Spider* by Grant Stockbridge or Norvell W. Page, *The Avenger* by Kenneth Robeson, *The Phantom Detective* by Robert Wallace, *Secret Agent X* by Brant House, *Dr. Death* by Zorro, *Dusty Ayres and his Battle Birds* by Robert Sidney Bowen, *Operator 5* by Curtis Steele, *The Phantom* by Lee Falk, *Buck Rogers* by William Francis Nowlan, *Flash Gordon* by Alex Raymond, and many others.

The first mass-market fantasy paperbacks were published by Pocket Books in 1939. That year Pocket came out with no less than five outstanding fantasy reprint selections: *Lost Horizon* by James Hilton (Pocket #1, the very first book in its series) where we were introduced to mythical Shangri-La; *Topper* by Thorne Smith (Pocket #4), ghosts come back to haunt and humor an old gent; *Green Mansions* by W.H. Hudson (Pocket #16), a female Tarzan in the South American jungle; *Pinocchio* by Carlo Collodi (Pocket #18), a wooden puppet that wants to become a real boy; and *A Christmas Carol* by Charles Dickens (Pocket #29), presenting the ghosts of Christmas Past, Present, and Future. All classic fantasy, then and now. Since then, fantastic fiction has exploded in popularity, and the paperback book has been there right beside most readers with every turn of the page.

	G	VG	F

Ackerman, Forest, *Best From Famous Monsters of Filmland, The,* Paperback Library #52-290, 1964, first book edition, #1 in series of 3, horror magazine reprints with info and photos. 📷
    $10   **$30**   **$100**

--- *Son of Famous Monsters of Filmland,* Paperback Library #52-504, 1965, first book edition, cover shows Frankenstein monster, horror photos, #2 in series.
    $10   **$35**   **$100**

--- *Famous Monsters of Filmland Strike Back!,* Paperback Library #52-813, 1965, first book edition, photo cover, contains over 150 photos, #3 in series.
    $15   **$40**   **$120**

Aldiss, Brian, *Bow Down to Nul,* Ace Book #D-443, 1960, paperback original, Ace Double backed with *The Dark Destroyers* by Manly Wade Wellman.
    $6   **$20**   **$50**

--- *Male Response, The,* Beacon Book #305, 1961, paperback original, cover by Robert Stanley.   **$14**   **$40**   **$120**

Anderson, Poul, *After Doomsday,* Ballantine Book #579, 1962, cover by Ralph Brillhart. 📷 **$3**   **$15**   **$40**

--- *Three Hearts and Three Lions,* Avon Book #G1127, 1961, paperback original.
    $5   **$20**   **$75**

--- *Virgin Planet,* Beacon Book #270, 1960, cover by Robert Stanley, male bondage cover. 📷
    $16   **$75**   **$150**

Anonymous, *Tales From the Crypt,* Ballantine Book #U2106, 1964, first book edition, cover by Frank Frazetta, EC horror comic reprints. 📷
    $10   **$30**   **$100**

--- *Tales of the Incredible,* Ballantine Book #U2140, 1964, first book edition, cover by Frank Frazetta, reprints EC comics horror stories. 📷
    $10   **$35**   **$120**

--- *Vault of Horror, The,* Ballantine Book #U2107, 1965, first book edition, EC horror comic reprints.
    $12   **$30**   **$100**

Asimov, Iaasc, *1,000-Year Plan, The,* Ace Book #D-110, 1955, reprint of Foundation, Ace Double backed with *No World of Their Own* by Poul Anderson, 1955, paperback original.
    $6   **$20**   **$60**

--- *2nd Foundation: Galactic Empire,* Avon Book #T-232, 1958, cover by Richard Powers, retitled *Second Foundation.*   **$2**   **$15**   **$40**

--- *Caves of Steel,* The, Signet Book #S1240, 1955, cover by Robert Schulz.
    $4   **$20**   **$50**

--- *Currents of Space, The,* Signet Book #1082, 1953.   **$4**   **$20**   **$40**

--- *End of Eternity, The,* Signet Book #S1493, 1958.   **$4**   **$18**   **$45**

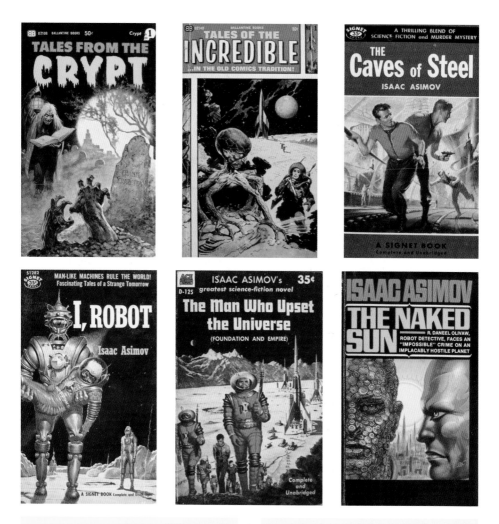

	G	VG	F		G	VG	F

--- *I, Robot*, Signet Book #S1282, 1956, cover by Robert Schulz.
     $5   **$20**   **$60**

--- *Man Who Upset the Universe, The*, Ace Book #D-125, 1955, first paperback printing, original title *Foundation and Empire*. **$6** **$20** **$50**

--- *Naked Sun*, The, Lancer Book #72-753, 1964, cover by Ed Emsh.
    $3   **$15**   **$35**

Bachman, Richard, *Long Walk, The,* Signet Book #J8754, 1979, paperback original; pseudonym of Stephen King.
    $10   **$30**   **$100**

--- *Rage*, Signet Book #W7645, 1981, paperback original.
    $15   **$100**   **$225**

--- *Roadwork*, Signet Book #E-9668, 1981, paperback original.
    $12   **$50**   **$120**

--- *Running Man, The*, Signet Book #AE-15008, 1981, paperback original.
    $12   **$40**   **$110**

Ballard, J. G., *Billenium*, Berkley Book #F667, 1962, first book edition, cover by Richard Powers, collection.
    $10   **$30**   **$90**

--- *Burning World, The*, Berkley Book #F961, 1964, paperback original, cover by Richard Powers, novel.
    $10   **$30**   **$100**

	G	VG	F

--- *Drowned World, The,* Berkley Book #F655, 1962, paperback original, cover by Richard Powers, SF disaster novel.
$10 $30 $100

--- *Impossible Man, The,* Berkley Book #F1204, 1966, first book edition, collection, cover by Richard Powers.
$10 $25 $90

--- *Passport to Eternity,* Berkley Book #F823, 1963, first book edition, cover by Richard Powers, collection.
$10 $25 $90

--- *Terminal Beach,* Berkley Book #F928, 1964, first book edition, cover by Richard Powers, collection.
$10 $30 $120

--- *Vermilion Sands,* Berkley Book #S1980, 1971, first book edition, cover by Richard Powers, collection.
$10 $20 $75

--- *Voices of Time and Other Stories, The,* Berkley Book #F607, 1962, first book edition, collection, cover by Richard Powers. $10 $25 $90

--- *Wind From Nowhere, The,* Berkley Book #F600, 1962, paperback original, cover by Richard Powers, his first book and first novel. 📷
$15 $40 $120

Beach, Rex, *Tower of Flame, The* with *Jaragu of the Lost Islands,* LA Bantam #19, 1940, paperback original, fantasy, rare. $95 $180 $375

Beagle, Peter, *Fine and Private Place, A,* Ballantine Book #01502, 1969, his first novel. $6 $20 $50

--- *Last Unicorn, The,* Ballantine Book #01503, 1969, cover by Gervasio Gallardo, highly regarded fantasy novel.
$5 $20 $40

Beaumont, Charles, *Hunger and Other Stories, The,* Bantam Book #A1917, 1959, cover by Hieronymus Bosch, horror collection. $8 $25 $90

--- *Night Ride and Other Journeys,* Bantam Book #A2087, 1960, first book edition, horror collection.
$7 $20 $75

--- *Yonder,* Bantam Book #A1759, 1958, first book edition, horror collection.
$6 $20 $75

	G	VG	F

Bellamy, Francis Rufus, *Atta,* Ace Book #D-79, 1954, Ace Double backed with *The Brain-Stealers* by Murray Leinster. 📷
$5 $20 $50

Bernard, Allan, *Cleopatra's Nights,* Dell Book #414, 1950, cover by Ray Johnson shows sexy Cleopatra, anthology.
$3 $20 $75

Bester, Alfred, *Demolished Man, The,* Signet Book #1105, 1954. 📷
$5 $20 $90

Binder, Otto, *Avengers Battle the Earth-Wrecker, The,* Bantam Book #F3569, 1967, paperback original, intro by Stan Lee, Marvel Comics hero novel.
$8 $20 $90

Blackwood, Algernon, *Selected Stories of Algernon Blackwood,* Armed Service Edition #S-26, no date, circa 1945, first book edition, horror.
$20 $55 $110

Bloch, Robert, *Atoms and Evil,* Gold Medal Book #s1231, 1962, first book edition, scarce collection. $5 $20 $80

--- *Living Demons, The,* Belmont Book #B50-787, 1967, paperback original, horror. $5 $25 $90

Bowen, John, *After the Rain,* Ballantine Book #284K, 1959, paperback original, cover by John Blanchard, apocalyptic novel. 📷 $3 $15 $35

Bowen, Robert Sidney, *Black Invaders vs The Battlebirds,* Cornith Book #CR-148, 1966, first book edition, cover by Robert Bonfils, #5 in the series of at least five Dusty Ayres hero pulp reprints, each book: $8 $20 $45

Brackett, Leigh, *Best of Planet Stories #1, The,* Ballantine Book #24334, 1975, first book edition, cover by Kelly Freas, pulp anthology. $4 $15 $40

--- *People of the Talisman* with *The Secret of Sinharat,* Ace Book #M-101, 1964, paperback original, both covers by Ed Emsh, Ace Double. 📷
$3 $20 $40

Bradbury, Edward P., *Barbarians of Mars,* Lancer Book #72-127, 1966, first U.S. edition, cover by Gray Morrow, #3 in Mars trilogy; pseudonym of Michael Moorcock. $3 $15 $30

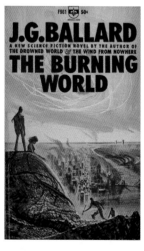

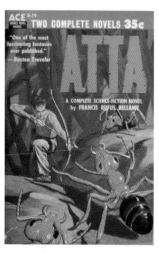

	G	VG	F

--- *Blades of Mars*, Lancer Book #72-122, 1966, first U.S. edition, cover by Gray Morrow, #2 in Mars trilogy.
$3 $15 $30

--- *Warriors of Mars*, Lancer Book #72-118, 1966, first U.S. edition, cover by Gray Morrow, #1 in Mars trilogy. 📷
$3 $15 $30

Bradbury, Ray, *Autumn People, The,* Ballantine Book #U2141, 1965, first book edition, cover by Frank Frazetta, reprints classic EC comics horror stories.
$10 $25 $75

--- *Fahrenheit 451*, Ballantine Book #41, 1953, paperback original, preceded hardcover and is the true first edition, rare in condition.
$10 $75 $400

--- *Illustrated Man, The*, Bantam Book #991, 1952, cover by Charles Binger, collection.
$4 $20 $90

--- *Martian Chronicles, The*, Bantam Book #886, 1951. 📷
$4 $30 $85

--- *Memory of Murder, A*, Dell Book #15559, 1984, first book edition, fantasy and horror pulp collection. 📷
$3 $20 $45

--- *October Country, The*, Ballantine Book #F139, 1956, collection, scare in condition. 📷
$10 $40 $150

--- *Tomorrow Midnight*, Ballantine Book #U2142, 1966, first book edition, cover by Frank Frazetta, reprints EC comics horror stories.
$10 $30 $100

Bradley, Marion Zimmer, *Bloody Sun, The,* Ace Book #F-303, 1964, paperback original, a Darkover novel.
$7 $20 $60

--- *Castle Terror*, Lancer Book #72-983, 1965, paperback original, gothic novel, uncommon.
$6 $20 $65

--- *Colors of Space, The*, Monarch Book #368, 1963, paperback original, cover by Ralph Brillhart.
$3 $20 $45

--- *Door Through Space, The*, Ace Book #F-117, 1961, first book edition, her first book, Ace Double with *Rendezvous On a Lost World* by A Betram Chandler.
$10 $30 $90

Brent, Lynton Wright, *Sex Demon of Jangal, The,* Brentwood Book #1007, 1964, paperback original, Aztec sex demon jungle fantasy. 📷
$15 $60 $125

Brown, Fredric, *Honeymoon in Hell,* Bantam Book #A1812, 1958, first book edition, cover by Hieronoymus Bosch.
$6 $30 $100

--- *Martians, Go Home*, Bantam Book #A1546, 1956, first paperback printing.
$6 $25 $75

--- *Martians, Go Home*, Ballantine Book #25314, 1976, reprint, cover by Kelly Freas shows classic little green man originally done for Astounding Stories in the 1950s. 📷
$5 $20 $45

	G	VG	F		G	VG	F

--- *Madball*, Dell First Edition #2E, 1953, paperback original, cover by Griffith Foxley, carnival horror novel. 📷
$20 $80 $225

--- *Madball*, Gold Medal Book #s1132, 1961, cover by Mitchell Hooks, reprints Dell First Edition.
$15 $40 $135

--- *Nightmares and Geezenstacks*, Bantam Book #J2296, 1961, first book edition.
$7 $30 $80

--- *Rogue in Space*, Bantam Book #A1701, 1957, cover by Richard Powers.
$5 $20 $55

--- *Space on My Hands*, Bantam Book #877, 1952, cover by Barye Phillips.
$8 $25 $90

--- *Starshine*, Bantam Book #1423, 1956.
$6 $25 $65

--- *What Mad Universe*, Bantam Book #835, 1950, cover by Herman Bischoff. 📷
$8 $30 $75

Buchard, Robert, *Thirty Seconds Over New York,* Belmont Book #51181, second printing circa 1976, chilling cover art shows commercial jet sent to crash into World Trade Center, first printing does not have this cover art, scarce. 📷
$15 $50 $100

Budrys, Algis, *Amsirs and the Iron Thorn, The,* Gold Medal Book #d1852, 1967, first book edition, cover by Frank Frazetta.
$4 $15 $40

--- *False Night*, Lion Book #230, 1954, paperback original, his first novel. 📷
$12 $30 $100

--- *Rogue Moon*, Gold Medal Book #s1057, 1960, paperback original, cover by Richard Powers.
$4 $15 $40

Burgess, Anthony, *Clockwork Orange, A,* Ballantine Book #U5032, 1965, predates the film. 📷 **$8 $40 $100**

Burroughs, Edgar Rice, *Cave Girl,* Dell Book #320, 1949, Map Back, cover by Jean Des Vignes. 📷
$15 $40 $125

--- *John Carter of Mars*, Ballantine Book #U2041, 1965, first paperback printing, cover by Bob Abbett, John Carter #11. 📷
$3 $15 $40

--- *Man Eater, The*, Fantasy Reader #5, 1974, first separate edition, cover by Robert Kline.   **$10 $20 $75**

--- *Mastermind of Mars*, Ace Book #F-181, 1963, cover by Roy Krenkel, #6 in John Carter series. Ace published dozens of Burroughs paperbacks in the 1960s in their F series, most with Frank Frazetta or Roy Krenkel cover art, each book: 📷
$3 $15 $30

--- *Return of Tarzan, The*, Armed Service Edition #0-22, no date, circa 1945, the scarcer of the two Tarzan ASE editions.
$100 $250 $750

	G	VG	F

--- *Tarzan and the Lost Empire*, Dell Book #536, 1951, Map Back, cover by Robert Stanley. 📷 **$12 $35 $100**

--- *Tarzan in the Forbidden City*, LA Bantam #23, 1940, text cover, abridged, rare. **$100 $200 $550**

--- *Tarzan in the Forbidden City*, LA Bantam #23, 1940, illustrated cover, abridged, rare. 📷 **$300 $750 $1,500**

--- *Tarzan of the Apes*, Armed Service Edition #M-16, no date, circa 1944. 📷 **$65 $150 $450**

--- *Thuvia, Maid of Mars*, Ballantine Book #F-770, 1963, cover by Bob Abbett, #4 in John Carter series of 11 books, first printing, each book: **$3 $15 $30**

--- *Thuvia, Maid of Mars*, Ballantine Book #01524, third printing 1969, cover by Bob Abbett, #4 in John Carter series, new cover art, scarce. 📷 **$10 $30 $100**

Campbell, John W., *Who Goes There and Other Stories?,* Dell Book #D150, 1955, cover by Richard Powers. **$6 $20 $75**

Campbell, Ramsey, *Doll Who Ate His Mother, The,* Jove Book #M4483, 1978, first edition thus, collection, subject to scuffing so Fine copies uncommon. **$10 $20 $100**

Card, Orson Scott, *Capitol,* Ace Book #09136, 1979, first book edition, Cards' first book. 📷 **$10 $20 $90**

Chambers, Robert W., *King in Yellow, The,* Ace Book #M-132, 1965, cover by Jack Gaughan, a key horror novel. **$4 $20 $45**

Chappell, Fred, *Dagon,* St Martin's Press, #90676, 1987, first paperback printing, cover by Peter Caras, Lovecraftian horror novel, die-cut cover. **$5 $20 $50**

Charteris, Leslie, *Saint's Choice of Impossible Crimes, The,* Bonded Book #11, 1945, first book edition, digest-size, text cover, SF anthology. **$12 $45 $100**

Chesterton, G. K., *Man Who Was Thursday, The,* Armed Service Edition #984, no date, circa 1946. **$15 $65 $135**

--- *Man Who Was Thursday, The,* Ballantine Book #02305, 1971, cover by Gervasio Gallardo. **$12 $40 $100**

Clark, Curt, *Anarchaos,* Ace Book #F-421, 1967, paperback original, cover by Lynch; pseudonym of Donald Westlake. **$10 $25 $90**

Clarke, Arthur C., *Reach For Tomorrow,* Ballantine Book #135, 1956, first book edition, cover by Richard Powers, collection, unique sideways cover. 📷 **$10 $25 $100**

--- *Sands of Mars,* Perma Book #M4149, 1959, cover by Robert Schulz. 📷 **$3 $15 $40**

Clement, Hal, *Mission of Gravity,* Galaxy SF Novel #33, 1958, cover by Wally Wood; pseudonym of Henry Clement Stubbs. 📷 **$7 $20 $75**

Coblentz, Stanton A., *Into Plutonian Depths,* Avon Book #281, 1950, paperback original. 📷 **$10 $30 $100**

Collier, John, *Green Thoughts and Other Strange Tales,* Armed Service Edition #871, no date, circa 1946, first book edition, literary collection. **$10 $45 $125**

Collins, Hunt, *Tomorrow and Tomorrow,* Pyramid Book #G214, 1956, paperback original, cover by Bob Lavin; pseudonym of Evan Hunter. 📷 **$10 $30 $90**

Collins, Wilkie, *Haunted Hotel and 25 Other Ghost Stories, The,* Avon Book no number (#6), 1941, with Globe endpapers only, anthology. **$25 $75 $225**

Collodi, Carlo, *Pinocchio,* Pocket Book #18, 1939. **$25 $85 $220**

Conklin, Geoff, *In the Grip of Terror,* Perma Book #P-117, 1951, includes Lovecraft, cover shows creepy bogeyman threatening woman. 📷 **$6 $20 $50**

--- *Science Fiction Terror Tales,* Pocket Book #1045, 1955. First book edition, cover by Stanley Meltzoff. **$5 $15 $40**

Cook, Glen, *Heirs of Babylon, The,* Signet Book #Q5299, 1972, paperback original, his first SF book. **$5 $30 $75**

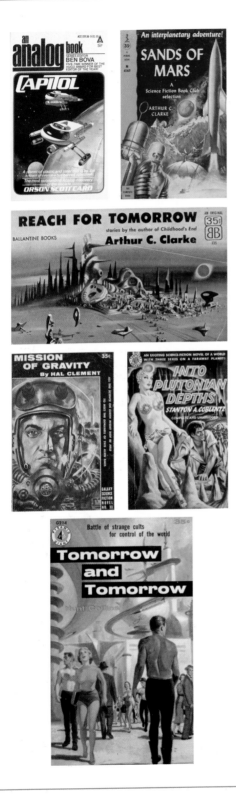

	G	VG	F

Copper, Basil, *Great White Space, The,* Manor Book #12400, 1976, Lovecraftian horror novel. **$5 $20 $45**

Crumley, Thomas W., *Star Trail,* Vega Book #VSF-14, 1966, paperback original, cover by Bill Edwards. 📷 **$4 $20 $50**

Cummings, Ray, *Brigands of the Moon,* Ace Book #D-324, 1958, cover by Ed Emsh, space pirate novel. **$3 $15 $35**

--- *Exiles of Time, The,* Ace Book #F-343, 1965, first paperback printing, cover by Alex Schomberg. 📷 **$3 $15 $30**

--- *Princess of the Atom, The,* Avon Fantasy Novel #1, 1950, sexy woman cover art, the world of the sub-atomic was never like this! 📷 **$15 $50 $125**

--- *Tama, Princess of Mercury,* Ace Book #F-406, 1966, cover by Jerome Podwil. **$3 $14 $30**

da Vinci, Leonardo, *Deluge, The,* Lion Book #233, 1954, paperback original, cover may be by Robert Maguire, written by the "editor" Robert Payne but based on da Vinci's writings. 📷 **$10 $30 $75**

deCamp, L. Sprague, *Cosmic Manhunt,* Ace Book #D-61, 1954, first book edition, Ace Double backed with *Ring Around the Sun* by Clifford D. Simak. **$8 $25 $70**

--- *Rogue Queen,* Dell Book #600, 1951, cover by Mike Ludlow, classic purple alien woman cover. 📷 **$10 $30 $120**

--- *Spell of Seven, The,* Pyramid Book #R-1192, 1965, first book edition, cover by Virgil Finlay, classic sword and sorcery anthology. 📷 **$4 $15 $40**

Delaney, Samuel R., *Fall of the Towers, The,* Ace Book #22640, 1966, first edition thus, cover by Kelly Freas, combines trilogy in one volume with notes and afterword. 📷 **$6 $20 $75**

--- *Heavenly Breakfast,* Bantam Book #12796, 1979, paperback original, science fiction essay and memoirs, scarce. **$10 $30 $100**

	G	VG	F		G	VG	F

--- *Jewels of Aptor, The*, Ace Book #F-173, 1962, paperback original, his first book, Ace Double backed with *Second Ending* by James White. **$4 $20 $65**

--- *Tides of Lust, The*, Lancer Book #71344, 1973, paperback original, drug-sex book by SF author.
$20 $100 $200

de Lint, Charles, *Drink Down the Moon*, Ace Book #16861, 1990, paperback original, scarce. **$6 $20 $50**

--- *Greenmantle*, Ace Book #30295, 1988, paperback original, scarce.
$6 $20 $55

--- *Moonheart*, Ace Book #53719, 1984, paperback original, cover by David Mattingly. **$6 $25 $60**

--- *Mulengro*, Ace Book #54484, 1985, paperback original.
$6 $20 $60

--- *Riddle of the Wren, The*, Ace Book #72229, 1984, paperback original, fantasy novel, author's first book.
$10 $30 $75

--- *Svaha*, Ace Book #79098, 1989,

paperback original, cyberpunk SF novel.
$5 $20 $55

--- *Wolf Moon*, Signet Book #AE5487, 1988, paperback original, werewolf novel. **$5 $20 $60**

--- *Yarrow*, Ace Book #94000, 1986, paperback original, cover by Segreles.
$5 $25 $60

del Rey, Lester, *Eleventh Commandment, The*, Regency Book #RB113, 1962, paperback original, cover by Leo and Diane Dillon. **$6 $20 $90**

--- *Nerves*, Ballantine Book #151, 1956, paperback original, cover by Richard Powers. **$5 $15 $55**

Derleth, August, *Sleep No More*, Armed Service Edition #R-33, no date, circa 1944, edited anthology or horror, contains H.P. Lovecraft.
$20 $75 $135

--- *Strange Ports of Call*, Berkley Book #G-131, 1958, SF anthology contains Ray Bradbury, Clark Ashton Smith, Henry Kuttner, A.E. Van Vogt.
$4 $15 $40

	G	VG	F		G	VG	F

--- *Time to Come*, Berkley Book #G-189, 1958, cover by Robert Schulz, SF anthology contains Philip K. Dick, Charles Beaumont, Clark Ashton Smith. **$4 $20 $45**

Dick, Philip K., *Clans of the Alphane Moon*, Ace Book #F-309, 1964, paperback original. 📷 **$10 $20 $80**

--- *Cosmic Puppets, The*, Ace Book #D-249, 1957, paperback original, Ace Double backed with *Sargasso of Space* by Andrew North (Andre Norton), cover by Ed Emsh. **$15 $40 $120**

--- *Crack in Space, The*, Ace Book #F-377, 1966, paperback original, cover by Jerome Podwil. **$10 $20 $90**

--- *Do Androids Dream of Electric Sleep?*, Signet Book #T3800, 1969, first paperback printing, novel made into film Bladerunner, scarce in first printing. **$8 $20 $100**

--- *Dr. Futurity*, Ace Book #D-421, 1960, paperback original, Ace Double backed with *Slavers of Space* by John Brunner. **$15 $30 $110**

--- *Eye in the Sky*, Ace Book #D-211, 1957, paperback original. **$15 $25 $100**

--- *Flow My Tears, the Policeman Said*, DAW Book #146, 1975, cover by Hans Ulrich and Ute Osterwalder. **$10 $20 $85**

--- *Galactic Pot Healer*, Berkley Book #X-1705, 1969, paperback original, cover by Sandy Kossin. **$10 $20 $90**

--- *Game Players of Titan, The*, Ace Book #F-251, 1963, paperback original, cover by Jack Gaughan. 📷 **$14 $25 $100**

--- *Ganymede Takeover, The*, Ace Book #G-637, 1967, paperback original, cover by Jack Gaughan, written with Ray Nelson. **$12 $20 $75**

--- *Golden Man, The*, Berkley Book #04268X, 1980, first book edition, cover by Walter Velez, collection of 15 stories with intro and notes by Dick, uncommon. **$8 $20 $80**

--- *Man in the High Castle, The*, Popular Library #SP250, 1964, first paperback printing but scarce. 📷 **$12 $30 $100**

--- *Man Who Japed, The*, Ace Book #D-193, 1956, paperback original, Ace Double backed with *The Space-Born* by E. C. Tubb. 📷 **$16 $35 $100**

--- *Martian Time-Slip*, Ballantine Book #U2191, 1964, paperback original. **$10 $25 $100**

--- *Preserving Machine, The*, Ace Book #67800, 1968, paperback original. **$10 $20 $80**

--- *Simulacra, The*, Ace Book #F-301, 1964, paperback original, cover by Ed Emsh. 📷 **$15 $30 $100**

--- *Solar Lottery*, Ace Book #D-103, 1955, paperback original, Dick's first book, Ace Double backed with *The Big Jump* by Leigh Brackett. **$20 $65 $175**

	G	VG	F

--- *Solar Lottery*, Ace Book #D-340, 1959, reprints Ace D-103 in first single edition.
$10 $20 $75

--- *Variable Man and Other Stories, The*, Ace Book #D-261, 1957, paperback original. 📖 **$10 $30 $100**

--- *Vulcan's Hammer*, Ace Book #D-457, 1960, paperback original, Ace Double backed with *The Skynappers* by John Brunner. 📖 **$12 $30 $100**

--- *World Jones Made, The*, Ace Book #D-150, 1956, paperback original, Ace Double backed with *Agent of the Unknown* by Margaret St. Clair.
$12 $40 $110

Dickens, Charles, *Christmas Carol, A,*

Pocket Book #29, 1939.
$15 $40 $125

Drachman, M. D., Theodore S., *Cry Plague!*, Ace Book #D-13, 1952, first paperback printing, Ace Double backed with *The Judas Goat* by Leslie Edgley, a mystery novel. This is the first science fiction Ace book, but not the first Ace SF Double. 📖 **$25 $90 $225**

Dunsany, Lord, *Guerrilla*, Armed Service Edition #Q-14, no date, circa 1944.
$10 $40 $105

Dutourd, Jean, *Dog's Head, A*, Lion Book #196, 1954, fantasy novel. 📖
$10 $30 $100

	G	VG	F

Dwyer, Deanna, *Demon Child*, Lancer Book #75-201, 1971, paperback original, horror novel; pseudonym of Dean Koontz, scarce. **$10 $30 $100**

Ehrlich, Max, *Big Eye, The*, Popular Library #273, 1950, cover by Earle Bergey, classic giant eye in sky cover terrorizes city.  **$6 $20 $75**

Ellison, Harlan, *Man With Nine Lives, The*, with *A Touch of Infinity*, Ace Book #D-413, 1960, paperback original, Ellison Ace Double. **$20 $75 $200**

--- *Shatterday*, Berkley Book #05370, 1982, cover by Walter Velez shows Ellison. **$4 $20 $75**

Endore, Guy, *Werewolf of Paris, The*, Pocket Book #97, 1941, scarce. **$30 $100 $275**

--- *Werewolf of Paris, The*, Avon Book #354, 1951, classic werewolf attacking woman cover art. **$12 $40 $125**

--- *Werewolf of Paris, The*, Ace Book #K-160, 1962. **$4 $15 $45**

English, Charles, *Lovers: 2075*, Scorpion Book #104, 1964, paperback original, cover by Gus Albet, SF-sleaze novel of sex in 21st Century. **$10 $20 $60**

Falk, Lee, *Mystery of the Sea Horse, The*, Avon Book #15867, 1973, paperback original, cover by George Wilson, Lee Falk's original story adapted by Frank S. Shawn, this is #7 in The Phantom series of at least 15 books written by various authors, each book: **$4 $15 $25**

Farley, Ralph M., *An Earthman on Venus*, Avon Book #285, 1951. **$20 $100 $250**

Farmer, Philip Jose, *Blown*, Essex House #0139, 1967, paperback original, sex novel by SF writer. **$60 $225 $550**

--- *Cache From Outer Space, The*, with *The Celestial Blueprint*, Ace Book #F-165, 1962, paperback original, Farmer Ace Double. **$5 $20 $60**

--- *Feast Unknown, A*, Essex House #0121, 1966, paperback original, mixes SF with sex. **$30 $120 $320**

--- *Fire and the Night*, Regency Book #RB-118, 1962, paperback original cover by Leo and Diane Dillon. **$16 $60 $175**

--- *Flesh*, Beacon Book #277, 1960, paperback original, cover by Gerald McConnel. **$20 $80 $200**

--- *Image of the Beast, The*, Essex House #0108, 1968, paperback original, mixes SF with sex. **$25 $100 $325**

--- *Love Song*, Brandon House #6134, 1970, paperback original, rare sex novel by SF writer. **$150 $350 $800**

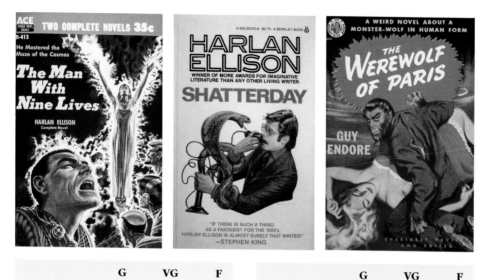

	G	VG	F		G	VG	F

--- *Mad Goblin, The* with *Lord of the Trees*, Ace Book #51375, 1970, paperback original, cover by Gray Morrow, Farmer's take on pulp heroes Tarzan and Doc Savage, Ace Double.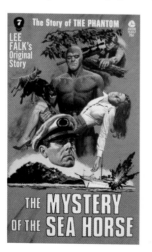

$5 $15 $50

--- *Woman a Day, A*, Beacon Book #291, 1960, paperback original, cover by Gerald McConnel. **$24 $100 $250**

Fast, Julius, *Out of This World*, Penguin Book #537, 1944, early SF anthology.

$6 $20 $75

Fessier, Michael, *Fully Dressed and in His Right Mind*, Lion Book #214, 1954, fantasy novel. **$15 $50 $100**

Finney, Jack, *Body Snatchers, The*, Dell First Edition #42, 1955, paperback original, cover by John McDermott.

$12 $65 $150

--- *Third Level, The*, Dell Book #D274, 1959, cover Richard Powers.

$6 $20 $75

Fles, Barthold, *Post Fantasy Stories*, Avon Book #389, 1951, first book edition, stories from the Saturday Evening Post.  **$5 $30 $100**

Forstchen, William, *Rally Cry*, ROC Book #45007, 1990, paperback original, book #1 in Lost Regiment alternate world SF series of nine PBOs, each book:

$6 $20 $45

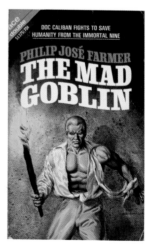

	G	VG	F		G	VG	F

Foster, Richard, *Rest Must Die, The,* Gold Medal Book #s853, 1959, paperback original, cover by Richard Powers, apocalyptic novel set in New York City subways; pseudonym of Kendall Foster Crossen. **$4 $15 $40**

Frank, Pat, *Mr. Adam,* Armed Service Edition #1217, no date, circa 1947. **$14 $45 $100**

Garrett, Randall and Harris, Larry M., *Pagan Passions,* Beacon Book #263, 1959, paperback original, cover by Robert Stanley, "Forced to make love to beautiful women! This is adult science fiction at its best." 📷 **$10 $40 $100**

Garton, Ray, *Darklings,* Pinnacle Book #42368, 1985, paperback original, horror novel. **$6 $20 $65**

--- *Live Girls,* Pocket Book #62628, 1987, paperback original, cover by Ron Lesser, vampire horror, scarce. 📷 **$8 $35 $75**

--- *Seductions,* Pinnacle Book #42309, 1984, paperback original, horror, author's first book. **$10 $30 $100**

Geis, Richard E., *Sex Machine, The,* Brandon House #1070, 1967, paperback original, mixes SF and sex. **$10 $30 $100**

Gibson, Walter B., *Return of the Shadow,* Belmont Book #90-298, 1963, paperback original, a new novel, not a pulp reprint; as far as I know this is the only Shadow novel under the author's true name. Also see Maxwell Grant. 📷 **$8 $35 $90**

Gibson, William, *Neuromancer,* Ace Book #56956, 1984, paperback original, Gibson's first book, began the SF cyberpunk movement. **$15 $50 $175**

Goulart, Ron, *Bloodstalk,* Warner Book #76-928, 1975, paperback original, #1 in series of six Vampirella novels, each book: 📷 **$5 $15 $40**

	G	VG	F

	G	VG	F

Grant, Maxwell, *Mark of the Shadow,*
Belmont Book #B50-663, 1966,
paperback original, written by Dennis
Lynds. **$5** **$20** **$40**

--- *Night of the Shadow,* Belmont Book
#B50-725, 1966, paperback original,
written by Dennis Lynds.
$5 **$20** **$35**

--- *Shadow and the Voice of Murder,
The,* LA Bantam #21, 1940, first book
edition, text cover, written by Walter B.
Gibson, rare. **$175** **$400** **$750**

--- *Shadow and the Voice of Murder,
The,* LA Bantam #21, 1940, first book
edition, illustrated cover, written by
Walter B. Gibson, rare. 📷
$300 **$900** **$2,000**

--- *Shadow: Destination Moon,
The,* Belmont Book #B50-737, 1966,
paperback original, written by Dennis
Lynds. **$6** **$20** **$40**

--- *Shadow Go Mad,* Belmont Book
#B50-709, 1966, paperback original,

written by Dennis Lynds.
$5 **20** **$35**

--- *Shadow's Revenge, The,* Belmont
Book #B50-647, 1965, paperback
original, written by Dennis Lynds.
$5 **$20** **$40**

--- *Living Shadow, The,* Pyramid Book
#N3597, 1974, cover by James Steranko,
written by Walter B. Gibson. The
Pyramid and Jove Shadow series ran 23
books. Steranko did all the covers; for
the Jove reprints of the Pyramids he did
new cover art. Gibson wrote all. Some
higher numbers are worth more; each
book: **$5** **$15** **$30**

--- *Living Shadow, The,* Jove Book
#V4576, 1977, new cover by James
Steranko shows classic "Yellow Peril" art,
written by Walter B. Gibson. 📷
$5 **$20** **$50**

--- *Living Shadow, The,* Bantam Book
#H-4463, 1969, first book edition, cover
by Sandy Kossin, #1 of seven written by
Walter B. Gibson, each book:
$5 **$15** **$30**

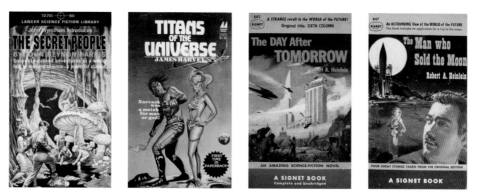

	G	VG	F		G	VG	F

Grazier, James, *Runts of 61 Cygni C,* Belmont Book #B75-2062, 1970, paperback original, title is a mouthful but the naked cyclops alien cover art is a favorite. 📷 **$6 $20 $45**

Grimm, Brothers, *Grimm's Fairy Tales,* LA Bantam #16, 1940, rare. **$50 $150 $275**

Haggard, H. Rider, *King Solomon's Mines,* Armed Service Edition #795, no date, circa 1947. **$12 $35 $100**

--- *She,* Armed Service Edition #881, no date, circa 1947. **$15 $42 $100**

--- *She,* Dell Book #339, 1949, Map Back, cover by Lou Marchetti, alluring image of She-Who-Must-Be-Obeyed bathing in living fire. 📷 **$4 $20 $50**

Hamilton, Edmond, *Beyond the Moon,* Signet Book #812, 1950. 📷 **$5 $20 $50**

Hamilton, Laurell K., *Guilty Pleasures,* Ace Book #30483, 1993, paperback original, first Anita Blake vampire hunter novel. **$10 $30 $90**

--- *Nightseer,* Roc Book #45143, 1992, paperback original, her first novel. **$10 $30 $100**

--- *Ravenloft: Death of a Dark Lord*, TSR Book #0112, 1995, paperback original, #11 in Ravenloft series, scarce. **$5 $20 $65**

Hanlon, Jon, *Death's Loving Arms and Other Terror Tales,* Corinth Book #CR-147, 1966, first book edition, cover by Robert Bonfils, anthology of pulp stories,

Terror Tales #2. **$20 $90 $200**

--- *Doctor Death and Other Terror Tales*, Corinth Book #CR-129, 1965, first book edition, cover Robert Bonfils, anthology of pulp stories, #4 in Doctor Death series. **$15 $75 $125**

--- *House of Living Death and Other Terror Tales, The,* Corinth Book #CR-143, 1966, first book edition, cover by Robert Bonfils, Terror Tales #1. 📷 **$25 $75 $150**

Harmon, Jim, *Man Who Made Maniacs!, The,* Epic Book #107, 1961, paperback original, depraved vampire cult sleaze novel. **$12 $60 $125**

Harris, John Benyon, *Secret People, The,* Lancer Book #72-701, 1964, first book edition, cover by Frank Frazetta; pseudonym of John Wyndham. 📷 **$5 $15 $40**

Harrison, Harry, *Deathworld,* Bantam Book #A2160, 1960, paperback original, first Deathworld book, uncommon. **$5 $20 $65**

--- *Stainless Steel Rat, The,* Pyramid Book #F672, 1961, first book edition, cover by John Schoenherr, first Stainless Steel Rat book. **$5 $20 $50**

Harvey, James, *Titans of the Universe,* Manor Book #15371, 1978, paperback original, plagiarized edition of Gardner F. Fox's Escape Across the Cosmos (Paperback Library, 1964), almost word-for-word copy of Fox's novel, all copies recalled and destroyed, credited inside as by "Moonchild," scarce. 📷 **$3 $15 $40**

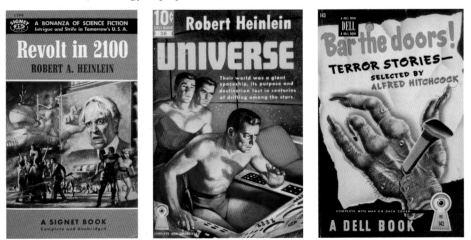

	G	VG	F

	G	VG	F

Healy, Raymond J., *New Tales of Space and Time*, Pocket Book #908, 1952, cover by Frank Charles, early SF anthology.
    $3   **$16**   **$35**

Heinlein, Robert A., *Day After Tomorrow, The*, Signet Book #882, 1951. 📷
    $4   **$20**   **$75**

--- *Door Into Summer, The*, Signet Book #S1639, 1959, cover by Paul Lehr.
    $4   **$18**   **$50**

--- *Green Hills of Earth, The*, Signet Book #943, 1952, cover by Stanley Meltzoff. Meltzoff told me he painted himself into this cover; he is the middle spaceman with the moustache.
    $4   **$20**   **$65**

--- *Man Who Sold the Moon, The*, Signet Book #847, 1951. 📷
    $5   **$20**   **$75**

--- *Revolt In 2100*, Signet Book #1194, 1955. 📷 **$5**   **$20**   **$65**

--- *Tomorrow the Stars*, Signet Book #1044, 1953, cover by Stanley Meltzoff, first anthology edited by Heinlein.
    $2   **$15**   **$45**

--- *Universe*, Dell Ten-Cent Book #36, 1950, cover by Robert Stanley shows two-headed mutant. 📷
    $15   **$75**   **$175**

--- *Waldo: Genius In Orbit*, Avon Book #T-261, 1958, original title: *Waldo and Magic Inc.* **$4**   **$15**   **$45**

Hill, John, *Long Sleep, The*, Popular Library #00325, 1975, paperback original; pseudonym of Dean Koontz.
    $10   **$25**   **$65**

Hilton, James, *Lost Horizon*, Pocket Book #1, 1st printing 1939, the first book in the numbered Pocket Book series and the first mass-market paperback sold to the public, only 10,000 copies printed and distributed in New York only, fantasy novel. 📷 **$100** **$375** **$1,000**

--- *Lost Horizon*, Pocket Book #1, second printing 1939. **$10**   **$25**   **$100**

Hitchcock, Alfred, *Bar the Doors*, Dell Book #143, 1946, first book edition, Map Back, cover by Gerald Gregg, horror anthology. 📷 **$6**   **$20**   **$75**

Hodgson, William Hope, *House on the Borderland, The*, Ace Book #D-553, 1962, horror. **$5**   **$20**   **$50**

--- *Night Land, The*, Ballantine Book #02669 and 02670, 1972, covers by Robert Lo Grippo, in two volumes, horror, each book: **$5**   **$20**   **$40**

Hogan, Robert J., *Bat Staffel, The*, Berkley Book #X1734, 1969, first book edition, #1 of eight in G-8 and His Battle Aces pulp reprint series. First three feature cover art by James Steranko, last five have pulp magazine cover art, each book: 📷 **$8**   **$15**   **$30**

Horlak, E. E., *Still Life*, Bantam Book #27656, 1989, paperback original, fantasy horror novel; pseudonym of Sheri S. Tepper. **$5**   **$15**   **$40**

House, Brant, *Sinister Scourge, The*, Corinth Book #CR-146, 1966, first book edition, cover by Robert Bonfils, book #7 in the Secret Agent X pulp reprint series of at least seven books, each book: 📷
    $10   **$18**   **$40**

Howard, Robert E., *Almuric*, Ace Book #F-305, 1964, first book edition, cover by Jack Gaughan. 📷 **$6**   **$20**   **$65**

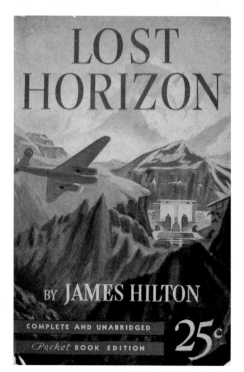

LOST HORIZON

BY JAMES HILTON

COMPLETE AND UNABRIDGED

Pocket BOOK EDITION

25¢

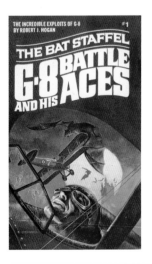

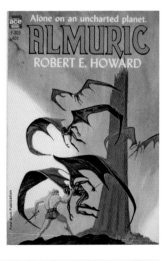

	G	VG	F

	G	VG	F

--- *Almuric*, Ace Book #91750, reprint 1970, new cover by Jeff Jones.

| | **$5** | **$20** | **$40** |

--- *Conan*, Lancer Book #73-685, 1967, cover by Frank Frazetta, #5 in the Lancer Conan series of 11 books (with L. Sprague de Camp and Lin Carter), each book:

| | **$4** | **$15** | **$30** |

--- *Conan the Conqueror*, Ace Books Double #D-36, 1953, first paperback printing, the first Conan paperback, Ace Double backed with *The Sword of Rhiannon* by Leigh Brackett. 📷

| | **$15** | **$50** | **$140** |

--- *Dark Man and Others, The*, Lancer Book #75-265, 1972.

| | **$6** | **$20** | **$40** |

--- *Hand of Kane, The*, Centaur Press, 1970, cover by Jeff Jones, Solomon Kane #1.

| | **$5** | **$20** | **$75** |

--- *King Kull*, Lancer Book #73-650, 1967, first book edition, cover by Roy Krenkel, scarce. 📷

| | **$5** | **$25** | **$70** |

--- *Moon of Skulls, The*, Centaur Press, 1969, cover by Jeff Jones, Solomon Kane #2, preceded Hand of Kane.

| | **$8** | **$20** | **$75** |

--- *Solomon Kane*, Centaur Press, 1971, cover by Jeff Jones, Solomon Kane #3.

| | **$6** | **$20** | **$75** |

--- *Wolfshead*, Lancer Book #73-721, 1968, cover by Frank Frazetta.

| | **$5** | **$20** | **$50** |

Hubbard, L. Ron, *Death's Deputy*, Leisure Book #00059, 1970, cover by Al Anderson.

| | **$8** | **$20** | **$60** |

--- *Fear*, Galaxy Novel #29, 1957, digest-size.

| | **$15** | **$40** | **$125** |

--- *Fear and the Ultimate Adventure*, Berkley Book #S1811, 1970, cover by Paul Lehr.

| | **$4** | **$20** | **$60** |

--- *Final Blackout*, Leisure Book #00032, 1970, cover by Nick Gallaway.

| | **$10** | **$40** | **$85** |

--- *Ole Doc Methuselah*, DAW Book #20, 1970, first book edition, cover by Tim Kirk.

| | **$5** | **$15** | **$35** |

--- *Return to Tomorrow*, Ace Book #S-66, 1954, paperback original. 📷

| | **$10** | **$25** | **$90** |

--- *Seven Steps to the Arbiter*, Major Book #3018, 1975, first book edition.

| | **$4** | **$16** | **$40** |

--- *Slaves of Sleep*, Lancer Book #73-573, 1967, cover by Kelly Freas. 📷

| | **$4** | **$15** | **$40** |

--- *Slaves of Sleep*, Dell Book #17646, 1979, cover by San Julian.

| | **$3** | **$14** | **$30** |

Hudson, Jan, *Those Sexy Saucer People*, Greenleaf Classic #GC220, 1967, paperback original, cover by Robert Bonfils, sleaze novel combines sex with SF; pseudonym of George H. Smith.

| | **$15** | **$75** | **$200** |

	G	VG	F		G	VG	F

Hudson, W. H., *Green Mansions,* Pocket Book #16, 1939, female "Tarzan."
$10 **$45** **$120**

Huxley, Aldous, *Brave New World,* Bantam Book #A1071, 1952, cover by Barye Phillips. 🎦 **$5** **$20** **$65**

Iverson, Eric, *Wereblood,* Belmont Book #51354, 1979, paperback original, #1 in Gerin series of two books; pseudonym of Harry Turledove, his first book.
$8 **$40** **$120**

--- *Werenight,* Belmont Book #51365, 1979, paperback original, Gerin #2.
$8 **$30** **$100**

Jackson, Shirley, *Lottery, The,* Lion Book #14, 1950, fantasy novel, "the adventure of a demon lover." 🎦 **$10** **$50** **$120**

Jakes, John, *Brak the Barbarian,* Avon Book #S363, 1968, first book edition, cover by Frank Frazetta, Conan-type hero. **$3** **$15** **$50**

James, M. R., *Selected Ghost Stories,* Armed Service Edition #O-28, no date, circa 1944, first book edition.
$15 **$50** **$120**

Jenkins, Will F., *Murder of the U.S.A., The,* Handi-Book #62, 1947, text cover, SF novel marketed as a mystery.
$8 **$30** **$100**

	G	VG	F

Johnson, David, *Jungle Nymph,* Scorpion Book #106, 1964, paperback original, sleaze novel about a female Tarzan-type; pseudonym of Charles Nuetzel. 📷 $15 $45 $125

Jones, Raymond F., *Deviates, The,* Beacon Book #242, 1959, cover by Robert Stanley. 📷 $8 $30 $100

Judd, Cyril, *Outpost Mars,* Dell Book #760, 1954, cover by Richard Powers, SF novel; pseudonym of C. M. Kornbluth and Judith Merrill. $4 $15 $30

--- *Sin in Space,* Beacon Book #312, 1961, cover by Robert Stanley. 📷 $15 $60 $150

Kastle, Herbert D., *Reassembled Man, The,* Gold Medal Book #L1494, 1964, paperback original, cover by Frank Frazetta. $4 $25 $65

Keene, Day and Pruyn, Leonard, *World Without Men,* Gold Medal Book #s975, 1960, paperback original, only SF novel by crime writer Day Keene. $6 $25 $75

Kennerley, Juba, *Terror of the Leopard Men, The,* Avon Book #339, 1951, strange discoveries of monsters, werewolves, leopard men. 📷 $10 $25 $90

Kersh, Gerald, *Nightshades & Damnations,* Gold Medal Book #r1887, 1968, first book edition, cover by Leo and Diane Dillon, horror collection, introduction by Harlan Ellison. $5 $20 $75

Ketchum, Jack, *Hide and Seek,* Ballantine Book #31237, 1984, paperback original, horror novel; pseudonym of Dallas Mayr. $10 $20 $65

--- *Off Season,* Ballantine Book #29427, 1981, paperback original, horror novel, his first book. $10 $30 $100

Key, Samuel M., *Angel of Darkness,* Jove Book #10422, 1990, paperback original, horror novel, first of three written under this pseudonym by Charles de Lint, each book: 📷 $5 $20 $45

Kline, Otis Adelbert, *Jan of the Jungle,* Ace Book #F-400, 1966, cover by Stephen Holland, jungle hero in India inspired by Tarzan. $4 $15 $30

--- *Maza of the Moon,* Ace Book #F-321, 1965, cover by Frank Frazetta. $5 $20 $40

--- *Outlaws of Mars,* Ace Book #G-693, 1968. $3 $15 $30

--- *Planet of Peril,* Ace Book #F-211, 1963, cover by Roy Krenkel, a Venus novel. 📷 $4 $20 $40

--- *Port of Peril, The,* Ace Book #F-294, 1964, cover by Roy Krenkel, a Venus novel. $4 $20 $40

--- *Prince of Peril,* Ace Book #F-259, 1964, cover by Roy Krenkel, a Venus novel. $4 $20 $40

--- *Swordsman of Mars, The,* Ace Book #D-516, 1961. 📷 $4 $20 $40

| | G | VG | F | | G | VG | F |

Knight, Damon, *Hell's Pavement,* Lion Library #LL13, 1955, first book edition, cover by Richard Powers.
    $5   **$20**   **$60**

--- *People Maker, The,* Zenith Book #ZB-14, 1959, first book edition of A Is For Anything, cover by Richard Powers.
    $4   **$18**   **$40**

Koman, Victor, *Starship Women,* Hustler Book #10-190, 1980, paperback original, his first book, SF porn.
    $5   **$30**   **$120**

Koontz, Dean, *Anti-Man,* Paperback Library #63-384, 1970, paperback original, cover by Steele Savage, scarce.   **$10**   **$30**   **$100**

--- *Beastchild,* Lancer Book #74719, 1970, paperback original, cover by Bernard Szafran. **$10**   **$35**   **$100**

--- *Crimson Witch, The,* Curtis Book #7156, 1971, first book edition.
   $30   **$100**   **$250**

--- *Darkness in My Soul, A,* DAW Book #12, 1972, paperback original, cover by Jack Gaughan. **$10**   **$30**   **$90**

--- *Dark of the Woods* with *Soft Come the Dragons,* Ace Book #13793, 1970, first book edition, Koontz Ace Double.
   $10   **$35**   **$100**

--- *Dark Symphony, The,* Lancer Book #74-621, 1970, paperback original.
   $10   **$30**   **$125**

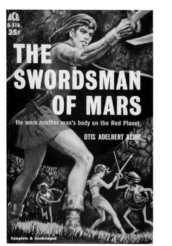

	G	VG	F

--- *Demon Seed*, Bantam Book #N7190, 1973, paperback original, cover by Jeff Jones. **$10　$30　$100**

--- *Flesh in the Furnace, The*, Bantam Book #S6977, 1972, paperback original. **$10　$30　$90**

--- *Fear That Man*, Ace Book #23140, 1969, paperback original, cover by Jack Gaughan, Ace Double backed with *Toyman* by E.C. Tubb, cover by Kelly Freas. **$10　$30　$100**

--- *Haunted Earth, The*, Lancer Book #75445, 1973, paperback original. **$10　$35　$100**

--- *Hell's Gate*, Lancer Book #74656, 1970, paperback original, cover by Kelly Freas. **$10　$40　$120**

--- *Nightmare Journey*, Berkley Book #02923, 1975, paperback original, cover by Paul Lehr. **$10　$30　$90**

--- *Star Blood*, Lancer Book #75306, 1972, paperback original, cover by Charles Moll. **$10　$35　$100**

--- *Star Quest*, Ace Book #H-70, 1968, paperback original, cover by Gray Morrow, Koontz's first novel, Ace Double backed with *Doom of the Green Planet* by Emil Petaja. **$8　$40　$130**

--- *Time Thieves*, Ace Book #00990, 1972, paperback original, Ace Double backed with *Against Arcturus* by Susan K. Putney.  **$10　$30　$90**

--- *Warlock*, Lancer Book #75386, 1972, paperback original. **$10　$40　$120**

--- *Werewolf Among Us, A*, Ballantine Book #3055, 1973, paperback original, cover by Bob Blanchard. **$10　$30　$90**

Kornbluth, Cyril M., *Syndic, The*, Bantam Book #1317, 1955. 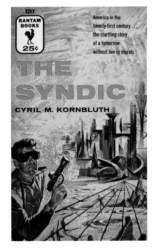 **$3　$15　$30**

Kress, Nancy, *Prince of Morning Bells, The*, Timescape Book#31146, 1981, paperback original, cover by Carl Lundgren, her first novel. **$4　$20　$50**

Kuttner, Henry, *Dark World, The*, Ace Book #F-327, 1965, first book edition, cover by Gray Morrow. **$5　$20　$60**

--- *Dr. Cyclops*, Popular Library #02485, 1970, first book edition, short SF novel not related to the film or Will Garth version done for Centaur Press, includes SF pulp stories by Bryce Walton, Edmond Hamilton. **$6　$25　$75**

Lansdale, Joe, *Act of Love*, Zebra Book #89083, 1981, paperback original, his first novel, horror. **$15　$60　$150**

--- *By Bizarre Hands*, Avon Book #71205, 1991, paperback original. **$6　$20　$75**

--- *Savage Season*, Bantam Book #28563, 1990, paperback original, cover by Alan Ayers. 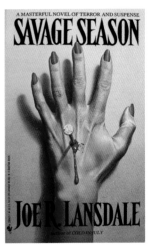 **$8　$25　$90**

	G	VG	F		G	VG	F

Laymon, Richard, *Cellar, The,* Paperjacks Book #00755, 1987, first U.S. edition.
$8 $30 $100

--- *Beast House, The,* Paperjacks Book #00684, 1987, first U.S. edition, horror novel, scarce. $8 $30 $100

--- *Flesh,* Tor Book #52110, 1988, paperback original, horror novel. 📷
$6 $25 $75

--- *Funland,* Onyx Book #40182, 1990, paperback original, horror novel.
$3 $18 $45

--- *Night Show,* Tor Book #52106, 1986, first U.S. edition, cover by Jill Bauman.
$6 $30 $90

--- *Out Are the Lights,* Warner Book #90519, 1993, scarce.
$20 $40 $120

--- *Resurrection Dreams,* Onyx Book #40136, 1989, paperback original, horror novel. $3 $30 $75

--- *Tread Softly,* Tor Book #52108, 1987, paperback original, cover by Jill Bauman, horror novel. $5 $30 $90

Lee, Edward, *Chosen, The,* Zebra Book #74372, 1993, paperback original.
$15 $40 $100

--- *Coven,* Berkley Diamond Book #73422, 1991, paperback original, horror.
$10 $25 $65

	G	VG	F

--- *Creekers*, Zebra Book #74568, 1994, paperback original, horror.
$12 $35 $90

--- *Incubi*, Berkley Diamond Book #73541, 1991, paperback original.
$10 $25 $60

Leguin, Ursula K., *Planet of Exile,* Ace Book #G-597, 1966, paperback original, cover by Jerome Podwil, Ace Double backed with *Mankind Under the Leash* by Thomas M. Disch, 1966, first book edition, cover by Kelly Freas.
$8 $20 $90

Leiber, Fritz, *Conjure Wife,* Lion Book #179, 1953, paperback original, cover by Robert Maguire.
$15 $45 $120

--- *Green Millennium, The,* Lion Library #LL7, 1954, first paperback printing.
$5 $15 $50

--- *Sinful Ones, The,* Giant Edition #5, 1953, first book edition, fantasy novel, double book with *Bulls, Blood and Passion* by David Williams.
$10 $30 $100

Leinster, Murray, *Fight For Life,* Prize Science Fiction Novel #10, 1949, first book edition, digest-size; pseudonym of Will F. Jenkins.   **$6 $25 $80**

--*Forgotten Planet, The,* Ace Book #D-528, 1961, first book edition.
$4 $15 $40

--- *Four From Planet 5,* Gold Medal Book #s937, 1959, paperback original, cover by Paul Lehr.
$4 $20 $40

--- *Monster From Earth's End, The,* Gold Medal Book #s832, 1959, paperback original, cover by Muni.
$4 $20 $50

--- *Pirates of Zan, The* with *The Mutant Weapon,* Ace Book #D-403, 1959, first book edition, cover by Ed Emsh, Leinster Ace Double.   **$4 $20 $55**

--- *War With the Gizmos, The,* Gold Medal Book #751, 1958, paperback original, cover by Richard Powers.
$4 $20 $50

Lewis, C. S., *Out of the Silent Planet,* Avon Book #195, 1949, cover by Ann Cantor shows amazing alien beaver creature.
$10 $30 $100

--- *Perelandra,* Avon Book #277, 1950, classic cover shows man confronting giant nude aliens.
$12 $35 $110

Long, Frank Belknap, *Mating Center,* Chariot Book #CB162, 1961, paperback original, sleaze SF novel about forbidden love.   **$5 $20 $65**

--- *Space Station #1,* Ace Book #D-242, 1957, paperback original, cover by Ed Emsh, Ace Double backed with *Empire of the Atom* by A.E. Van Vogt.
$4 $20 $45

--- *Woman From Another Planet,* Chariot Book #CB-123, 1960, paperback original, cover by Basil Gogot.
$5 $25 $75

Loomis, Noel, *City of Glass,* Double-Action Pocketbook, no number, 1955, first book edition, cover by Ed Emsh, digest-size.
$6 $20 $65

Lovecraft, H. P., *Cry Horror!,* Avon Book #T-284, 1958, cover by Richard Powers, reprints The Lurking Fear and Other Stories, with new title and cover art.
$6 $20 $45

--- *Doom That Came to Sarnath, The,* Ballantine Book #02146, 1971.
$6 $20 $50

--- *Dunwich Horror and Other Weird Tales, The,* Armed Service Edition #730, no date, circa 1945, first edition thus, collection.   **$22 $75 $155**

--- *Dunwich Horror, The,* Bart House Book #12, 1945. **$10 $30 $120**

--- *Fungi From Yuggoth,* Ballantine Book #02147, 1971, horror poetry, uncommon.
$8 $20 $90

--- *Lurking Fear and Other Stories, The,* Avon Book #136, 1947, classic cover by A. R. Tilburne shows graveyard ghoul among the tombstones, scarce in Fine.
$20 $50 $150

--- *Weird Shadow Over Innsmouth, The,* Bart House Book #4, 1944, first book edition.   **$15 $45 $120**

Lowther, George, *Adventures of Superman, The,* Armed Service Edition #656, no date, circa 1945, one of the rarest and most expensive ASEs.
$135 $600 $1,000

	G	VG	F

Lumley, Brian, *Burrowers Beneath, The*, DAW Book #91, 1974, paperback original, cover by Tim Kirk, Lovecraftian horror, Lumley's first book.

$4 **$20** **$75**

Lupoff, Richard A., *One Million Centuries*, Lancer Book #74-892, 1967, paperback original, cover by Jack Gaughan, author's first novel. **$3** **$15** **$40**

MacDonald, John D., *Planet of the Dreamers*, Pocket Book #943, 1953, cover by Rod Dunham, retitled *Wine of the Dreamers*, mystery author's early SF. **$4** **$18** **$45**

--- *Girl, the Gold Watch and Everything, The*, Gold Medal Book #s1259, 1962, paperback original, fantasy novel.

$8 **$40** **$125**

Machen, Arthur, *Great God Pan and Other Weird Stories, The*, Armed Service Edition #940, about 1946. **$15** **$45** **$125**

Maine, Eric Charles, *World Without Men*, Ace Book #D-274, 1958, paperback original, cover by Ed Emsh. 📷

$10 **$30** **$100**

Margulies, Leo, *Weird Tales*, Pyramid Book #R-1029, 1964, first book edition, cover by Virgil Finlay, anthology of classic pulp horror stories. **$4** **$20** **$60**

--- *Weird Tales*, Pyramid Book #V4472, reprint 1977, cover by Virgil Finlay. 📷

$3 **$15** **$30**

--- *Worlds of Weird*, Jove Book #4826, reprint 1978, new cover by Margaret Brundage shows her famous bat-girl cover. 📷 **$4** **$20** **$50**

	G	VG	F

Martin, George R. R., *Sandkings,*
Timescape Book #42663, 1981, first
book edition, cover by Rowena Morrill,
collection.  **$3** **$20** **$65**

Matheson, Richard, *Bid Time Return,*
Ballantine Book #24810, 1970, paperback
original, romance and SF, movie tie-in
edition retitled as *Somewhere in Time.*
$10 **$40** **$145**

--- *Hell House,* Bantam Book #N7277,
1972, horror novel given Gothic cover
treatment, scarce. **$6** **$25** **$85**

--- *I Am Legend,* Gold Medal #417, 1954,
paperback original, cover by Stanley
Meltzoff.  **$20** **$100** **$250**

--- *Shock,* Dell First Edition #B195, 1961,
first book edition, cover by Richard
Powers, collection. **$4** **$20** **$60**

--- *Shock III,* Dell Book #7830, 1966,
first book edition, cover by Neal Adams,
collection. **$4** **$20** **$50**

--- *Shrinking Man, The,* Gold Medal
Book #s577, 1956, paperback original,
cover by Mitchell Hooks.
$20 **$100** **$225**

--- *Shrinking Man, The,* Gold Medal
Book #d1203, second printing 1962,
cover by Mitchell Hooks, image reduced
from first printing with title enlarged in
red. **$10** **$25** **$75**

--- *Shrinking Man, The,* Bantam Book
#H3970, 1969, cover shows man battling
giant spider. **$4** **$20** **$50**

--- *Stir of Echoes, A,* Crest Book #S-308,
1959, cover Mitchell Hooks, horror.
$4 **$30** **$90**

--- *Third From the Sun,* Bantam Book
#1294, 1955, cover by Barye Phillips,
collection.  **$4** **$30** **$90**

--- *Third From the Sun,* Bantam Book
#J2467, second printing 1962, new cover
art.  **$3** **$20** **$45**

McCaffrey, Anne, *Cooking Out of This
World,* Ballantine Book #23413,
1973, paperback original, SF writer's
cookbook, scarce.
$20 **$75** **$150**

	G	VG	F		G	VG	F

--- *Dragonflight*, Ballantine Book #U6124, 1968, first book edition, Pern #1. **$12** **$30** **$90**

--- *Restoree*, Ballantine Book #U6108, 1967, paperback original, her first book, early SF romance novel. **$10** **$20** **$100**

McClary, Thomas Calvert, *Rebirth*, Bart House Book #6, 1944, machines run wild. **$9** **$20** **$65**

Merrill, Judith, *Galaxy of Ghouls*, Lion Library #LL25, 1955, first book edition, cover by B. Thomas, fantasy anthology with Ray Bradbury, Fred Brown. **$4** **$18** **$45**

--- *Human?*, Lion Book #205, 1954, first book edition, anthology.  **$10** **$30** **$100**

--- *Shot in the Dark, A*, Bantam Book #751, 1950, cover by H. E. Bischoff, early science fiction anthology. **$5** **$20** **$75**

Merritt, A., *Burn Witch Burn*, Avon Murder Mystery Monthly #5, 1942, digest-size. **$10** **$30** **$90**

--- *Burn Witch Burn*, Avon Book #43, 1944. **$10** **$20** **$70**

--- *Burn Witch Burn*, Avon Book #392, 1951. **$10** **$20** **$65**

--- *Creep Shadow Creep*, Avon Murder Mystery Monthly #11, 1943, digest-size. **$15** **$45** **$120**

--- *Creep Shadow Creep*, Avon Book #117, 1947. **$10** **$30** **$80**

--- *Dwellers in the Mirage*, Avon Murder Mystery Monthly #24, 1944, digest-size, cover by Paul Stahr. **$10** **$50** **$125**

--- *Dwellers in the Mirage*, Avon Book #413, 1952, giant octopus attacks naked blonde cover art. **$10** **$25** **$80**

--- *Face in the Abyss, The*, Avon Murder Mystery Monthly #29, 1945, digest-size, cover by Paul Stahr. **$10** **$45** **$120**

--- *Fox Woman, The*, Avon Book #214, 1949, first book edition, oddball cover art shows pointy-eared creature with sexy woman. **$10** **$30** **$90**

--- *Metal Monster, The*, Avon Murder Mystery Monthly #41, 1946, paperback original, digest-size. **$10** **$45** **$110**

--- *Metal Monster, The*, Avon Book #315, 1951. **$6** **$25** **$75**

--- *Metal Monster, The*, Avon Book #T-172, 1957, cover by Richard Powers. **$3** **$15** **$30**

--- *Moon Pool, The*, Avon Book #370, 1951, cover art shows giant frog with scantily clad blonde, "What secret compulsion made this lovely girl the handmaiden to unnatural horrors?" **$10** **$40** **$100**

--- *Seven Footprints to Satan*, Avon Murder Mystery of the Month #1, 1942, digest-size. **$10** **$55** **$125**

--- *Seven Footprints to Satan*, Avon Book #26, 1943. **$8** **$20** **$65**

--- *Seven Footprints to Satan*, Avon Book #235, 1950, new cover art. **$6** **$25** **$75**

	G	VG	F			G	VG	F

--- *Seven Footprints to Satan*, Avon Book #T-115, 1956, reuses bondage/torture cover art from Europa by Robert Briffault, Avon #272.

$8 — $25 — $75

--- *Ship of Ishtar, The*, Avon Murder Mystery Monthly #34, 1945, digest-size, cover by Paul Stahr.

$10 — $40 — $100

--- *Ship of Ishtar, The*, Avon Book #324, 1951, brutal bondage and torture cover art. 📷 $12 — $40 — $100

Merwin Jr., Sam, *Sex War, The*, Beacon Book #264, 1960, paperback original, cover by Gerald McConnel.

$12 — $30 — $100

Mitchell, Kirk, *Cry Republic*, Ace Book #12389, 1989, paperback original, cover by Jim Gurney, #3 in Rome trilogy.

$3 — $20 — $45

--- *New Barbarians*, Ace Book #57101, 1986, paperback original, cover by Jim Gurney, #2 in Rome trilogy. 📷

$4 — $20 — $50

--- *Procurator*, Ace Book #68029, 1984, paperback original, cover by Jim Gurney, #1 in alternate history trilogy where Rome never fell. $6 — $25 — $60

Moorcock, Michael, *Stealer of Souls, The*, Lancer Book #73-545, 1967, first U.S. edition, the first Elric book.

$5 — $20 — $60

	G	VG	F

--- *Stormbringer*, Lancer Book #73-579, 1967, first U.S. edition, Elric novel. **$4** **$15** **$50**

Moore, C. L., *Jirel of Joiry*, Paperback Library #63166, 1969. **$3** **$15** **$45**

Munro, H. H., *She-Wolf and Other Stories, The*, Bantam Book #143, 1948, Superior reprint in dust jacket. 🎞 **$20** **$75** **$175**

Niven, Larry, *Ringworld*, Ballantine Book #02046, 1970, paperback original, error has planet's rotation backwards, corrected next printing, cover by Dean Ellis. **$4** **$25** **$90**

Noel, Sterling, *I Killed Stalin*, Eton Book #E119, second printing 1952, new cover art, fantasy novel. 🎞 **$10** **$30** **$100**

Norden, Eric, *Ultimate Solution, The*, Warner Book #75-154, 1973, paperback original, cover by Seymour Chwast, SF crime novel where Nazis won World War II. 🎞 **$15** **$30** **$75**

Norman, John, *Blood Brothers of Gor*, DAW Book #504, 1982, paperback original, cover by Ken W. Kelly, Gor #18; pseudonym of John Frederick Lange Jr. **$10** **$30** **$80**

--- *Dancer of Gor*, DAW Book #77301, 1985, paperback original, Gor #22. **$10** **$30** **$85**

	G	VG	F

--- *Guardsmen of Gor*, DAW Book #456, 1981, paperback original, cover by Ken W. Kelly, Gor #16. **$6** **$25** **$75**

--- *Imaginative Sex*, DAW Book #UJ1146, 1974, paperback original, sexual fantasy scenarios. **$20** **$90** **$200**

--- *Kajira of Gor*, DAW Book #520, 1983, paperback original, cover by Ken W. Kelly, Gor #20. **$10** **$40** **$100**

--- *Magician of Gor*, DAW Book #746, 1988, paperback original, cover by Ken W. Kelly, Gor #25. **$10** **$45** **$125**

--- *Mercenaries of Gor*, DAW Book #617, 1985, paperback original, cover by Ken W. Kelly, Gor #22. 🎞 **$10** **$30** **$90**

--- *Players of Gor*, DAW Book #568, 1984, paperback original, cover by Ken W. Kelly, Gor book #21. **$10** **$40** **$90**

--- *Renegades of Gor*, DAW Book #77112, 1986, paperback original, cover by Ken W. Kelly, Gor #23. **$10** **$30** **$90**

--- *Savages of Gor*, DAW Book #472, 1982, paperback original, cover by Ken W. Kelly, Gor #17. **$8** **$25** **$80**

--- *Tarnsmen of Gor*, Ballantine #U6071, 1966, paperback original, cover by Robert Foster, Gor #1. **$5** **$20** **$75**

| | G | VG | F | | G | VG | F |

--- *Vagabonds of Gor*, DAW Book collector #701, 1987, paperback original, cover by Ken W. Kelly, Gor #24.
$10 **$45** **$100**

North, Andrew, *Voodoo Planet* with *Plague Ship*, Ace Book #D-345, 1959, paperback original, cover by Ed Emsh, Ace Double, early pseudonym of Mary Alice Norton, aka Andre Norton.
$5 **$20** **$60**

North, Eric, *Ant Men, The,* MacFadden Book #60-277, 1967, cover by Jack Faragasso, giant ants terrorize Australian outback.  **$4** **$15** **$40**

Norton, Andre, *Daybreak – 2250 A.D.,* Ace Book #D-69, 1954, Ace Double backed with *Beyond Earth's Gates* by Lewis Padgett (Henry Kuttner and C. L. Moore), 1954, paperback original; pseudonym of Mary Alice Norton. **$5** **$20** **$50**

--- *Daybreak – 2250 A.D.,* Ace Book #D-534, 1961, reprint, first single edition.
$3 **$15** **$35**

--- *Last Planet, The,* Ace Book #D-96, 1955, Ace Double backed with *A Man Obsessed* by Alan E. Nourse, paperback original, cover by Harry Barton.
$5 **$15** **$50**

--- *Last Planet, The,* Ace Book #D-96, 1955, "Special Edition" first separate printing. **$5** **$15** **$40**

--- *Spell Of the Witch World*, DAW Book #1, 1972, first book edition, cover by Jack Gaughan, the first DAW book.
$5 **$20** **$65**

--- *Witch World*, Ace Book #F-197, 1963, paperback original, cover by Jack Gaughan. **$4** **$15** **$45**

Nowlan, Philip Francis, *Armageddon 2419 A.D.,* Ace Book #F-188, 1963, first book edition, cover by Ed Emsh, the original "Buck Rogers" novel.
$4 **$18** **$45**

Page, Spider, *Blue Steel*, Python Book #002-7, 1979, paperback original, cover by George Gross, the last pulp novel in the Spider series, "Slaughter, Inc." by Donald Cormac, written for the pulp magazine but never published, published under this title and byline due to copyright problems at the time, the Gross cover was to have been used on the fourth Operator 5 paperback from Freeway Press, which also was never published, uncommon.
$10 **$30** **$100**

Philips, Rog, *Time Trap*, Century Book #116, 1947, the first science fiction paperback original novel, gorgeous alien woman with three eyes cover art.
$14 **$50** **$125**

--- *World of If*, Merit Book #B-13, 1951, paperback original, digest-size, novel.
$5 **$18** **$45**

--- *Worlds Within*, Century Book #124, 1950, paperback original, cover by Malcolm Smith. **$10** **$30** **$100**

Piper, H. Beam, *Cosmic Computer, The,* Ace Book #F-274, 1964, first book publication under this title. **$5** **$15** **$40**

--- *Crisis in 2140*, Ace Book #D-227, 1957, first book edition, written with John J. MaGuire, Ace Double backed with *Gunner Cade* by Cyril Judd (C. M. Kornbluth and Judith Merrill).
$6 **$20** **$50**

--- *Fuzzies and Other People*, Ace Book #26176, 1984, paperback original, cover by Michael Whelan, long-lost third book in series discovered after the author's suicide. **$8** **$20** **$60**

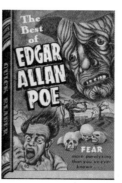

	G	VG	F

--- *Little Fuzzy*, Avon #F-118, 1962, paperback original, cover by Victor Kalin. **$6** **$30** **$75**

--- *Space Viking*, Ace Book #F-225, 1963, paperback original.  **$5** **$20** **$50**

Poe, Edgar Allen, *Best of Edgar Allen Poe, The*, Quick Reader #149, 1945. **$10** **$30** **$75**

--- *Selected Stories of Edgar Allen Poe*, Armed Service Edition #J297, no date, circa 1944, first edition thus, collection. **$22** **$90** **$155**

--- *Great Tales and Poems of Edgar Allen Poe, The*, Armed Service Edition #767, no date, circa 1945, reprints ASE #J297 with new title. **$12** **$55** **$150**

--- *Tales and Poems of Mystery and Imagination*, Pocket Book #39, 1940. **$7** **$25** **$75**

Pohl, Fred, *Beyond the End of Time*, Perma Book #P145, 1952, early SF anthology. **$5** **$15** **$40**

--- *Slave Ship*, Ballantine Book #192, 1957, paperback original. **$3** **$15** **$50**

Pohl, Fred and Kornbluth, C. M., *Space Merchants, The*, Ballantine Book #21, 1952, paperback original, cover by Richard Powers. **$6** **$20** **$60**

--- *Town Is Drowning, A*, Ballantine Book #123, 1955, paperback original, cover by Ed Emsh, disaster novel, uncommon. **$10** **$40** **$120**

Quinn, Seabury, *Adventures of Jules de Grandin, The*, Popular Library #00394, 1976, first book edition, cover by Vincent DiFate, six-book series of occult detective pulp stories from Weird Tales,

	G	VG	F

each book: **$5** **$15** **$35**

--- *Devil's Bride, The*, Popular Library #00424, 1976, first book edition, cover by Vincent DiFate, toughest book in de Grandin series. **$10** **$30** **$75**

Rathbone, Basil, *Strange Tales*, Belmont Book #B50-633, 1965, first book edition, cover art shows Basil Rathbone, anthology. **$4** **$15** **$40**

Reed, David V., *Thing That Made Love, The*, Uni-Book #15, 1951, first book edition, digest-size, SF-horror novel. **$12** **$40** **$100**

Rivere, Alec, *Lost City of the Damned*, Pike Book #101, 1961, paperback original, cover by Albert Nuetzel, sleaze adventure SF novel; pseudonym of Charles Nuetzel. **$10** **$60** **$125**

Robeson, Kenneth, *Jiu San* with *The Black, Black Witch*, Bantam Book #14901, 1981, first book edition, Doc Savage Double #107-108, there are many Doc Savage "Doubles" and "Omnibus" editions in this series, each book: **$20** **$40** **$90**

--- *Man of Bronze, The*, Bantam Book #E2853, 1964, first book edition, cover by James Bama, #1 in the Doc Savage series of hero pulp reprints, begins series of 100+ paperbacks, almost all first book editions, most written by Lester Dent under the Robeson house name, first printings only each book: **$4** **$15** **$25**

Russell, Eric Frank, *Sentinels of Space*, Ace Book #D-44, 1954, cover by Robert Schulz, Ace Double backed with *The Ultimate Invader and Other Stories*, edited by Donald A. Wollheim, anthology. **$4** **$18** **$60**

	G	VG	F		G	VG	F

--- *Six Worlds Yonder* with *The Space Willies*, Ace Book #D-315, 1958, first book edition, Ace Double. **$4** **$20** **$50**

--- *Three to Conquer*, Ace Book #D-215, 1957, Ace Double backed with *Doomsday Eve* by Robert Moore Williams. 🐛 **$4** **$15** **$45**

Sale, Richard, *Lazarus #7*, Handi-Book #13, 1943. **$20** **$50** **$125**

--- *Not Too Narrow...Not Too Deep*, Armed Service Edition #S-7, no date, circa 1944. **$18** **$50** **$90**

Salten, Felix, *Bambi*, Pocket Book #10, 1939, only 10,000 copies sold in New York City area. **$45** **$200** **$450**

Saunders, Charles R., *Imaro*, DAW Book collector #459, 1981, paperback original, cover by Ken W. Kelly. Two versions of this PBO exist, the scarce one references a black Tarzan on cover and back cover and subject of legal action by the Edgar Rice Burroughs estate. That book was pulled and "Tarzan" replaced with "jungle hero" on subsequent copies, scarce. **$30** **$75** **$150**

Savage, Hardley, *Jetman Meets the Mad Madam*, Bee-Line Book #118, 1966, paperback original, SF-sleaze novel. **$15** **$40** **$120**

	G	VG	F

Scott, R. T. M., *Spider Strikes, The,* Berkley Book #X1735, 1969, first book edition, cover by James Steranko, book #1 in this four-book Berkley Spider pulp reprint series, the last two books are bylined Grant Stockbridge, each book:
| | $5 | $15 | $25 |

Scott, Warwick, *Doomsday,* Lion Book #148, 1953, paperback original, end-of-world SF novel.
| | $7 | $20 | $75 |

Sellers, Connie, *Red Rape!,* Headline Book #105, 1960, paperback original, Cold War SF sleaze novel; pseudonym of Con Sellers.
| | $8 | $25 | $75 |

Shea, Michael, *Quest For Simbilis, A,* DAW Book #88, 1974, paperback original, cover by George Barr, author's first book, authorized novel continues Jack Vance's Dying Earth series.
| | $4 | $20 | $60 |

Shelley, Mary, *Frankenstein,* Armed Service Edition #909, no date, circa 1946.
| | $40 | $150 | $325 |

--- *Frankenstein,* Lion Book #146, 1953, horror novel gets sexy cover treatment.
| | $10 | $40 | $100 |

Sherman, Harold M., *Green Man, The,* Century Book #104, 1946, first book edition, digest-size.
| | $18 | $90 | $200 |

Shirley, John, *Dracula in Love,* Zebra Book #5020, 1979, paperback original.
| | $8 | $25 | $80 |

	G	VG	F

Simak, Clifford D., *City,* Ace Book #D-283, 1958.
| | $4 | $15 | $50 |

--- *First He Died,* Dell Book #680, 1953, retitled *Time and Again.*
| | $4 | $15 | $40 |

Siodmak, Curt, *Donovan's Brain,* Armed Service Edition #0-9, no date, circa 1944.
| | $15 | $50 | $120 |

--- *Donovan's Brain,* Bantam Book #819, 1950.
| | $4 | $30 | $90 |

Smith, Clark Ashton, *City of the Singing Flame, The,* Timescape Book #83415, 1981, first book edition, cover by Rowena Morrill, collection.
| | $6 | $20 | $50 |

--- *Hyperborea,* Ballantine Book #02206, 1971, cover by Bill Martin.
| | $10 | $25 | $75 |

--- *Last Incantation, The,* Timescape Book #83542, 1982, first book edition, cover by Rowena Morrill, collection.
| | $8 | $20 | $45 |

--- *Monster of the Prophecy, The,* Timescape Book #83544, 1983, first book edition, collection.
| | $6 | $20 | $50 |

--- *Poseidonis,* Ballantine Book #03353, 1973, cover by Gervasio Gallardo.
| | $10 | $35 | $65 |

--- *Xiccarph,* Ballantine Book #02501, 1972, cover by Gervasio Gallardo, scarce, low print run.
| | $10 | $40 | $100 |

	G	VG	F		G	VG	F

--- *Zothique*, Ballantine Book #01938, 1970, cover by George Barr.
$10 $25 $75

Smith, Cordwainer, *Conquest of the Three Worlds,* Ace Book #F-402, 1966, first book edition, cover by Gray Morrow.
$6 $20 $50

--- *You Will Never Be the Same*, Regency Book #R309, 1963, first book edition, cover by Ron Bradford, collection.
$8 $30 $100

Smith, Edward E. E. "Doc," *Galaxy Primes, The,* Ace Book #F-328, 1965, first book edition, cover by Ed Valigursky.
$4 $20 $45

Smith, George H., *Coming of the Rats, The,* Pike Book #203, 1961, paperback original, cover by Albert Nuetzel, apocalyptic sleaze SF novel.
$18 $100 $250

--- *Doomsday Wing*, Monarch Book #338, 1963, paperback original, cover by Earl Mayan. $3 $12 $30

--- *Scourge of the Blood Cult*, Epic Book #110, 1961, paperback original, fantasy novel. $12 $50 $125

--- *Unending Night, The*, Monarch Book #464, 1964, paperback original, cover by Ralph Brillhart, disaster novel.
$3 $14 $40

--- *1976 The Year of Terror*, Epic Book #103, 1961, paperback original, cover by Doug Weaver, United States in reign of terror in this sleaze SF shocker.
$10 $30 $100

Smith, George O., *Operation Interstellar,* Merit Book #B-10, 1950, paperback original, cover by Malcolm Smith, digest-size. $5 $20 $75

--- *Troubled Star*, Beacon Book #256, 1959, paperback original, cover by Ed Emsh. $10 $30 $100

Smith, Martin, *Indians Won, The,* Belmont Book #B95-2045, 1970, paperback original, alternate history novel, author's full name is Martin Cruz Smith, his first book, scarce. $50 $100 $200

Smith, Thorne, *Night Life of the Gods,* Armed Service Edition #S-28, no date, circa 1944. $10 $45 $100

--- *Passionate Witch, The*, Armed Service Edition #953, no date, circa 1946.
$10 $65 $125

--- *Rain in the Doorway*, Armed Service Edition #922, no date, circa 1946, fantasy-humor. $10 $45 $100

--- *Topper*, Pocket Book #4, first printing 1939, only 10,000 copies printed and distributed in the New York City area, rare. $50 $240 $650

Sohl, Jerry, *Altered Ego, The,* Pennant Book #P-75, 1954, surreal SF cover art.
$4 $15 $40

--- *Haploids, The*, Lion Book #118, 1953, paperback original, cover by Raphael DeSoto, skull and hypodermic needle cover art. $10 $30 $100

Spinrad, Norman, *Agent of Chaos,* Belmont Book #B50-139, 1967, paperback original.
$4 $20 $40

Stapledon, Olaf, *Odd John,* Beacon Book #236, 1959, cover by Robert Stanley.
$6 $35 $100

	G	VG	F		G	VG	F

Steele, Curtis, *Army of the Dead, The,* Corinth Book #CR-120, 1966, first book edition, cover by Robert Bonfils, book #2 in the Operator 5 series of at least eight books, each book: 🎲
$10 $20 $40

Steffanson, Con, *Space Circus, The,* Avon Book #19695, 1974, paperback original, cover by George Wilson, originally a comic strip created by Alex Raymond, #3 in six-book Flash Gordon series; pseudonym of Ron Goulart. Goulart wrote the first three books in the series as Con Steffanson; Bruce Cassidy (as Carson Bingham) wrote the last three, each book: 🎲 **$4 $15 $30**

Stevens, Francis, *Citadel of Fear, The,* Paperback Library #65-401, 1970, cover by Steele Savage, pre-Lovecraftian horror novel.   **$6 $20 $65**

Stevenson, Robert Louis, *The Strange Case of Dr. Jekyll and Mr. Hyde,* Armed Service Edition #885, no date, circa 1945. 🎲
$15 $35 $100

--- *Dr. Jekyll and Mr. Hyde, The,* Quick Reader #142, 1945.
$10 $25 $80

Stewart, George R., *Storm,* Bantam Book #155, 1948, Penguin Book in Bantam dust jacket.   **$30 $75 $165**

Stine, Hank, *Season of the Witch,* Essex House #0112, 1968, paperback original, early fantasy and transgender novel where rapist turns into woman.
$30 $125 $300

--- *Thrill City,* Essex House #0141, 1969, mixes SF with sex.
$20 $100 $200

Stirling, S. M., *Marching Through Georgia,* Baen Book #65407, 1988, paperback original, cover by Kevin Davies, scarce.
$5 $20 $60

Stockbridge, Grant, *Death Reign of the Vampire King,* Pocket Book #77952, 1975, first book edition, cover by Robert Maguire, #1 in Pocket Books Spider series of four pulp reprints, all were updated, each book: 🎲
$4 $15 $30

Stoker, Bram, *Dracula,* Armed Service Edition #L-25, no date, circa 1944, reprinted as ASE 851.
$22 $100 $225

--- *Dracula,* Armed Service Edition #851, no date, circa 1947.
$15 $55 $150

--- *Dracula,* Pocket Book #452, 1947, not a movie tie-in edition. 🎲
$10 $35 $100

Stuart, W. J., *Forbidden Planet,* Paperback Library #52-572, 1967, illustrated cover shows Robby the Robot.
$6 $20 $65

Sturgeon, Theodore, *Cosmic Rape, The,* Dell First Edition #B120, 1958, first book edition, cover by Richard Powers, collection.   **$5 $20 $55**

--- *Some of Your Blood,* Ballantine Book #458K, 1961, paperback original, horror novel.   **$15 $30 $100**

--- *Sturgeon In Orbit,* Pyramid Book #F-974, 1964, first book edition, cover by Ed Emsh shows author, collection. 🎲
$4 $15 $45

	G	VG	F			G	VG	F

--- *Way Home, A*, Pyramid Book #G-184, 1956, first book edition, cover by Mel Hunter, collection. 📷

| | **$5** | **$15** | **$60** |

Swanson, Logan, *Earthbound,* Playboy Book #21144, 1982, paperback original, horror novel; pseudonym of Richard Matheson. **$10** **$25** **$90**

Tepper, Sheri S., *Flight of Mavin Manyshaped, The,* Ace Book #24092, 1985, paperback original, #2 in shapeshifter trilogy, uncommon.

| | **$5** | **$20** | **$60** |

--- *Search of Mavin Manyshaped, The,* Ace Book #75712, 1985, paperback

original, #3 in shapeshifter trilogy.

| | **$5** | **$20** | **$60** |

--- *Song of Mavin Manyshaped, The,* Ace Book #77523, 1985, paperback original, cover by Kinyoko Craft, book #1 in shapeshifter trilogy. 📷

| | **$6** | **$20** | **$65** |

Tolkien, J. R. R., *Hobbit, The,* Ballantine Book #U7039, 1965, first authorized paperback printing, uncommon in condition. **$8** **$25** **$90**

--- *Fellowship of the Ring, The,* Ace Book #A-4, 1965, unauthorized, first U.S. edition, cover by Jack Gaughan, #1 in Lord of the Rings trilogy, scarce. 📷

| | **$10** | **$35** | **$100** |

	G	VG	F

--- *Return of the King, The*, Ace Book #A-6, 1965, unauthorized, first U.S. edition, cover by Jack Gaughan, #3 in Lord of the Rings trilogy, scarce.
$10 $40 $100

--- *Two Towers, The*, Ace Book #A-5, 1965, unauthorized, first U.S. edition, cover by Jack Gaughan, #2 in Lord of the Rings trilogy, scarce.
$6 $40 $100

Tubb, E. C., *Temple of Truth, The*, DAW Book #77059, 1985, paperback original, cover by Ken W. Kelly, #31 and last mass-market edition in Dumarest series dropped by DAW Books.
$20 $40 $100

Tucker, Wilson, *Long Loud Silence, The*, Dell Book #791, 1954, cover by Richard Powers. **$4 $15 $50**

--- *Tomorrow Plus X*, Avon Book #T-168, 1957, cover by Richard Powers, aka Time Bomb. 📷 **$3 $15 $40**

Twain, Mark, *Connecticut Yankee in King Arthur's Court, A*, Armed Service Edition #E139, no date, circa 1944.
$20 $50 $125

--- *Connecticut Yankee in King Arthur's Court, A*, Pocket Book #497, 1948.
$5 $20 $75

Vance, Jack, *Big Planet* with *Slaves of the Klau*, Ace Book #D-295, 1958, paperback original, cover by Ed Emsh, a Vance Ace Double. **$10 $30 $100**

	G	VG	F

--- *Dying Earth, The*, Hillman Book #41, 1950, first book edition, Vance's first book, not a paperback original as is often listed in error. 📷
$35 $125 $500

--- *Five Gold Bands* with *The Dragon Masters*, Ace Book #F-185 1963, paperback original, a Vance Ace Double.
$5 $20 $80

--- *Space Pirate, The*, Toby Press, no number, 1953, paperback original, digest-size. 📷 **$10 $30 $100**

Van Vogt, A. E., *Away and Beyond*, Avon Book #548, 1953, first book edition, collection. **$4 $15 $40**

--- *Destination: Universe*, Signet Book #1007, 1953, cover by Stanley Meltzoff.
$4 $20 $45

--- *Mating Cry, The*, Beacon Book #298, 1960, paperback original, cover by Gerald McConnel, bondage cover. 📷
$20 $90 $200

--- *Mission: Interplanetary*, Signet Book #914, 1952. 📷 **$3 $15 $40**

--- *Slan*, Dell Book #696, 1953, classic SF novel. **$3 $12 $30**

Von Harbou, Thea, *Metropolis*, Ace Book #F-246, 1963, cover by Jack Gaughan.
$3 $14 $40

Vonnegut Jr., Kurt, *Canary in a Cat House*, Gold Medal Book #s1153, 1961, paperback original, cover by Leo and Diane Dillon. **$15 $100 $250**

	G	VG	F

--- *Mother Night*, Gold Medal Book #s1191, 1962, paperback original, cover by Leo and Diane Dillon.

    $20   **$150**   **$250**

--- *Sirens of Titan, The*, Dell First Edition #B-138, 1959, paperback original, cover by Richard Powers. 📷

    $12   **$60**   **$135**

--- *Utopia 14*, Bantam Book #A1262, 1954, first paperback version with different title for *Player Piano*, his first book. 📷   **$10**   **$30**   **$120**

Wagner, Karl Edward, *Darkness Weaves,* Powell Book #PP-213, 1970, paperback original, fantasy. **$10**   **$30**   **$100**

Wallace, F. L., *Address: Centauri*, Galaxy SF Novel #32, 1958, cover by Wally Wood, paperback size. 📷 **$6**   **$15**   **$45**

Wallace, Robert, *Vampire Murders, The,* Corinth Book #CR-101, 1965, first book edition, cover by Robert Bonfils, book #1 in the Phantom Detective hero pulp series of at least 19 books, each book: 📷

    $6   **$15**   **$40**

Walton, Evangeline, *Witch House,* Monarch Book #264, 1962, cover by Ralph Brillhart. **$5**   **$25**   **$75**

Welles, Orson, *Invasion From Mars,* Dell Book #305, 1949, Map Back, cover by Malcolm Smith, anthology. 📷

    $6   **$20**   **$75**

Wellman, Manly Wade, *Sherlock Holmes's War of the Worlds,* Warner Book #76-982, 1975, paperback original, cover by Frank Accanero, written with his son, Wade Wellman. **$15**   **$40**   **$125**

--- *Sojarr of Titan*, Prize Science Fiction Novel #11, 1949, first book edition, digest-size, classic space fantasy cover art, uncommon. 📷

    $10   **$40**   **$120**

--- *Twice In Time*, Galaxy SF Novel #34, 1958, cover by Wally Wood, paperback size. **$10**   **$30**   **$85**

Wells, H. G., *First Men in the Moon, The,* Dell Book #201, 1947, Map Back, cover by Earl Sherman. **$5**   **$15**   **$60**

--- *Food of the Gods, The*, Armed Service Edition #958, no date, circa 1945.

    $15   **$30**   **$100**

--- *Island of Dr. Moreau, The*, Armed Service Edition #698, no date, circa 1946.

    $15   **$35**   **$100**

--- *Time Machine, The*, Armed Service Edition #T-2, no date, circa 1944.

    $16   **$50**   **$120**

--- *War of the Worlds, The*, Armed Service Edition #745, no date, circa 1945, reprinted as ASE #1091.

    $20   **$65**   **$160**

--- *War of the Worlds, The*, Armed Service Edition #1091, no date, circa 1947.

    $20   **$50**   **$100**

--- *War of the Worlds, The*, Airmont Book #CL45, 1964. 📷 **$2**   **$14**   **$30**

Werper, Barton, *Tarzan and the Abominable Snow Men,* Gold Star Book #IL7-60, 1964, paperback original, series of five unauthorized Tarzan novels. 📷

    $10   **$20**   **$60**

	G	VG	F
	G	VG	F

--- *Tarzan and the Cave City*, Gold Star Book #IL7-49, 1964, paperback original. **$10** **$20** **$50**

--- *Tarzan and the Silver Globe*, Gold Star Book #IL7-42, 1964, paperback original. **$10** **$20** **$50**

--- *Tarzan and the Snake People*, Gold Star Book #IL7-54, 1964, paperback original. **$10** **$20** **$55**

--- *Tarzan and the Winged Invaders*, Gold Star Book #IL7-65, 1964, paperback original. **$10** **$25** **$60**

West, Owen, *Funhouse*, Jove Book #5726, 1990; pseudonym of Dean Koontz, novelization by Koontz based on Lawrence Block screenplay. **$4** **$20** **$60**

White, Ted, *Great Gold Steal, The*, Bantam Book #F3780, 1968, paperback original, Captain America novel based on Marvel comic book hero. **$5** **$20** **$65**

Willeford, Charles, *Machine In Ward Eleven, The*, Belmont Book #90-286, 1963, first book edition, cover by Robert Maguire. **$10** **$35** **$125**

Williams, Herbert, *Terror At Night*, Avon Book #110, 1947, cover by George Mayers, anthology contains Lovecraft. **$10** **$30** **$100**

Williams, Robert Moore, *Chaos Fighters, The*, Ace Book #S-90, 1955, paperback original. **$4** **$15** **$40**

	G	VG	F

--- *Day They H-Bombed Los Angeles, The*, Ace Book #D-530, 1961, paperback original, end-of-world SF novel with mushroom cloud cover art.

	$5	**$25**	**$75**

Williamson, Jack, *Dragon's Island*, Popular Library #447, 1952, cover by Walter Popp.

	$8	**$30**	**$90**

--- *Dome Around America*, Ace Book #D-118, 1955, first book edition, Ace Double backed with *The Paradox Men* by Charles L. Harness.

	$6	**$20**	**$65**

--- *Green Girl, The*, Avon Fantasy Novel #2, 1950, cover artist unknown but

	G	VG	F

surely one of the strangest SF covers as a green woman is abducted by a giant alien orchid.

	$20	**$100**	**$200**

Wolfe, Aaron, *Invasion*, Laser Book #9, 1976, paperback original, cover by Kelly Freas; pseudonym of Dean Koontz.

	$8	**$25**	**$65**

Wollheim, Donald A., *Girl With the Hungry Eyes, The*, Avon Book #184, 1949, first book edition, cover by Ann Cantor, early anthology.

	$10	**$35**	**$120**

--- *Pocket Book of Science Fiction, The*, Pocket Book #214, 1943, the first

	G	VG	F			G	VG	F

paperback to use the term "science fiction" in the title. 📷 **$10 $30 $120**

Wylie, Philip, *Gladiator*, Avon Book #216, 1949, inspired the creation of Superman.
$6 $20 $75

Wylie, Phillip and Balmer, Edwin, *When Worlds Collide*, Armed Service Edition #801, no date, circa 1945.
$10 $40 $100

--- *When Worlds Collide*, Dell Book #627, 1952, cover by Robert Stanley. 📷
$4 $20 $80

Wyndham, John, *Midwich Cuckoos, The*, Ballantine Book #299K, 1957, first U.S.

edition.   **$4 $20 $75**

--- *Revolt of the Triffids*, Popular Library #411, 1952, cover by Earle Bergey giant plants attack London. 📷
$10 $30 $100

Zelazny, Roger, *Dream Maker, The*, Ace Book #F-403, 1966, first book edition, cover by Kelly Freas.   **$4 $15 $50**

Zorro, *Grey Creatures, The*, Corinth Book #CR-121, 1966, first book edition, cover by Robert Bonfils shows face of Corinth editor Earl Kemp, Doctor Death book #2. 📷   **$20 $75 $145**

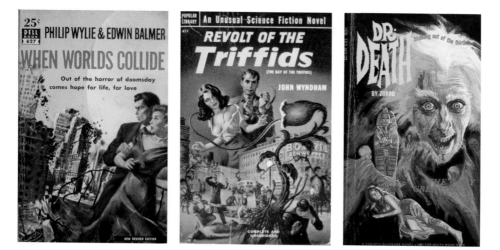

MYSTERIES:
Crime, Detective, Hard-boiled, Noir, Spy, and Suspense

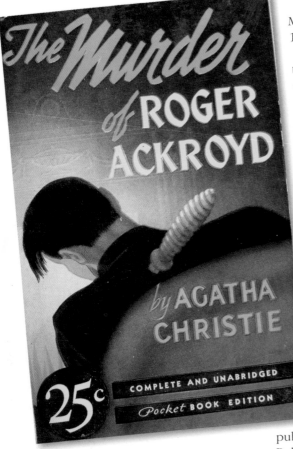

Mickey Spillane (Signet Books, 1949).

The mystery genre makes up the largest section in this book and deservedly so because it was the genre that made the mass-market paperback a success in the early days, and hence a lot of classic work, and key collectible editions, were published in the paperback format.

Some of the many highlights here include all the various Dashiell Hammett and Raymond Chandler first book editions in digest format, the Pocket Book edition of Hammett's *Maltese Falcon* in dust jacket, the Clayton Rawson Yogi Mystery digest, the two All-Picture Mystery digests, Gold Medal Books paperback originals of David Goodis, and all the Lion Books paperback originals of Jim Thompson, including *The Killer Inside Me*. Lion also published PBOs of David Goodis, Robert Bloch, and Richard Matheson. There's a lot to choose from here and I've barely scratched the surface. There are also three Perma and one Popular Library editions of early James Bond novels. Then there are the 0008 James Bond spy spoofs by Clyde Allison that offer spectacular sexy adventures, most graced by beautiful Robert Bonfils covers.

Some of the best Popular Library crime covers were originally painted for pulp magazines. Many of these

The advent of the mass-market paperback also heralded in a golden age for the traditional mystery novel beginning with Pocket Book #5, *The Murder of Roger Ackroyd* by Agatha Christie (1939), and a bit later in the 1940s, for the hard-boiled private eye paperback with work by Dashiell Hammett and Raymond Chandler. There were many more later examples, one of the most important and influential being *I, the Jury* by

classic covers by Rudolph Belarski originally appeared on Popular Library pulps. These crime paperbacks are avidly collected for their cover art alone, irrespective of the author or book. Earle Bergey also contributed many fine covers. Dell Books displayed the high quality and stylish airbrushed work of Gerald Gregg and later, the pulp-inspired art of Robert Stanley, which helps make these Dell editions collectible. Beginning with Dell Book #5 in 1943 and running until 1952, there were a total of 577 Map Back editions published by Dell Books with glorious "scene of the crime" maps and art on the back cover. These books are mostly mysteries but all of them are very collectible. They are simply lovely and command premium prices when in "Fine" condition.

The mystery genre seemed to excel in interesting and exciting cover art motifs. Skull cover art was often seen on classic mystery paperbacks. Many Dell Map Backs contain outrageous skull cover art, sometimes surreal in design, but always effective. Women in peril were another staple of traditional mystery and later hard-boiled paperback cover art. These pulp-inspired covers abounded and are popular today with collectors. Sometimes the cover artist turned the tables on the men, and we see them in peril at the hands of women! Then we are introduced to images of lovely but dangerous femme fatales. There are also all manner of depictions of murder, where guns and knives

reign supreme in every conceivable permutation. The generic blonde with a gun is a favorite, but also there are some interesting implements, such as on the cover of *Pick Your Victim*, where a yard pick is used. Murder in bathtubs is another motif that seems to be used more often than you would think. There are many others, and browsing through the covers in this section you will see many of the most popular and eye-catching covers ever painted for a mystery paperback. Colorful, lovely, and sexy, sometimes grotesque or violent, these images are just amazing, and fans and collectors love them.

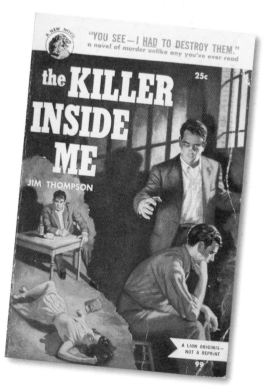

	G	VG	F

Abbot, Anthony, *About the Murder of the Night Club Lady,* Green Dragon #27, 1945, surreal cover art; pseudonym of Fulton Oursler. 📷 **$4 $15 $50**

--- *The Creeps,* Dell Book #88, 1945.
$10 $30 $100

--- *Murder of the Clergyman's Mistress,* Popular Library #286, 1950, women in peril cover with a difference, the killer has a knife, but she has a gun! 📷
$6 $20 $70

Adams, Cleve F., *No Wings On a Cop,* Handi-Book #112, 1950, paperback original, expanded by Robert Leslie Bellem from Adams' novelette.
$10 $30 $120

--- *Private Eye, The,* Signet Book #1405, 1957, cover by Robert Maguire, one of his classic and most effective covers 📷 .
$4 $20 $50

Alexander, David, *Dead, Man, Dead,* Dell Book #D362, 1960, cover by Robert Maguire, voodoo murder in Manhattan.
$4 $15 $45

Allingham, Margery, *Death of a Ghost,* Penguin Book #503, 1942, in dust jacket. 📷 **$30 $100 $220**

Allison, Clyde, *0008 Meets Gnatman,* Leisure Book #1140, 1966, paperback original, cover by Robert Bonfils, 0008 novel, sexy soft-core adult series spoofs James Bond; pseudonym of William Knoles. **$25 $60 $200**

--- *0008 Meets Modesta Blaze,* Leisure Book #1169, 1966, paperback original, cover by Robert Bonfils, 0008 novel.
$50 $100 $300

--- *Desdamona Affair, The,* Ember Library #EL-317, 1966, paperback original, cover by Robert Bonfils, 0008 novel. **$40 $75 $250**

--- *Desert Damsels, The,* Candid Reader #CA-930, 1968, paperback original, cover by Robert Bonfils.
$55 $150 $350

--- *For Your Sighs Only,* Ember Library #EL-329, 1966, paperback original, cover by Robert Bonfils, 0008 novel.
$50 $100 $250

--- *From Rapture With Love,* Leisure Book #1180, paperback original, 1966, cover by Robert Bonfils, 0008 novel.
$60 $100 $275

--- *Gamefinger,* Ember Library #EL-321, 1966, paperback original, cover by Robert Bonfils, 0008 novel. 📷
$35 $80 $175

--- *Go-Go Sadisto,* Ember Library #EL-313, 1966, paperback original, cover by Robert Bonfils, 0008 novel.
$40 $90 $200

--- *Ice Maiden, The,* Ember Library #EL-365, 1967, paperback original, cover by Robert Bonfils, 0008 novel.
$40 $100 $275

--- *Lost Bomb, The,* Ember Library #EL-333, 1966, paperback original, cover by Robert Bonfils, 0008 novel. 📷
$35 $100 $275

--- *Merciless Mermaids, The,* Leisure Book #1159, 1966, paperback original, cover by Robert Bonfils, 0008 novel.
$50 $125 $320

--- *Mondo Sadisto,* Leisure Book #1160, 1966, paperback original, cover by Robert Bonfils, 0008 novel.
$50 $150 $300

--- *Nautipuss,* Ember Library #EL-309, 1965, paperback original, cover by Robert Bonfils, 0008 novel.
$35 $100 $225

--- *Our Girl From Mephisto,* Ember Library #EL-305, 1965, paperback original, cover by Robert Bonfils, 0008 novel. 📷 **$40 $125 $300**

--- *Our Man From Sadisto,* Ember Library #EL-301, 1965, paperback original, cover by Rober Bonfils, first 0008 novel. **$40 $125 $300**

--- *Platypussy,* Nightstand Book #1877, 1968, paperback original, cover by Darryl Milsap, 0008 novel.
$50 $125 $400

--- *Roberta the Conqueress,* Leisure Book #1176, 1966, paperback original, cover by Robert Bonfils, 0008 novel.
$55 $100 $250

	G	VG	F			G	VG	F

--- *Sadisto Royale*, Ember Library #EL-325, 1966, paperback original, cover by Robert Bonfils, 0008 novel.
$40 **$110** **$175**

--- *Sex Ray, The,* Leisure Book #1174, 1966, paperback original, cover by Robert Bonfils, 0008 novel.
$50 **$150** **$300**

--- *Sin Funnel, The,* Candid Reader #CA-901, 1967, paperback original, cover by Robert Bonfils, 0008 novel.
$50 **$150** **$400**

Alter, Robert Edmond, *Carny Kill,* Gold Medal Book #d1611, 1966, paperback original. **$5** **$20** **$75**

--- *Swamp Sister*, Gold Medal Book #s1095, 1961, paperback original, cover by Mitchell Hooks, rural noir.
$5 **$30** **$90**

Anderson, W.W., *Kill One, Kill Two,* Atlas Mystery, no number, 1944, digest-size.
$8 **$30** **$100**

Anonymous, *Chillers Illustrated, The,* Quick Reader #104, 1943, first book edition, cover by Axelrod, includes a Sherlock Holmes story. 🎲
$8 **$25** **$65**

--- *Horror and Homicide,* Checker Book #5, 1949, first book edition, early crime anthology includes Dashiell Hammett, Cornell Woolrich, Vincent Starrett, Sax Rohmer. **$10** **$30** **$100**

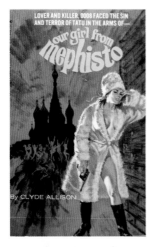

LOVER AND KILLER, 0008 FACED THE SIN
AND TERROR OF TATU IN THE ARMS OF—

our girl from
mephisto

By CLYDE ALLISON

MYSTERY MASTERS

DOROTHY SAYERS
W. W. Jacobs
Amelia B. Edwards
A. Conan Doyle

THE CHILLERS
Illustrated

4 SPINE-TINGLING STORIES THAT WILL
MAKE YOU SHUDDER AND GASP—FOR MORE!

A GANG KILLER MEETS HIS
MATCH IN A TNT BLONDE

BRAIN GUY
25c

BENJAMIN
APPEL

"A TENDER AND TERRIBLE TALE OF NEW
YORK'S HELL'S KITCHEN"—NELSON ALGREN

LION BOOK
39

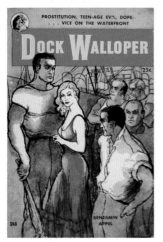

PROSTITUTION, TEEN-AGE EVIL, DOPE
. . . VICE ON THE WATERFRONT

DOCK WALLOPER
25c

BENJAMIN
APPEL

166

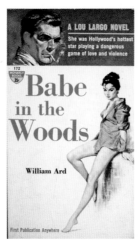

A LOU LARGO NOVEL

She was Hollywood's hottest
star playing a dangerous
game of love and violence

172

Babe
in the
Woods

William Ard

First Publication Anywhere

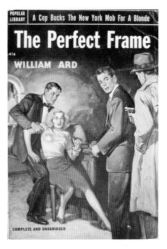

POPULAR
LIBRARY

A Cop Bucks The New York Mob For A Blonde

The Perfect Frame
416
WILLIAM ARD

COMPLETE AND UNABRIDGED

POPULAR
LIBRARY   25¢

Hoodlums On The Waterfront—Women On The Town

559

A PRIVATE PARTY

William Ard   "Fast, tough and
always exciting."
St. Louis POST DISPATCH

Complete and
Unabridged

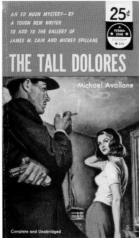

AN ED NOON MYSTERY—BY
A TOUGH NEW WRITER
TO ADD TO THE GALLERY OF
JAMES M. CAIN AND MICKEY SPILLANE

25¢
PERMA
STAR

THE TALL DOLORES

Michael Avallone

Complete and Unabridged

A MISSING MAN AND A STRANGLED GIRL STARTS
HOMICIDE HANNAH ON ANOTHER WILD "KILLER" HUNT

THE
GORGEOUS GHOUL
MURDER CASE
DWIGHT V. BABCOCK

SPECIALLY REVISED AND EDITED

	G	VG	F

--- *I, Mobster!*, Gold Medal Book #171, 1951, paperback original. **$5** **$20** **$75**

Appel, Benjamin, *Brain Guy,* Lion Book #39, 1950. 📷 **$5** **$20** **$75**

--- *Brain Guy,* Lion Library #LL151, 1957, cover by Mort Kunsler, reprints Lion #39 with new cover art. **$5** **$15** **$40**

--- *Dock Walloper,* Lion Book #166, 1953, paperback original, crime on the docks. 📷 **$6** **$25** **$90**

Ard, William, *All I Can Get,* Monarch Book #124, 1959, paperback original. **$10** **$30** **$100**

--- *Babe in the Woods,* Monarch Book #172, 1960, paperback original, completed by Lawrence Block. 📷 **$12** **$50** **$125**

--- *Diary, The,* Popular Library #477, 1953. **$10** **$35** **$90**

--- *Like Ice She Was,* Monarch Book #147, 1960, paperback original. **$10** **$40** **$100**

--- *Perfect Frame, The,* Popular Library #416, 1958, "a cop bucks the New York mob for a blonde." 📷 **$5** **$20** **$75**

--- *Private Party, A,* Popular Library #569, 1954. 📷 **$8** **$30** **$75**

--- *Sins of Billy Serene, The,* Monarch Book #152, 1960, paperback original, cover by Robert Maguire. **$10** **$35** **$100**

--- *You Can't Stop Me,* Popular Library #526, 1953, paperback original. **$5** **$18** **$55**

Asimov, Isaac, *Death Dealers, The,* Avon Book #T-287, 1958, paperback original, his first mystery novel. **$10** **$35** **$100**

Avallone, Michael, *Case of the Violent Virgin, The* with *The Case of the Bouncing Betty,* Ace Book #D-259, 1957, paperback original, Avallone Ace Double, scarce in condition. **$8** **$30** **$85**

--- *Crazy Mixed-Up Corpse, The,* Gold Medal Book #718, 1957, paperback original, cover by John Floherty. **$5** **$15** **$45**

--- *Dead Game,* Perma Book #M3012, 1955, cover by James Meese. **$5** **$18** **$50**

--- *High Noon at Midnight,* Paperjacks Book #00993, 1988, paperback original, cover by Frank Hamilton, Avallone's last Ed Noon novel. **$4** **$18** **$45**

--- *Meanwhile Back at the Morgue,* Gold Medal Book #1024, 1960, paperback original, photo cover. **$5** **$15** **$50**

--- *Tall Dolores, The,* Perma Book #244, 1953, cover by "DS" Daniel Schwartz, the first Ed Noon novel. Avallone had the original painting hanging in his New Jersey home. 📷 **$4** **$20** **$55**

--- *Voodoo Murders, The,* Gold Medal Book #703, 1957, paperback original, cover by Mitchell Hooks. **$5** **$15** **$50**

Babcock, Dwight V., *Gorgeous Ghoul Murder Case, The,* Avon Book, no number (#30), 1943. **$10** **$40** **$120**

--- *Gorgeous Ghoul Murder Case, The,* Avon Book #320, 1951, new cover art. 📷 **$4** **$30** **$90**

--- *Homicide For Hannah, A,* Avon Book #68, 1945, cover by Paul Stahr. **$4** **$25** **$75**

Baldwin, Linton, *Sinner's Game,* Lion Book #227, 1954, paperback original, author's only novel, "a tough kid – a con man – and a TNT blonde." 📷 **$12** **$40** **$100**

Ballard, W. T., *Murder Can't Stop,* Graphic Book #65, 1953. 📷 **$4** **$14** **$45**

--- *Pretty Miss Murder,* Perma Book #M4228, 1961, paperback original. **$2** **$15** **$50**

--- *Seven Sisters, The,* Perma Book #M4258, 1962, paperback original, cover by Harry Bennett. **$4** **$15** **$50**

--- *Three For the Money,* Perma Book #M4297, 1963, first book edition, cover by Harry Bennett. **$5** **$20** **$50**

--- *Walk in Fear,* Gold Medal Book #259, 1952, first book edition. **$5** **$20** **$65**

	G	VG	F

Barnard, Allan, *Harlot Killer, The,* Dell Book #797, 1954, first book edition, cover by Bill George, stories about Jack the Ripper. **$5 $20 $80**

Barnes, Linda, *Blood Will Have Blood,* Avon Book #79368, 1982, paperback original, her first book, crime novel introduces Michael Sprague. **$6 $30 $100**

Barry, Joe, *Homicide Hotel,* Phantom Book #500, 1951, paperback original, digest-size, private eye novel, brutal bondage cover art; pseudonym of Joe Barry Lake. 📷 **$30 $120 $300**

Becker, Stephen, *Shanghai Incident,* Gold Medal Book #994, second printing 1960, reprints Gold Medal #456 under author's true name, cover by Robert McGinnis. **$4 $20 $60**

Beckman Jr., Charles, *Honky Tonk Girl,* Falcon Book #44, 1953, paperback original, digest size, hard-boiled novel, "it was the last stop for the scum of humanity on the road to hell!" 📷 **$20 $125 $275**

Bellem, Robert Leslie, *Window With the Sleeping Nude, The,* Handi-Book #118,

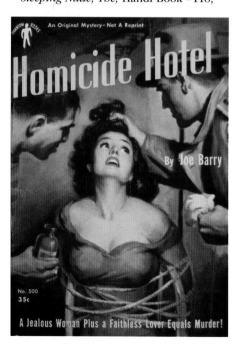

1950, his only U.S. vintage paperback. **$35 $75 $180**

Benson, O. G., *Cain's Woman,* Dell First Edition #A200, 1960, paperback original, cover by Darcy, the author's only novel, classic noir. 📷 **$20 $40 $125**

Berkley, Anthony, *Trial and Error,* Pocket Book #307, 1945, cover by Roswell Keller, in dust jacket. **$25 $100 $200**

Bezzerides, A. I., *They Drive By Night,* Dell Book #416, 1949, Map Back, cover by Robert Stanley. **$6 $25 $75**

--- *Thieves Market,* Bantam Book #750, 1950. **$6 $20 $65**

--- *Tough Guy,* Lion Book #153, 1953. 📷 **$10 $40 $120**

Biggers, Earl Derr, *Agony Column, The,* Avon Book no number (#17), 1942. **$8 $40 $100**

--- *Agony Column, The,* Avon Book #337, 1951, new cover art and number, a Charlie Chan novel. **$5 $25 $65**

--- *Chinese Parrot, The,* Avon Book #344, 1951, classic cover art, a Charlie Chan mystery. 📷 **$8 $25 $100**

--- *Seven Keys to Baldpate,* Quick Reader #131, 1945, cover by Axelrod, scarce. **$10 $30 $90**

Bliss, Tip, *Broadway Butterfly Murders, The,* Checker Book #2, 1949, cover by Leon H. Leiderman shows face of Boris Karloff, who introduces story. 📷 **$10 $40 $100**

Blizard, Marie, *Men in Her Death, The,* Green Dragon #32, 1946, surreal cover art. 📷 **$5 $20 $55**

Bloch, Robert, *Dead Beat, The,* Popular Library #G-532, 1961. **$8 $30 $100**

--- *Kidnaper, The,* Lion Book #185, 1954, paperback original. **$35 $85 $300**

--- *Scarf, The,* Avon Book #494, 1952, reprints *The Scarf of Passion* with shorter title. **$10 $35 $100**

--- *Scarf of Passion, The,* Avon Monthly Novel #9, 1948, digest-size, photo cover. **$20 $125 $255**

	G	VG	F

--- *Scarf of Passion, The*, Avon Special, no # (#7), 1951, photo cover, digest-size, very scarce. **$35 $150 $400**

--- *Scarf of Passion, The*, Avon Book #211, 1949, photo cover. **$20 $60 $155**

--- *Shooting Star with Terror in the Night*, Ace Book #D-265, 1958, paperback original, Ace Double. **$20 $65 $160**

--- *Spiderweb*, Ace Book #D-59, 1954, paperback original, Ace Double backed with *The Corpse in My Bed* by David Alexander. **$15 $60 $175**

--- *Will to Kill, The*, Ace Book #S-67, 1954, paperback original, cover by Rafael DeSoto. **$20 $100 $240**

--- *Yours Truly, Jack the Ripper*, Belmont Book #L92-527, 1962, paperback original. **$12 $50 $110**

Blochman, Lawrence G., *Bengal Fire*, Dell Book #311, 1949, Map Back. **$4 $15 $50**

--- *Bombay Mail*, Dell Book #488, 1951, Map Back, cover by Robert Stanley. **$4 $15 $40**

--- *Pursuit*, Handi-Book #128, 1951, paperback original. **$5 $15 $45**

--- *Wives to Burn*, Dell Book #134, 1947, Map Back. **$5 $16 $40**

	G	VG	F

Block, Lawrence, *Death Pulls a Doublecross*, Gold Medal Book #s1162, 1961, paperback original, photo cover. **$10 $50 $130**

--- *Girl With the Long Green Heart, The*, Gold Medal Book #k1555, 1965, paperback original. **$8 $40 $100**

--- *Here Comes a Hero*, Gold Medal Book #r2008, 1968, paperback original, cover by Robert McGinnis. **$6 $25 $75**

--- *Mona*, Gold Medal Book #s1085, 1961, paperback original, his first book. **$10 $60 $175**

--- *Ronald Rabbit is a Dirty Old Man*, Manor Book #12241, 1974. **$22 $100 $250**

--- *Sins of the Fathers*, Dell Book #7991, 1976, paperback original, the first Matt Scudder book. **$25 $80 $175**

--- *Specialists, The*, Gold Medal Book #r2067, 1969, paperback original. **$8 $40 $120**

--- *Tanner's Tiger*, Gold Medal Book #d1940, 1968, paperback original. **$10 $40 $125**

--- *Thief Who Couldn't Sleep, The*, Gold Medal Book #d1722, 1966, paperback original, photo cover. **$10 $45 $140**

Bogar, Jeff, *My Gun, Her Body*, Lion Book #79, 1952, paperback original, cover by Robert Maguire. **$5 $25 $75**

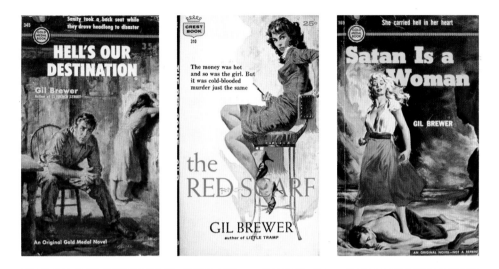

	G	VG	F

--- *Tigress, The*, Lion Book #72, 1951.
$5 $20 $70

Boucher, Anthony, *Case of the Crumpled Knave, The*, Popular Library #154, 1949, cover by Rudolph Belarski.
$10 $35 $125

--- *Case of the Seven Sneezes, The*, Dell Book #334, 1949, Map back.
$5 $20 $80

--- *Rocket to the Morgue*, Dell Book #591, 1952, cover by Robert Stanley, murder at a science fiction convention.
$4 $15 $60

Boyer, Richard L., *Giant Rat of Sumatra, The*, Warner Book #88-107, 1976, paperback original, excellent Sherlock Holmes pastiche novel.
$20 $50 $120

Braly, Malcolm, *Felony Tank*, Gold Medal Book #s1075, 1961, paperback original, prison crime novels by former convict.
$10 $40 $125

--- *On the Yard*, Crest Book #T1163, 1968, first paperback printing.
$8 $30 $100

--- *Shake Him Till He Rattles*, Gold Medal Book #k1311, 1963, paperback original, cover by Harry Bennett.
$10 $30 $100

Brandel, Marc, *Maniac Rendezvous*, Avon Book #387, 1951.
$10 $30 $85

Branson, H. C., *I'll Eat You Last*, Bonded Mystery #5, 1946, murder mystery has great hard-boiled title.
$4 $20 $50

Brewer, Gil, *13 French Street*, Gold Medal Book #211, 1951, paperback original.
$15 $35 $135

--- *And the Girl Screamed*, Crest Book #147, 1956, paperback original.
$10 $35 $85

--- *Angel*, Avon Book #866, 1960, paperback original.
$12 $55 $135

--- *Backwoods Teaser*, Gold Medal Book #950, 1960, paperback original, cover by Robert McGinnis, bad-girl noir.
$15 $50 $150

--- *Bitch, The*, Avon Book #830, 1958, paperback original.
$15 $60 $135

--- *Brat, The*, Gold Medal Book #708, 1957, paperback original, cover by Barye Philips. $10 $50 $100

--- *Flight Into Darkness*, Gold Medal Book #277, 1952, paperback original, cover by Barye Phillips.
$10 $25 $100

--- *Girl From Hateville, The*, Zenith Book #ZB-7, 1958. $10 $55 $140

--- *Hell's Our Destination*, Gold Medal Book #345, 1953, paperback original, cover by James Meese.
$15 $60 $155

	G	VG	F

--- *Killer is Loose, A,* Gold Medal Book #380, 1954, paperback original, cover by Lu Kimmel. **$20 $75 $145**

--- *Memory of Passion,* Lancer Book #70-008, 1962, paperback original. **$20 $65 $160**

--- *Nude on Thin Ice,* Avon Book #T-470, 1960, paperback original. **$15 $60 $165**

--- *Play It Hard,* Monarch Book #168, 1960, paperback original, cover by Rafael DeSoto. **$14 $65 $125**

--- *Red Scarf, The,* Crest Book #310, 1959, cover by Robert McGinnis. **$15 $50 $120**

--- *Satan Is a Woman,* Gold Medal Book #169, 1951, paperback original, cover by Barye Phillips. **$15 $60 $150**

--- *Sin For Me,* Banner Book #B50-108, 1967, paperback original. **$20 $100 $250**

--- *Some Must Die,* Gold Medal Book #409, 1954, paperback original, cover by Ray Johnson. **$20 $65 $175**

--- *So Rich, So Dead,* Gold Medal Book #196, 1951, paperback original, cover by Barye Philips. **$10 $40 $140**

--- *Squeeze, The,* Ace Book #D-123, 1955, paperback original, Ace Double backed with *Love Me to Death* by Frank Diamond. **$15 $40 $125**

--- *Sugar,* Avon Book #T-335, 1959, paperback original. **$20 $60 $125**

--- *Taste For Sin, A,* Berkley Book #G-509, 1961, cover by Harry Schaare. **$25 $65 $155**

--- *Tease, The,* Banner Book #B50-102, 1967, paperback original. **$25 $80 $200**

--- *Vengeful Virgin, The,* Crest Book #238, 1958, paperback original. **$15 $40 $100**

--- *Wild to Possess,* Monarch Book #107, 1959, paperback original, cover by Robert Maguire. **$10 $60 $150**

Brown, Carter, *Hellcat, The,* Signet Book #S2122, 1962, first U.S. edition, cover by Robert McGinnis, who did dozens of Carter Brown covers. **$4 $18 $50**

--- *Jade-Eyed Jungle, The,* Signet Book #G2355, 1963, first U.S. edition, cover by Robert McGinnis, great sexy cover art. **$5 $20 $40**

--- *Sex Clinic, The,* Signet Book #T4658, 1971, first U.S. edition, cover by Robert McGinnis, sexy hippie chick cover art. **$5 $20 $50**

Brown, Fredric, *Bloody Moonlight, The,* Bantam Book #783, 1950, cover by Harry Schaare. **$5 $30 $85**

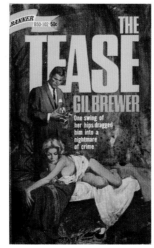

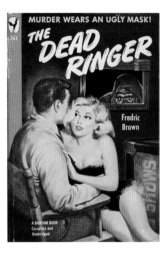

	G	VG	F

--- *Case of the Dancing Sandwiches, The,* Dell Ten-Cent Book #33, 1951, paperback original, cover by Robert Stanley.  **$75 $200 $650**

--- *Compliments of a Fiend,* Bantam Book #876, 1951. **$8 $25 $100**

--- *Dead Ringer, The,* Bantam Book #361, 1949, cover by Robert Stanley. **$6 $30 $100**

--- *Deep End, The,* Bantam Book #1215, 1954, cover by Charles Binger. **$6 $25 $80**

--- *Death Has Many Doors,* Bantam Book #1040, 1952, cover by Barye Philips. **$8 $35 $90**

--- *Death Has Many Doors,* Bantam Book #1567, 1957, new cover art by Barye Philips. **$5 $20 $50**

--- *Fabulous Clipjoint, The,* Bantam Book #302, 1948, cover by Ed Grant. **$10 $45 $100**

--- *Far Cry, The,* Bantam Book #1133, 1953, cover by James Avati. **$8 $45 $150**

--- *Five Day Nightmare,* Tower Book #42-502, 1962, photo cover. **$10 $30 $100**

--- *Here Comes a Candle,* Bantam Book #943, 1951, cover by Earl Mayan. **$15 $50 $120**

--- *Knock Three-Two-One,* Bantam Book #A2135, 1960, cover by Barye Phillips. **$5 $25 $75**

--- *Late Lamented, The,* Bantam Book

	G	VG	F

#2030, 1960. **$5 $20 $75**

--- *Lenient Beast, The,* Bantam Book #1712, 1958. **$5 $24 $80**

--- *Night of the Jabberwock,* Bantam Book #990, 1952. **$10 $35 $100**

--- *One For the Road,* Bantam Book #1990, 1959, cover by Barye Phillips. **$6 $25 $75**

--- *Plot For Murder, A,* Bantam Book #735, 1949, photo cover. **$7 $30 $100**

--- *Screaming Mimi, The,* Bantam Book #831, 1950. **$8 $40 $100**

--- *Wench is Dead, The,* Bantam Book #1565, 1957, cover by Mitchell Hooks. **$10 $50 $135**

Brown, Wenzell, *Hoods Ride In, The,* Pyramid Book #G-439, 1959, paperback original, cover by Harry Schaare, mafia and JD crime novel. **$5 $20 $60**

Browne, Howard, *Thin Air,* Dell Book #894, 1956, cover by Bill George, also see John Evans. **$4 $15 $60**

Brackett, Leigh, *No Good From a Corpse,* Handi-Book #32, 1944. **$10 $60 $150**

Bryan, Michael, *Intent to Kill,* Dell First Edition #FE88, 1956, paperback original, cover by Richard Powers; pseudonym of Brian Moore. **$15 $35 $100**

--- *Murder in Majorca,* Dell First Edition #A-145, 1957, paperback original. **$15 $65 $165**

	G	VG	F		G	VG	F

Burke, Richard, *Here Lies the Body,*
Popular Library #310, 1951, "a hot
redhead meets a cold corpse." 📷
$4 $20 $80

Burnett, W. R., *Asphalt Jungle, The,* Pocket
Book #74, 1950. $6 $25 $100

--- *Cool Man, The,* Gold Medal Book
#d1890, 1968, paperback original, cover
by Bob Abbett, ghost-written by Robert
Silverberg. $8 $30 $60

--- *High Sierra,* Bantam Book #826,
1950, cover by Harry Schaare.
$5 $20 $80

--- *Iron Man,* Avon Book #212, 1949.
$6 $20 $90

--- *Little Caesar,* Avon Book #66, 1945,
cover by Paul Stahr. 📷
$10 $30 $120

--- *Little Caesar,* Avon Book #329,
1951. 📷 $4 $20 $75

--- *Nobody Lives Forever,* Avon Murder
Mystery Monthly #33, 1945, digest-size.
$12 $55 $145

--- *Nobody Lives Forever,* Bantam Book
#888, 1951. 📷 $5 $20 $55

--- *Round the Clock At Volari's,* Gold
Medal Book #s1145, 1961, paperback
original, ghost-written by Robert
Silverberg. $4 $20 $65

Butler, Gerald, *Lurking Man, The,* Lion
Book #81, 1953. $8 $25 $90

--- *Kiss the Blood Off My Hands,* Dell
Book #197, 1947, Map Back, cover by
Gerald Gregg. $10 $25 $75

Cain, James M., *Career in C Major,* Avon
Book #141, 1947. $5 $20 $75

--- *Double Indemnity,* Armed Service
Edition #766, no date, circa 1945,
includes Career In C Major and The
Embezzler. $14 $75 $135

--- *Double Indemnity,* Avon Murder
Mystery Monthly #16, 1943, paperback
original, digest-size.
$35 $150 $275

--- *Double Indemnity,* Avon Book #60,
1945. 📷 $6 $25 $90

	G	VG	F

--- *Double Indemnity*, Avon #137, 1947, cover by T. Varaday.

	$4	$20	$60

--- *Double Indemnity*, Signet Book #784, 1950, not a film tie-in but cover art shows the famous door scene with Fred MacMurray, Edward G. Robinson, and Barbara Stanwyck. 📷

	$5	$20	$75

--- *Embezzler, The*, Avon Murder Mystery Monthly #20, 1944, paperback original, cover by Jack Deckler, digest-size.

	$25	$110	$275

--- *Embezzler, The*, Avon Book #99, 1946.

	$6	$30	$90

--- *Jealous Woman*, Avon Monthly Novel #17, 1949, paperback original, digest-size.

	$25	$100	$400

--- *Jealous Woman*, Avon Book #348, 1951.

	$6	$25	$100

--- *Love's Lovely Counterfeit*, Avon Murder Mystery Monthly #44, 1947, cover by Don Milsop, digest-size.

	$18	$55	$125

--- *Love's Lovely Counterfeit*, Avon Book #161, 1948.

	$5	$25	$75

--- *Love's Lovely Counterfeit*, Signet Book #1445, 1957, typical bad-girl noir cover art by an unknown artist. 📷

	$5	$15	$60

--- *Postman Always Rings Twice, The*, Armed Service Edition #Q-2, no date, circa 1944.

	$14	$55	$120

--- *Postman Always Rings Twice, The*, Armed Service Edition #1058, no date, circa 1946, reprints ASE #Q-2.

	$12	$40	$75

--- *Postman Always Rings Twice, The*, Avon Murder Mystery Monthly #6, 1942, digest-size.

	$25	$90	$275

--- *Sinful Woman*, Avon Monthly Novel #1, 1947, paperback original, digest-size, cover by Barye Philips.

	$40	$120	$375

--- *Sinful Woman*, Avon Book #174, 1948.

	$8	$30	$90

Cain, Paul, *Fast One*, Bonded Book #10, 1943, digest-size.

	$20	$150	$325

--- *Fast One*, Avon Book #178, 1948. 📷

	$15	$70	$150

--- *Fast One*, Avon Book #496, 1952, cover by Victor Olson, reprints Avon #178 with new cover art. 📷

	$12	$30	$120

--- *Seven Slayers*, Chartered Books #21, 1946, first book edition, pulp crime collection.

	$75	$250	$700

--- *Seven Slayers*, Avon Book #268, 1950, pulp crime collection.

	$20	$80	$160

Canning, Victor, *Chasm, The*, Bantam Book #313, 1948, in dust jacket.

	$55	$125	$350

Cannon, Curt, *I Like 'Em Tough*, Gold Medal Book #743, 1958, first book edition, cover by Jerry Powell, reprints *Manhunt* magazine stories; pseudonym of Evan Hunter.

	$8	$40	$100

	G	VG	F

--- *I'm Cannon – For Hire*, Gold Medal Book #814, 1958, first book edition, cover by Milton Charles. 📷

| | $10 | $45 | $125 |

Carr, John Dickson, *Below Suspicion,* Bantam Book #1119, 1953. 📷

| | $3 | $15 | $50 |

--- *Case of the Constant Suicides, The,* Berkley Book #G-60, 1957, cover by Robert Maguire. $4 $20 $65

--- *Corpse in the Waxworks,* Avon Book, no # (#33), 1943 $5 $25 $100

--- *Curse of the Bronze Lamp,* Armed Service Edition #991, no date, circa 1945.

| | $15 | $35 | $100 |

--- *Four False Weapons, The,* Popular Library #282, 1950. 📷

| | $5 | $30 | $100 |

--- *Hag's Nook,* Penguin Book #532, 1943. 📷 $5 $30 $85

--- *Hag's Nook,* Berkley Book #G-129, 1958, cover by Robert Maguire.

| | $5 | $20 | $55 |

--- *New Exploits of Sherlock Holmes, The,* Ace Book #D-181, 1954, cover by Vern Tossey, new Holmes stories written by Carr and Adrian Conan Doyle.

| | $5 | $25 | $85 |

--- *Poison In Jest,* Popular Library #349, 1951. 📷 $5 $35 $100

--- *Problem of the Green Capsule, The,* Bantam Book #101, 1947, photo cover.

| | $6 | $15 | $50 |

--- *Sleeping Sphinx, The,* Armed Service Edition #1280, no date, circa 1947.

| | $12 | $45 | $100 |

Carter, Nick, *Rendezvous With Dead Men,* Atlas Mystery #1, circa 1947, digest-size.

| | $12 | $35 | $100 |

--- *Yellow Disc Murder Case, The,* Atlas Mystery #3, circa 1948, digest-size.

| | $12 | $40 | $120 |

Caspary, Vera, *Laura,* Armed Service Edition, #666, no date, circa 1945, classic noir. $10 $40 $100

Chaber, M. E., *Don't Get Caught,* Popular Library #482, 1953; pseudonym of Kendell Foster Crossen.

| | $3 | $15 | $40 |

--- *Splintered Man, The,* Perma Book #M3080, 1957, cover by Robert Schulz, "the commies were out to break

America's toughest secret agent," needle and torture cover art. 📷

| | $5 | $20 | $90 |

Chambers, Dana, *She'll Be Dead By Morning,* Popular Library #238, 1950.

| | $15 | $30 | $75 |

Chambers, Whitman, *Come-On, The,* Pyramid Book #74, 1953, cover by Victor Olsen. $4 $15 $55

--- *In Savage Surrender,* Monarch Book #139, 1959, paperback original.

| | $5 | $15 | $45 |

--- *Season For Love,* Monarch Book #122, 1959, paperback original, cover by Robert Maguire. $5 $20 $60

Chandler, Raymond, *5 Murderers,* Avon Murder Mystery Monthly #19, 1944, first book edition, digest-size.

| | $30 | $100 | $300 |

--- *5 Murderers,* Avon Book #63, 1944. 📷 $12 $60 $125

--- *Big Sleep, The,* Armed Service Edition #751, no date, circa 1945.

| | $40 | $100 | $265 |

--- *Big Sleep, The,* Avon Murder Mystery Monthly #7, 1942, first paperback printing, digest-size. 📷

| | $35 | $100 | $400 |

--- *Big Sleep, The,* Pocket Book #696, 1950, cover by Harvey Kidder.

| | $4 | $20 | $75 |

--- *Big Sleep, The,* Ballantine Book #02201, 1971, cover by Tom Adams. In the early 1970s Ballantine published 10 Chandler paperbacks each with Adams cover art, all are collectible, each book:

| | $5 | $20 | $45 |

--- *Farewell My Lovely,* Pocket Book #212, 1943, cover by H. Lawrence Hoffman. $5 $20 $75

--- *Finger Man,* Avon Book #219, 1950,

| | $18 | $80 | $175 |

--- *Finger Man, The,* Avon Murder Mystery Monthly #43, 1946, first book edition, digest-size, collects 4 pulp crime stories. 📷 $30 $120 $275

--- *Five Sinister Characters,* Avon Murder Mystery Monthly #28, 1945, cover by Paul Stahr, first book edition, digest-size.

| | $35 | $125 | $325 |

--- *Five Sinister Characters,* Avon Book #88, 1946. 📷 $15 $50 $150

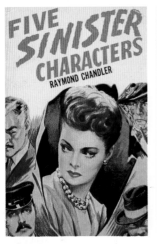

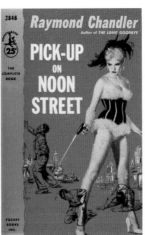

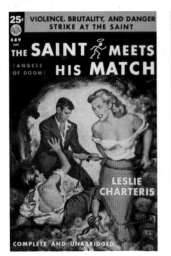

	G	VG	F

--- *Lady in the Lake, The*, Armed Service Edition #838, no date, circa 1945. **$35 $100 $200**

--- *Playback*, Cardinal Book #C-375, 1960, cover by William Rose. **$5 $20 $75**

--- *Pick-Up on Noon Street*, Pocket Book #846, 1952, cover by Tom Dunn. **$4 $20 $85**

--- *Pick-Up on Noon Street*, Pocket Book #2846, sixth printing 1957, cover by Robert Maguire, new cover art. **$5 $15 $50**

--- *Trouble Is My Business*, Pocket Book #823, 1951, cover by Herman Geisen. **$4 $35 $100**

Charteris, Leslie, *Saint Goes On, The*, Avon #34, 1943. **$5 $25 $100**

--- *Saint In Action, The*, Avon Book #118, 1947. **$5 $20 $90**

--- *Saint In Europe, The*, Avon Book #611, 1954. **$4 $15 $35**

--- *Saint Meets His Match, The*, Avon Book #489, 1952, cover by Norman

Saunders, original title *Angels of Doom*. **$5 $20 $60**

--- *Saint Overboard*, Popular Library no number (#1), 1943, first Popular Library paperback, cover by Hoffman. **$20 $70 $200**

--- *Saint Overboard*, Avon Book #432, 1952. **$4 $20 $65**

Chase, James Hadley, *I'll Get You For This*, Avon Monthly Novel #18, 1950, digest-size. **$35 $100 $185**

--- *Kiss My Fist!*, Eton Book #E-112, 1952, paperback original, one of the most brutal paperback covers ever. **$10 $65 $150**

--- *Marijuana Mob, The*, Eton Book #E116, 1952, crime and drugs with politics. **$25 $100 $225**

--- *No Orchids For Miss Blandish*, Avon Book #355, 1951, photo cover, classic gangster novel. **$8 $25 $90**

--- *Villain and the Virgin, The*, Avon Monthly Novel #4, 1948, digest-size, new title for *No Orchids For Miss Blandish*. **$30 $90 $200**

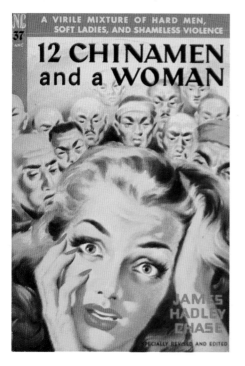

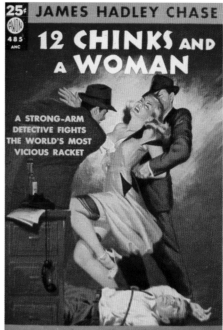

	G	VG	F

--- *Villain and the Virgin, The*, Novel Library #11, 1949, gangster novel, new title for *No Orchids For Miss Blandish* with sexy cover art.

| | $6 | $25 | $90 |

--- *You're Lonely When You're Dead*, Popular Library #378, 1951.

| | $5 | $30 | $75 |

--- *12 Chinamen and a Woman*, Novel Library #37, 1950, new title for *12 Chinks and a Woman* to make it less offensive. 📷

| | $18 | $75 | $135 |

--- *12 Chinks and a Woman*, Handi-Book

	G	VG	F

no number (#3), 1942.

| | $16 | $80 | $225 |

--- *12 Chinks and a Woman*, Avon Monthly Novel #7, 1948, digest-size, photo cover.

| | $45 | $125 | $275 |

--- *12 Chinks and a Woman*, Avon Book #485, 1952, brutal new cover art. 📷

| | $12 | $65 | $155 |

Chaze, Elliott, *Black Wings Has My Angel*, Gold Medal Book #296, 1953, paperback original, cover by Lu Kimmel, classic bad-girl cover art, "she had the face of a Madonna and a heart made of dollar bills," high demand. 📷

| | $100 | $350 | $1,000 |

	G	**VG**	**F**

--- *One For the Money*, Berkley Book #Y658, 1962, cover by Charles Copeland, reprints *Black Wings Has My Angel* with new title and cover art, scarce.

| | $40 | $125 | $275 |

Cheyney, Peter, *Case of the Dark Hero, The,* Avon Book #123, 1947, WWII spy novel. | $5 | $15 | $50 |

--- *Dark Street Murders, The,* Avon #93, 1946, | $6 | $20 | $50 |

--- *London Spy Murders, The,* Avon Book #49, 1944. | $6 | $20 | $60 |

--- *Sinister Errand,* Avon Book #114, 1947. | $4 | $15 | $40 |

Chidsey, Donald Barr, *Nobody Heard the Shot,* LA Bantam #25, 1941, rare, text cover. | $40 | $100 | $175 |

--- *Nobody Heard the Shot,* LA Bantam #25, 1941, illustrated cover, rare.

| | $100 | $200 | $400 |

Christie, Agatha, *And Then There Were None,* Pocket Book #261, 1944, cover by Leo Manso. | $4 | $15 | $50 |

--- *And Then There Were None,* Reader's League For US Red Cross, no date, circa 1945, no number, cover by Leo Manso, reprints Pocket Book #261.

| | $10 | $40 | $100 |

--- *Appointment With Death,* Dell Book #105, 1946, Map Back, surreal cover art by Gerald Gregg. | $5 | $15 | $65 |

--- *Big Four, The,* Avon Book no number (#3), 1941, with Globe endpapers.

| | $50 | $100 | $275 |

	G	VG	F

--- *Big Four, The*, Avon #690, seventh printing no date, 1956, new cover art by Everett Raymond Kinstler who told me the model on the cover wore her dress backwards to get more effect in the bustline. 🎥 **$4 $15 $40**

--- *Blue Geranium and Other Tuesday Club Murders, The*, LA Bantam #26, 1940, rare, text cover. **$50 $125 $300**

--- *Blue Geranium and Other Tuesday Club Murders, The*, LA Bantam #26, 1940, rare, illustrated cover. 🎥 **$100 $200 $500**

--- *Death Comes As the End*, Pocket Book #465, 1947, Egyptian-theme cover art. 🎥 **$4 $15 $45**

--- *Death in the Air*, Avon Book #89, 1946, cover by Robert Cole. **$4 $20 $75**

--- *Death on the Nile*, Avon Book #46, 1944. **$8 $25 $90**

--- *Moving Finger, The*, Avon Book #164, 1948, photo cover. **$4 $20 $50**

--- *Murder in the Calais Coach*, Pocket Book #79, 1940. **$5 $20 $90**

--- *Murder in Three Acts*, Avon Book #61, 1945. **$5 $20 $90**

--- *Murder of Roger Ackroyd*, Pocket Book #5, 1939, only 10,000 copies distributed in NYC area, rare. 🎥 **$350 $1,800 $7,500**

--- *Murder of Roger Ackroyd*, Pocket Book #5, second printing, 1939. **$10 $40 $100**

--- *Mysterious Mr. Quin, The*, Dell Book #570, 1952, Map Back, cover by Robert Jonas. **$5 $20 $65**

--- *Poirot Loses a Client*, Avon Book #70, 1945. **$8 $20 $90**

--- *Secret Adversary, The*, Avon Book #100, 1946, cover by Carl Bower. **$4 $20 $65**

--- *Tuesday Club Murders, The*, Dell Book #8, 1943. **$12 $40 $125**

Clark, Al C., *Crime Partners,* Holloway House #67445, 1974, paperback original; pseudonym of Donald Goines, his first novel, Goines wrote some of his 16 novels under this pen-name, all later reprinted by Holloway under his true name, each book. **$20 $00 $200**

--- *Death List*, Holloway House #67443, 1974, paperback original, . **$20 $60 $150**

Clark, Dale, *Blonde, the Gangster and the Private Eye,* The, Avon Murder Mystery Monthly #47, 1947, digest-size, cover by Ann Cantor. **$50 $165 $350**

Clarke, Donald Henderson, *Louis Beretti,* Novel Library #19, 1949, gangster novel. **$6 $20 $65**

--- *Louis Beretti*, Avon Book #384, 1951, gangster novel. 🎥 **$4 $15 $50**

	G	VG	F			G	VG	F

Cohen, Octavus Roy, *Bullet For My Love, A,* Popular Library #462, 1952, "Valerie had everything but morals."
$4 $15 $60

--- *Dangerous Lady*, Popular Library #264, 1950, cover by Rudolph Belarski.
$5 $20 $80

--- *Don't Ever Love Me*, Popular Library #222, 1951, "she was loveable, kissable... and killable." 📷 **$5 $25 $100**

--- *More Beautiful Than Murder*, Popular Library #427, 1952. 📷
$4 $20 $65

--- *There's Always Time to Die*, Popular Library #196, 1949.
$4 $15 $55

Colby, Robert, *Captain Must Die, The,* Gold Medal Book #835, 1959, paperback original, cover by Wexler, a noir classic.
$5 $30 $75

--- *Deadly Desire, The*, Gold Medal Book #940, 1959, paperback original.
$5 $20 $65

--- *Lament For Julie*, Monarch Book #196, paperback original, cover by Harry Barton.   **$4 $20 $75**

Conroy, Albert, *Mob Says Murder, The,* Gold Medal Book #780, 1958, paperback original, bondage cover art; pseudonym of Marvin Albert.   **$4 $18 $60**

	G	VG	F

--- *Nice Guys Finish Dead*, Gold Medal Book #676, 1957, paperback original, cover by Mitchell Hooks. **$4 $20 $55**

--- *Road's End, The*, Gold Medal Book #231, 1952, paperback original. **$4 $20 $60**

Conway, John, *Hell Is My Destination*, Monarch Book #128, 1959, paperback original; pseudonym of Joseph Chadwick, revenge crime novel. **$4 $15 $50**

Coxe, George Harmon, *Fashioned For Murder*, Dell Book #678, 1953. **$5 $18 $50**

--- *Flash Casey, Hard-Boiled Detective*, Avon Book #143, 1948, collects 4 pulp stories. 📷 **$4 $20 $75**

--- *Four Frightened Women*, Dell Book #5, 1943, cover by Gerald Gregg, first Dell Map Back. **$20 $60 $120**

--- *Four Frightened Women*, Dell Told In Pictures #2, 1950, in comic book format, cover by Robert Stanley. **$60 $150 $350**

--- *One Minute Past Eight*, Dell Book #D346, 1960, cover is by Robert Maguire, book credits Freeman Eliot inside in error. **$4 $20 $50**

Craig, Jonathan, *Alley Girl*, Lion Book #206, 1954, paperback original, cover by Robert Maguire. **$10 $25 $100**

--- *Case of the Brazen Beauty*, Gold Medal Book #d1706, 1966, paperback original. **$5 $20 $65**

--- *Renegade Cop*, Berkley Diamond #D-2015, 1959, uncommon. **$10 $25 $75**

Crais, Robert, *Monkey's Raincoat, The*, Bantam Book #26336, 1987, paperback original, his first novel and the first Elvis Cole mystery. **$10 $30 $100**

Crane, Francis, *Applegreen Cat, The*, Popular Library #344, 1951, cover by Rudolph Belarski. 📷 **$6 $20 $100**

Crofts, Freeman Wills, *Cask, The*, Penguin Book #575, 1946, in dust jacket. **$45 $125 $225**

--- *Cold-Blooded Murder*, Avon Book #126, 1947. 📷 **$5 $20 $75**

--- *Losing Game, A*, Popular Library

#121, 1947, cover by Im-Ho. **$4 $15 $40**

--- *Wilful and Premeditated*, Avon Book no number (#9), 1941, with Globe endpapers. **$25 $125 $255**

Crooker, Herbert, *Man About Broadway*, Yogi Mysteries no number, 1940, digest-size. 📷 **$20 $60 $150**

Cussler, Clive, *Mediterranean Caper, The*, Pyramid Book #V-3179, 1973, paperback original. **$25 $100 $350**

Daniels, Norman, *Bedroom in Hell*, Rainbow Book #117, 1952, paperback original, digest-size, cover by George Gross. **$25 $90 $250**

--- *Mistress On a Deathbed*, Falcon Book #29, 1952, paperback original, cover by George Gross, digest-size. **$30 $100 $225**

--- *Sweet Savage*, Falcon Book #38, 1952, paperback original. **$35 $100 $250**

Darby, J.N., *Murder In the House With the Blue Eyes*, Thrilling Mystery Novel (Atlas), 1944, digest-size. 📷 **$10 $35 $110**

Davis, Dorothy Salisbury, *Judas Cat, The*, Bantam Book #927, 1951, first paperback printing, two cover variants with same date and number, each book: 📷 **$6 $20 $50**

Davis, Frederick C., *Deadly Miss Ashley, The*, Pocket Book #804, 1951, cover by Victor Kalin. **$8 $20 $75**

Davis, Gordon, *Counterfeit Kill*, Gold Medal Book #k1348, 1963, paperback original; pseudonym of E. Howard Hunt. **$4 $15 $40**

--- *House Dick*, Gold Medal Book #s1103, 1961, paperback original. **$4 $20 $60**

Davis, Norbert, *Dead Little Rich Girl*, Handi-Book #40, 1945. **$20 $100 $200**

--- *Oh, Murderer Mine*, Handi-Book #54, 1946, paperback original. 📷 **$65 $200 $450**

Day, Lula M., *Mystery of the Red Suitcase, The*, Hip Books, no number, 1946, paperback original, one-shot done in the early Pocket Book format, scarce. 📷 **$20 $75 $200**

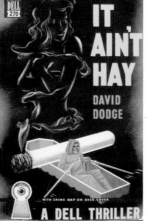

	G	VG	F

Demaris, Ovid, *Hoods Take Over, The,* Gold Medal Book #s1088, 1961, paperback original, cover by Barye Phillips, mob novel. **$5 $20 $75**

--- *"Lucky" Luciano,* Monarch Book #MA302, 1960, paperback original, photo cover of Luciano, true crime. **$10 $40 $100**

--- *Slasher, The,* Gold Medal Book #s910, 1959, paperback original, cover by Barye Phillips. **$6 $25 $75**

DeMille, Nelson, *Hammer of God, The,* Leisure Book #2122K, 1974, paperback original, #2 in Ryker series. **$5 $25 $90**

--- *Smack Man, The,* Manor Book #12259, 1975, paperback original, crime and drug novel, #1 in Keller series. 🎥 **$6 $35 $100**

--- *Sniper, The,* Leisure Book #1942K, 1974, paperback original, #1 in Ryker series. **$4 $25 $85**

Deming, Richard, *Fall Girl,* Zenith Book #ZB-20, 1959, paperback original. **$4 $20 $50**

--- *Kiss and Kill,* Zenith Book #ZB-36, 1960, paperback original. **$5 $20 $50**

--- *This Game Is Murder,* Monarch #439, 1964, paperback original, cover by Harry Barton, early serial killer novel, meat cleaver cover. **$4 $15 $50**

	G	VG	F

--- *Vice Cop,* Belmont Book #221, 1961, paperback original, cover by Paul Rader. **$5 $15 $60**

Dent, Lester, *Cry At Dusk,* Gold Medal Book #247, 1952, paperback original. **$14 $30 $85**

--- *High Stakes,* Ace Book #D-21, 1952, Ace Double backed with *Nightshade* by John N. Makris. **$10 $30 $90**

--- *Lady in Peril,* Ace Book #D-357, 1959, paperback original, Ace Double backed with *Wired For Scandal* by Floyd Wallace. **$10 $25 $80**

Dewey, Thomas B., *Every Bet's a Sure Thing,* Avon Book #564, 1954, dope and murder novel. **$5 $20 $60**

--- *Handle With Fear,* Graphic Book #73, 1954, cover by Walter Popp. 🎥 **$5 $20 $60**

Dickson, Carter, *My Late Wives,* Armed Service Edition #1246, no date, circa 1947; pseudonym of John Dickson Carr. **$15 $45 $100**

--- *Plague Court Murders, The,* Avon Book no number (#7), 1941, cover by Robert Cole, with Globe endpapers. **$25 $75 $155**

--- *Scotland Yard: The Department of Queer Complaints,* Dell Book #65, 1944, cover by Gerald Gregg. **$35 $100 $225**

	G	VG	F

Dietrich, Robert, *Cheat, The,* Pyramid Book #135, 1954, paperback original; pseudonym of E. Howard Hunt.
$8 $30 $100

--- *One For the Road,* Pyramid Book #235, 1957, paperback original.
$6 $25 $75

Dodge, David, *It Ain't Hay,* Dell Book #270, 1949, cover by Gerald Gregg, marihuana and murder, cover art shows woman forming out of marihuana smoke. 📷
$20 $70 $160

--- *Red Tassel, The,* Dell Book #565, 1952, Map Back, cover by Robert Stanley.
$5 $20 $60

Dodge, Steven, *Shanghai Incident,* Gold Medal Book #456, 1955, paperback original, spy novel; pseudonym of Stephen Becker. $5 $25 $100

Doyle, Arthur Conan, *Case Book of Sherlock Holmes, The,* Pocket Book #670, 1950, cover by Charles Skoggs.
$5 $20 $65

--- *Hound of the Baskervilles, The,* Bantam Book #366, 1949, cover by William Shoyer, bondage cover art, a Sherlock Holmes novel. 📷
$5 $30 $80

--- *Memoirs of Sherlock Holmes, The,* Bantam Book #704, 1949.
$4 $20 $60

--- *Sherlock Holmes,* Mayfair Editions, no number, 1950, pulp magazine size.
$35 $100 $175

--- *Sherlock Holmes Pocket Book, The,* Pocket Book #95, 1941, first book edition. $10 $40 $100

--- *Sherlock Holmes Pocket Book, The,* Pocket Book #95, 11th printing 1944, variant cover art version, scarce.
$30 $60 $125

--- *Valley of Fear, The,* Bantam Book #733, 1950. $4 $20 $60

Duff, James, *Who Dies There?,* Graphic Book #134, 1956, paperback original, cover by Walter Popp, who told me his wife, Marie, was the model for the woman on the cover. 📷
$4 $15 $40

Duke, Will, *Fair Prey,* Graphic Book #142, 1956, paperback original, cover by Oliver Brabbins; pseudonym of William Campbell Gault. $5 $20 $75

Eberhart, Mignon, *Hangman's Whip, The,* Popular Library #293, 1950. 📷
$5 $25 $100

--- *Hasty Wedding,* Popular Library #73, 1946, cover by H. Lawrence Hoffman.
$5 $15 $45

--- *Pattern For Murder,* Popular Library #167, 1948, cover by Rudolph Belarski. 📷 $10 $30 $100

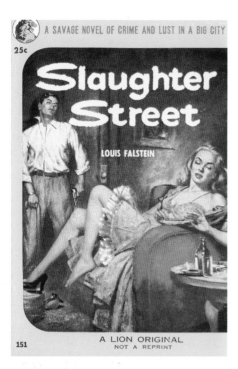

A SAVAGE NOVEL OF CRIME AND LUST IN A BIG CITY

25c

Slaughter Street

LOUIS FALSTEIN

A LION ORIGINAL
NOT A REPRINT

151

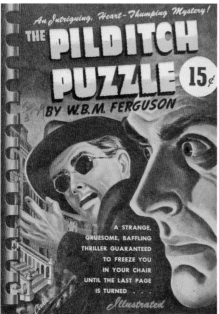

An Intriguing, Heart-Thumping Mystery!

THE **PILDITCH PUZZLE** 15¢

BY W.B.M. FERGUSON

A STRANGE, GRUESOME, BAFFLING THRILLER GUARANTEED TO FREEZE YOU IN YOUR CHAIR UNTIL THE LAST PAGE IS TURNED . . . . *Illustrated*

	G	VG	F
--- *Strangers in Flight*, LA Bantam #28, 1940, paperback original, text cover, rare.	$50	$100	$200
--- *Strangers in Flight*, LA Bantam #28, 1940, paperback original, illustrated cover, rare.	$75	$150	$400
Ellin, Stanley, *Big Night, The*, Lion Book #41, 1950.	$5	$25	$100
Elliott, Bruce, *One is a Lonely Number*, Lion Book #100, 1952, paperback original, "An escaped con seeks refuge – finds jailbait!"	$10	$25	$90
Elliott, Paul, *Mysterious Mickey Finn*, Avon Murder of the Month #2, 1942, digest-size.	$20	$65	$135
Ellroy, James, *Brown's Requiem*, Avon Book #78741, 1981, paperback original, his first book.	$12	$45	$125
--- *Clandestine*, Avon Book #81141, 1982, paperback original, his scarce second book.	$15	$40	$120
--- *Silent Terror*, Avon Book #89934, 1986, paperback original.	$10	$30	$90
Endore, Guy, *Furies In Her Body, The*, Avon Book #323, 1951, aka *Nightmare*.	$5	$20	$55
--- *Nightmare*, Dell Book #D183, 1956, cover by Victor Kalin.	$5	$15	$40
Engle, William, *Enter the G-Men*, LA Bantam #9, 1940, paperback original, rare.	$60	$150	$250
Estleman, Loren, *Oklahoma Punk, The*, Major Book #3052, 1976, paperback original, his first book, crime novel about Baby Face Nelson.	$50	$100	$250
Evans, John, *Halo For Satan*, Bantam Book #800, 1950; pseudonym of Howard Browne. 📓	$5	$20	$65
--- *Halo In Blood*, Bantam Book #74, 1946.	$6	$20	$75
--- *Halo In Brass*, Bantam Book #709, 1950, cover by Mike Ludlow, private eye Paul Pine with lesbian plot.	$5	$25	$80
--- *If You Have Tears*, Handi-Book #74, 1948, aka Lona.	$15	$40	$100
--- *Lona*, Lion Book #94, 1952, cover by Earle Bergey. 📓	$10	$30	$100

	G	VG	F			G	VG	F

Fair, A. A., *Bats Fly at Dusk,* Dell Book #D-348, 1960, cover by Robert McGinnis; pseudonym of Erle Stanley Gardner.
$4   **$15**   **$35**

--- *Beware the Curves,* Pocket Book #1258, 1959, one of four U.S. Pocket Books only distributed in Europe, rare.
$30   **$100**   **$200**

--- *Give 'Em the Ax,* Dell Book #389, 1950, Map Back, leg art cover with dead guy in bath tub. 📷**$4**   **$15**   **$65**

--- *Gold Comes in Bricks,* Dell Book #84, 1945, Map Back, cover by Gerald Gregg.
$5   **$15**   **$55**

--- *Spill the Jackpot,* Dell Book #109, 1946.   **$4**   **$15**   **$50**

Falstein, Louis, *Slaughter Street,* Lion Book #151, 1953, paperback original, cover by Lou Marchetti. 📷 **$5**   **$20**   **$65**

Fearing, Kenneth, *Big Clock, The,* Armed Service Edition #1215, no date, circa 1946.   **$18**   **$55**   **$100**

--- *Big Clock, The,* Bantam Book #738, 1949.   **$5**   **$15**   **$50**

Ferguson, W. B. M., *Pilditch Puzzle, The,* Trophy Book #402, 1946, abridged, cover by Cirkle, one of only two books in this scarce series. 📷 **$20**   **$100**   **$200**

	G	VG	F

Finney, Jack, *5 Against the House,* Pocket Book #1078, 1955, cover by George Erickson, gambling-caper novel. 📷
     $5 $20 $75

--- *House of Numbers, The,* Dell First Edition #A-139, 1957, paperback original.
     $10 $50 $120

Fischer, Bruno, *Bleeding Scissors, The,* Signet Book #1256, 1955, cover by Robert Maguire. 📷 $5 $20 $60

--- *Dead Men Grin,* Pyramid Book #22, 1950, first paperback printing, scarce in condition. $10 $25 $100

--- *Fast Buck, The,* Gold Medal Book #270, 1952, paperback original, cover by Barye Phillips. $6 $25 $100

--- *Fast Buck, The,* Gold Medal Book #s783, second printing 1958, new cover by James Meese. 📷 $5 $15 $50

--- *Fingered Man, The,* Ace Book #D-27, 1950, cover by Norman Saunders, Ace Double backed with *Double Take* by Mel Colton, cover by Julian Paul.
     $5 $25 $75

--- *Fools Walk In,* Gold Medal Book #209, 1951, paperback original.
     $5 $35 $90

--- *House of Flesh,* Gold Medal Book #123, 1950, paperback original, ravenous dog cover art. $10 $35 $120

--- *Restless Hands, The,* Signet Book #780, 1950, sexy woman insert is a version of the "keyhole" cover. 📷
     $5 $20 $50

--- *So Much Blood,* Golden Willow Book #52, 1946, first paperback printing, digest-size, uncommon.
     $10 $40 $120

--- *Stairway to Death,* Pyramid Book #29, 1951, first paperback printing, cover by Frederick Meyer.
     $10 $25 $75

Fisher, Steve, *Be Still My Heart,* Red Seal Book #21, 1952, paperback original.
     $25 $60 $150

--- *Homicide Johnny,* Popular Library #229, 1950, cover by Rudolph Belarski. 📷 $15 $75 $200

--- *I Wake Up Screaming,* Handi-Book #27, 1944. $100 $200 $400

--- *I Wake Up Screaming,* Popular Library #129, 1947. $30 $90 $200

--- *Night Before Murder, The,* Mystery Novel of the Month, no number (6), 1939, digest-size. $30 $75 $175

--- *Night Before Murder, The,* Popular Library #317, 1951, cover by Rudolph Belarski, scarce. $20 $90 $200

--- *Sheltering Night, The,* Gold Medal Book #219, 1952, paperback original, scarce. $20 $75 $200

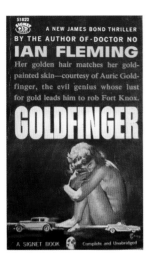

	G	VG	F

--- *Take All You Can Get*, Popular Library #781, 1956, cover by Mitchell Hooks.
$15 $60 $150

--- *Winter Kill*, Popular Library #361, 1951, cover by Rudolph Belarski.
$20 $90 $200

Flaming, I. M., *Snakefinger*, All Star Book #80, 1966, paperback original, sexy James Bond spoof.
$16 $40 $100

Fleischman, A. S., *Counterspy Express*, Ace Book #D-57, 1954, paperback original, Ace Double backed with *Treachery in Trieste* by Charles I. Leonard.
$5 $25 $100

--- *Look Behind You Lady*, Gold Medal Book #223, 1952, paperback original.
$5 $20 $55

--- *Shanghai Flame*, Gold Medal Book #514, 1955.   **$5 $20 $60**

Fleming, Ian, *Diamonds Are Forever*, Perma Book #M-3084, 1957, cover by William Rose.   **$15 $65 $200**

--- *Diamond Smugglers, The*, Collier Book #AS544V, 1964, first book edition, cover by Bob Eichinger, true crime.
$10 $30 $60

--- *Dr. No*, Signet Book #S-1670, 1959.
$20 $45 $100

--- *From Russia With Love*, Signet Book #S1563, 1958, cover by Barye Phillips.
$15 $35 $90

	G	VG	F

--- *Goldfinger*, Signet Book #S1822, 1960, cover by Barye Phillips, predates film with sexy golden-girl cover.
$3 $20 $50

--- *Live and Let Die*, Perma Book #M3048, 1956, cover by James Meese, early James Bond paperback.
$16 $70 $150

--- *Octopussy*, Signet Book #P3200, 1967, cover shows Ian Fleming.
$5 $20 $60

--- *Too Hot to Handle*, Perma Book #M-3070, 1956, first edition thus, cover by Lou Marchetti, aka Moonraker.
$75 $200 $500

--- *You Asked For It*, Popular Library #660, 1955, paperback original, aka Casino Royale.   **$65 $200 $700**

Fl*m*ng, I*n, *Alligator*, Vanitas Book #V-4402, 1963, paperback original, states first printing, James Bond parody in Signet Books format, 25-cents cover price, has two tiny staple holes above top staple to indicate it was removed from Harvard Lampoon magazine where it originally appeared, only four known to exist, rare.   **$100 $250 $600**

--- *Alligator*, Vanitas Book #V-4402, second printing 1963, first and only separate edition from magazine, 50-cents cover price, same book number and cover as first.   **$20 $50 $100**

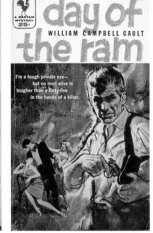

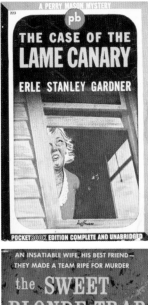

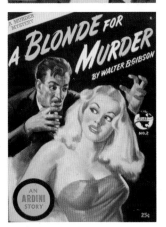

	G	VG	F

Foster, Richard, *Invisible Man Murders, The,* Five Star Mystery #5, 1945, digest-size; pseudonym of Foster Kendall Crossen. **$6** **$20** **$60**

Fox, James M., *Death Commits Bigamy,* Dell Book #845, 1955, cover by Mike Privatello. **$5** **$18** **$55**

--- *Lady Regrets, The,* Dell Book #338, 1949, Map Back, cover by Robert Stanley. 📷 **$6** **$15** **$65**

Frances, William, *Corruptors, The,* Lion Book #174, 1953, paperback original. **$4** **$20** **$70**

--- *Don't Dig Deeper,* Lion Book #123, 1953, paperback original. **$5** **$20** **$75**

Fray, Al, *Built For Trouble,* Dell First Edition #A167, 1958, paperback original, cover by Robert McGinnis, noir novel. **$6** **$25** **$55**

--- *Come Back For More,* Dell First Edition #A161, 1958, paperback original, crime-trucker novel. **$6** **$20** **$55**

--- *Dame's the Game, The,* Popular Library #G431, 1960, paperback original, cover by Harry Schaare, private eye in Las Vegas gambling scheme. 📷 **$6** **$20** **$75**

Freeman, R. Austin, *Adventures of Dr. Thorndyke, The,* Popular Library #122, 1947, cover by Fiedler, collection. **$6** **$20** **$65**

--- *Dr. Thorndyke's Discovery,* Avon Book, no number (#10), 1941, with Globe endpapers. **$25** **$100** **$175**

--- *Unconscious Witness, The,* Avon Book #122, 1947. 📷 **$6** **$20** **$75**

Frome, David, *Mr. Pinkerton Passage For One,* Quick Reader #134, 1945. **$5** **$16** **$45**

Gardner, Erle Stanley, *Case of the Calendar Girl, The,* Pocket Book #1275, 1960, Perry Mason novel, one of four U.S. Pocket Books only distributed in Europe, rare. **$50** **$100** **$200**

--- *Case of the Caretaker's Cat, The,* Pocket Book #138, 1942. **$4** **$20** **$80**

--- *Case of the Howling Dog, The,* Pocket Book #116, 1941. **$5** **$25** **$90**

--- *Case of the Lame Canary, The,* Pocket Book #223, 1943, cover by H. Lawrence Hoffman. 📷 **$4** **$20** **$65**

--- *Case of the Substitute Face, The,* Pocket Book #242, 1943, cover by Leo Manso. **$5** **$20** **$60**

Gat, Dimitri, *Nevsky's Demon,* Avon Book #82248, 1983, paperback original, a charge that it was a plagiarism of John D. MacDonald's The Dreadful Lemon Sky caused the book to be recalled. **$5** **$20** **$60**

Gault, William Campbell, *Day of the Ram,* Bantam Book #1638, 1957, cover by Mitchell Hooks. 📷 **$4** **$15** **$40**

--- *Death Out of Focus,* Dell Book #1012, 1960, first paperback printing, cover by Robert McGinnis. **$4** **$20** **$50**

--- *Don't Cry For Me,* Dell Book #672, 1953, cover by James Meese. 📷 **$5** **$16** **$45**

--- *End of a Call Girl,* Crest Book #248, 1958, paperback original, a Joe Puma novel. **$8** **$35** **$90**

--- *Hundred-Dollar Girl, The,* Signet Book #S2205, 1962, a Joe Puma novel. **$6** **$20** **$65**

--- *Million Dollar Tramp,* Crest Book #361, 1960, paperback original, a Joe Puma novel. **$8** **$25** **$90**

--- *Murder In the Raw,* Dell Book #926, 1957, cover by Victor Kalin. **$5** **$20** **$55**

--- *Night Lady,* Crest Book #260, 1958, paperback original, a Joe Puma novel. **$5** **$25** **$90**

--- *Sweet Blonde Trap, The,* Zenith Book #ZB-25, 1959. 📷 **$8** **$30** **$100**

--- *Sweet Wild Wench,* Crest Book #309, 1959, paperback original, a Joe Puma novel. **$8** **$25** **$90**

--- *Wayward Widow, The,* Crest Book #281, 1959, paperback original, a Joe Puma novel. **$10** **$25** **$85**

Gibson, Walter B., *Blonde For Murder, A,* Atlas Mystery #2, 1948, paperback original, digest-size. 📷 **$16** **$55** **$165**

	G	VG	F

--- *Looks That Kill*, Atlas Mystery #5, 1948, paperback original, digest-size. **$14 $45 $125**

Gilbert, Elliott, *Vice Trap*, Avon Book #T-266, 1958, paperback original, cover by Harry Schaare, hard crime and drug noir. **$6 $20 $65**

Givens, Charles, *Big Mike*, Pyramid Book #104, 1953, first book edition, cover by Julian Paul, underrated Hammett-type novel. **$5 $20 $75**

Goines, Donald, *Death List*, Holloway House, #BH070, 1974 reprint of his second novel under his true name, originally written as by Al C. Clark. Holloway printed all 16 novels by Goines, each book: **$5 $15 $50**

Goodis, David, *Black Friday*, Lion Book #224, 1954, paperback original. **$45 $125 $250**

--- *Behold This Woman*, Bantam Book #407, 1948. **$12 $60 $150**

--- *Behold This Woman*, Popular Library #775, 1956, cover by Owen Kampen. **$20 $75 $180**

--- *Blonde on the Street Corner, The*, Lion Book #186, 1954, paperback original, cover by Robert Maguire. 📷 **$40 $150 $400**

--- *Burglar, The*, Lion Book #124, 1953, paperback original. 📷 **$35 $150 $350**

	G	VG	F

--- *Cassidy's Girl*, Gold Medal Book #189, 1951, paperback original, cover by Owen Kampen. **$50 $140 $350**

--- *Cassidy's Girl*, Gold Medal Book #544, 1955, second printing, cover by Owen Kampen, reprints Gold Medal #189. **$22 $75 $155**

--- *Dark Chase, The*, Lion Book #133, 1953, paperback original. 📷 **$30 $100 $250**

--- *Dark Passage*, Dell Book #221, 1948, Map Back. **$30 $100 $250**

--- *Down There*, Gold Medal Book #623, 1956, paperback original, cover by Mitchell Hooks. **$35 $150 $400**

--- *Fire in the Flesh*, Gold Medal Book #691, 1957, paperback original, cover by Barye Philips. **$25 $90 $200**

--- *Moon In the Gutter, The*, Gold Medal Book #348, 1953, paperback original. 📷 **$20 $90 $200**

--- *Nightfall*, Bestseller Mystery #B-121, 1949, digest-size. **$25 $75 $145**

--- *Night Squad*, Gold Medal Book #s1083, 1961, paperback original. **$15 $80 $150**

--- *Of Missing Persons*, Pocket Book #833, 1951, cover by Roy App. 📷 **$15 $60 $150**

--- *Of Tender Sin*, Gold Medal Book #226, 1952, paperback original. **$30 $75 $175**

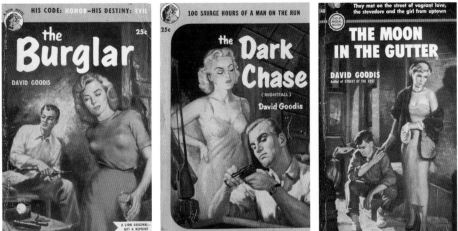

	G	VG	F			G	VG	F

--- *Of Tender Sin*, Gold Medal Book #626, 1956, reprints Gold Meal #226.
$20 $40 $90

--- *Somebody's Done For*, Banner Book #B60-111, 1967, paperback original.
$20 $80 $200

--- *Street of No Return*, Gold Medal Book #428, 1954, paperback original, cover by Barye Philips. $35 $90 $200

--- *Street of the Lost*, Gold Medal Book #652, 1957, cover by Barye Philips.
$25 $90 $350

--- *Wounded and the Slain, The*, Gold Medal Book #530, 1955, paperback original, cover by Ernest Chiriaka.
$35 $120 $300

Gould, Chester, *Dick Tracy and the Woo-Woo Sisters*, Dell Books, no number, 1947, paperback original.
$35 $100 $250

Gray, Russell, *Lustful Ape, The*, Lion Book #38, 1950, paperback original, cover by Julian Paul; pseudonym of Bruno Fischer.
$15 $50 $100

Greene, Graham, *Brighton Rock*, Bantam Book #315, 1949. $5 $20 $60

--- *Brighton Rock*, Bantam Book #315, 1949, in dust jacket.
$35 $125 $225

--- *Confidential Agent, The*, Armed Service Edition #873, no date, circa 1946.
$20 $65 $120

--- *Confidential Agent, The*, Bantam Book #971, 1952, cover by Mitchell Hooks. 📖 $5 $15 $50

--- *Man Within, The*, Bantam Book #355, 1948, first edition thus, in dust jacket.
$25 $100 $200

--- *Orient Express*, Bantam Book #1333, 1955, cover by George Gross. 📖
$4 $15 $40

Grey, Harry, *Hoods, The*, Signet Book #S999, 1953, true gangsters, scarce in condition. $8 $20 $90

Grantland, Keith, *Run From the Hunter*, Gold Medal Book #701, 1957, paperback original; pseudonym of Charles Beaumont. $15 $40 $120

Gruber, Frank, *Hungry Dog Murders*, Avon Murder Mystery Monthly #12, 1943, digest-size. $25 $75 $145

--- *Laughing Fox, The*, Penguin Book #538, 1943, in dust jacket.
$65 $150 $300

--- *Mighty Blockhead, The*, Bantam Book #144, 1948, Superior reprint in dust jacket. 📖 $45 $160 $250

--- *Navy Colt, The*, Bantam Book #151, 1948, Superior reprint in dust jacket.
$45 $100 $200

--- *Talking Clock, The*, Penguin Book #454, 1946, in dust jacket.
$55 $165 $350

	G	VG	F		G	VG	F

--- *Whispering Master, The*, Signet Book #726, 1949, cover by Leonard. 📷
$3 $15 $45

--- *Yellow Overcoat, The*, Popular Library #188, 1949. 📷 **$4 $20 $85**

Hamilton, Donald, *Death of a Citizen*, Gold Medal Book #957, 1960, paperback original, the first Matt Helm novel. 📷
$8 $35 $120

--- *Murder Twice Told*, Dell Book #577, 1952, Map Back, cover by Robert Stanley.
$4 $20 $75

--- *Night Walker*, Dell First Edition #27, 1954, paperback original, cover by Carl Bobertz. 📷 **$8 $35 $100**

--- *Removers, The*, Gold Medal Book #s1082, 1961, paperback original, cover by Barye Phillips, Matt Helm #3.
$5 $25 $90

--- *Wrecking Crew, The*, Gold Medal Book #1025, 1960, paperback original, Matt Helm #2. **$8 $30 $100**

Hammett, Dashiell, *$106,000 Blood Money*, Bestseller Mystery #B-40, 1943, first book edition, digest-size.
$65 $125 $275

--- *Adventures of Sam Spade, The*, Bestseller Mystery #B50, 1944, his first collection. **$65 $100 $250**

--- *Big Knockover, The*, Jonathan Press #J-36, 1947, digest-size, retitled *$106,000 Blood Money*. **$15 $50 $100**

--- *Blood Money*, Dell Book #53, 1944, Map Back, cover by Gerald Gregg.
$10 $50 $150

--- *Blood Money*, Dell Book #486, 1951, Map Back, cover by Robert Stanley, reprints Dell #53 with new cover art. 📷
$12 $40 $85

--- *Continental Op, The*, Bestseller Mystery #B-62, 1945, first book edition, digest-size. **$45 $100 $200**

--- *Continental Op, The*, Jonathan Press #J-40, 1947, digest-size.
$15 $50 $125

--- *Continental Op, The*, Dell Book #129, 1946, Map Back, cover by Gerald Gregg.
$10 $40 $125

--- *Creeping Siamese, The*, Jonathan Press #J-48, 1950, digest-size.
$18 $100 $200

--- *Creeping Siamese, The*, Dell Book #538, 1951, Map Back, cover by Robert Stanley. 📷 **$12 $60 $120**

--- *Dain Curse, The*, Pocket Book #295, 1945. **$5 $25 $75**

--- *Dead Yellow Women*, Jonathan Mystery #J-29, 1947, digest-size.
$25 $100 $200

--- *Dead Yellow Women*, Dell Book #308, 1949, Map Back. **$10 $60 $150**

--- *Dead Yellow Women*, Dell Book #421, 1950, reprint, Map Back, scarce in condition. **$20 $50 $150**

--- *Hammett Homicides*, Bestseller Mystery #B-81, 1946, first book edition, digest-size. **$25 $100 $225**

--- *Hammett Homicides*, Dell Book #223, 1948, Map Back, cover by Gerald Gregg. 📷 **$12 $60 $135**

--- *Maltese Falcon, The*, American Red Cross Readers League of America, no number, (#3), circa 1945.
$12 $55 $125

--- *Maltese Falcon, The*, Pocket Book #268, 1944, no dust jacket, first printing scarce in condition. 📷
$10 $20 $100

--- *Maltese Falcon, The*, Pocket Book #268, 1945, cover by Stanley Meltzoff, in dust jacket. 📷 **$50 $150 $400**

--- *Man Called Spade, A*, Dell Book #452, 1950. **$10 $25 $90**

--- *Man Called Spade and Other Stories, A*, Dell Book #90, 1945.
$20 $100 $175

--- *Man Called Spade and Other Stories, A*, Dell Book #411, 1950, cover by Robert Stanley. **$15 $55 $120**

--- *Man Named Thin, A*, Mercury Mystery #233, 1962, paperback original, digest-size, cover by George Salter.
$15 $100 $200

--- *Nightmare Town*, Mercury Mystery #120, 1948, first book edition, abridged, digest-size, cover by George Salter.
$15 75 $150

--- *Nightmare Town*, Dell Book #379, 1950, cover by Robert Stanley.
$15 $50 $120

--- *Red Brain, The*, Belmont Book #239, 1961, paperback original, anthology edited by Hammett. **$10 $25 $65**

	G	VG	F

--- *Red Harvest*, Perma Book #M3043, 1956, cover by Lou Marchetti.
$8 $20 $65

--- *Return of the Continental Op, The*, Jonathan Press #J-17, 1945, first book edition, digest-size, cover by George Salter.   **$45 $100 $200**

--- *Return of the Continental Op, The*, Dell Book #154, 1947, Map Back, cover by Gerald Gregg. **$15 $45 $150**

--- *They Can Only Hang You Once*, Mercury Mystery #131, 1944, digest-size, cover by George Salter.
$12 $75 $155

--- *Thin Man, The*, American Red Cross Readers League of America, no number, (#2), circa 1945. **$12 $35 $100**

--- *Woman in the Dark*, Jonathan Press #J-59, 1951, paperback original, digest-size.   **$22 $85 $200**

Harlow, Alvin F., *True Murders Not Quite Solved*, Quick Reader #123, 1944, cover by Axelrod, early true crime book.
$5 $25 $55

Harrigan, Steve, *Dope Doll and Bigamy Kiss, The,* Universal Giant Editions #4, 1953, paperback original, thick digest-size double volume, bondage cover art. 📷   **$20 $75 $150**

Harrison, Chip, *Make Out With Murder*, Gold Medal Book #m3029, 1974, paperback original, cover by Elaine; pseudonym of Lawrence Block, there are four Gold Medal Chip Harrisons, each book: **$6 $30 $100**

Harrison, Joel L., *Bloody Wednesday: The True Story of the Ramon Navarro Murder,* Major Book #41215, 1978, paperback original, true crime, scarce.
$75 $150 $300

Harrison, Whit, *Violent Night,* Phantom Book #511, 1952, paperback original, cover by George Gross, digest-size; pseudonym of Harry Whittington, scarce.
$100 $200 $500

Heard, H. F., *Taste For Honey, A,* Avon Book #108, 1946, Sherlockian.
$6 $20 $90

Hecht, Ben, *Florentine Dagger, The,* Checker Book #9, 1949.
$8 $35 $100

Held, Peter, *Take My Face,* Pyramid Book #G-327, 1958, first paperback printing, cover by John Floherty Jr.; pseudonym of Jack Vance, scarce.
$15 $75 $150

Highsmith, Patrica, *Strangers On a Train,* Bantam Book #905, 1951, cover by Stanley Zuckerberg. 📷
$5 $20 $90

Himes, Chester, *All Shot Up,* Avon Book #T-434, 1960, first English language edition.   **$12 $70 $155**

--- *Big Gold Dream, The,* Avon Book #T-384, 1960, first English language edition.
$14 $75 $165

--- *Crazy Kill, The,* Avon Book #T-357, 1959, first English language edition, Coffin Ed and Grave Digger Jones. 📷
$12 $55 $155

--- *For Love of Imabelle,* Gold Medal Book #717, 1957, paperback original, cover by Mitchell Hooks, first Coffin Ed and Gravedigger Jones novel.
$15 $75 $200

--- *If He Hollers Let Him Go*, Signet Book #756, 1949, first U.S. edition, cover by James Avati, Himes' first American paperback. 📷   **$15 $85 $175**

--- *If He Hollers Let Him Go*, Berkley Book #G-6, 1955, photo cover.
$10 $50 $100

--- *If He Hollers Let Him Go*, Berkley Book #G-139, 1958, cover by Rudy Nappi, scarce.   **$15 $60 $120**

--- *Primitive, The*, Signet Book #1264, 1955, paperback original.
$10 $80 $200

--- *Real Cool Killers, The*, Avon Book #T-328, 1959, first English language edition.
$12 $65 $160

Hoch, Edward D., *City of Brass and Other Simon Ark Stories, The,* Leisure Book #LB29S, 1971, first book edition, collection.   **$20 $50 $100**

--- *Judges of Hades and Other Simon Ark Stories, The,* Leisure Book #LB33, 1971, first book edition, cover by James Dietz, collection.   **$20 $40 $90**

--- *Shattered Raven, The,* Lancer Book #74-525, 1969, paperback original, novel, murder at a mystery writers dinner, his first book.   **$20 $75 $150**

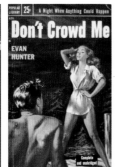

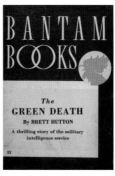

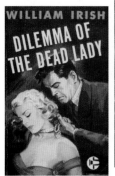

	G	VG	F

--- *Shattered Raven, The,* Prestige/ Magnum Book #74-525, 1976, reprints Lancer. This was a pirate edition; the author told me he was never paid for it. **$4 $20 $60**

Holding, Elizabeth Sax, *Net of Cobwebs,* Bantam Book #26, 1948, in dust jacket. **$15 $60 $125**

Holmes, H. H., *Rocket to the Morgue,* Phantom Mystery #1, 1942, paperback original, cover by Shayn, digest-size; pseudonym of Anthony Boucher.  **$20 $80 $225**

Hopley, George, *Fright,* Popular Library #424, 1952, cover by Rudolph Belarski; pseudonym of Cornell Woolrich. **$15 $75 $200**

--- *Night Has 1,000 Eyes,* Dell Book #679, 1953. **$16 $60 $150**

Household, Geoffrey, *Rogue Male,* Bantam Book #9, 1945, in dust jacket. **$25 $100 $175**

Hughes, Dorothy B., *Bamboo Blonde, The,* Pocket Book #394, 1946. **$3 $15 $50**

--- *Johnnie,* Bonded Mystery #11, no date, 1940s, abridged, male bondage cover art. **$8 $25 $80**

Hunt, Howard, *Bimini Run,* Avon Book #457, 1952, cover by George Erickson, crime noir. **$5 $20 $50**

--- *Judas Hour, The,* Gold Medal Book #167, 1951, paperback original. **$5 $30 $75**

	G	VG	F

--- *Lovers Are Losers,* Gold Medal Book #297, 1953, paperback original, cover by Barye Phillips. **$10 $40 $100**

--- *Violent Ones, The,* Gold Medal Book #113, 1950, paperback original, cover by Barye Phillips. **$4 $20 $75**

--- *Whisper Her Name,* Gold Medal Book #268, 1952, paperback original, two versions exist: one with no price, one with 35 cents cover price, each: **$6 $20 $75**

Hunter, Evan, *Don't Crowd Me,* Popular Library #478, 1953, paperback original, cover by Walter Popp. **$4 $25 $90**

--- *Evil Sleep, The,* Falcon Book #41, 1952, paperback original, digest-size, his first book. **$90 $300 $750**

Hutton, Brett, *Green Death and Other Stories, The,* LA Bantam #22, 1940, text cover, same design on all text cover LA Bantams, rare. **$75 $150 $255**

--- *Green Death and Other Stories, The,* LA Bantam #22, 1940, illustrated cover, rare. **$160 $300 $550**

Hynd, Alan, *Pinkerton Case Book, The,* Penguin Signet Book #667, 1948, cover by Robert Jonas, true crime. **$3 $20 $55**

--- *We Are the Public Enemies,* Gold Medal Book #101, 1949, paperback original, third Gold Medal Book, first Gold Medal original. **$10 $25 $90**

	G	VG	F

Irish, William, *And So to Death,* Jonathan Press #J-31, 1947, digest-size; pseudonym of Cornell Woolrich.
| | **$25** | **$90** | **$175** |

--- *After-Dinner Story,* Armed Service Edition #S-20, no date, about 1945.
| | **$15** | **$45** | **$120** |

--- *Bluebeard's Seventh Wife,* Popular Library #473, 1952, collection.
| | **$14** | **$60** | **$120** |

--- *Borrowed Crime,* Avon Murder Mystery Monthly #42, 1946, paperback original, digest-size.
| | **$60** | **$175** | **$355** |

--- *Dancing Detective, The,* Popular Library #309, 1951, collection. 📷
| | **$15** | **$75** | **$160** |

--- *Deadline at Dawn,* Armed Service Edition #878, no date, circa 1945.
| | **$12** | **$55** | **$125** |

--- *Deadline at Dawn,* Bestseller Mystery #B-90, 1946, digest-size.
| | **$10** | **$50** | **$100** |

--- *Deadline at Dawn,* Graphic Book #16, 1949.
| | **$6** | **$30** | **$85** |

--- *Deadly Night Call,* Graphic Book #31, 1951, cover shows falling woman, scarce in high grade.
| | **$8** | **$30** | **$100** |

--- *Dilemma of the Dead Lady,* Graphic Book #20, 1950, strangulation cover art. 📷
| | **$10** | **$40** | **$120** |

--- *If I Should Die Before I Wake,* Avon Murder Mystery Monthly #31, 1945, paperback original.
| | **$30** | **$130** | **$255** |

--- *If I Should Die Before I Wake,* Avon Book #104, 1946, collection.
| | **$15** | **$35** | **$125** |

--- *I Married a Dead Man,* Avon Book #220, 1950, gruesome cover art shows corpse-like groom with bride.
| | **$15** | **$90** | **$200** |

--- *I Wouldn't Be In Your Shoes,* Armed Service Edition #1173, no date, circa 1946.
| | **$20** | **$75** | **$175** |

--- *Marihuana,* Dell Ten-Cent #11, 1951, first book edition, cover by Bill Fleming, drugs and murder. 📷
| | **$75** | **$200** | **$500** |

--- *Nightmare,* Readers Choice Library #12, 1950. 📷
| | **$10** | **$50** | **$125** |

--- *Phantom Lady,* Pocket Book #253, 1944, cover by Leo Manso. 📷
| | **$5** | **$25** | **$90** |

--- *Phantom Lady,* Readers League of America, no number, no date, 1944, reprints Pocket Book #253 with same cover art but with white border.
| | **$8** | **$35** | **$100** |

--- *Phantom Lady,* American Red Cross Readers League of America, no number (#4), circa 1945.
| | **$10** | **$40** | **$100** |

--*Six Nights of Mystery,* Popular Library #258, 1950, first book edition, cover by Rudolph Belarski, collection. 📷
| | **$20** | **$100** | **$225** |

--- *Six Times Death,* Popular Library #137, 1948, collection.
| | **$15** | **$60** | **$150** |

--- *Strangler's Serenade,* Popular Library #431, 1952, cover by Rudolph Belarski.
| | **$16** | **$90** | **$200** |

--- *Waltz into Darkness,* Ace Book #D-40, 1954, abridged, Ace Double backed with *Scylla* by Malden Grange Bishop.
| | **$10** | **$35** | **$120** |

--- *You'll Never See Me Again,* Dell Ten-Cent #26, 1951, first book edition, cover by Robert Stanley. 📷 **$25** **$100** **$200**

Jackson, Gregory, *Mystery At Spanish Hacienda,* Avon Book, no number (#13), 1942, with Globe endpapers.
| | **$25** | **$75** | **$155** |

Jaediker, Kermit, *Hero's Lust,* Lion Book #156, 1953, paperback original, cover by Lou Marchetti. **$5** **$20** **$65**

--- *Tall Dark and Dead,* Lion Book #51, 1951, cover by Robert Maguire. 📷
| | **$5** | **$20** | **$75** |

Janson, Hank, *Lady, Mind That Corpse,* Checker Book #10, 1949, cover by Reginald Heade; pseudonym of Steven Francis. **$35** **$120** **$250**

--- *Nympho Named Sylvia, A,* Gold Star Book #IL7-48, 1965, paperback original, #16 in new Hank Janson series of at least 17 books, each book: 📷
| | **$5** | **$15** | **$50** |

	G	VG	F

Jenkins, Will F., *Man Who Feared, The,* Hangman's House #4, 1946, digest-size. 📷 $10 $30 $100

Johns, Veronica Parker, *Singing Widow, The,* Atlas Mystery, no number, 1945, digest-size. $10 $35 $90

Kane, Frank, *Slay Ride,* Popular Library #400, 1952. $10 $25 $65

Kane, Henry, *Deadly Doll, The,* Zenith Book #ZB-19, 1959, paperback original. $5 $20 $55

--- *Until You Are Dead*, Dell Book #580, 1952, Map Back, cover by Victor Kalin. 📷 $3 $20 $50

Karp, David, *Big Feeling, The,* Lion Book #93, 1952, paperback original. $10 $35 $110

--- *Brotherhood of Velvet, The,* Lion Book #105, 1953, paperback original. 📷 $10 $30 $100

--- *Cry Flesh*, Lion Book #132, 1953, paperback original. $15 $50 $125

--- *Escape to Nowhere*, Lion Library #LL10, 1955, hypodermic needle cover art. $5 $25 $80

--- *Girl on Crown Street, The,* Lion Library #LB86, 1956, cover by Robert Stanley. $4 $20 $50

--- *Hardman*, Lion Book #119, 1953, paperback original, cover by Piezio. 📷 $6 $30 $100

Kay, Cameron, *Thieves Fall Out,* Gold Medal Book #311, 1953, paperback original, cover by Barye Philips; pseudonym of Gore Vidal. $20 $100 $300

Keenan, James, *Run, Mann, Run,* Major Book #3035, 1975, paperback original, plagiarizes John McPartland's *I'll See You In Hell.* 📷 $5 $15 $50

Keene, Day, *Big Kiss-off, The,* Berkley Diamond #D2003, 1959, cover by Darcy. $6 $40 $100

--- *Bring Him Back Dead*, Gold Medal Book #603, 1958, paperback original, cover by Barye Phillips. $8 $40 $120

--- *Bring Him Back Dead* with *There Was a Crooked Man*, Lancer Book #72-655, 1963, a Lancer 2-For-1 Book. 📷 $8 $25 $75

--- *Dangling Carrot, The,* Ace Book #D-129, 1955, paperback original, cover by Rudy Nappi, Ace Double backed with *Silenced Witness* by Norman C. Rosenthal. $10 $35 $100

--- *Dead Dolls Don't Talk*, Crest Book #286, 1959, paperback original, photo cover. $8 $35 $90

--- *Dead In Bed*, Pyramid Book #G-448, 1959, paperback original, cover by Harry Schaare. $6 $30 $100

--- *Death House Doll*, Ace Book #D-41, 1953, paperback original, Ace Double backed with *Mourning After* by Thomas D. Dewey, cover by Victor Olsen. 📷 $10 $40 $125

--- *Flight By Night*, Ace Book #D-170, 1956, paperback original, Ace Double backed with *Black Fire* by Lawrence Goldman. $10 $30 $100

--- *His Father's Wife*, Pyramid Book #138, 1954, paperback original, cover by Carl Bobertz. $10 $50 $120

--- *Homicidal Lady*, Graphic Book #87, 1954, paperback original. $7 $35 $100

--- *Home Is the Sailor*, Gold Medal Book #225, 1952, paperback original. $10 $55 $130

--- *Hunt the Killer*, Phantom Book #507, 1951, paperback original, digest-size. $45 $135 $355

--- *Hunt the Killer*, Avon Book #705, 1956, reprints Phantom #507. $8 $25 $70

--- *If the Coffin Fits*, Graphic Book #43, 1952, paperback original, brutal torture and hypodermic needle cover. 📷 $8 $45 $120

--- *Joy House*, Lion Book #210, 1954, paperback original. $9 $35 $100

--- *Joy House*, Lancer Book #72-628, 1962, combined with *City of Sin* by Milton K. Ozaki. $5 $30 $65

	G	VG	F

--- *Love Me and Die!*, Phantom Book #504, 1951, paperback original, digest-size, pulp story expanded to novel length by Gil Brewer. **$75** **$150** **$350**

--- *Moran's Woman*, Zenith Book #ZB-24, 1959, paperback original.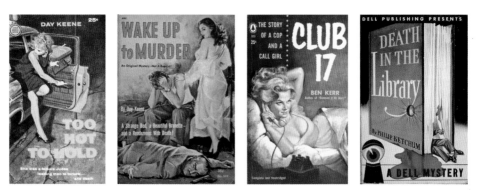
$15 **$50** **$140**

--- *Mrs. Homicide*, Ace Book #D-11, 1952, paperback original, cover by Norman Saunders, Ace Double backed with *Dead Ahead* by William L. Stuart.
$10 **$60** **$130**

--- *Murder On the Side*, Gold Medal Book #622, 1956, paperback original, cover by Barye Philips.
$10 **$45** **$125**

--- *My Flesh is Sweet*, Lion Book #68, 1951, paperback original.
$10 **$50** **$150**

--- *Naked Fury*, Phantom Book #509, 1952, paperback original, digest-size.
$55 **$125** **$325**

--- *Naked Fury*, Berkley Diamond Book #D2020, 1959, cover by Milo.
$10 **$50** **$120**

--- *Notorious*, Gold Medal Book #372, 1954, paperback original, carnival murder, scarce in condition.
$10 **$45** **$150**

--- *Passage to Samoa*, Gold Medal Book #823, 1958, paperback original.
$8 **$35** **$100**

--- *Passion Murders*, The, Avon Book #684, 1955. **$5** **$30** **$75**

--- *Sleep With the Devil*, Lion Book #204, 1954, paperback original.
$10 **$60** **$150**

--- *Sleep With the Devil*, Berkley Diamond #D2024, 1959.
$7 **$30** **$90**

--- *Take a Step to Murder*, Gold Medal Book #874, 1959, paperback original, cover by Bob Abbett.
$6 **$40** **$100**

--- *There Was a Crooked Man*, Gold Medal Book #405, 1954, paperback original, cover by Ray Johnson.
$8 **$55** **$125**

--- *This is Murder, Mr. Herbert*, Avon Book #159, 1948, first book edition, collection. **$10** **$50** **$125**

--- *Too Black For Heaven*, Zenith Book #ZB-31, 1959, paperback original.
$8 **$35** **$110**

--- *Too Hot to Hold*, Gold Medal Book #931, 1959, paperback original.
$10 **$30** **$120**

--- *To Kiss, Or Kill*, Gold Medal Book #206, 1951, paperback original, cover by Barye Phillips. **$6** **$50** **$130**

--- *Wake Up to Murder*, Phantom Book #513, 1952, paperback original, digest-size. **$30** **$125** **$275**

--- *Wake Up to Murder*, Berkley Book #G-258, 1959, cover by Robert Maguire.
$6 **$25** **$65**

--- *Who Was Wilma Lathrop?*, Gold Medal Book #494, 1955, paperback original, cover by Barye Phillips.
$10 **$35** **$100**

	G	VG	F

--- *Who Was Wilma Lathrop?* with *Murder on the Side*, Lancer Double Book #72-633, 1962, first book edition. **$5 $20 $50**

Kerr, Ben, *Blonde and Johnny Malloy, The,* Popular Library Eagle Book #EB104, 1958, paperback original; pseudonym of William Ard. **$10 $40 $90**

--- *Club 17*, Popular Library #803, 1957, paperback original. **$10 $25 $75**

--- *Down I Go*, Popular Library #653, 1955, paperback original, cover by Rafael DeSoto. **$10 $25 $85**

--- *Shakedown*, Popular Library #467, 1952. **$10 $30 $75**

Kersh, Gerald, *Dishonor,* Avon Book #T-111, 1955, aka Night and the City. **$4 $18 $40**

--- *Prelude to a Certain Midnight*, Lion Book #98, 1952. **$5 $30 $100**

Kesserling, Joseph, *Arsenic and Old Lace,* Pocket Book #199, 1943, very scarce in first printing and in any Pocket Books printing. **$25 $50 $125**

Ketchum, Philip, *Death in the Library,* Dell Book #1, 1943, cover by William Strohmer, not a Map Back, the first book in the Dell series. **$20 $100 $255**

King, Rufus, *Murder in the Willett Family,* Popular Library #55, 1945, cover by H. Lawrence Hoffman. **$4 $20 $55**

King, Sherwood, *If I Should Die Before I Wake,* Mystery Novel of the Month, 1940, digest-size, noir classic. **$60 $175 $400**

	G	VG	F

--- *If I Should Die Before I Wake*, Ace Book #D-9, 1952, Ace Double backed with *Decoy* by Michael Morgan. **$15 $35 $100**

Kline, Otis Adelbert, *Man Who Limped, The,* Chartered Books #22, 1946, paperback original, digest-size. **$50 $125 $400**

Knight, Adam, *I'll Kill You Next,* Signet Book #1276, 1956, cover by Robert Maguire. **$4 $15 $50**

Knight, David, *Pattern For Murder,* Graphic Book #48, 1952, paperback original; pseudonym of Richard S. Prather. **$4 $30 $75**

Koehler, Robert Portner, *Road House Murders, The,* Hangman House #17, 1946. **$4 $20 $45**

Koontz, Dean, *After the Last Race,* Crest Book #Q2650, 1975, heist novel. **$6 $35 $85**

Kuttner, Henry, *Murder of a Mistress,* Perma Book #M4082, 1957, paperback original, cover by Paul Bacon. **$10 $30 $100**

--- *Murder of Ann Avery, The*, Perma Book #3058, 1956, paperback original, cover by James Meese. **$10 $20 $90**

--- *Murder of a Wife*, Perma Book #M4096, 1958, paperback original, cover by William Rose. **$10 $35 $110**

--- *Murder of Eleanor Pope, The*, Perma Book #M3046, 1956, paperback original, cover by Alfred Gescheidt. **$10 $20 $75**

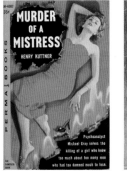

	G	VG	F

Lacey, Ed, *Woman Aroused, The,* Avon Book #342, 1951, actually Ed Lacy; publisher misspelled "Lacy" as "Lacey," pseudonym of Len Zinberg.
        $15   **$35**   **$100**

Lacy, Ed, *Blonde Bait,* Zenith Book #ZB-18, 1959, paperback original, cover by Rudy Nappi; pseudonym of Len Zinberg.
        $15   **$50**   **$100**

--- *Dead End,* Pyramid Book #G-471, 1960, cover by Darcy, crooked cop novel.   **$10**   **$20**   **$75**

--- *Enter Without Desire,* Avon Book #561, 1954, cover by Robert Schulz.
        $10   **$20**   **$60**

--- *Lead With Your Left,* Perma Book #M3106, 1958, cover by Robert Schulz.
        $10   **$25**   **$70**

--- *Visa to Death,* Perma Book #M3036, 1956, cover by Robert Maguire.
        $10   **$25**   **$75**

L'Amour, Louis, *Hills of Homicide, The,* Carroll & Graf #88184, 1983, first book edition, reprints five hard-boiled pulp stories, unauthorized edition.
        $10   **$25**   **$90**

--- *Hills of Homicide, The,* Bantam Book #24134, 1983, first book edition, reprints C&G edition but adds three stories and author introduction and notes, authorized edition.   **$5**   **$20**   **$60**

Lange, John, *Drug of Choice,* Signet Book #P4116, 1970, paperback original; pseudonym of Michael Crichton.
        $30   **$100**   **$250**

--- *Easy Go,* Signet Book #P3374, 1968, paperback original, his third novel.
        $20   **$80**   **$175**

--- *Grave Descend,* Signet Book #T4214, 1970, paperback original.
        $15   **$50**   **$135**

--- *Odds On,* Signet Book #P3068, 1966, paperback original, his first book.
        $75   **$180**   **$400**

--- *Scratch One,* Signet Book #P3238, 1967, paperback original, photo cover, his second novel.   **$15**   **$50**   **$125**

--- *Zero Cool,* Signet Book #P3746, 1969, paperback original.
        $15   **$75**   **$160**

Latimer, Jonathan, *Fifth Grave, The,* Popular Library #301, 1950, first book edition, abridged version of hard-boiled cult novel *Solomon's Vineyard.*
        $6   **$30**   **$100**

--- *Lady in the Morgue,* Pocket Book #246, 1943, cover by Leo Manso, features alcoholic detective William Crane.
        $4   **$20**   **$75**

--- *Sinners and Shrouds,* Pocket Book #1136, 1956, cover by James Meese, brutal murder scene cover art.
        $5   **$25**   **$80**

Leonard, Elmore, *Big Bounce, The,* Gold Meal Book #R2079, 1969, paperback original, cover by Robert McGinnis.
        $15   **$80**   **$175**

--- *Elmore Leonard Reader, The,* Avon Books, no number, 1983, first edition thus, giveaway, advance preview to coincide with release of his novel *Stick.*
        $8   **$20**   **$65**

	G	VG	F

--- *Maximum Leonard*, Dell Books, no number, 1993, first edition thus, no price, giveaway sampler, thin paperback excerpts his novels, photo cover shows author. **$5** **$15** **$40**

Lipsky, Eleazar, *Hoodlum, The*, Lion Book #161, 1953, aka The Kiss of Death. **$15** **$45** **$125**

--- *Kiss of Death, The*, Penguin Book #642, 1947, true first edition, cover by Robert Jonas. **$12** **$40** **$125**

--- *Kiss of Death, The*, Dell Book #D396, 1961, cover by Bob Abbett, crime classic. 📷 **$8** **$15** **$50**

Long, Julius, *Murder in Her Big Blue Eyes*, Avon Murder Mystery Monthly #48, 1950, cover by Ann Cantor, digest-size. **$45** **$150** **$325**

Longbaugh, Harry, *No Way to Treat a Lady*, Gold Medal Book #k1384, 1964, paperback original, byline taken from the real name of the Sundance Kid; pseudonym of William Goldman. **$8** **$40** **$150**

Lorenz, Frederick, *Hot*, Lion Library #LB144, 1956, paperback original, cover by Rudy Nappi. **$5** **$20** **$50**

--- *Rage At Sea, A*, Lion Book #152, 1953, paperback original, cover by Robert Maguire. **$5** **$30** **$90**

--- *Savage Chase, The*, Lion Book #223, 1954, paperback original. 📷 **$5** **$25** **$75**

Lustgarten, Edgar, *Blondie Iscariot*, Avon Book #179, 1949, "siren of the Underworld." 📷 **$4** **$20** **$65**

--- *One More Unfortunate*, Bantam Book #360, 1949, in dust jacket. **$45** **$140** **$275**

MacDonald, John D., *All These Condemned*, Gold Medal Book #420, 1954, paperback original, cover by James Meese. **$15** **$100** **$225**

--- *Area of Suspicion*, Dell First Edition #12, 1954, paperback original, cover by Stanley Borack. **$10** **$60** **$165**

--- *Beach Girls, The*, Gold Medal Book #s907, 1959, paperback original. **$9** **$50** **$145**

--- *Border Town Girl*, Popular Library #750, 1956, paperback original, scarce in condition. **$14** **$90** **$300**

--- *Brass Cupcake, The*, Gold Medal Book #124, 1950, paperback original, his first novel, cover by Barye Phillips. 📷 **$20** **$100** **$350**

--- *Bullet For Cinderella, A*, Dell First Edition #62, 1955, paperback original, cover by George Gross. **$10** **$40** **$125**

--- *Cry Hard, Cry Fast*, Popular Library #675, 1955, paperback original, cover by Ray Johnson. **$15** **$75** **$155**

--- *Damned, The*, Gold Medal Book #240, 1952, paperback original. **$18** **$60** **$175**

--- *Dead Low Tide*, Gold Medal Book #298, 1953, paperback original, cover by Barye Phillips. **$15** **$65** **$250**

--- *Deadly Welcome*, Dell First Edition #B-127, 1959, paperback original, cover by Robert McGinnis. **$10** **$60** **$120**

--- *Deep Blue Good-By, The*, Gold Medal Book #k1405, 1964, paperback original, cover by Ron Lesser, the first Travis McGee novel. **$14** **$60** **$155**

--- *I Could Go On Singing*, Gold Medal Book #k1291, 1963, paperback original, only edition, never reprinted, scarce. **$20** **$75** **$150**

--- *Judge Me Not*, Gold Medal Book #186, 1951, paperback original, cover by Barye Phillips. **$20** **$80** **$200**

--- *Murder For the Bride*, Gold Medal Book #164, 1951, paperback original, cover by Barye Phillips. **$15** **$75** **$275**

--- *Murder in the Wind*, Dell First Edition #A-113, 1956, paperback original, cover by George Gross. **$15** **$60** **$145**

--- *Neon Jungle, The*, Gold Medal Book #323, 1953, paperback original, JD crime, rare in condition. **$25** **$125** **$750**

--- *Price of Murder, The*, Dell First Edition #A-152, 1957, paperback original, cover by Victor Kalin. **$10** **$60** **$140**

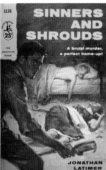

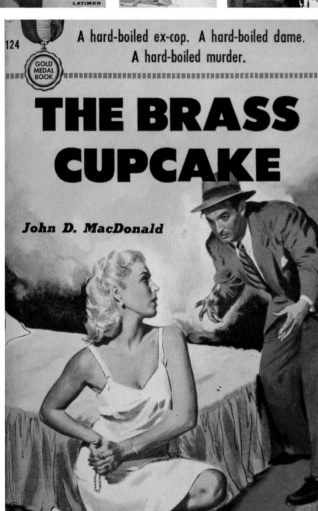

A hard-boiled ex-cop. A hard-boiled dame.
A hard-boiled murder.

THE BRASS CUPCAKE

John D. MacDonald

	G	VG	F

--- *Seven*, Gold Medal Book #t2412, 1971, first book edition, photo cover shows author, reprints stories from *Playboy*.

| | **$10** | **$40** | **$100** |

--- *Soft Touch*, Dell First Edition #B-117, 1958, paperback original, cover by Mitchell Hooks.

| | **$8** | **$45** | **$100** |

--- *Weep For Me*, Gold Medal Book #200, 1951, paperback original, cover by Owen Kampen.

| | **$20** | **$100** | **$300** |

--- *You Kill Me*, Popular Library #G507, 1961, reprint under new title, photo cover, aka *You Live Once*. 📷

| | **$10** | **$45** | **$90** |

--- *You Live Once*, Popular Library #737, 1956, first edition.

| | **$15** | **$50** | **$125** |

Macdonald, John Ross, *Drowning Pool, The*, Pocket Book #821, 1951, cover by Roy App. 📷

| | **$5** | **$30** | **$100** |

--- *Marked For Murder*, Pocket Book #971, 1953, cover by Robert Maguire. 📷

| | **$4** | **$20** | **$75** |

--- *Meet Me at the Morgue*, Pocket Book #1020, 1954, cover by Clark Hulings.

| | **$4** | **$20** | **$70** |

--- *Name Is Archer, The*, Bantam Book #1295, 1955, paperback original, cover by Mitchell Hooks.

| | **$10** | **$60** | **$155** |

Macdonald, Philip, *Rasp, The*, Penguin Book #586, 1946, in dust jacket.

| | **$25** | **$100** | **$265** |

--- *Renox Murder Mystery, The*, Bantam Book #146, 1948, Superior reprint in dust jacket.

| | **$45** | **$100** | **$200** |

--- *Warrant For X*, Pocket Book #328, 1945. 📷

| | **$5** | **$15** | **$60** |

MacIvers, Donald, *Cult of Killers, The*, Leisure Book #364DK, 1976, paperback original, uncredited cover, novel. 📷

| | **$10** | **$30** | **$60** |

MacNeil, Neil, *Death Ride, The*, Gold Medal Book #1055, 1960, paperback original; pseudonym of W. T. Ballard.

| | **$3** | **$15** | **$40** |

--- *Death Takes An Option*, Gold Meal Book #807, 1958, paperback original, cover by Powell.

| | **$3** | **$15** | **$45** |

--- *Hot Dam*, Gold Medal Book #964, 1960, paperback original.

| | **$3** | **$20** | **$45** |

--- *Third On a Seesaw*, Gold Medal Book #s844, 1959, paperback original, cover by Powell.

| | **$3** | **$20** | **$45** |

Mara, Bernard, *Bullet For My Lady, A*, Gold Medal Book #472, 1955, paperback original, cover by James Meese; pseudonym of Brian Moore.

| | **$30** | **$75** | **$250** |

--- *French For Murder*, Gold Medal Book #402, 1954, paperback original, cover Clark Hulings.

| | **$30** | **$75** | **$225** |

--- *This Gun For Gloria*, Gold Medal Book #562, 1956, paperback original.

| | **$20** | **$65** | **$150** |

Mark, Ted, *I Was a Teeny-Bopper For the C.I.A.*, Berkley Book #X1496, 1967, paperback original, sexy spy spoof in the Man From O.R.G.Y. series; pseudonym of Ted Gottfried. 📷

| | **$5** | **$20** | **$50** |

Markham, Robert, *Colonel Sun*, Berkley Book #S4408, 1969, first paperback printing, a James Bond novel; pseudonym of Kingsly Amis.

| | **$4** | **$16** | **$40** |

Marlowe, Dan J., *Name of the Game Is Death, The*, Gold Medal Book #s1184, 1962, paperback original, cited by Stephen King as one of the best noir crime novels.

| | **$12** | **$50** | **$125** |

--- *Route of the Red Gold*, Gold Medal Book #d1791, 1967, paperback original.

| | **$5** | **$25** | **$75** |

Marlowe, Stephen, *Blonde Bait*, Avon Book #T-330, 1959, paperback original cover by Darcy; pseudonym of Milton Lesser, uncommon.

| | **$15** | **$30** | **$100** |

--- *Catch the Brass Ring*, Ace Book #D-77, 1954, paperback original, aka known as Milton Lesser, Ace Double backed with *Stranger At Home* by George Sanders, which was written by Leigh Brackett.

| | **$8** | **$30** | **$90** |

--- *Death Is My Comrade*, Gold Medal Book #986, 1960, paperback original.

| | **$4** | **$20** | **$65** |

	G	VG	F

--- *Jeopardy Is My Job*, Gold Medal Book #s1214, 1962, paperback original.
$4 $20 $60

--- *Mecca For Murder*, Gold Medal Book #575, 1956, paperback original, cover by James Meese.   **$4 $25 $75**

--- *Model For Murder*, Graphic Book #94, 1954, paperback original, cover by Walter Popp, who told me his wife, Marie, was the model for the woman, he just gave her blonde hair. Popp is the guy at the typewriter; the guy with the glasses was based on a then-obscure Texas politician named Lyndon B. Johnson. 📷
$5 $20 $65

--- *Peril Is My Pay*, Gold Medal Book #1018, 1960, paperback original.
$5 $25 $75

--- *Terror Is My Trade*, Gold Medal Book #813, 1958, paperback original, cover by Powell.   **$5 $25 $75**

--- *Turn Left For Murder*, Ace Book #D-89, 1955, paperback original, Ace Double backed with *Death Watch* by Ruth and Alexander Wilson. 📷
$8 $20 $65

Marquand, John P., *Think Fast, Mr. Moto*, Pocket Book #59, 1940, cover by A. Pope.   **$4 $25 $85**

Marsh, Ngaio, *Colour Scheme*, Armed Service Edition #882, no date, circa 1946.
$15 $45 $120

--- *Final Curtain*, Armed Service Edition #1269, no date, circa 1947.
$12 $35 $100

Marsten, Richard, *Even the Wicked*, Perma Book #M3117, 1958, paperback original, cover by Jerry Allison; pseudonym of Evan Hunter.   **$10 $40 $100**

--- *Murder In the Navy*, Gold Medal Book #507, 1955, paperback original, cover by Clark Hulings, scarce in condition.   **$10 $40 $150**

--- *Runaway Black*, Gold Medal Book #415, 1954, paperback original, cover by Lu Kimmel, racial crime novel.
$12 $50 $150

--- *Vanishing Ladies*, Perma Book #M-3097, 1957, paperback original, cover by James Meese.   **$8 $30 $100**

Mason, Van Wyck, *Shanghai Bund Murders, The*, Century Book #32, 1945, first edition thus, revised, cover by

Malcolm Smith, digest-size.
$12 $75 $165

Masur, Harold Q., *Bury Me Deep*, Pocket Book #558, 1948, cover by William Wirts, the first Scott Jordan novel and author's first book. Masur told me he wrote it while stationed in China in World War II. 📷   **$5 $20 $50**

--- *Dolls Are Murder*, Lion Library #LB152, 1957, first book edition, anthology with John D. MacDonald, Raymond Chandler, Ellery Queen, Rex Stout.   **$4 $20 $65**

--- *You Can't Live Forever*, Dell Book #D329, 1959, cover by Robert McGinnis.
$5 $20 $50

Matheson, Richard, *Fury on Sunday*, Lion Book #180, 1953, paperback original. 📷
$60 $200 $525

--- *Ride the Nightmare*, Ballantine Book #301K, 1959, paperback original, photo cover.   **$40 $100 $280**

--- *Someone is Bleeding*, Lion Book #137, 1953, paperback original. 📷
$60 $200 $500

McBain, Ed, *Con Man, The*, Perma Book #M3055, 1957, paperback original, cover by James Meese, 87th precinct novel #4; pseudonym of Evan Hunter.
$12 $60 $150

--- *Cop Hater*, Perma Book #M3037, 1956, paperback original, the first book in the 87th Precinct series. 📷
$15 $100 $200

--- *Killer's Choice*, Perma Book #M3108, 1957, paperback original, cover by Robert Schulz, 87th Precinct novel #5.
$10 $30 $85

--- *Killer's Payoff*, Perma Book #M3113, 1958, paperback original, cover by Robert Schulz, 87th Precinct novel #6.
$10 $30 $100

--- *Killer's Wedge*, Perma Book #M-4150, 1959, paperback original, cover by Darcy.
$15 $35 $120

--- *Lady Killer*, Perma Book #M3119, 1958, paperback original, cover by Charles Binger, 87th Precinct novel #7.
$8 $35 $80

--- *Mugger, The*, Perma Book #M3061, 1956, paperback original, cover by Lou Marchetti, 87th Precinct novel #2.
$10 $55 $155

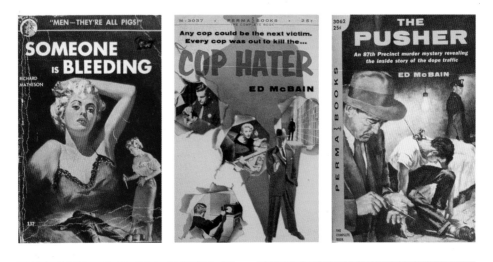

	G	VG	F

--- *Pusher, The,* Perma Book #M3062, 1956, paperback original, cover by Charles Binger, 87th Precinct novel #3, drug novel. 📷 **$14** **$100** **$175**

McCloy, Helen, *Panic,* Dell Book #369, 1950, Map Back, cover image shows shadow of giant hand threatening woman. 📷 **$5** **$20** **$65**

--- *Through a Glass, Darkly,* Dell Book #519, 1951, Map Back, cover by Robert Stanley. **$5** **$15** **$65**

McCoy, Horace, *Corruption City,* Dell First Edition #A-188, 1959, paperback original. **$5** **$30** **$75**

--- *I Should Have Stayed Home,* Berkley Book #328, 1955, noir. **$4** **$20** **$80**

--- *No Pockets In a Shroud,* Signet Book #690, 1948, first U.S. edition, cover by "TV." 📷 **$4** **$20** **$75**

--- *They Shoot Horses Don't They?,* Berkley Book #108, 1955, Depression era dance marathon noir novel. **$5** **$25** **$75**

McCready, Jack, *Raper, The,* Monarch Book #229, 1961, paperback original, cover by Rafael DeSoto; pseudonym of Talmage Powell. **$10** **$30** **$100**

McCrumb, Sharon, *Bimbos of the Death Sun,* TSR Windwalker Book #88038, 1987, paperback original, cover by Jeff Easley, murder at a SF convention. 📷 **$6** **$20** **$75**

	G	VG	F

McDowell, Emmett, *Bloodline For Murder* with *In At the Kill,* Ace Book #D-445, 1960, Ace Double, paperback original. **$5** **$18** **$45**

McGerr, Pat, *Pick Your Victim,* Dell Book #307, 1949, Map Back, incredible cover art. 📷 **$5** **$15** **$65**

McGivern, William P., *Big Heat, The,* Pocket Book #981, 1954, photo cover by Bill Hughes. 📷 **$4** **$15** **$60**

--- *Waterfront Cop,* Pocket Book #1105, 1956, cover by Clark Hulings, "a one-man police force without a badge!" **$5** **$20** **$60**

McKimmey, James, *24 Hours to Kill,* Dell First Edition #B169, 1961, paperback original, cover by Robert McGinnis. **$8** **$25** **$80**

--- *Cornered!,* Dell First Edition #B157, 1960, paperback original, cover by Harry Schaare. 📷 **$6** **$25** **$75**

--- *Long Ride, The,* Dell First Edition #B211, 1961, first book edition, cover by Bob Abbett. **$6** **$20** **$55**

--- *Wrong Ones, The,* Dell First Edition #B192, 1961, paperback original, cover by Robert McGinnis. **$6** **$25** **$75**

McPartland, John, *I'll See You In Hell,* Gold Medal Book #571, 1956, paperback original, cover by Barye Phillips. **$5** **$25** **$75**

	G	VG	F		G	VG	F

Meredith, Scott and Sidney, *Best From Manhunt, The,* Perma Book #M3111, 1958, first book edition, cover by Ernest Chiriaka, anthology. 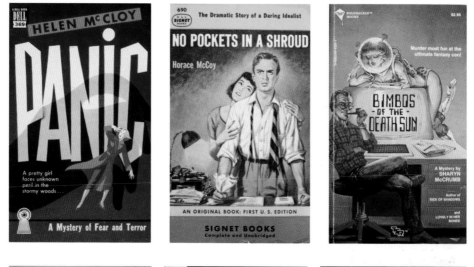 **$5**   **$25**   **$80**

Merwin Jr., Sam, *Big Frame, The,* Handi-Book #12, 1943. **$15**   **$35**   **$90**

--- *Creeping Shadow, The,* Gold Medal Book #227, 1952, paperback original. **$5**   **$25**   **$75**

Meskil, Paul S., *Sin Pit,* Lion Book #198, 1954, paperback original, his only novel and a crime classic. **$20**   **$60**   **$140**

Millar, Kenneth, *Blue City,* Dell Book #363, 1950, Map Back. **$5**   **$20**   **$75**

--- *Dark Tunnel, The,* Lion Book #48, 1950, "the story of a homosexual spy." **$10**   **$40**   **$125**

--- *I Die Slowly,* Lion Library #LL52, 1955, reprints Lion #48 with new title and cover art, cover by Clark Hullings. **$4**   **$20**   **$65**

--- *Trouble Follows Me,* Lion Book #47, 1950. **$5**   **$30**   **$100**

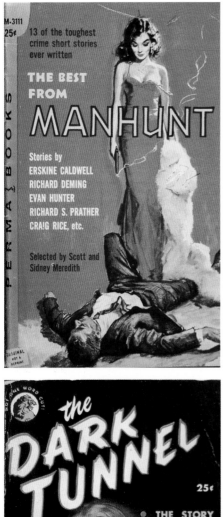

M-3111
25¢

13 of the toughest
crime short stories
ever written

THE BEST
FROM

MANHUNT

Stories by
ERSKINE CALDWELL
RICHARD DEMING
EVAN HUNTER
RICHARD S. PRATHER
CRAIG RICE, etc.

Selected by Scott and
Sidney Meredith

PERMA BOOKS

ORIGINAL
NOT A
REPRINT

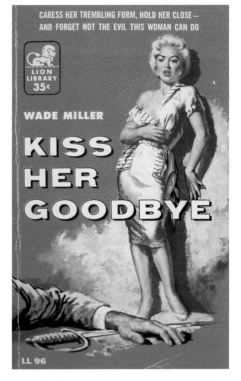

CARESS HER TREMBLING FORM, HOLD HER CLOSE—
AND FORGET NOT THE EVIL THIS WOMAN CAN DO

LION LIBRARY 35¢

WADE MILLER

KISS HER GOODBYE

LL 96

the

DARK TUNNEL

NOT ONE WORD CUT!

25¢

• THE STORY
OF A
HOMOSEXUAL
SPY •

KENNETH MILLAR

LION BOOKS
48

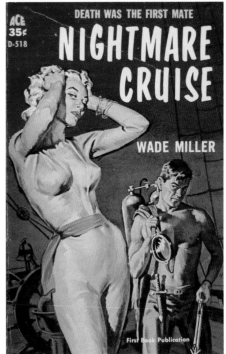

ACE
35¢
D-518

DEATH WAS THE FIRST MATE

NIGHTMARE CRUISE

WADE MILLER

First Book Publication

	G	VG	F		G	VG	F

Miller, Wade, *Big Guy, The,* Gold Medal Book #279, 1953, cover by John Floherty Jr.; pseudonym of Robert Wade and Bill Miller. **$5** **$25** **$100**

--- *Branded Woman,* Gold Medal Book #257, 1952, paperback original. **$10** **$30** **$90**

--- *Devil May Care,* Gold Medal Book #108, 1950, paperback original. **$12** **$40** **$100**

--- *Killer, The,* Gold Medal Book #152, 1951, paperback original. **$10** **$25** **$100**

--- *Kiss Her Goodbye,* Lion Library #LL96, 1956, paperback original, cover by Richard Copeland. 📷 **$5** **$25** **$90**

--- *Kitten With a Whip,* Gold Medal Book #s845, 1959, paperback original. **$9** **$30** **$90**

--- *Nightmare Cruise,* Ace Book #D-518, 1961, paperback original. 📷 **$5** **$20** **$75**

--- *Stolen Woman,* Gold Medal Book #139, 1950, paperback original, cover by Barye Phillips. **$5** **$26** **$60**

--- *Tiger's Wife, The,* Gold Medal Book #173, 1951, paperback original. **$5** **$20** **$75**

--- *Uneasy Street,* Signet Book #722, 1949, cover by James Avati. 📷 **$4** **$20** **$60**

Moore, Brian, *Sailor's Leave,* Pyramid Book #94, 1953, first U.S. edition, hard-boiled noir. 📷 **$35** **$125** **$375**

Moran, Mike, *Double Cross,* Popular Library #494, 1953, paperback original; pseudonym of William Ard. **$10** **$25** **$90**

Morelli, Spike, *Take It and Like It,* Archer Book #3, 1951, cover by Reginald Heade; pseudonym of William Newton. **$8** **$35** **$100**

--- *You'll Never Get Me,* Archer Book #8, 1951, cover by Reginald Heade. **$8** **$35** **$100**

Nebel, Frederick, *Six Deadly Dames,* Avon Book #264, 1950, collection of 6 Black Mask pulp stories. 📷 **$20** **$60** **$160**

Nelson, Kent, *Straight Man, The,* Black Lizard Book #11-1, 1978, paperback original, the first Black Lizard book; pseudonym of Barry Gifford. **$10** **$30** **$100**

Nisbet, Jim, *Gourmet, The,* Pinnacle Book #41-523, 1981, paperback original, cover by Earl Norem, author's first book. **$10** **$40** **$100**

Nyland, Gentry, *Hot Bullets For Love,* Double Action Detective Novel #2, 1943, digest-size, classic title is augmented by grinning skull cover art. 📷 **$8** **$30** **$90**

	G	VG	F

O'Farrell, William, *Causeway to the Past,* Dell Book #555, 1951, Map Back, cover by Robert Stanley, noir murder.

	$6	$20	$75

O'Flaherty, Liam, *Informer, The,* Bantam Book #150, 1948, Superior reprint in dust jacket. 📷

	$20	$75	$145

Oppenheim, E. Phillips, *Lion and the Lamb, The,* Popular Library #339, 1951, cover art predates 1954 Hitchcock film *Dial M For Murder.* 📷

	$6	$25	$100

Otis, G.H., *Bourbon Street,* Lion Book #131, 1953, paperback original, "a loot-mad thug takes New Orleans apart," underrated author.

	$10	$30	$85

--- *Hot Cargo,* Lion Book #171, 1953, paperback original.

	$15	$45	$110

Oursler, Will, *As Tough As They Come,* Perma Book #P118, 1951, early hard-boiled anthology includes Dashiell Hammett, James M. Cain, Day Keene. 📷

	$5	$30	$100

Ozaki, Milton K., *Case of the Deadly Kiss,* Gold Medal Book #715, 1957, paperback original, Japanese-American also wrote as Robert O. Saber.

	$5	$20	$60

	G	VG	F

--- *Dressed to Kill*, Graphic Book #79, 1954, cover by Walter Popp. 📷
| | $5 | $15 | $50 |

--- *Inquest*, Gold Medal Book #981, 1960, paperback original.
| | $6 | $20 | $65 |

Packer, Vin, *3 Day Terror*, Gold Medal Book #689, 1957, paperback original, cover by Louis Glanzman, who told me the model for the woman on the cover was his wife, Fran; uncommon in condition; pseudonym of Marijane Meaker.
| | $10 | $30 | $125 |

--- *Come Destroy Me*, Gold Medal Book #363, 1954, paperback original.
| | $7 | $35 | $120 |

--- *Damnation of Adam Blessing, The*, Gold Medal Book #s1074, 1961, paperback original, cover by Robert McGinnis.
| | $5 | $30 | $100 |

--- *Something in the Shadows*, Gold Medal Book #s1146, 1961, paperback original, cover by Leo and Diane Dillon.
| | $8 | $40 | $120 |

--- *Whisper His Sin*, Gold Medal Book #426, 1954, paperback original.
| | $8 | $30 | $100 |

Padgett, Lewis, *Day He Died, The*, Bantam Book #306, 1948.
| | $4 | $20 | $65 |

--- *Murder in Brass*, Bantam Book #107, 1947; pseudonym of Henry Kuttner. 📷
| | $5 | $25 | $80 |

Pagano, Joe, *Die Screaming*, Zenith Book #ZB-4, 1958. 📷
| | $5 | $15 | $55 |

--- *Condemned, The*, Perma Book #286, 1954, noir classic.
| | $10 | $25 | $70 |

Palmer, Stuart, *Before It's Too Late*, Dell Book #601, 1952, Map Back, cover by Willard Downes, first publication under author's true name. 📷
| | $5 | $25 | $75 |

--- *Monkey Murder, The*, Bestseller Mystery #B-128, 1950, first edition, digest-size.
| | $40 | $80 | $175 |

--- *Riddles of Hildegard Withers, The*, Jonathan Press Mystery #J-26, 1947, first edition, digest-size.
| | $40 | $85 | $225 |

Park, Jordan, *Man of Cold Rages*, Pyramid Book #368, 1958, paperback original, cover by Harry Schaare; pseudonym of C. M. Kornbluth.
| | $15 | $75 | $160 |

Patrick, Q., *Death Goes to School*, Banner Mysteries #2, 1945, digest-size, uncommon. 📷
| | $10 | $35 | $100 |

Patterson, James, *Season of the Machete*, Ballantine Book #27105, 1977, paperback original, his scarce second book.
| | $15 | $35 | $120 |

Paul, F. W., *Lay of the Land, The*, Lancer Book #74553, 1969, paperback original, photo cover shows artist Frank Frazetta as model, Man From STUD #8; pseudonym of Paul W. Fairman.
| | $20 | $50 | $100 |

--- *Planned Parenthood Caper, The*, Lancer Book #74531, 1969, paperback original, photo cover shows artist Frank Frazetta as model, Man From STUD #7.
| | $20 | $50 | $100 |

Paul, Gene, *Big Make, The*, Lion Library #LL158, 1957, cover by Robert Maguire. 📷
| | $8 | $15 | $55 |

--- *Little Killer*, Lion Book #104, 1952, paperback original, "a young gunpunk goes brute-wild over a woman."
| | $5 | $25 | $80 |

--- *Naked in the Dark*, Lion Book #154, 1953, paperback original.
| | $6 | $20 | $75 |

Pelrine, Eleanor and Dennis, *Ian Fleming: Man With the Golden Pen*, Swan Book #S102, 1966, paperback original, on James Bond and his creator.
| | $10 | $30 | $90 |

Pendleton, Don, *War Against the Mafia*, Pinnacle Book #P001S, 1969, paperback original, first Mack Bolan the Executioner, first Pinnacle Book.
| | $4 | $20 | $65 |

Pentecost, Hugh, *Cat and Mouse*, Quick Reader #128, 1944, cover by Axelrod; pseudonym of Judson Phillips. 📷
| | $6 | $20 | $55 |

--- *Chinese Nightmare*, Dell Ten-Cent #31, 1950, first book edition, cover by Rafael DeSoto, communist Chinese terror cover art. 📷
| | $10 | $30 | $100 |

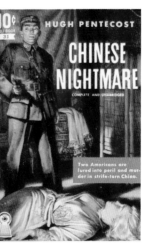

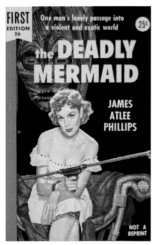

	G	VG	F

--- *Dead Man's Tale, The*, Quick Reader #145, 1945, cover by Axelrod.

	$8	$25	$65

Phillips, James Atlee, *Deadly Mermaid, The*, Dell First Edition #26, 1954, first book edition, cover by Bill George. 📷

	$4	$25	$75

--- *Green Wound, The*, Gold Medal Book #k1321, 1963, paperback original, cover by Harry Bennett, the first Joe Gall novel.

	$5	$20	$65

--- *Suitable For Framing*, Pocket Book #725, 1950, cover by Harry Barton, cover frame imitates Avon Books of that time. 📷

	$4	$20	$60

Powell, Talmage, *Girl Who Killed Things, The*, Zenith Book #ZB-37, 1960, paperback original.

	$4	$20	$60

Prather, Richard S., *Bodies In Bedlam*, Gold Medal Book #147, 1951, paperback original.

	$4	$20	$70

--- *Case of the Vanishing Beauty*, Gold Medal Book #127, 1950, paperback original, first Shell Scott book. 📷

	$5	$30	$125

--- *Dagger of Flesh*, Falcon Book #30, 1952, paperback original, cover by Rudy Nappi, digest-size.

	$50	$175	$450

--- *Dagger of Flesh*, Crest Book #142, 1956, cover by James Meese.

	$3	$15	$50

--- *Dagger of Flesh*, Crest Book #277, 1959, reprints Crest #142 with new cover art.

	$3	$15	$40

--- *Darling, It's Death*, Gold Medal Book #265, 1952, paperback original, cover by Barye Phillips.

	$5	$15	$65

--- *Everybody Had a Gun*, Gold Medal Book #165, 1951, paperback original, bondage cover art.

	$5	$20	$100

--- *Lie Down, Killer,* Lion Book #85, 1952, paperback original. 📷

	$10	$35	$120

--- *Pattern For Panic*, Berkley Book #362, 1960, cover by Robert Maguire. 📷

	$3	$20	$75

--- *Pattern For Panic*, Berkley Book #G-98, 1958, cover by Paul Rader.

	$3	$20	$75

--- *Scrambled Yeggs, The*, Gold Medal Book #770, 1958, first edition thus, aka Pattern For Murder.

	$3	$15	$40

--- *Wailing Frail, The*, Gold Medal Book #592, 1956, paperback original, cover by Barye Phillips.

	$4	$18	$40

--- *Way of a Wanton*, Gold Medal Book #233, 1952, paperback original.

	$3	$15	$45

	G	VG	F		G	VG	F

Queen, Ellery, *Calendar of Crime,* Pocket Book #960, 1953, cover by Richard Powers, collection. **$5** **$15** **$45**

--- *Chinese Orange Mystery, The,* Pocket Book #17, 1939. **$12** **$40** **$100**

--- *French Powder Mystery, The,* Pocket Book #71, 1940, cover by Allen Pope. **$10** **$30** **$90**

--- *Four Johns, The,* Pocket Book #4706 and #6229, 1964, two variants, both are paperback originals with same date and cover but different number and cover price, written by Jack Vance, each book: **$10** **$30** **$100**

--- *Halfway House,* Pocket Book #259, 1944, regular edition.**$6** **$20** **$45**

--- *Halfway House,* Pocket Book #259, 1944, variant, bound oblong at top. **$90** **$200** **$500**

--- *Inspector Queen's Own Case,* Pocket Book #1167, 1957, cover by Lou Marchetti. 📷 **$5** **$15** **$45**

--- *Kill As Directed,* Pocket Book #4704, 1963, paperback original. **$6** **$25** **$70**

--- *Lamp of God, The,* Dell Ten-Cent #23, 1950, first book edition, cover by George Mayers. 📷 **$5** **$20** **$75**

--- *Madman Theory, The,* Pocket Book #50496, 1966, paperback original, written by Jack Vance. **$6** **$30** **$100**

--- *Queens Award Fifth Series, The,* Ace Book #D-493, 1961, first book edition, anthology, cover by Robert Maguire. **$4** **$15** **$50**

--- *Spanish Cape Mystery, The,* LA Bantam #1, 1940, rare. **$75** **$250** **$600**

--- *Spanish Cape Mystery, The,* Pocket Book #146, 1942. **$5** **$20** **$90**

--- *Tragedy of X, The,* Avon Book #425, 1952. 📷 **$6** **$20** **$65**

Rabe, Peter, *Agreement to Kill,* Gold Medal Book #670, 1957, paperback original, cover by Barye Phillips. **$15** **$35** **$100**

--- *Anatomy of a Killer,* Berkley Book #G-541, 1961, first paperback printing, photo cover. **$10** **$40** **$100**

--- *Benny Muscles In,* Gold Medal Book #520, 1955, paperback original, cover by Lu Kimmel. **$15** **$75** **$175**

--- *Black Mafia,* Gold Medal Book #m2939, 1974, paperback original. **$10** **$40** **$120**

--- *Blood on the Desert,* Gold Medal Book #s825, 1958, paperback original, cover by Richard Powers, spy novel. **$6** **$35** **$90**

--- *Box, The,* Gold Medal Book #s1262, 1962, paperback original. **$10** **$45** **$120**

	G	VG	F

--- *Bring Me Another Corpse*, Gold Medal Book #864, 1959, paperback original, photo cover. **$15 $45 $150**

--- *Code Name Gadget*, Gold Medal Book #d1830, 1967, paperback original, cover by Harry Bennett. **$6 $25 $75**

--- *Cut of the Whip, The*, Ace Book #D-297, 1958, paperback original, Ace Double backed with *Kill One, Kill Two* by Robert H. Kelston.
$10 $30 $125

--- *Dig My Grave Deep*, Gold Medal Book #612, 1956, paperback original, cover by Lu Kimmel. **$10 $40 $125**

--- *His Neighbor's Wife*, Beacon Book #B542F, 1962, paperback original.
$8 $35 $100

--- *Journey Into Terror*, Gold Medal Book #710, 1957, paperback original, cover by Mitchell Hooks.
$8 $20 $75

--- *Kill the Boss Good-By*, Gold Medal Book #594, 1956, paperback original, cover by Bayre Philips.
$12 $40 $100

--- *Murder Me for Nickels*, Gold Medal Book #996, 1960, paperback original, cover by Robert McGinnis.
$8 $40 $120

--- *Out Is Death, The*, Gold Medal Book #657, 1957, paperback original, cover by Mitchell Hooks. **$8 $40 $110**

--- *Shroud For Jesso, A*, Gold Medal Book #528, 1955, paperback original, cover by Lu Kimmel, scarce in condition.
$20 $50 $200

--- *Stop This Man!*, Gold Medal Book #506, 1955, paperback original, cover by Lu Kimmel, Rabe's first book.
$10 $55 $160

--- *Time Enough to Die*, Gold Medal Book #939, 1959, paperback original, photo cover. **$10 $30 $90**

Rawlings, Frank, *Lisping Man, The*, Thrilling Mystery Novel, no number, (Atlas), 1944, abridged, digest-size.
$6 $30 $100

Rawson, Clayton, *Death From a Top Hat*, Dell Book #69, 1945, cover by Gerald Gregg. **$25 $75 $175**

--- *Headless Lady, The*, Dell Book #176, 1947, Map Back.
$5 $25 $100

Reasoner, James, *Texas Wind*, Manor Book #23201, 1980, paperback original, his rare first novel. **$30 $75 $200**

Reed, Mark, *Lay Down and Die!*, Falcon Book #26, 1952, paperback original, digest-size, a tough cop meets a tougher dame. **$35 $125 $250**

--- *Sins of the Flesh*, Falcon Book #32, 1952, paperback original, digest-size, cover by George Gross.
$25 $100 $200

Reid, Ed, *Mafia*, Signet Book #1151, 1954, cover by James Avati, mob rubout cover art. **$5 $15 $50**

Reilly, Helen, *Doll's Trunk Murder, The*, Popular Library #211, 1949, cover by Rudolph Belarski, notorious bondage cover art. **$25 $100 $300**

--- *Murder At Arroways*, Dell Book #576, 1952, Map Back. **$4 $15 $40**

--- *Silver Leopard, The*, Dell Book #287, 1949, Map Back. **$4 $15 $60**

Rhode, John, *Dead of the Night*, Popular Library #99, 1946, cover art by Im-Ho.
$4 $15 $50

--- *Dr. Priestly Investigates*, Avon Book no number (#5), 1941, with Globe endpapers. **$20 $65 $145**

--- *Poison For One*, Avon Books, no number (35), 1943. **$12 $40 $100**

Rice, Craig, *April Robin Murders, The*, Dell Book #D306, 1959, first paperback printing, cover by Robert McGinnis, written with Ed McBain.
$5 $20 $100

--- *Big Midget Murders, The*, Pocket Book #528, 1948, cover by Harvey Kidder. **$4 $15 $45**

--- *Corpse Steps Out, The*, Pocket Book #476, 1947. **$4 $20 $60**

--- *Having a Wonderful Crime*, Pocket Book #289, 1945. **$4 $15 $45**

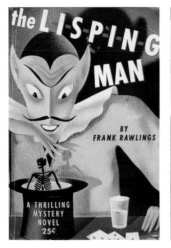

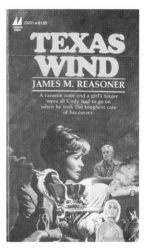

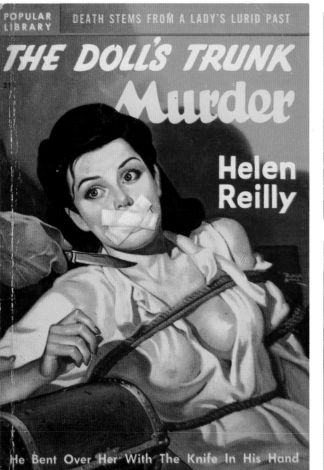

	G	VG	F		G	VG	F

--- *Los Angeles Murders*, Armed Service Edition #1313, no date, circa 1947, anthology. **$20** **$55** **$120**

--- *Lucky Stiff, The*, Pocket Book 391, 1947, electric chair cover art. 📷 **$4** **$20** **$50**

--- *Name Is Malone, The*, Pyramid Book #G-350, 1958, paperback original. **$10** **$35** **$120**

--- *Sunday Pigeon Murders, The*, Armed Service Edition #1074, no date, circa 1945. **$15** **$40** **$100**

--- *Sunday Pigeon Murders, The*, Banner Mysteries #1, 1945, cover by Mac Raboy,

digest-size. **$15** **$50** **$120**

--- *Trial By Fury*, Pocket Book #237, 1943, cover by Leo Manso. **$4** **$20** **$60**

--- *Wrong Murder, The*, Popular Library #45, 1945, cover by H. Lawrence Hoffman. **$10** **$25** **$65**

--- *Yesterday's Murder*, Popular Library #253, no date, 1950. 📷 **$6** **$30** **$100**

Richards, Wm., *Dead Man's Tide*, Graphic Book #60, 1953, paperback original; pseudonym of Day Keene. 📷 **$10** **$30** **$90**

	G	VG	F

Rifkin, Shepard, *Desire Island,* Ace Book #D-444, 1960, paperback original, his first crime novel. The fight in the story is said to have actually taken place between mystery novelist Patricia Highsmith and her girlfriend at the time.   **$8 $25 $75**

--- *Ladyfingers,* Gold Medal Book #r2035, 1969, early serial killer novel.   **$4 $20 $45**

Rinehart, Mary Roberts, *Bat, The,* Dell #652, 1953, classic black and yellow cover art by Walter Brooks.   **$4 $18 $50**

--- *Case of Jennie Brice, The,* Dell Book #404, 1950, Map Back, brutal murder mystery.   **$4 $20 $60**

--- *Curve of the Catenary, The,* Quick Reader #121, 1944, cover by Axelrod, very scarce.   **$15 $40 $120**

--- *Door, The,* Pocket Book #140, 1942.   **$4 $20 $60**

--- *Sight Unseen,* Avon Book #83, 1946, skull cover art by Renaldo Epworth. 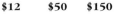   **$4 $25 $75**

Ring, Douglas, *Peddler, The,* Lion Book #110, 1952, paperback original; pseudonym of Richard S. Prather, who told me he chose the name Douglas "King" because he wanted to be the king, but the publisher thought the "K" was an "R," so "King" became "Ring."    **$15 $50 $150**

Robbins, Harold, *Stiletto,* Dell First Edition #C-115, 1960, paperback original, cover by Bob Abbett.   **$4 $20 $75**

Roberts, John Maddox, *S.P.Q.R.,* Avon Book #75993, 1990, paperback original, historical mystery, his first book, #1 in SPQR series.   **$10 $40 $130**

--- *Catiline Conspiracy, The,* Avon Book #75995, 1991, paperback original, #2 in SPQR series.   **$6 $30 $90**

Rogers, Joel Townsley, *Red Right Hand, The,* Pocket Book #385, 1946, first printing is Canadian only.   **$4 $30 $85**

Rohmer, Sax, *Daughter of Fu Manchu,* Avon Book #189, 1949, cover by Ann Cantor; pseudonym of Arthur Sarsfield Ward. 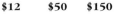   **$10 $50 $135**

--- *Emperor Fu Manchu,* Gold Medal Book #s929, 1959, paperback original, cover by Bob Abbett. 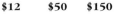   **$8 $40 $130**

--- *Fire Goddess, The,* Gold Medal Book #283, 1952, first book edition.   **$10 $50 $135**

--- *Nude In Mink,* Gold Medal Book #105, 1950, first book edition, first appearance of Sumuru.   **$12 $50 $150**

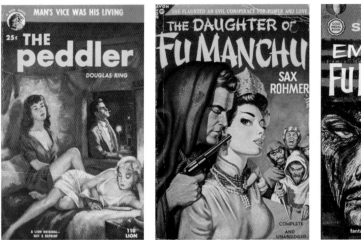

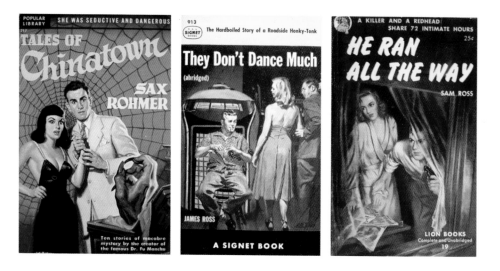

	G	VG	F		G	VG	F

--- *Return of Sumuru*, Gold Medal Book #408, 1952, first book edition, cover by James Meese. **$8 $50 $135**

--- *Sinister Madonna*, Gold Medal Book #555, 1956, first book edition, cover by Charles Binger. **$8 $55 $150**

--- *Sumuru*, Gold Medal Book #199, 1951, first book edition, cover by Barye Phillips. **$10 $55 $155**

--- *Tales of Chinatown*, Popular Library #217, 1950, cover by Rudolph Belarski. **$12 $75 $150**

Ronns, Edward, *Catspaw Ordeal*, Gold Medal Book #133, 1950, paperback original; pseudonym of Edward S. Aarons. **$4 $20 $65**

--- *Decoy, The*, Gold Medal Book #194, 1951, paperback original. **$4 $25 $90**

--- *I Can't Stop Running*, Gold Medal Book #166, 1951, paperback original, cover by Barye Phillips. **$4 $20 $65**

--- *Lady, the Guy is Dead*, Avon Murder Mystery Monthly #49, 1950, digest-size. **$35 $135 $275**

--- *Million Dollar Murder*, Gold Medal Book #110, 1950, paperback original. **$5 $25 $75**

Ross, James, *They Don't Dance Much*, Signet Book #913, 1952, first paperback printing, abridged, author's only novel. **$10 $35 $100**

Ross, Sam, *He Ran All the Way*, Lion Book #19, 1950. **$5 $20 $65**

Rubel, James L., *No Business For a Lady*, Gold Medal Book #114, 1950, paperback original, first paperback female detective, Eli Donovan. **$5 $20 $60**

Saber, Robert O., *Deadly Lover, The*, Phantom Book #502, 1951, paperback original, digest-size; pseudonym of Milton K. Ozaki. **$22 $100 $165**

--- *Murder Doll*, Phantom Book #510, 1952, paperback original, digest-size, private eye Carl Good. **$20 $100 $200**

--- *No Way Out*, Phantom Book #512, 1952, paperback original, digest-size. **$25 $120 $225**

Sale, Richard, *Death At Sea*, Popular Library #163, 1948, cover by Rudolph Belarski. **$6 $30 $100**

--- *Home Is the Hangman*, Popular Library #205, 1949, first book edition, cover by Rudolph Belarski. **$6 $40 $100**

--- *Murder At Midnight*, Popular Library #275, 1950. **$6 $25 $100**

--- *Passing Strange*, Ace Book #D-23, 1953, paperback original, Ace Double backed with *Bring Back Her Body* by Stuart Brock. **$8 $30 $100**

114 Meet Eli Donovan, lady detective, and
easily the most beautiful shamus living

GOLD MEDAL BOOK

NO BUSINESS
FOR A LADY

JAMES L. RUBEL

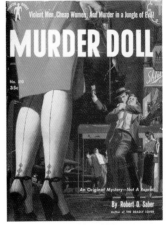

Violent Men, Cheap Women, And Murder in a Jungle of Evil!

MURDER DOLL

No. 510
35¢

An Original Mystery—Not A Reprint.

By Robert O. Saber
Author of THE DEADLY LOVER

POPULAR LIBRARY

MURDER ABOARD A STRICKEN SHIP

163

DEATH at SEA
by RICHARD SALE

POCKET BOOK

Dorothy L. Sayers

Busman's Honeymoon

He stared at
the clock . .
would it strike
the hour of
death?

COMPLETE AND
UNABRIDGED

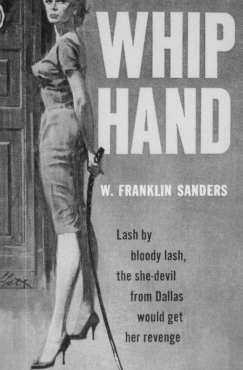

s1087

GOLD
MEDAL
BOOK

35¢

WHIP
HAND

W. FRANKLIN SANDERS

Lash by
bloody lash,
the she-devil
from Dallas
would get
her revenge

378 Meet Jerry Nelson, a tough private eye,
who knew what to feed a public enemy

GOLD MEDAL BOOK

Let Them Eat Bullets

Howard Schoenfeld

HOTEL
ST. CHARLES

An Original Gold Medal Novel
NOT A REPRINT

	G	VG	F

	G	VG	F

Sanders, Daphne, *To Catch a Thief*, Handi Book #26, 1944, first paperback printing; pseudonym of Georgiana Ana Randolph Craig, aka Craig Rice.
$12 $40 $100

Sanders, George, *Crime On My Hands*, Armed Service Edition #R-15, no date, circa 1945. $10 $30 $90

Sanders, W. Franklin, *Whip Hand*, Gold Medal Book #s1087, 1961, paperback original, cover by Bob Abbett, ghost written by Charles Willeford. 📷
$50 $125 $350

Sayers, Dorothy L., *Busman's Honeymoon*, Pocket Book #324, 1946, in dust jacket, cover by Don Lupo. 📷
$15 $50 $135

--- *Have His Carcase*, Pocket Book #163, 1942, cover by Im-Ho.
$5 $20 $75

--- *Nine Tailors, The*, Pocket Book #185, 1942, cover by Bilpen.
$4 $20 $75

--- *Strong Poison*, Avon Book #328, 1951.
$5 $25 $80

--- *Suspicious Characters*, Avon Book #23, 1943. $6 $35 $100

Schoenfeld, Howard, *Let Them Eat Bullets*, Gold Medal Book #378, 1954, paperback original, cover by Barye Philips, author's only novel. 📷 $5 $30 $90

Scott, Roney, *Shakedown*, Ace Book #D-17, 1953, paperback original, cover by Norman Saunders; pseudonym of William Campbell Gault, Ace Double backed with *The Darkness Within* by Walter Erikson; pseudonym of Howard Fast writing under the Blacklist. 📷
$6 $30 $100

Shore, Julian, *Rattle His Bones*, Thrilling Mystery Novel, no number (Atlas), 1944, abridged, digest-size. 📷
$8 $30 $100

Slesar, Henry, *Gray Flannel Shroud, The*, Zenith Book #ZB-33, 1959, paperback original. $6 $30 $100

Slim, Iceberg, *Mama Black Widow*, Holloway House #HH176, 1969, paperback original.
$15 $60 $120

--- *Pimp, the Story of My Life*, Holloway House #HH139, 1967, paperback original, the first of the "Black Experience" crime novels; pseudonym of Robert Beck. $30 $100 $200

Snelling, O. F., *007 James Bond, a Report*, Signet Book #D-2652, 1965, the lowdown on James Bond. $15 $20 $65

Spain, John, *Death Is Like That*, Popular Library #178, 1949, cover by Rudolph Belarski; pseudonym of Cleve Adams.
$5 $20 $75

	G	VG	F

--- *Evil Star, The*, Popular Library #239, 1950. 📷 **$4** **$20** **$65**

Spatz, Donald H., *Murder With Long Hair*, Atlas Mystery, no number, 1944, digest-size. **$6** **$35** **$100**

Spillane, Mickey, *Big Kill, The*, Signet Book #915, 1951, first paperback printing. 📷 **$5** **$20** **$75**

--- *I, the Jury*, Signet Book #699, 1948, Spillane's first paperback and a first paperback printing, cover by Lu Kimmel, the first Mike Hammer novel.
$10 **$40** **$125**

--- *Kiss Me Deadly*, Signet Book #1000, 1953, first paperback printing, cover by James Meese. **$4** **$20** **$65**

--- *Long Wait, The*, Signet Book #932, 1952, first paperback printing, male bondage cover art. 📷 **$5** **$25** **$70**

--- *My Gun Is Quick*, Signet Book #791, 1950, first paperback printing, cover by Lu Kimmel. **$5** **$25** **$75**

--- *One Lonely Night*, Signet Book #888, 1951, first paperback printing, cover by Lu Kimmel, bondage cover art.
$5 **$25** **$70**

--- *Vengeance Is Mine*, Signet Book #852, 1951, first paperback printing, cover by Lu Kimmel. **$5** **$20** **$65**

Stark, Richard, *Green Eagle Score, The*, Gold Medal Book #d1861, 1967, paperback original.
$15 **$35** **$100**

--- *Handle, The*, Pocket Book #50220, 1966, paperback original; pseudonym of Donald Westlake. **$10** **$35** **$100**

--- *Hunter, The*, Perma Book #M4272, 1962, paperback original, cover by Harry Bennett, first Parker book.
$12 **$40** **$125**

--- *Man With the Getaway Face, The*, Pocket Book #6180, 1963, paperback original, cover by Harry Bennett, second Parker book. **$6** **$30** **$100**

--- *Mourner, The*, Perma Book #M-4298, 1963, paperback original, scarce.
$12 **$40** **$135**

--- *Outfit, The*, Perma Book #M-4292, 1963, paperback original, cover by Harry Bennett. **$10** **$40** **$120**

--- *Point Blank*, Gold Medal Book #d1856, no date, 1966, reprint of *The Hunter* under new title.
$6 **$25** **$65**

--- *Rare Coin Score, The*, Gold Medal Book #d1803, 1967, paperback original.
$15 **$35** **$120**

--- *Score, The*, Pocket Book #35014, 1964, paperback original.
$10 **$50** **$100**

--- *Sour Lemon Score, The*, Gold Medal Book #r2037, 1966, paperback original, cover by Robert McGinnis, bondage cover art. 📷 **$10** **$40** **$125**

Steel, Kurt, *Murder Goes to College*, Atlas Mystery, no number, 1944, digest-size.
$9 **$46** **$115**

	G	VG	F

Stokes, Manning Lee, *Case of the Winking Buddha, The,* All-Picture Mystery, no number (#1), 1950, paperback original, digest-size, story in comic book format.

	$60	**$175**	**$375**

Stone, Grace Zaring, *Cold Journey, The,* Bantam Book #44, 1948, in dust jacket.

	$35	**$100**	**$220**

Storme, Michael, *Dame in My Bed,* Archer Book #5, 1951, cover by Reginald Heade, digest-size.

	$6	**$30**	**$90**

--- *Hot Dames on Cold Slabs,* Leisure Library #5, no date, circa 1954, digest-size, cover by Reginald Heade. 📷

	$8	**$35**	**$120**

--- *Make Mine a Harlot,* Archer Book

	G	VG	F

#84, 1952, cover by Pollack, digest-size.

	$7	**$30**	**$100**

Stout, Rex, *Alphabet Hicks,* Dell Book #146, 1947, Map Back.

	$5	**$20**	**$80**

--- *Black Orchids,* Avon Book #95, 1946.

	$8	**$28**	**$100**

--- *Broken Vase, The,* Dell Book #115, 1946, Map Back, cover by Gerald Gregg. 📷

	$10	**$20**	**$75**

--- *Broken Vase, The,* Dell Book #674, 1953, new cover by Carl Bobertz.

	$4	**$15**	**$45**

--- *Case of the Black Orchids, The,* Avon Book #256, 1950, reprints Avon Book #95 *Black Orchids* with new cover art and title. 📷

	$5	**$25**	**$90**

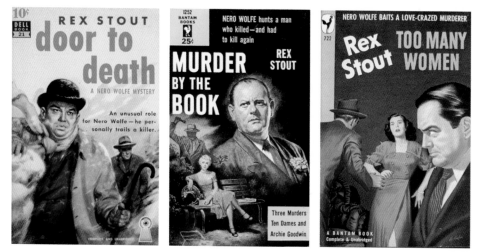

	G	VG	F		G	VG	F

--- *Death Times Three*, Bantam Book #25425, 1985, first book edition, collects three Nero Wolfe stories previously only published in anthologies, uncommon.
$12 $40 $100

--- *Door to Death*, Dell Ten-Cent #21, 1950, first book edition, cover by Robert Stanley. 📖 **$8 $35 $100**

--- *Double For Death*, Dell Book #9, 1943, Map Back. **$12 $35 $100**

--- *Fer-de-Lance*, Pocket Book #34, 1941.
$22 $60 $175

--- *How Like a God*, Lion Library #LL23, 1955. **$5 $20 $75**

--- *League of Frightened Men, The*, Avon Book, no number (#20), 1942.
$10 $35 $120

--- *Murder By the Book*, Bantam Book #1252, 1954. 📖 **$4 $20 $60**

--- *Not Quite Dead Enough*, Armed Service Edition #P-6, no date, circa 1944.
$12 $55 $150

--- *Not Quite Dead Enough*, Armed Service Edition #906, no date, circa 1946, reprints ASE #P-6.
$12 $35 $75

--- *Not Quite Dead Enough*, Jonathan Press, #J27, circa 1944, cover by George Salter. **$10 $60 $125**

--- *Over My Dead Body*, Avon Book #62, 1945. **$5 $25 $75**

--- *Red Box, The*, Avon Book #82, 1946
$5 $25 $85

--- *Red Bull, The*, Dell Book #70, 1944, Map Back, cover by Gerald Gregg.
$6 $35 $100

--- *Red Threads, The*, LA Bantam #1, 1940, in illustrated cover only, rare. 📖
$100 $255 $800

--- *Rubber Band, The*, Pocket Book #208, 1943. **$4 $25 $80**

--- *Silent Speaker*, The, Armed Service Edition #1222, no date, circa 1947.
$18 $65 $155

--- *Too Many Women*, Bantam Book #722, 1949, cover by Hy Rubin. 📖
$4 $25 $90

--- *Where There's a Will*, Avon Book #103, 1946, first book edition.
$5 $30 $75

Sylvester, Robert, *Big Boodle, The*, Perma Book #M3022, 1955, cover by Robert Schulz. 📖 **$4 $15 $50**

Taylor, Phoebe Atwood, *Diplomatic Corpse*, Avon Book #A439, 1952, spooky graveyard murder scene cover art; pseudonym of Alice Tilton. 📖
$5 $20 $65

--- *Perennial Border, The*, Penguin Book #618, 1947, in dust jacket.
$75 $150 $350

--- *Six Iron Spiders, The*, Pennant Mystery #2, no date, 1940s, digest-size.
$12 $55 $135

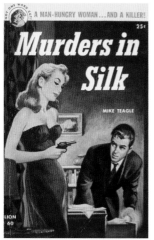

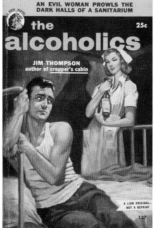

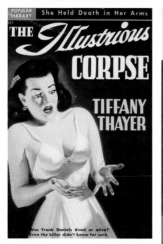

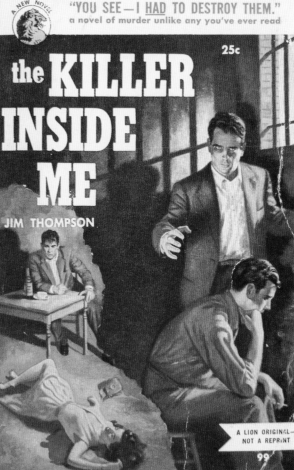

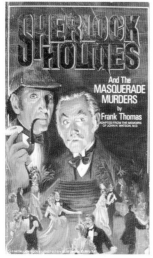

	G	VG	F		G	VG	F

--- *Spring Harrowing*, Dell Book #98, 1946, Map Back, skull cover art by Gerald Gregg. **$5 $15 $55**

Taylor, Samuel W., *Grinning Gismo, The*, Ace Book #D-1, 1952, first paperback printing, the first Ace Book and the first Ace Double, cover by Norman Saunders, backed with *Too Hot For Hell* by Keith Vining. **$60 $200 $500**

Teagle, Mike, *Murders in Silk*, Lion Book #60, 1951. 📷 **$4 $20 $65**

Tey, Josephine, *Franchise Affair, The*, Berkley Book #S1962, 1971, photo cover shows head of the model Deborah Harry in a box of chocolates before the rock band Blondie. **$4 $20 $50**

Thayer, Tiffany, *Illustrious Corpse, The*, Popular Library #227, 1950, cover by Rudolph Belarski, blood-on-her-hands cover art. 📷 **$5 $20 $85**

Thomas, Frank, *Sherlock Holmes and the Masquerade Murders*, Medallion Book #017, 1986, paperback original, cover by Jeani Brunnick, scarce Sherlock Holmes pastiche novel. 📷 **$10 $25 $90**

Thompson, Jim, *After Dark, My Sweet*, Popular Library #716, 1955, paperback original, cover by Ray Johnson. **$60 $150 $475**

--- *Alcoholics*, Lion Book #127, 1953,

paperback original. 📷 **$45 $100 $425**

--- *Bad Boy*, Lion Book #149, 1953, paperback original. **$50 $120 $400**

--- *Child of Rage*, Lancer Book #75-342, 1972, paperback original. **$60 $175 $650**

--- *Criminal, The*, Lion Book #184, 1953, paperback original. 📷 **$55 $175 $500**

--- *Cropper's Cabin*, Lion Book #108, 1952, paperback original. **$50 $150 $500**

--- *Cropper's Cabin*, Pyramid Book #G-336, 1958, cover by Clark Hulings. **$25 $90 $290**

--- *Getaway, The*, Signet Book #1584, 1959, paperback original. **$50 $200 $400**

--- *Golden Gizmo, The*, Lion Book #192, 1954, paperback original. 📷 **$45 $125 $400**

--- *Grifters, The*, Regency Book #RB-322, 1963, paperback original. **$100 $200 $650**

--- *Hell of a Woman, A*, Lion Book #218, 1954, paperback original. **$75 $200 $750**

	G	VG	F
--- *Hell of a Woman, A*, Lion Library #LB138, 1956, reprints Lion #218 with new cover art.	$18	$55	$140
--- *Killer Inside Me, The*, Lion Book #99, 1952, paperback original, his first book for Lion, a cornerstone of crime fiction and the author's favorite of all his books. 📷	$100	$400	$1,200
--- *Killer Inside Me, The*, Gold Medal Book #k1522, 1965.	$20	$50	$100
--- *Kill-Off, The*, Lion Library #LB-142, 1957, paperback original, cover by William Rose.	$25	$100	$225
--- *Nothing Man, The*, Dell First Edition #22, 1954, paperback original, cover by Stanley Borack.	$25	$85	$180
--- *Nothing More Than Murder*, Hillman Book #38, 1949.	$25	$130	$250
--- *Pop. 1280*, Gold Medal Book #k1438, 1964, paperback original, cover by Robert McGinnis. 📷	$40	$100	$300
--- *Recoil*, Lion Book #120, 1953, paperback original.	$65	$140	$350
--- *Recoil*, Lion Library #LL124, 1956, reprints Lion #210 with new cover art by Robert Maguire.	$20	$75	$140
--- *Roughneck*, Lion Book #201, 1954, paperback original.	$65	$150	$375
--- *Savage Night*, Lion Book #155, 1953, paperback original.	$65	$175	$600
--- *South of Heaven*, Gold Medal Book #1793, 1967, paperback original.	$35	$100	$300
--- *Swell-Looking Babe, A*, Lion Book #212, 1954, paperback original. 📷	$65	$150	$375
--- *Transgressors, The*, Signet Book #S-2034, 1961, paperback original.	$65	$155	$500
--- *Texas By the Tail*, Gold Medal Book #k1502, 1965, paperback original, cover by Barye Philips.	$20	$75	$200
--- *Wild Town*, Signet Book #1461, 1957, paperback original, cover by Robert Maguire.	$40	$125	$300
Tiger, John, *Death Hits the Jackpot*, Avon Book #605, 1954, paperback original, spy novel; pseudonym of Walter Wager, his first book. 📷	$5	$20	$60
Towne, Stuart, *Death From Nowhere*, Yogi Mystery #1, 1940, digest-size; pseudonym of Clayton Rawson. 📷	$125	$600	$1,500
Tracy, Don, *Cheat, The*, Lion Book #69, 1951, cover by Harry Schaare, original title *Criss-Cross*.	$8	$25	$100
Trail, Armitage, *Scarface*, Dell Book #D-336, 1995, paperback original, cover by Victor Kalin shows Al Capone. 📷	$4	$15	$50

	G	VG	F			G	VG	F

Treat, Lawrence, *Big Shot*, Bantam Book #1026, 1952, a tough cop goes wrong. 📖
$3 $15 $45

Trimble, Louis, *Blondes Are Skin Deep*, Lion Book #62, 1951, paperback original, "she taunted a dope fiend killer." 📖
$6 $30 $90

Turner, Robert, *Tobacco Auction Murders, The*, Ace Book #D-55, 1954, paperback original, cover by Robert Maguire, Ace Double backed with *Kill Box* by Michael Stark. $7 $30 $85

Ullman, Albert E., *Kidnappers, The*, Black

Knight Book #28, no date, 1940s. 📖
$5 $20 $55

Vance, John Holbrook, *Bad Ronald*, Ballantine Book #23477, 1973, paperback original, cover by Mort Engle; pseudonym of Jack Vance.
$20 $90 $200

--- *Pleasant Grove Murders, The*, Ace Book #67110, 1967.
$8 $30 $100

Van Dine, S. S., *Green Murder Case, The*, Pocket Book #256, 1944.
$4 $20 $100

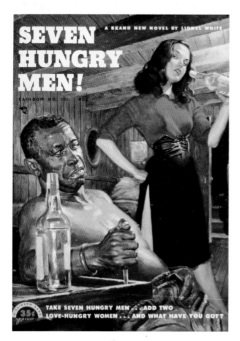

	G	VG	F

--- *Kennel Murder Case, The*, Bantam Book #60, 1946. 📷

| | $5 | $15 | $65 |

Wade, David, *Raise the Devil*, Falcon Book #35, 1952, paperback original, digest-size, early serial killer novel. 📷

| | $25 | $120 | $275 |

Walker, Shel, *Man I Killed, The*, Lion Book #112, 1952, paperback original.

| | $6 | $20 | $75 |

Walling, R. A. J., *Corpse in the Green Pyjamas, The*, Avon Book, no number (#8), 1941, with Globe endpapers.

| | $20 | $75 | $165 |

--- *Corpse With the Eerie Eye, The*, Popular Library #106, 1946. 📷

| | $4 | $20 | $60 |

--- *Murder At Midnight*, Avon Book, no number (#16), 1941, with Globe endpapers.

| | $22 | $70 | $150 |

Walton, Bryce, *Long Night, The*, Falcon Book #42, 1952, paperback original, digest-size.

| | $30 | $125 | $250 |

Waugh, Hillary, *Girl Who Cried Wolf, The*, Dell Book #0338, 1960, cover by Robert McGinnss, bondage cover. 📷

| | $5 | $25 | $75 |

Webb, Jack, *Damed Lovely, The*, Signet Book #1233, 1955, cover by Robert Maguire, this Webb was not the actor on the "Dragnet" TV series.

| | $4 | $15 | $60 |

Weller, Drake, *It Rhymes With Lust*, All-Picture Mystery, no number (#2), 1950, paperback original, digest-size, cover by Matt Baker, in comic book format, only two books in this series.

| | $90 | $200 | $450 |

Wellman, Manly, *Find My Killer*, Signet Book #1448, 1957, crime novel by fantasy writer Manly Wade Wellman. 📷

| | $4 | $25 | $75 |

Wells, Charlie, *Last Kill, The*, Signet Book #1225, 1955, paperback original, cover by Robert Maguire, author was protégé of Mickey Spillane, endorsed by "The Mick" on the cover. 📷

| | $4 | $15 | $50 |

Wentworth, Patricia, *Clock Strikes Twelve, The*, Popular Library #131, 1947, skull cover art.

| | $4 | $20 | $85 |

	G	VG	F

--- *Dark Threat*, Popular Library #382, 1951, cover by Rudolph Belarski.  **$4 $20 $100**

--- *Key, The*, Popular Library #232, 1950, man in mirror with gun terrorizes woman. **$4 $20 $75**

--- *Silence In Court*, Popular Library #283, 1950, women in peril cover art. **$4 $20 $85**

--- *Weekend With Death*, Popular Library #29, 1944, cover by H. Lawrence Hoffman, scarce. **$30 $100 $225**

Westlake, Donald E., *Two Much*, Crest Book #X2750, 1976, cover by Morgan Kane, interesting cover has pink fuzz on title and woman's bikini. **$4 $20 $65**

White, Lionel, *A Death At Sea* with *The Time of Terror*, Ace Book #F-155, 1961, paperback original, Ace Double. **$5 $20 $50**

--- *Big Caper, The*, Gold Medal Book #470, 1955, paperback original, cover by Barye Phillips. **$15 $35 $125**

--- *Death Takes the Bus*, Gold Medal Book #663, 1957, paperback original, cover by Mitchell Hooks. **$20 $60 $175**

--- *Flight into Terror*, Signet Book #1378, 1957, first paperback printing, cover by Robert Maguire. **$6 $25 $65**

--- *Hostage For a Hood*, Gold Medal Book #687, 1957, paperback original, cover by James Meese, bondage cover art. **$10 $35 $100**

--- *Killing, The*, Signet Book #1310, 1956, first paperback printing, cover by Robert Maguire. **$10 $30 $125**

--- *Lament For a Virgin*, Gold Medal Book #s949, 1960, paperback original, photo cover. **$10 $25 $90**

--- *Operation-Murder*, Gold Medal Book #606, 1956, paperback original, cover by James Meese. **$15 $35 $135**

--- *Run, Killer Run*, Avon Book #T-361, 1959. **$5 $25 $80**

--- *Seven Hungry Men*, Rainbow Book #121, 1952, paperback original, cover by George Gross, digest-size. **$35 $155 $300**

--- *Snatchers, The*, Gold Medal Book #304, 1953, paperback original, noir classic. **$18 $40 $200**

--- *Steal Big*, Gold Medal Book #998, 1960, paperback original, cover Bob Abbett. **$10 $25 $75**

--- *To Find a Killer*, Signet Book #1241, 1955, cover by Robert Maguire. **$5 $20 $65**

--- *Too Young to Die*, Gold Medal Book #786, 1958, paperback original. **$18 $35 $125**

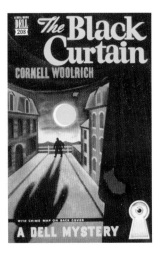

	G	VG	F

White, Stewart Edward, *Killer, The,* Quick Reader #102, 1943, cover by Axelrod.
$8 **$20** **$60**

Whitney, Hallam, *The Wild Seed,* Ace Book #S-153, 1956, paperback original; pseudonym of Harry Whittington.
$8 **$35** **$120**

Whittington, Harry, *Brass Monkey, The,* Handi-Book #138, 1951, paperback original. 📷 **$25** **$80** **$200**

--- *Brute in Brass,* Gold Medal Book #595, 1956, paperback original, cover by Mitchell Hooks. **$8** **$35** **$120**

--- *Call Me Killer,* Graphic Book #36, 1951, paperback original.
$15 **$30** **$90**

--- *Drawn to Evil,* Ace Book #D-5, 1952, paperback original, cover by Norman Saunders, Ace Double backed with *The Scarlet Spade* by Eaton W. Goldthwaite.
$20 **$90** **$175**

--- *Fires That Destroy,* Gold Medal Book #190, 1951, paperback original, illustrated cover, classic bad-girl noir. 📷
$15 **$60** **$160**

--- *God's Back Was Turned,* Gold Medal Book #s1134, 1961, paperback original.
$10 **$40** **$125**

--- *Haven For the Damned, A,* Gold Medal Book #s1190, 1962, paperback original, scarce. **$10** **$40** **$120**

--- *Humming Box, The,* Ace Book #D-185, 1956, paperback original, cover by Harry Barton, Ace Double backed with *Build My Gallows High* by Geoffrey Homes. **$12** **$35** **$120**

--- *Journey Into Violence,* Pyramid Book #G-578, 1961, paperback original, cover by Lou Marchetti. **$10** **$30** **$100**

--- *Lady Was a Tramp, The,* Handi-Book #131, 1951, paperback original.
$20 **$85** **$180**

--- *Married to Murder,* Phantom Book #503, 1951, paperback original, digest-size. 📷 **$35** **$160** **$400**

--- *Married to Murder,* Berkley Diamond #D-2019, 1959. 📷 **$15** **$50** **$120**

--- *Mourn the Hangman,* Graphic Book #41, 1951, paperback original.
$10 **$30** **$100**

--- *Naked Jungle, The,* Ace Book #S-95, 1955, paperback original.
$14 **$45** **$125**

--- *Night For Screaming, A,* Ace Book #D-472, 1960, paperback original, cover by Robert Maguire.
$20 **$75** **$175**

--- *One Deadly Dawn,* Ace Book #D-241, 1957, paperback original, cover by Ruddy Nappi, Ace Double backed with *The Hired Target* by Wilson Tucker.
$10 **$30** **$100**

	G	VG	F		G	VG	F

--- *One Got Away*, Ace Book #D-115, 1955, paperback original, cover by Harry Barton, Ace Double backed with *Shady Lady* by Cleve Adams, cover by Robert Schulz. **$12** **$30** **$120**

--- *Play For Keeps*, Ace Book #D-347, 1959, paperback original, Ace Double backed with *The Corpse Without a Country* by Louis Trinble. **$8** **$35** **$100**

--- *Prime Sucker*, Universal Giant Editions #1, 1952, paperback original, thick digest-size, with *The Hussy* by Idabel Williams. **$20** **$75** **$200**

--- *Satan's Widow*, Phantom Book #505, 1951, paperback original, digest-size. **$100** **$350** **$750**

--- *Shack Road Girl*, Berkley Diamond Book #D2004, 1959, cover by Robert McGinnis, scarce. **$15** **$75** **$200**

--- *Slay Ride For a Lady*, Handi-Book #120, 1950, paperback original, his first mystery. **$20** **$80** **$200**

--- *So Dead My Love!*, Ace Book #D-7, 1952, paperback original, cover by Rafael DeSoto shows bondage and torture, backed with *I, the Executioner* by Stephen Ransome. **$15** **$85** **$200**

--- *Strange Bargain*, Avon Book #T-347, 1959, paperback original. **$10** **$40** **$100**

--- *Strangers on Friday*, Zenith Book #ZB-30, 1959, paperback original. **$10** **$55** **$125**

--- *Ticket to Hell, A*, Gold Medal Book #862, 1959, paperback original, photo cover. **$10** **$45** **$150**

--- *Web of Murder*, Gold Medal Book #740, 1958, paperback original. **$10** **$50** **$120**

--- *Woman on the Place, A*, Ace Book #S-143, 1956, paperback original. **$10** **$40** **$150**

--- *You'll Die Next!*, Ace Book #D-63, 1954, paperback original, Ace Double backed with *Drag the Dark* by Frederick C. Davis. 📷 **$15** **$60** **$155**

Widmer, Harry, *Hardboiled Lineup, The*, Lion Library #LB130, 1956, first book edition, cover by Mort Kunsler, anthology contains Vin Packer, Gil Brewer. 📷 **$6** **$25** **$75**

Williams, Ben Ames, *Killer Among Us, A*, Lion Library #LL149, 1957, cover by Harry Schaare. **$3** **$15** **$45**

--- *Lady In Peril*, Popular Library #164, 1949, cover by Rudolph Belarski. 📷 **$4** **$20** **$85**

Williams, Charles, *Big City Girl*, Gold Medal Book #163, 1951, paperback original, cover by Bayre Phillips. **$8** **$60** **$150**

	G	VG	F

--- *Diamond Bikini, The*, Gold Medal Book #s607, 1956, paperback original. **$15 $80 $175**

--- *Girl Out Back*, Dell First Edition #B114, 1958, first book edition, cover by Darcy. 📷 **$8 $25 $100**

--- *Gulf Coast Girl*, Dell Book #D-337, 1960, cover by Robert McGinnis. **$10 $30 $100**

--- *Gulf Coast Girl*, Dell Book #898, second printing 1956, cover by Robert Maguire. **$10 $25 $75**

--- *Hell Hath No Fury*, Gold Medal Book #286, 1953, paperback original, cover by Barye Phillips. **$15 $75 $150**

--- *Hill Girl*, Gold Medal Book #141, 1951, paperback original, cover by Barye Phillips, author's first book. 📷 **$15 $60 $150**

--- *Nothing in Her Way*, Gold Medal Book #340, 1953, paperback original. **$12 $75 $185**

--- *Touch of Death, A*, Gold Medal Book #434, 1954, first book edition, cover by Saul Tepper. **$5 $35 $75**

Wills, Thomas, *Mine to Avenge*, Gold Medal Book #490, 1955, paperback original, cover by John Floherty; pseudonym of William Ard. **$5 $20 $65**

--*You'll Get Yours*, Lion Book #87, 1952. **$5 $25 $85**

Wolfson, P.J., *Bodies Are Dust*, Lion Book #83, 1952, classic hard-boiled novel. 📷 **$20 $50 $120**

Woolrich, Cornell, *Beware the Lady*, Pyramid Book #80, 1953, cover by C. Doore. **$12 $75 $225**

--- *Beyond the Night*, Avon Book #T-354, 1959, paperback original. **$8 $50 $100**

--- *Black Alibi*, Bestseller Mystery #B-198, no date, circa 1950, digest-size. **$8 $40 $100**

--- *Black Alibi*, Handi-Book #14, 1943. **$40 $90 $325**

--- *Black Angel, The*, Bestseller Mystery #B-206, no date, circa 1950, digest-size. **$8 $45 $100**

--- *Black Angel, The*, Avon Murder Mystery Monthly #27, 1944, digest-size. **$25 $100 $200**

--- *Black Angel, The*, Avon Book #96, 1946. **$10 $45 $125**

--- *Black Curtain, The*, Dell Book #208, 1948, Map Back, cover by George A. Frederikson. 📷 **$10 $40 $135**

--- *Black Path of Fear, The*, Avon Book #106, 1946. 📷 **$10 $30 $100**

--- *Death Is My Dancing Partner*, Pyramid Book #G-374, 1959, paperback original, cover by Ed Schmidt. **$12 $65 $180**

--- *Doom Stone, The*, Avon Book #T-408, 1960, paperback original. **$10 $30 $90**

--- *Rendezvous in Black*, Pocket Book #570, 1949, cover by William Wirts. 📷 **$5 $30 $90**

--- *Savage Bride*, Gold Medal Book #136, 1950, cover by Barye Philips. 📷 **$10 $40 $125**

--- *Time of Her Life, The*, Mayfair Editions, no number, no date, probably 1930s, pulp magazine size, text cover. **$45 $150 $350**

Worts, George F., *Overboard*, Popular Library #292, 1950, cover by Rudolph Belarski, incredible pulp bondage cover art is definitely over the top. 📷 **$20 $100 $250**

Wylie, Philip, *Danger Mansion*, LA Bantam #27, 1940, rare, text cover, also contains "A Resourceful Lady." **$50 $125 $300**

--- *Danger Mansion*, LA Bantam #27, 1940, rare, illustrated cover. 📷 **$100 $250 $650**

--- *Savage Gentleman, The*, Avon Book #390, 1951. **$6 $25 $100**

Zinberg, Len, *Walk Hard-Talk Loud*, Lion Book #29, 1950, cover by Reynold Brown, "a Negro prizefighter in a savage white world," Zinberg is better known under his pseudonym of Ed Lacy. 📷 **$10 $25 $80**

WESTERNS:
AN EVER-POPULAR GENRE

an adventure story where good and evil fought their war on an expansive frontier canvas and where good always triumphed. A lot has changed since those days of yesteryear, but the western continues to be popular, and western books are avidly read and collected by fans.

The western speaks to that something special inside the heart and soul of men and women everywhere. Tales of courage and self-sacrifice, shoot-outs, pioneers, cowboys, and American Indians abounded. Writers like Zane Grey and Max Brand popularized the genre; writers like Louis L'Amour, Ernest Haycox, Luke Short, and many others filled out the western landscape.

It was through the myriad paperback reprints of the 1940s and paperback originals of the 1950s and1960s where most readers became familiar with western books and the many fine writers who created the wonderful stories.

At one time, western stories and novels were the largest-selling category of fiction, more popular than today's leading romance, mystery, science fiction, fantasy, or horror genres. The western spoke to something that was quintessential American – independence, self-reliance, boldness, and action, all in

There were also artists who did many fine covers for western paperbacks, some of whom worked on westerns exclusively. Masterful illustrators like Norman Saunders,

Louis S. Glanzman, Robert Stanley, and Tom Dunn worked in many genres but did stunning western work. Then you had a group of paperback artists who seemed to work in the western genre almost exclusively and their work is treasured today. These artists included Sam Cherry, A. Leslie Ross, Malcolm Smith, Frank McCarthy, Kirk Wilson, John Leone, Ron Lesser, and Tom Ryan. There are many more, and all created wonderful works that cause them to have avid followings today among fans of the genre.

A key cover art motif was that of the tough, no-nonsense cowboy as western hero. Another popular cover motif was that of a man and woman (hero and heroine) fighting together side by side. Much western paperback cover art showed a battle between two strong men, the sheriff and the outlaw, usually tense action scenes with fists or guns. All these images were perennially popular with western fans, and some outstanding work was created for these books by a host of incredibly talented artists.

This category contains western fiction and a few western fact books, with many collectible high points. These include the early Louis L'Amour titles (under his byline and as Jim Mayo), Armed Service Editions, dust jacketed editions – including *Concannon* – which is probably the highest-valued mass-market paperback western. There are also key paperback originals by Elmore Leonard, Elmer Kelton, and books under pseudonyms. Lion Books westerns seem to be getting scarce in best condition, and interest is growing for them.

1065

THE COMPLETE BOOK

THE TENDERFOOT

A Western Novel by MAX BRAND

POCKET BOOKS INC.

	G	VG	F

Allison, Sam, *Trouble on Crazyman,* Lion Book #183, 1963. 📷
$5 $20 $75

Appell, George C., *Ambush Hell,* Lion Book #199, 1954, paperback original, cover by John Leone. **$5 $20 $55**

--- *Gunman's Grudge,* Lion Book #139, 1953, paperback original.
$5 $15 $54

--- *Shadow on the Border,* Ballantine Book #185, 1957, paperback original, cover by Mel Crair. 📷
$6 $20 $65

Arnold, Elliott, *Blood Brother,* Armed Service Edition #1273, 1947, Apache warfare. **$15 $55 $100**

Arthur, Burt, *Two-Gun Texan,* Lion Book #189, 1954, paperback original.
$5 $20 $55

Austin, Brett, *Gambler's Gun Luck,* Lion Book #20, 1950. 📷
$4 $20 $60

Bellah, James Warner, *Apache, The,* Gold Medal Book #155, 1951, first book edition. **$3 $15 $50**

--- *Massacre,* Lion Book #43, 1950. 📷
$4 $20 $55

Bower, B. M., *Flying U's Last Stand, The,* Popular Library #118, 1946, cover by Fielder. 📷 **$3 $16 $40**

Brand, Max, *Flaming Irons,* Pocket Book #687, 1950, cover by Frank McCarthy.
$2 $15 $40

--- *Gunman's Gold,* Pocket Book #877, 1952, cover by A. Leslie Ross.
$2 $15 $35

--- *Hunted Riders,* Pocket Book #744, 1950, cover by John Floherty Jr.
$3 $15 $40

--- *Rancher's Revenge,* Popular Library #152, 1948. **$2 $15 $40**

--- *Rustlers of Beacon Creek,* Pocket Book #781, 1951, cover by Frank McCarthy. **$2 $15 $35**

--- *Streak,* The, Pocket Book #910, 1952, cover by Verne Tossey.
$3 $15 $35

--- *Tenderfoot, The,* Pocket Book #1065, 1055, cover by Tom Ryan. 📷
$3 $15 $45

--- *Timbal Gulch Trail,* Popular Library #445, 1952. **$3 $14 $40**

Burke, James Lee, *Two For Texas,* Pocket Book #44112, 1982, paperback original, cover by Robert Maguire.
$10 $50 $120

Burnett, W. R., *Stretch Dawson,* Gold Medal Book #106, 1950, paperback original, western by hard-boiled author. 📷 **$8 $30 $90**

Cain, James M., *Past All Dishonor,* Signet Book #690, 1948, cover by T. V., by hard-boiled author. 📷 **$3 $30 $75**

Claussen, W. Edmunds, *El Paso,* Lion Book #55, 1951, paperback original.
$10 $25 $75

--- *Gun Devil,* Lion Book #28, 1950, paperback original, cover by Robert Stanley. 📷 **$4 $20 $75**

Coburn, Walt, *Mavericks,* Popular Library #250, 1950, cover by J. Dreany.
$3 $14 $35

--- *Pardners of the Dim Trails,* Popular Library #415, 1952, "she was his until his guns gave out." 📷 **$3 $16 $35**

Cody, Al, *Big Corral, The,* Popular Library #253, 1951, cover by Kirk Wilson, art shows team-up of the hero and the heroine. 📷 **$3 $15 $40**

--- *Marshal of Deer Creek,* The, Avon Book #378, 1951, cover by C. Doare.
$3 $18 $40

--- *Outlaw Justice at Hangman's Coulee,* Avon Book #460, 1952, cover by C. Doare. **$4 $16 $35**

Cole, Jackson, *Guns of Mist River,* Popular Library #298, 1950. 📷
$4 $15 $40

--- *Texas Tornado,* Pyramid Book #108, 1954, paperback original, a Jim Hatfield pulp western. **$3 $15 $40**

Conway, John, *Apache Wars, The,* Monarch Book #MA309, 1961, paperback original, cover by Robert Stanley; pseudonym of Joseph Chadwick.
$4 $18 $35

--- *Sioux Indian Wars, The,* Monarch Book #MA324, 1962, paperback original, cover by Robert Stanley shows Sioux war chief Crazy Horse. 📷 **$5 $20 $55**

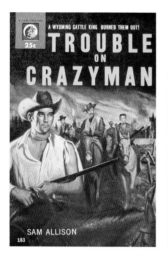

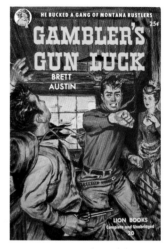

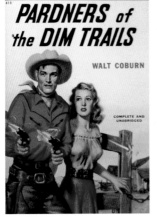

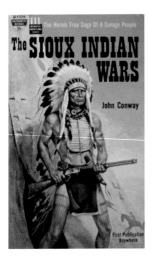

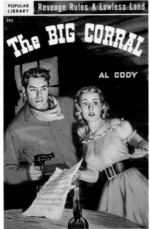

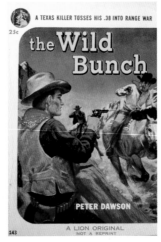

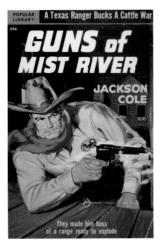

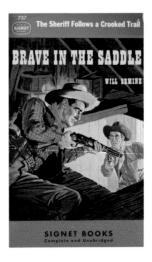

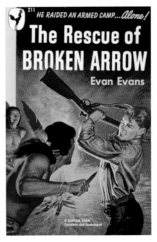

	G	VG	F

--- *Texas Rangers, The*, Monarch Book #MM333, 1963, paperback original, photo cover. **$5** **$35** **$100**

Crawford, Oliver, *Blood on the Branches*, Ace #S-141, 1956, paperback original. **$4** **$15** **$55**

Dawson, Peter, *Canyon, Hell*, Lion Book #10, 1949. **$4** **$30** **$80**

--- *Guns of Santa Fe*, Lion Book #37, 1950, cover by Robert Stanley. **$5** **$20** **$75**

--- *Wild Bunch, The*, Lion Book #143, 1853. 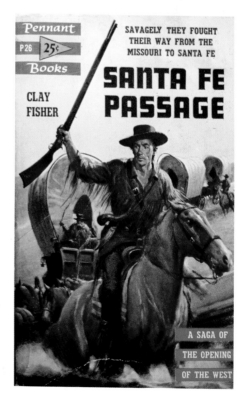 **$5** **$25** **$80**

Dodge, Gil, *Flint*, Signet Book #S1414, 1957, paperback original, author admits he based story on Jim Thompson's Savage Night; pseudonym of Arnold Hano, who was Thompson's editor at Lion Books, scarce. **$20** **$55** **$125**

Durst, Paul, *Bloody River*, Lion Book #178, 1953, paperback original. **$5** **$20** **$65**

--- *Die, Damn You!*, Lion Book #75, 1953. **$7** **$28** **$85**

Early, Tom, *Sons of Texas #1*, Berkley Book, 1989, paperback original, written by Elmer Kelton. **$10** **$25** **$60**

--- *Raiders, The*, Berkley Book, 1989, paperback original, Sons of Texas #2, written by Elmer Kelton. **$10** **$25** **$60**

--- *Rebels, The*, Berkley Book, 1989, paperback original, Sons of Texas #3, written by Elmer Kelton. **$10** **$30** **$90**

--- *Defiant, The*, Berkley Book, 1993, paperback original, Sons of Texas #6, written by James and Livia Reasoner. **$10** **$20** **$50**

Ermine, Will, *Brave in the Saddle*, Signet Book #737, 1949. **$3** **$15** **$30**

--- *Outlaw on Horseback*, Dell Book #284, 1949, Map Back, cover by Bob Meyers. **$3** **$16** **$40**

--- *Silver Star, The*, Dell Book #684, 1953, cover by Robert Stanley. **$4** **$12** **$30**

Evans, Evan, *Border Bandit, The*, Bantam Book #254, 1948, cover by Norman Saunders; pseudonym of Frederick Faust, aka Max Brand. **$4** **$18** **$40**

	G	VG	F

--- *Montana Rides*, Penguin Book #600, 1946, cover by Getz. **$3** **$20** **$60**

--- *Montana Rides Again*, Penguin Book #620, 1947, cover by Robert Jonas. **$3** **$15** **$40**

--- *Rescue of Broken Arrow, The*, Bantam Book #211, 1949, cover by Bob Doares. **$3** **$18** **$35**

Fast, Howard, *Last Frontier, The*, Avon Book #205, 1949, the last stand of 300 Cheyenne Indians. **$3** **$20** **$45**

Fisher, Clay, *Santa Fe Passage*, Pennant Book #P-26, 1953. **$3** **$15** **$30**

Fleischman, A.S., *Yellowleg*, Gold Medal Book #958, 1960, paperback original. **$4** **$20** **$50**

Fles, Barthold, *Saturday Evening Post Western Stories, The*, Avon Book #311, 1951, first book edition, anthology, contains Ernest Haycox. **$4** **$15** **$50**

Pennant
P 26 25¢
Books

CLAY FISHER

SAVAGELY THEY FOUGHT THEIR WAY FROM THE MISSOURI TO SANTA FE

SANTA FE PASSAGE

A SAGA OF THE OPENING OF THE WEST

	G	VG	F

Floren, Lee, *Gunslammer, The,* Lion Book #169, 1953, paperback original.
                 $5 $20 $60

Flynn, T. T., *Man From Laramie, The,* Dell First Edition #14, 1954, cover by Stanley Borack. $3 $15 $30

--- *Two Faces West,* Dell First Edition #33, paperback original, cover by Verne Tossey, expands magazine story.
                 $4 $20 $35

Foreman, L. L., *Arrow in the Dust,* Dell First Edition #11, 1954, first book edition, cover by Robert Stanley.
                 $3 $15 $30

Foster, Bennett, *Badlands,* Bantam Book #255, 1948, cover by Norman Saunders. $3 $20 $50

--- *Barbed Wire,* Bantam Book #252, 1948, in dust jacket.
             $20 $125 $200

--- *Dust of the Trail,* Lion Book #17, 1950, cover by Norman Saunders.
                 $5 $20 $75

--- *Man Tracks,* Lion Book #35, 1950, cover by Robert Stanley.
                 $5 $18 $75

Frazee, Steve, *Lawman's Feud,* Lion Book #150, 1953, paperback original.
                 $5 $20 $85

--- *Pistolman,* Lion Book #90, 1952, paperback original.
                 $5 $20 $85

--- *Sharp the Bugle Calls,* Lion Book #130, 1953, paperback original. $5 $20 $90

Friend, Oscar J., *Guns of Powder River,* Bonded Book #10B, 1945, digest-size.
                 $8 $20 $65

--- *Round-Up, The,* Avon Book #299, 1951. $3 $20 $50

Garfield, Brian, *Apache Canyon,* Ace Book #F-324, 1963, first paperback printing.
                 $4 $20 $60

Garland, Bennett, *7 Brave Men,* Monarch Book #292, 1962, paperback original, cover by Robert Stanley, novel about Cook Canyon Massacre; pseudonym of Brain Garfield. $8 $40 $100

Garst, Shannon, *Buffalo Bill,* Pocket Book Junior #J48, 1950, cover by Louis S. Glanzman. $5 $15 $35

Gregory, Jackson, *Ace in the Hole,* Popular Library #337, 1951.
                 $4 $15 $35

--- *Sudden Bill Dorn,* Popular Library #226, 1950, cover by Sam Cherry.
                 $3 $15 $30

Grey, Zane, *Last of the Plainsmen, The,* Pennant Book #2, 1953, cover by Harry Schaare. $3 $16 $35

--- *Raiders of Spanish Peaks,* Cardinal Book #C-385, 1960, cover by Jerry Allison. $2 $14 $30

	G	VG	F		G	VG	F

Grinstead, J. E., *Ranger Justice,* Prize Western #57, 1947, cover by Malcolm Smith. 📷 **$3** **$18** **$50**

Gruber, Frank, *Broken Lance,* Bantam Book #1198, 1954. **$2** **$16** **$35**

--- *Gunsight,* Lion Book #163, 1953. **$6** **$25** **$80**

--- *Lone Gunhawk,* The, Lion Book #157, 1953. **$5** **$25** **$70**

--- *Quantrell's Raiders,* Ace Book #D-39, 1953, paperback original, cover by Norman Saunders, Ace Double backed with *Gruber's Rebel Road.* 📷 **$8** **$25** **$80**

Halleran, E. E., *Colorado Creek,* Lion Book #134, 1953, paperback original. **$5** **$20** **$70**

Hamilton, Donald, *Texas Fever,* Gold Medal Book #1035, 1960, paperback original. **$6** **$35** **$100**

Harrison, C. William, *Eat Dog or Die!,* Lion Book #103, 1952, paperback original, cover by Rafael DeSoto, scarce. 📷 **$8** **$40** **$100**

--- *Missouri Maiden,* The, Lion Book #84, 1952. **$5** **$20** **$70**

Haycox, Ernest, *Adler Gulch,* Dell Book #450, 1950, Map Back, cover by Bob Meyers. 📷 **$3** **$15** **$40**

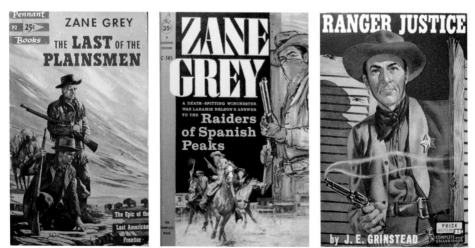

	G	VG	F

--- *Bugles in the Afternoon*, Bantam Book #25, 1946.   **$4**   **$15**   **$35**

--- *Deep West*, Pocket Book #594, 1949, cover by Joseph Camana.   **$3**   **$12**   **$35**

--- *Grim Canyon, The*, Popular Library #537, 1953, first book edition, collection.   **$3**   **$15**   **$40**

--- *Guns Up*, Popular Library #589, 1954, cover by A. Leslie Ross.   **$3**   **$18**   **$40**

--- *Head of the Mountain*, Popular Library #442, 1952.   **$3**   **$18**   **$35**

--- *Man in the Saddle*, Dell Book #120, 1946, Map Back. 📖   **$3**   **$20**   **$45**

--- *Return of a Fighter*, Dell Book #598, 1952, cover by Robert Stanley, collection.   **$3**   **$18**   **$40**

--- *Riders West*, Popular Library #271, 1950, cover by Sam Cherry. 📖   **$4**   **$18**   **$35**

--- *Rim of the Desert*, Pocket Book #446, 1947.   **$2**   **$14**   **$35**

--- *Rough Justice*, Pocket Book #790, 1951, cover by Warren Baumgartner.   **$2**   **$16**   **$35**

--- *Silver Desert, The*, Popular Library #360, 1951, cover by Sam Cherry. 📖   **$3**   **$18**   **$35**

--- *Starlight Rider*, Popular Library #235, 1950, "he was too tough to kill."   **$3**   **$18**   **$40**

--- *Sundown Jim*, Pocket Book #573, 1949, cover by John Blaine. 📖   **$2**   **$20**   **$35**

--- *Trail Town*, Dell Book #748, 1954, cover by Robert Stanley.   **$2**   **$15**   **$30**

--- *Trouble Shooter*, Popular Library #450, 1952.   **$3**   **$18**   **$40**

--- *Whispering Range*, Popular Library #199, 1949.   **$4**   **$20**   **$40**

--- *Wild Bunch, The*, Bantam Book #261, 1949, cover by Norman Saunders. 📖   **$3**   **$15**   **$50**

Heckelmann, Charles N., *Guns of Arizona*, Lion Book #34, 1950, cover by Earl Eugene Mayan; the author was also an editor at Popular Library, founder of Monarch Books. 📖   **$6**   **$35**   **$100**

	G	VG	F		G	VG	F

--- *Six-Gun Outcast*, Bantam Book #128, 1947. **$2** **$16** **$35**

--- *Two-Bit Rancher*, Signet Book #842, 1951. **$2** **$15** **$30**

Hendryx, James B., *Blood of the North*, Pony Book #66, 1946, a novel of the Canadian Northwest. 📷 **$3** **$16** **$45**

Henry, Will, *Reckoning at Yankee Flat*, Bantam Book #A1935, 1959. **$2** **$16** **$35**

Hogan, Robert J., *Challenge of Smoke Wade, The*, Avon Book #454, 1952, cover by Bob Doare. **$3** **$16** **$40**

Hopson, William, *Apache Greed*, Lion Book #195, 1954, cover by Robert Schulz. 📷 **$5** **$25** **$90**

--- *Arizona Round-up*, Avon Western Novel Monthly #3, 1950, cover by Norman Saunders, digest-size. **$6** **$35** **$100**

--- *Hang Tree Range*, Lion Library #LB156, 1957, cover by Robert Schulz. **$4** **$15** **$35**

--- *Killers Five*, Lion Book #65, 1951. 📷 **$5** **$20** **$75**

--- *Ranch Cat*, Lion Book #66, 1951, cover by Mitchell Hooks. **$5** **$20** **$75**

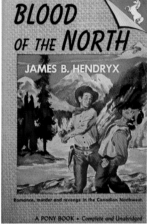

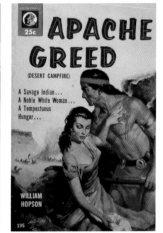

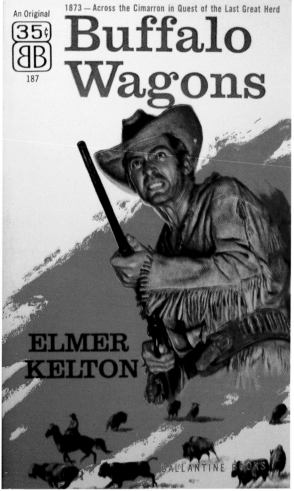

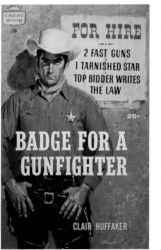

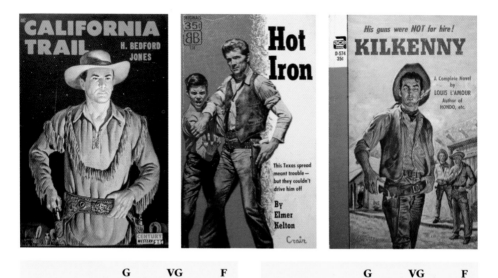

	G	VG	F		G	VG	F

--- *Yucca City Outlaw*, Avon Book #723, 1956. **$3** **$15** **$40**

Huffaker, Clair, *Badman*, Crest Book #167, 1957, paperback original, cover by Lu Kimmel, made into a John Wayne film. **$2** **$16** **$40**

--- *Badge For a Gunfighter*, Crest Book #158, 1957, paperback original, cover by James Meese. 📷 **$3** **$15** **$40**

--- *Guns of Rio Conchos*, Gold Medal Book #733, 1958, paperback original. **$3** **$15** **$45**

--- *Profiles of the American West*, Pocket Book #80711, 1976, cover by Robert Schulz, true stories about lawmen and outlaws. **$3** **$15** **$35**

--- *Rider From Thunder Mountain*, Crest Book #193, 1957, paperback original. **$3** **$18** **$40**

Jenkins, Will F., *Son of the Flying 'Y'*, Gold Medal Book #161, 1951, paperback original, cover by A. Leslie Ross, author better known as Murray Leinster. **$10** **$35** **$100**

Jessup, Richard, *Chuka*, Gold Medal Book #s1105, 1961, paperback original. **$3** **$15** **$40**

Jones, H., Bedford, *California Trail*, Century Western #133, 1950, cover by Malcolm Smith, pulp adventure author. 📷 **$8** **$25** **$75**

Kelton, Elmer, *Buffalo Wagons*, Ballantine Book #187, 1956, paperback original, his scarce second book. 📷 **$8** **$50** **$125**

--- *Barbed Wire*, Ballantine #247, 1957, paperback original, cover by Mel Crair. **$12** **$50** **$135**

--- *Captain's Rangers*, Ballantine Book #70703, 1969. **$6** **$25** **$65**

--- *Horse Head Crossing*, Ballantine Book #Y735, 1963. **$10** **$30** **$90**

--- *Hot Iron*, Ballantine Book #128, 1956, paperback original, cover by Mel Crair, his first book. 📷 **$15** **$75** **$175**

--- *Llano River*, Ballantine Book #U2306, 1966, paperback original. **$10** **$40** **$100**

--- *Shadow of a Star*, Ballantine Book #304K, 1969, paperback original. **$8** **$35** **$90**

L'Amour, Louis, *Burning Hills, The*, Bantam Book #1486, 1956. **$6** **$30** **$75**

--- *Crossfire Trail*, Ace Book #D-52, 1954, paperback original, backed with *Boomtown Buccaneers* by William Colt MacDonald. **$20** **$110** **$300**

--- *Guns of the Timberlands*, Bantam Book #1390, 1955. **$8** **$40** **$100**

--- *Heller With a Gun*, Gold Medal Book #478, 1955, paperback original, cover by Walter Baumfofer. **$12** **$60** **$150**

	G	VG	F

--- *Hondo,* Gold Medal Book #347, 1953, paperback original.
     $14   **$75**   **$200**

--- *Kilkenny,* Ace Book #S-82, 1954, paperback original, cover by Bentley with red border. **$65**   **$225**   **$500**

--- *Kilkenny,* Ace Book #D-574, 1963, same cover art by Bentley with blue border, reprints Ace S-82.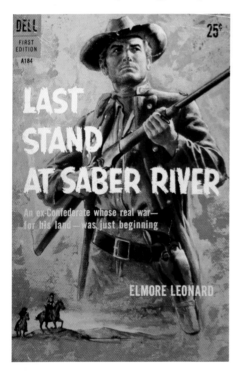
     $10   **$35**   **$90**

--- *Last Stand at Papago Wells,* Gold Medal Book #686, 1957, paperback original, cover by Frank McCarthy.
     $20   **$100**   **$225**

--- *Taggert,* Bantam Book #1977, 1959, paperback original.
     $6   **$30**   **$100**

--- *To Tame A Land,* Gold Medal Book #516, 1955, paperback original.
     $10   **$60**   **$200**

Lehman, Paul Evan, *Passion in the Dust,* Red Circle Book #6, 1949, paperback original, sexy saloon woman cover art, scarce pre-Lion Book.
     $8   **$30**   **$100**

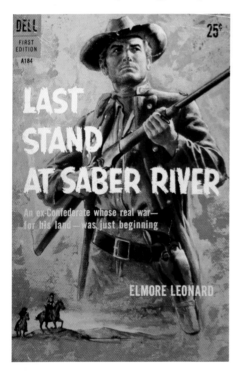

	G	VG	F

Leinster, Murray, *Outlaw Deputy,* Star Book #5, 1950, cover by Fred Claude Rodewald, digest-size; pseudonym of Will F. Jenkins. **$15**   **$35**   **$90**

--- *Outlaw Guns,* Star Book #3, 1950, digest-size. **$15**   **$30**   **$90**

--- *Texas Gun Slinger,* Star Book #1, 1950, cover by George Gross, digest-size.
     $20   **$40**   **$100**

Leonard, Elmore, *Bounty Hunters, The,* Ballantine Book #54, 1953, paperback original, his first book.
     $55   **$225**   **$600**

--- *Forty Lashes Less One,* Bantam Book #S6928, 1972, paperback original.
     $10   **$45**   **$120**

--- *Hombre,* Ballantine Book #526K, 1961, paperback original.
     $55   **$200**   **$450**

--- *Last Stand at Saber River,* Dell First Edition #A184, 1959.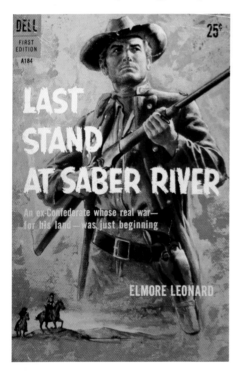
     $15   **$75**   **$175**

--- *Valdez Is Coming,* Gold Medal Book #r2238, 1970, paperback original.
     $10   **$40**   **$110**

MacDonald, William Colt, *Roaring Lead,* Century Western #61, 1945.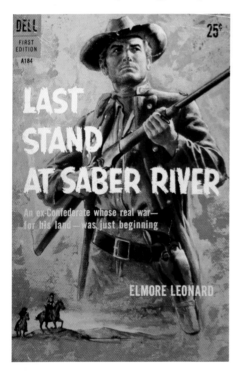
     $3   **$15**   **$45**

--- *Six-Gun Melody,* Avon Book #343, 1951, cover by Norman Saunders.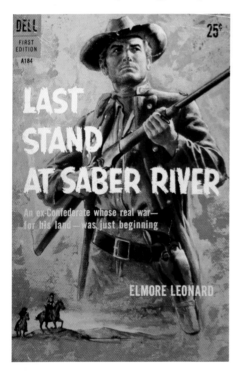
     $4   **$30**   **$65**

Mann, E. B., *Dead Man's Gorge,* Lion Book #27, 1950, cover by Bob Doares.
     $5   **$20**   **$75**

Marshall, Edison, *Bullets at Clearwater,* Popular Library #245, 1951, cover by Kirk Wilson. 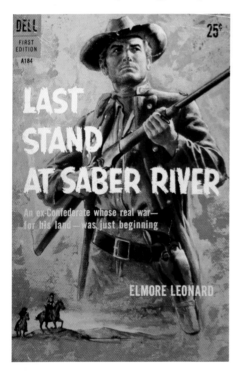 **$4**   **$15**   **$35**

--- *Deputy at Snow Mountain, The,* Popular Library #208, 1949.
     $4   **$16**   **$35**

--- *Trail's End,* Popular Library #272, 1950, cover by Sam Cherry, "they faced a cut-throat crew."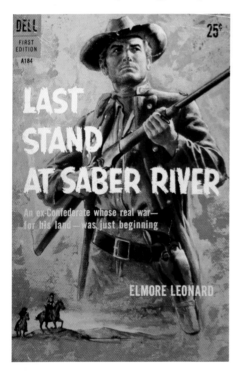
     $4   **$20**   **$40**

Martin, Charles M., *Lost River Buckaroos,* Checker Book #4, 1949, obscure publisher. **$10**   **$40**   **$100**

Mayo, Jim, *Showdown at Yellow Butte,* Ace Book #D-38, 1953; pseudonym of Louis L'Amour, covers by Norman Saunders,

	G	VG	F

Ace Double backed with *Outlaw River* by Bliss Lomax.  **$30** **$150** **$350**

--- *Utah Blaine*, Ace Book #D-48, 1954, paperback original, cover by Norman Saunders; pseudonym of Louis L'Amour, backed with *Desert Showdown* by Brad Ward. **$25** **$100** **$175**

McCulley, Johnston, *Gunsight Showdown,* Avon Book #748, 1956, original title *Texas Showdown.* **$4** **$15** **$45**

--- *Mark of Zorro, The,* Dell Book #553, 1951, cover by Robert Stanley.
$4 **$20** **$50**

--- *Reckless Range,* Century Western #131, 1950, cover by Malcolm Smith.
$5 **$16** **$40**

Morgan, Mark, *Fighting Man,* Lion Book #136, 1953, paperback original.
$5 **$20** **$65**

Mulford, Clarence E., *Bar 20 Rides Again, The,* Armed Service Edition #F-163, no date, circa 1844. **$12** **$40** **$100**

--- *Bar-20 Three, The,* Armed Service Edition #1141, no date, circa 1946.
$10 **$45** **$100**

--- *Corson of the JC,* Armed Service Edition #H-227, no date, circa 1945.
$10 **$30** **$75**

--- *Hopalong Cassidy's Protégé,* Armed Service Edition #I-257, no date, circa 1845. **$10** **$35** **$75**

	G	VG	F

--- *Hopalong Cassidy's Saddle Mate,* Popular Library #198, 1949, cover by A. Leslie Ross. **$8** **$35** **$100**

--- *Hopalong Cassidy Serves a Writ,* Armed Service Edition #C072, no date, circa 1944. **$10** **$35** **$90**

--- *Hopalong Cassidy Takes Cards,* Popular Library #146, 1948.
$5 **$25** **$75**

--- *Man From Bar-20, The,* Armed Service Edition #1072, no date, circa 1946.
$12 **$50** **$100**

--- *Man From Bar-20, The,* Graphic Book #23, 1950, a pupil of Hopalong in his own adventure.
$4 **$20** **$65**

--- *Mesquite Jenkins, Tumbleweed,* Popular Library #104, 1946, cover by Fielder. **$5** **$15** **$45**

--- *Tex,* Armed Service Edition #918, no date, circa 1946. **$10** **$35** **$75**

Montana, Duke, *Nevada Killing, Lion Book #78,* 1952, "Gold, whiskey, women – he wanted them all."
$5 **$20** **$65**

Nye, Nelson, *Bullet For Billy the Kid, A,* Avon Book #267, 1950, Billy the Kid in the Lincoln County War, original title *Pistols For Hire.* **$3** **$16** **$45**

--- *Salt River Ranny,* Pony Book #58, 1946. **$3** **$15** **$40**

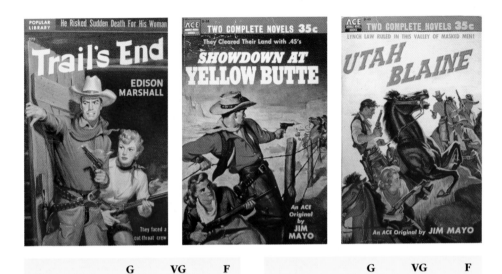

	G	VG	F			G	VG	F

Olsen, T. V., *Ramrod Rider,* Gold Medal Book #s1117, 1961, paperback original. **$3** **$20** **$45**

O'Rourke, Frank, *Concannon,* Ballantine book #10, 1952, paperback original, in dust jacket with art by Robert Maguire, the most valuable mass-market western paperback. 📷 **$150** **$400** **$1,000**

Owen, Dean, *Pistol Belt,* Monarch Book #204, 1961, paperback original, cover by Robert Stanley; pseudonym of Dudley Owen McGaughy. 📷 **$3** **$18** **$40**

--- *Sam Houston Story, The,* Monarch Book #MA308, 1961, paperback original,

cover by A. Leslie Ross, Texas history. **$3** **$20** **$50**

Patten, Lewis B., *Massacre at White River,* Ace Book #D-4, 1952, paperback original, backed with *Rimrock Rider* by Walter A. Tompkins, cover by Norman Saunders. **$8** **$25** **$100**

Patterson, Rod, *Whip Hand,* Lion Book #203, 1954. **$5** **$20** **$75**

Porter, Donald Clayton, *Red Stick,* Bantam Book #56142, 1994, paperback original, cover by Louis S. Glanzman, book #26 in the 28-book White Indian series, all are PBOs with Glanzman art, last four scarce, each: 📷 **$10** **$25** **$65**

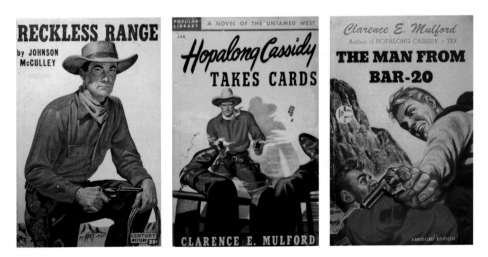

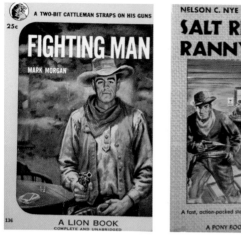

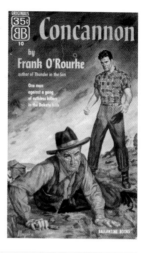

	G	VG	F			G	VG	F

Raine, William MacLeod, *Bandit Trail,* Dell Book #424, 1950, Map Back, cover by Robert Stanley.
$2 $15 $40

--- *Drygulch Trail,* Popular Library #256, 1950, cover by George Rozen.
$4 $16 $40

--- *Gunsight Pass,* Dell Book #629, 1952, cover by Robert Stanley.
$3 $14 $30

--- *Trail's End,* Dell Book #179, 1947, Map Back. $3 $15 $40

Ryan, Riley, *Dakota Deal, The,* Lion Book #187, 1954. $5 $30 $75

Sabin, Mark, *Winchester Cut,* Gold Medal Book #144, 1951, paperback original.
$5 $15 $35

Schaefer, Jack, *First Blood,* Ballantine Book #13, 1953, first book edition.
$4 $20 $75

--- *Shane,* Bantam Book #833, 1950, not a movie tie-in. $4 $15 $40

Shirreffs, Gordon D., *Brave Rifles, The,* Gold Medal Book #876, 1959, paperback original. $3 $18 $35

--- *Bugles on the Prairie,* Gold Medal Book #639, 1957, paperback original, cover by Frank McCarthy.
$4 $20 $40

	G	VG	F		G	VG	F

Short, Luke, *Barren Land Murders,* Gold Medal Book #159, 1951, first book edition, originally a pulp magazine serial; pseudonym of Frederick D. Glidden; Luke Short was also the name of a famous actual western gunman. **$4 $20 $50**

--- *Bought With a Gun*, Dell First Edition #68, 1955, paperback original, cover by Stanley Borack. **$5 $20 $40**

--- *Bounty Guns*, Dell Book #702, 1953, paperback original, cover by Stanley Borack. **$3 $14 $35**

--- *Hard Money*, Bantam Book #209, 1949, cover by Norman Saunders. **$4 $18 $40**

--- *Savage Range*, Dell Book #606, 1952, cover by Robert Stanley. **$2 $16 $30**

--- *Trumpet's West!*, Dell Ten-Cent Book #1, 1950, first book edition, cover by H. W. Scott. **$5 $25 $60**

Slater, Ray, *Texas Night Riders,* Leisure Book #2023, 1983, paperback original; pseudonym of Joe Lansdale. **$20 $45 $175**

Steeves, Harrison R., *Good Night, Sheriff,* Bantam Book #149, 1948, Superior reprint in dust jacket. **$40 $100 $200**

Stevens, Dan J., *Oregon Trunk,* Lion Book #50, 1951, first paperback printing. **$5 $20 $75**

	G	VG	F

Stewart, Logan, *Rails West,* Gold Medal Book #367, 1954, paperback original; pseudonym of Les Savage Jr.
$3 $18 $35

--- *Trail, The,* Gold Medal Book #193, 1951, paperback original.
$4 $20 $40

Striker, Fran, *Lone Ranger and the Secret of Thunder Mountain, The,* LA Bantam #14, 1940, rare.   **$125 $250 $650**

--- *Lone Ranger Rides Again, The,* Pinnacle Book #40-492, 1979, cover by Bruce Minney, #8 in the Lone Ranger series that reprints the original books in mass-market paperback, each book:
$5 $15 $30

Telfair, Richard, *Sundance,* Gold Medal Book #999, 1960, paperback original; pseudonym of Richard Jessup.
$3 $15 $40

--- *Wyoming Jones For Hire,* Gold Medal Book #883, 1959, paperback original.
$3 $15 $35

Trimnell, Robert L., *Wench and the Flame, The,* Lion Book #147, 1953, paperback original, cover by Rafael DeSoto.
$5 $20 $75

Tuttle, W. C., *Blind Trail at Sunrise,* Quick Reader #148, 1945, first book edition, cover by Cirkle.   **$10 $20 $45**

	G	VG	F

--- *Ghost Trails,* Armed Service Edition #D-123, no date, circa 1944.
$8 $32 $75

--- *Gun Feud,* Popular Library #354, 1951, cover by Sam Cherry, creator of the Hashknife Hartley western mystery novels.   **$3 $18 $50**

--- *Hidden Blood,* Popular Library #149, 1948.   **$4 $18 $40**

--- *Mystery of the Red Triangle, The,* Avon Book #53, 1944.
$5 $20 $60

--- *Mystery of the Red Triangle, The,* Armed Service Edition #I-245, no date, circa 1945.   **$10 $35 $85**

--- *Shotgun Gold,* Popular Library #297, 1950, cover by Kirk Wilson.
$4 $16 $35

--- *Tumbling River Range,* Armed Service Edition #D-94, no date, circa 1944.
$10 $40 $100

--- *Twisted Trails,* Popular Library #249, 1959, cover by Kirk Wilson.
$4 $18 $35

--- *Wild Horse Valley,* Popular Library #203, 1949, cover by A. Leslie Ross.
$4 $16 $35

Ward, Jonas, *Buchanan Gets Mad,* Gold Medal Book #803, 1958, paperback original.   **$4 $20 $55**

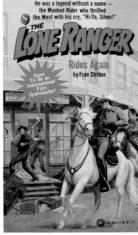

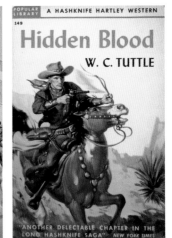

	G	VG	F		G	VG	F

--- *Buchanan On the Prod*, Gold Medal Book #k1576, 1960, paperback original.
$4 $20 $50

--- *Buchanan's Gun*, Gold Medal Book #d1926, 1968, paperback original, hard-boiled western series; pseudonym of William Ard only on books before 1961, this book ghost-written by Brian Garfield. $6 $50 $100

--- *Buchanan's Revenge*, Gold Medal #951, 1960, paperback original.
$5 $20 $60

--- *Name's Buchanan*, The, Gold Medal Book #604, 1956, paperback, cover by Lu Kimmel. $5 $30 $65

Watson, Will, *Wolf Dog Range*, Lion Book #61, 1951. 📷 $7 $30 $90

Wellman, Manly Wade, *Fort Sun Dance*, Dell First Edition #52, 1955, first book edition, scarce western novel by a famous fantasy author.
$3 $20 $75

White, Leslie Turner, *Log Jam*, Ace Book #D-494, 1961. 📷 $4 $10 $30

Whittington, Harry, *Hangrope Town*, Ballantine Book #U1021, 1964, paperback original. $5 $30 $75

--- *High Fury*, Ballantine Book #U1020, 1964, paperback original.
$8 $20 $60

--- *Prairie Raiders and Dry Gulch Town*, Ace Book #F-196, 1963, paperback original. $5 $20 $50

--- *Trap For Sam Dodge, A*, Ace Book #F-103, 1961, paperback original, Ace Double backed with *High Thunder* by Lee Floren. $5 $20 $60

--- *Wild Lonesome*, Ballantine Book #U1022, 1965, paperback original.
$4 $20 $60

Wister, Owen, *Virginian, The*, Cardinal Book #C-209, 1956, cover by James Meese, tough western classic made famous the phrase, "when you call me that, smile!" 📷 $2 $15 $35

SPORTS:
Baseball, Football, and Others

The next-best thing to playing sports is watching sports, and the next-best thing to watching sports is reading about sports and the heroes who make all the great records and spectacular plays.

Paperbacks about sports break down into roughly two categories: baseball books, which seems to be the largest sub-group of the early paperbacks, and books about all other sports. This is an interesting and popular genre because the books feature wonderful photos or artwork of major sports heroes on the covers. Many of these heroes have become legends today.

These are hot collectibles with great crossover potential and interest among sports and baseball collectors; the market is large and so is the demand for the key books in best condition. Many sports fans do not know of the existence of most of these books because most have never seen them until now. Many of these books are in demand – even by non-book collectors, especially in the larger non-book collecting sports market – because of the sports heroes shown on the covers or the great artwork depicting crucial plays in classic games.

Far larger than the paperback collecting market or even the antiquarian book market, the sports collecting market is filled with people very interested in many of these books if they knew what to look for and how to find them. This book will bring attention to a neglected area of sports collectibles. Listed here are many of the scarce and early vintage paperback editions that are collectible in best condition.

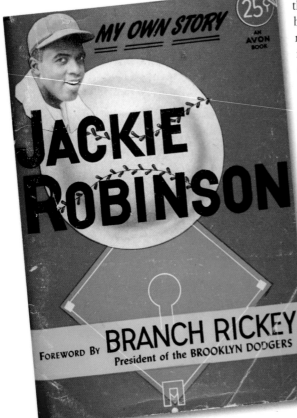

	G	VG	F		G	VG	F

Andretti, Mario, *What's It Like Out There?,* Bantam Book #N5916, 1971, written with Bob Collins, race car driver hero tells his own story. 📷   **$4**   **$15**   **$40**

Anonymous, *Big League Baseball,* Avon Book #307, 1950, anthology.   **$10**   **$30**   **$80**

Berkow, Ira, *Oscar Robertson,* MacFadden Book #183, 1972, cover art shows the famous basketball player.   **$3**   **$15**   **$45**

Borstein, Larry, *Ali,* Tower Book #T-095-88, 1971, paperback original, cover shows photo of Muhammad Ali.   **$10**   **$20**   **$55**

Brown, Warren, *Chicago Cubs, The,* Armed Service Edition #1197, about 1945.   **$25**   **$75**   **$155**

Carmichael, John F., *My Greatest Day in Baseball,* Armed Service Edition #1128, no date, circa 1945.   **$15**   **$35**   **$100**

--- *My Greatest Day in Baseball,* Bantam Book #500, 1948, cover by Hy Rubin. 📷   **$5**   **$25**   **$45**

David, Mac, *Sports Shorts,* Bantam Book #A1981, 1959.   **$2**   **$10**   **$35**

Davies, Valentine, *It Happens Every Spring,* Avon Book #249, 1950.   **$4**   **$15**   **$40**

DiMaggio, Joe, *Baseball For Everyone,* Signet Book #718, 1949. 📷   **$10**   **$30**   **$90**

--- *Lucky to Be a Yankee,* Bantam Book #506, 1949, cover by Hy Rubin shows the Yankee slugger, scarce in condition. 📷   **$15**   **$50**   **$125**

Enery, Russell G., *High Inside!,* Pocket Book Junior #J66, 1951.   **$5**   **$15**   **$35**

Farr, Finis, *Black Champion,* Gold Medal Book #t2092, first paperback printing 1969, cover by Peter Caras, story of Black boxer Jack Johnson. 📷   **$10**   **$30**   **$80**

Feller, Bob, *Bob Feller's Strikeout Story,* Bantam Book #510, 1948.   **$8**   **$20**   **$65**

--- *Strikeout Story,* Armed Service Edition #1316, no date, circa 1947.   **$22**   **$75**   **$155**

Fitzgerald, Ed, *Heroes of Sport,* Sport Magazine Extra, no number, 1961, cover shows photos of Mickey Mantle, Johnny Unitas, Bob Cousy.   **$6**   **$20**   **$55**

--- *Johnny Unitas,* Sport Magazine Library #1, 1960, cover shows photo of Unitas. 📷   **$5**   **$20**   **$50**

--- *Story of the Brooklyn Dodgers, The,* Bantam Book #556, 1949, cover by Hy Rubin. 📷   **$10**   **$30**   **$75**

Garreau, Garth, *Bat Boy of the Giants,* Comet Book #17, 1949, cover by Richard Powers, true story of 1940s bat boy. 📷   **$6**   **$15**   **$40**

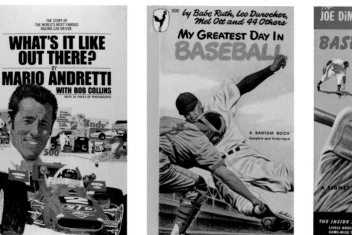

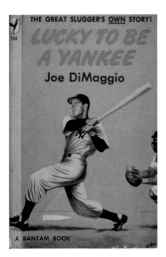

THE GREAT SLUGGER'S OWN STORY!

LUCKY TO BE A YANKEE

Joe DiMaggio

A BANTAM BOOK

The Explosive Story of Jack Johnson, Who Dared the World to Find The Great White Hope

BLACK CHAMPION

by Finis Farr
with photographs

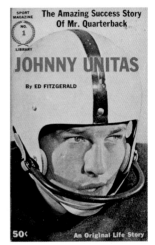

SPORT MAGAZINE NO. 1 LIBRARY

The Amazing Success Story Of Mr. Quarterback

JOHNNY UNITAS

By ED FITZGERALD

50¢   An Original Life Story

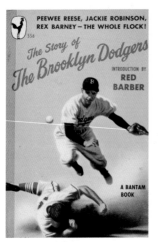

PEEWEE REESE, JACKIE ROBINSON, REX BARNEY — THE WHOLE FLOCK!

The Story of The Brooklyn Dodgers

INTRODUCTION BY RED BARBER

A BANTAM BOOK

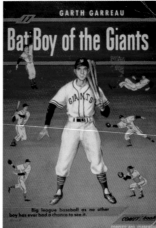

GARTH GARREAU

Bat Boy of the Giants

Big league baseball as no other boy has ever had a chance to see it.

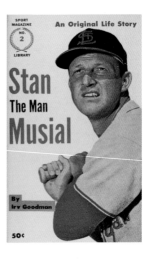

SPORT MAGAZINE NO. 2 LIBRARY

An Original Life Story

Stan The Man Musial

By Irv Goodman

50¢

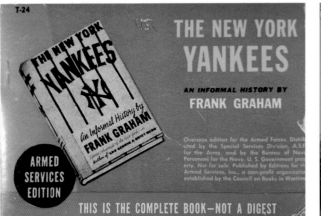

T-24

THE NEW YORK YANKEES

AN INFORMAL HISTORY BY FRANK GRAHAM

Overseas edition for the Armed Forces. Distributed by the Special Services Division, A.S.F., for the Army, and by the Bureau of Naval Personnel for the Navy. U. S. Government property. Not for sale. Published by Editions for the Armed Services, Inc., a non-profit organization established by the Council on Books in Wartime.

ARMED SERVICES EDITION

THIS IS THE COMPLETE BOOK—NOT A DIGEST

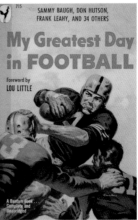

SAMMY BAUGH, DON HUTSON, FRANK LEAHY, AND 34 OTHERS

My Greatest Day in FOOTBALL

Foreword by LOU LITTLE

A Bantam Book Complete and Unabridged

	G	VG	F		G	VG	F

Goodman, Irv, *Stan "The Man" Musial,* Sports Magazine Library #2, 1961, photo cover of Stan Musial. 📷

| | $5 | $15 | $45 |

Goodman, Murray and Lewin, Leonard, *My Greatest Day in Football,* Bantam Book #715, 1949, cover by Norman Saunders. 📷 $5 $20 $60

Graham, Frank, *Brooklyn Dodgers, The, An Informal History,* Armed Service Edition #963, 1945. $25 $65 $145

--- *Lou Gehrig,* Armed Service Edition #J-277, no date, circa 1945, reprinted as ASE #781, cover shows Lou Gehrig.

| | $15 | $45 | $120 |

--- *Lou Gehrig,* Armed Service Edition #781, no date, circa 1946, reprints earlier #J-277. $10 $40 $100

--- *New York Yankees, The,* Armed Service Edition #T-24, 1944, reprinted as ASE #1170. 📷 $35 $75 $150

--- *New York Yankees, The,* Armed Service Edition #1170, 1945, reprints #T-24. $20 $50 $100

Haines, Donal Hamilton, *The Southpaw,* Comet Book #16, 1949.

| | $5 | $15 | $35 |

Hano, Arnold, *Willie Mays: The Say-Hey Kid,* Sport Magazine Library #6, paperback original May, 1961, photo cover of Willie Mays. 📷

| | $10 | $25 | $75 |

Harris, Mark, *Southpaw, The,* Perma Book #P-299, 1954. $3 $16 $40

Heinz, W. C., *Professional The,* Berkley Book #BG-197, 1959, boxing novel, Hemingway blurb says it's the only good novel he'd ever read about a fighter.

| | $10 | $20 | $60 |

Herndon, Booton, *Football's Greatest Quarterbacks,* Sports Magazine Library #10, 1961. $5 $20 $40

Heuman, William, *Wonder Boy,* Scholastic Book Services #T498, 1964, first paperback printing, cover by Albert Micolo. $4 $15 $40

Jacobs, Bruce, *Baseball Stars of 1950,* Lion Book #23, 1950, cover by Bob Doares, anthology, scarce in condition.

| | $10 | $40 | $135 |

--- *Baseball Stars of 1953,* Lion Book #125, 1953, anthology. 📷

| | $12 | $30 | $75 |

--- *Baseball Stars of 1954,* Lion Book #194, 1954, anthology.

| | $6 | $25 | $75 |

--- *Baseball Stars of 1955,* Lion Library #LL12, 1955, cover art shows Yogi Berra and Willie Mays. 📷

| | $5 | $25 | $65 |

--- *Baseball Stars of 1956,* Lion Library #LL74, 1956, cover by Robert Engle shows Duke Snider.

| | $8 | $20 | $60 |

--- *Baseball Stars of 1957,* Lion Library #LL150, 1957, cover by Robert Engle shows Mickey Mantle. 📷

| | $15 | $30 | $100 |

Lampell, Millard, *Hero, The,* Popular Library #278, 1950, cover by Earle Begey, steamy novel about football halfback on college team. 📷 $4 $16 $35

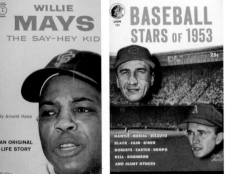

	G	VG	F

Lardner, Ring, *You Know Me, Al,* Armed Service Edition #J278 (reprinted as #782). 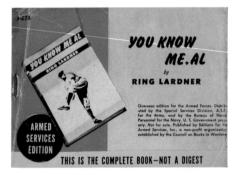 **$10 $20 $65**

--- *You Know Me, Al,* Armed Service Edition #782, 1945. **$5 $20 $45**

Lieb, Frederick G., *Boston Red Sox, The,* Armed Service Edition #1271, no date, circa 1947. **$35 $100 $160**

--- *Detroit Tigers, The,* Armed Service Edition #1260, no date, circa 1947. **$25 $75 $140**

--- *Saint Louis Cardinals, The,* Armed Service Edition #S-25, no date, circa 1945. **$25 $75 $150**

Linn, Ed, *Ted Williams, the Eternal Kid,* Sports Magazine Library #3, 1961, photo cover of Ted Williams. **$10 $25 $80**

Lucas, Robert, *Below the Belt,* Uni-Book #76, 1953, paperback original, digest-size, cover by Julian Paul, novel of a

black boxer. 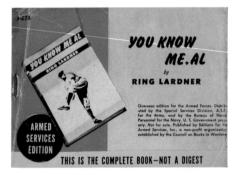 **$20 $80 $175**

Mailer, Norman, *Fight, The,* Bantam Book #Y2605, 1976, cover shows photo of Muhammad Ali, Mailer's version of the famous Ali and Foreman fight in Africa. **$2 $20 $50**

Mann, Arthur, *The Jackie Robinson Story,* F. J. Low, 1950, digest-size, tie-in with the film. **$75 $130 $300**

Marsh, Irwin and Ehre, Edward, Best Sports Stories of 1944, Armed Service Edition #913, no date, circa 1945. **$12 $35 $75**

Meany, Tom, *Babe Ruth,* Bantam Book #505, 1948, cover by Foxley shows Babe Ruth. **$12 $25 $65**

--- *Baseball's Greatest Players,* Dell Book #839, 1955, photo cover of players. **$3 $20 $45**

--- *Baseball's Greatest Teams,* Bantam Book #763, 1950, cover by Hy Rubin. 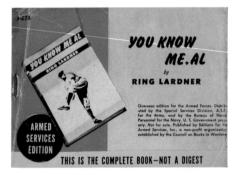 **$5 $18 $45**

Michael, D. J., *Win – Or Else!,* Lion Book #208, 1954, novel. 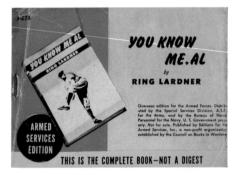 **$15 $40 $125**

Miller, Margary, *Joe Louis: American,* Armed Service Edition #1118, no date, circa 1947, boxing. **$15 $55 $100**

Moon, Bucklin, *Champs and Bums,* Lion Book #229, 1954, cover by George Gross, boxing stories by Ernest Hemingway, William Saroyan, Budd Schulberg, Nelson Algren. 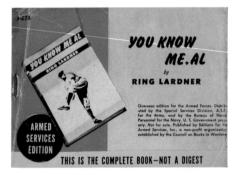 **$8 $30 $85**

	G	VG	F

Newcombe, Jack, *Floyd Patterson,* Sport Magazine Library #7, 1961, photo cover of famous boxer Patterson.
$6 $20 $75

Nickerson, Kate, *Ringside Jezebel,* Original Novels #725, 1953, paperback original, digest-size, sex and boxing fiction. 📕
$20 $75 $145

Nicklaus, Jack, *Best Way to Better Golf #1, The,* Gold Medal Book #r1788, 1966, first book edition, illustrated.
$5 $20 $50

--- *Best Way to Better Golf #2, The,* Gold Medal Book #r1919, 1968, first book edition, illustrated.
$5 $15 $40

--- *Best Way to Better Golf #3, The,* Gold Medal Book #r2058, 1969, third book in this classic golf series.
$5 $15 $40

Robinson, Ray, *Baseball Stars of 1958,* Pyramid Book #G-324, 1958, cover by Robert Engle, anthology. 📕
$3 $15 $45

--- *Baseball Stars of 1959,* Pyramid Book #G-392, 1959, photo cover.
$3 $15 $40

--- *Baseball Stars of 1961,* Pyramid Book #G-605, 1961, photo cover.
$3 $15 $40

--- *Baseball Stars of 1965,* Pyramid Book #R-1148, 1965, paperback original, photo cover shows Mickey Mantle.
$10 $30 $90

Rosenthal, Harold, *Baseball's Best Managers,* Sports Magazine Library #4, 1961, photo cover shows managers.
$5 $15 $35

Ruth, Babe, *Babe Ruth Story, The,* Pocket Book #562, 1948, the story of the "sultan of swat" told to Bob Considine. 📕
$10 $25 $80

--- *Major League Baseball of 1953,* digest-size, 1953, back cover shows Mickey Mantle.
$10 $35 $100

Salsinger, et. al., H.G., *Major League Baseball 1950,* digest-size, 1950, photo cover of Joe Page.
$10 $25 $50

Schaap, Dick, *Mickey Mantle, the Indispensable Yankee,* Sports Magazine Library #5, 1961, photo cover of Mickey Mantle. 📕
$20 $40 $120

Schacht, Al, *Clowning Through Baseball,* Bantam Book #507, 1949.
$5   20 $40

Schifer, Don, *1960 Pro Football Handbook,* Cardinal Book #GC97, 1960, first book edition, anthology, photo cover shows Johnny Unitas.
$5 $15 $40

Scholz, Jackson, *Batter Up,* Comet Book #2, 1948, cover by Robert Frankenberg. 📕
$4 $16 $40

--- *Gridiron Challenge,* Pocket Book Junior #J52, 1950, cover by Ray Quigley.
$5 $15 $35

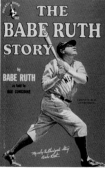

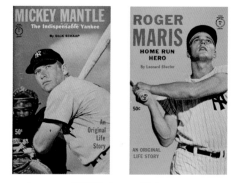

	G	VG	F		G	VG	F

Shecter, Leonard, *Roger Maris Home Run Hero,* Sport Magazine Library #11, 1961, photo cover shows Maris. 📷
$10 $40 $100

Silverman, Al, *Best From Sport,* Sport Magazine Library #8, 1961, photo cover of Babe Ruth and Joe Louis.
$4 $15 $45

--- *Warren Spahn,* Sports Magazine Library #9, 1961, photo cover of Spahn.
$5 $20 $60

Smith, Don, *Quarterbacks, The,* American Sports Library, #F120, 1964, pro football.
$5 $16 $40

Smith, H. Allen, *Rhubarb,* Pocket Book #695, 1950, cat inherits baseball team.
$3 $15 $30

Smith, Robert, *Runs, Hits & Errors,* Dell Book #292, 1949, Map Back shows 1887 World Series. 📷 $8 $20 $60

Smith, Wendell, *Jackie Robinson: My Own Story,* Avon Books, no number, 1949, digest-size, reprints Greenberg

hardcover, scarce. 📷
$30 $90 $250

Snead, Sam, *Sam Snead's Natural Golf,* Dell Book #774, 1954, cover by Phil Dormont. 📷 $5 $20 $60

Stern, Bill, *Bill Sterns' Favorite Baseball Stories,* Pocket Book #572, 1949.
$5 $15 $35

Stix, Thomas L., *Sporting Gesture, The,* Armed Service Edition #832, no date, circa 1945, anthology.
$10 $30 $70

Stockton, Roy J., *Gashouse Gang, The,* Armed Service Edition #1172, about 1948. $20 $55 $100

--- *Gashouse Gang, The,* Bantam Books #552, 1949. 📷 $10 $20 $45

Terrill, Rogers, *Argosy Book of Sports Stories, The,* Pennant Book #P-61, 1954, first book edition, anthology.
$3 $16 $35

Tully, Jim, *Bruiser, The,* Bantam Book #67, 1946, cover by Charles Andres, boxing classic. 📷 $5 $20 $40

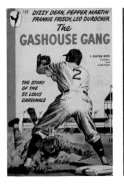
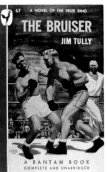
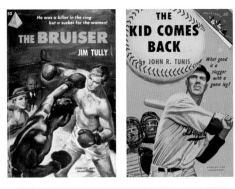

	G	VG	F		G	VG	F

--- *Bruiser, The*, Pyramid Book #53, 1952, cover by Mel Hunter. 📷
$8 $35 $65

Tulley, Walt, *Baseball Recorder*, Armed Service Edition #1083, 1946.
$20 $50 $110

Tunis, John, *Keystone Kids: A Baseball Story, The*, Armed Service Edition #Q-8, 1943, fiction. $12 $35 $90

--- *Kid Comes Back, The*, Pocket Book Junior #J67, 1951, cover by George Meyerriecks, baseball novel. 📷
$4 $15 $35

--- *Rookie of the Year*, Armed Service Edition #P-3, 1945, fiction.
$10 $25 $75

Ward, Arch, *Frank Leahy and the Fighting Irish*, Armed Service Edition #1037, no date, circa 1947, Notre Dame football.
$18 $55 $120

Werstein, Irving, *Roaring Road, The*, Automotive Periodicals, 1957, first book edition, auto racing stories, uncommon.
$10 $20 $65

Wise, Bill, *1965 Official Baseball Almanac*, Gold Medal Book #r1516, 1965, paperback original, edited anthology, photo cover shows Mickey Mantle.
$10 $25 $75

--- *1963 Official Pro Football Almanac*, Gold Medal Book #r1329, 1963, paperback original, photo cover.
$5 $15 $45

--- *1964 Official Pro Football Almanac*, Gold Medal Book #r1454, 1964, paperback original, photo cover.
$5 $15 $35

Zinkoff, Dave, *Go, Man,* Go!, Pyramid Book #PG17, 1958, written with Edgar Williams, cover art by Willard Mullen shows famous Harlem Globetrotters basketball team high jinks. 📷
$4 $15 $50

MEDIA-RELATED:
Movie and TV Tie-ins

They're images that are indelibly impressed upon our collective consciousness because of their broad appeal, and they're incredibly popular with readers and collectors even as they evoke wonderful nostalgic memories. They are media tie-in paperbacks, and they are growing in popularity.

These books cross over into almost every collectibles area as well as with fans and collectors of memorabilia on Hollywood stars and famous celebrities. The tie-in book is a genre (and some may say mini art form) all its own. The tie-in mass-market paperback has grown from humble origins in the 1950s and 1960s with an explosion that often puts them on bestseller lists today. It was made possible because paperback books can be published far more quickly and then directly targeted to their core audience more easily and faster than hardcover books. Tie-in paperbacks for hit TV shows and movies have become very collectible in recent years. Certain titles have become quite valuable. Many of these books, like the stars portrayed on their covers, have become well-remembered icons themselves and are instantly recognizable and cherished by the public as part of our collective popular culture.

Media tie-in paperbacks offer so much to choose from. Almost every hit TV show and most hit films from the 1950s to present have a paperback edition that was specifically published to tie in with that film or show. Paperback tie-ins for popular franchises like Star Trek, Star Wars, X-Files, Buffy the Vampire Slayer, 24, and many more are avidly collected.

I am sure movie and TV tie-in paperbacks will become even more collectible in the future. With covers featuring the biggest stars of Hollywood and of the small screen, and cover images from the hottest and most popular TV and film hits, these books are instantly recognizable nationwide (and increasingly through cable, satellite and the Internet, now worldwide). There is growing interest for key and scarce titles or series, or books that show big stars.

Since many of these books were published as paperback originals, most are actual first editions. While some media fans and paperback collectors have gotten the jump in this hot area of collectibles, there is still plenty of room for everyone to enjoy this segment of the hobby. There are still many great finds out there just waiting for the informed collector to come along.

Many of the movie tie-in paperbacks also include pages of photos from the film, including the stars. Some later TV tie-in books and star biographies also include photos.

The definition of a movie or TV tie-in is that it must always mention the film or show made from it, or that it was made from. A blurb announcing the forth-coming film, or telling the reader that the book is based upon the "hit TV series" will do. Many tie-ins, of course, go much further than a mere mention. Most have photo covers of stars or scenes from the film or show. Usually TV tie-ins are also paperback originals. Movie tie-ins are also often paperback originals, but if the film is taken from a famous novel – as many of them are often based upon – the tie-in paperback will be a reprint. Then there can be earlier editions, even first editions, which predate the film and do not tie in with it. However, the tie-in reprint for the film may be the first (and often only) edition of that book to tie in with that film, hence it can be collectible in its own right – even though it is a reprint!

Types of media tie-in books include: screenplays (where the screenplay, play script, or teleplay was reprinted); novelizations (where a script or screenplay has been rewritten and turned into a novel, in what is an entirely new edition); movie editions of existing novels made into films (reprints that tie in to the film); and original novels (based on a TV show or film but which are an entirely new work, a paperback original).

Condition is very important to the price value of these books. High prices can be paid for pristine copies, whereas copies in lesser condition are not in such demand.

C·248

35¢

THE
COMPLETE
BOOK

WILL ACTING SPOIL
Marilyn Monroe
?

Illustrated with
43 LUSCIOUS
PICTURES
which clearly prove
that NOTHING
could spoil
Marilyn

PETE MARTIN

	G	VG	F

Albert, Marvin H., *Law and Jake Wade, The,* Gold Medal Book #756, second printing 1958, photo cover shows stars Robert Taylor and Richard Widmark.
$2 $15 $30

--- *Pillow Talk,* Gold Medal Book #k1410, 1964, photo cover shows stars Doris Day and Rock Hudson.
$5 $15 $40

Alcott, Louisa May, *Little Women,* Dell Book #296, 1949, Map Back, photo cover shows stars of the MGM film.
$3 $15 $45

Anderson, Edward, *Your Red Wagon,* Bantam Book #350, 1948, in dust jacket, rare. **$100 $300 $550**

Anderson, K. J., *Sky Captain and the World of Tomorrow,* Onyx Book #41163, 2004, paperback original, pulp adventure novel, tie-in with Angelina Jolie, Gwyneth Paltrow, Jude Law film.
$2 $5 $20

Andrew, Matthew, *Let's Make Love,* Bantam Book #A2112, 1960, paperback original, cover photo shows Marilyn Monroe. **$12 $50 $120**

Anobile, Richard, *Mork & Mindy: A Video Novel,* Pocket Book #82754, 1979, paperback original, shows stars Robin Williams and Pam Dawber, all color photos with captions.
$4 $12 $30

Anonymous, *Celebrated Stories Made into Movies,* Quick Reader #127, 1944.
$8 $20 $50

--- *Voice of Experience, The,* LA Bantam #7, 1940, paperback original, "based on the famous radio series," rare.
$65 $150 $255

Anthony, Piers, *Total Recall,* Avon Book #70874, 1990, paperback original, cover shows star Arnold Schwarzenegger, novelization of Philip K. Dick short story.
$3 $15 $30

Armstrong, Louis, *Satchmo,* Signet Book #S1245, 1955, cover by Stanley Zuckerberg shows Armstrong.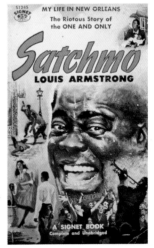
$3 $15 $50

Avallone, Michael, *Felony Squad,* Popular Library #60-8036, 1967, paperback original, photo cover shows stars Howard Duff and Ben Alexander.
$4 $14 $40

--- *Keith, the Hero,* Curtis Book #05005, 1970, paperback original, tie-in to the Partridge Family series, book #3.
$3 $12 $20

--- *Man From U.N.C.L.E., The,* Ace Book #G-553, 1965, paperback original, photo cover shows star Robert Vaughan, #1 in series. **$4 $14 $30**

--- *Mannix,* Popular Library #1156, 1968, paperback original, cover photo shows star Michael Conners.
$4 $15 $35

	G	VG	F		G	VG	F

--- *Terror In the Sun*, Signet Book #P3994, 1969, paperback original, book #2 in the book series based on the "Hawaii Five-O" TV series, photo cover shows star Jack Lord. **$5 $20 $40**

Axelrod, George, *Seven Year Itch, The,* Bantam Book #1371, 1955, cover photo of Marilyn Monroe. **$10 $35 $90**

Barbera, Joe and Hanna, Bill, *Yogi Bear Goes to College,* Dell First Edition #B-199, 1961, paperback original, cartoon TV series. **$2 $20 $45**

Barrett, William E., *Lillies of the Field,* Popular Library #PC1027, 1963, tie-in with Sidney Poitier film. **$2 $12 $25**

Bast, William, *James Dean,* Ballantine Book #180, 1956, early biography with photo cover showing James Dean. **$12 $45 $120**

Beach, Edward L., *Run Silent, Run Deep,* Perma Book #M4061, fourth printing 1958, submarines at war, photo cover shows stars Burt Lancaster and Clark Gable. 📷 **$2 $15 $40**

Bernard, Joel, *Thinking Machine Affair, The,* Ace Book #51704, 1967, paperback original, photo cover, #21 in the "Man From U.N.C.L.E." TV series, uncommon higher number in series. **$4 $20 $50**

Bevan, A. J., *Zarak,* Avon Book #T-150, 1956, paperback original, photo cover shows stars Antia Ekberg and Victor Mature. 📷 **$4 $25 $75**

Bingham, Carson, *Gorgo,* Monarch Book #MM603, 1960, paperback original, photo cover; pseudonym of Bruce Cassidy. 📷 **$12 $60 $125**

Black, Campbell, *Raiders of the Lost Ark,* Ballantine Book #29490, 1981, paperback original, photo cover shows star Harrison Ford as Indiana Jones. **$3 $15 $40**

Blish, James, *Spock Must Die,* Bantam Book #H5515, 1970, paperback original, photo cover of star Leonard Nimoy as Mr. Spock, the first original Star Trek novel. **$3 $20 $45**

--- *Star Trek*, Bantam Book #H5629, 1967, first book edition, cover by James Bama shows stars William Shatner and Leonard Nimoy, first Star Trek book, adapts scripts from original 1960s TV series. 📷 **$4 $20 $75**

Bloch, Robert, *Psycho,* Crest Book #S-385, 1961, cover photo shows the star, a terrified Janet Leigh. 📷 **$10 $30 $90**

Block, Lawrence, *Markham,* Belmont Book #236, 1961, paperback original, cover art shows star Ray Milland, early tie-in novel by major mystery novelist. 📷 **$10 $40 $125**

	G	VG	F		G	VG	F

Boorman, John, *Zardoz*, Signet Book #Q5830, 1974, paperback original, tie-in with cult film, cover art shows star Sean Connery. 🎬 **$8 $20 $60**

Boulle, Pierre, *Planet of the Apes*, Signet Book #P3399, 11th printing, 1968, photo cover shows star Charleton Heston. 🎬 **$2 $18 $40**

Boyd, Frank, *Johnny Staccato*, Gold Medal Book #980, 1960, paperback original, cover illustration shows John Cassavetes from the private eye TV series. **$3 $15 $45**

Brackett, Leigh, *Rio Bravo*, Bantam Book #1893, 1959, paperback original, cover shows stars John Wayne, Dean Martin, Ricky Nelson. **$15 $60 $125**

Bradbury, Ray, *Fahrenheit 451*, Ballantine Book #U5060, 14th printing 1968, photo cover shows stars Julie Harris and Oskar Werner. **$2 $15 $40**

Brewer, Gil, *Appointment in Cairo*, Ace Book #37600, 1970, paperback original, photo cover shows star Robert Vaughan, "It Takes a Thief" TV series, book #3. **$3 $20 $50**

	G	VG	F		G	VG	F

--- *Mediteranean Caper*, Ace Book #37599, 1969, paperback original, photo cover shows star Robert Vaughan, "It Takes a Thief" TV series, book #2.
$4 $15 $45

Brown, Will C., *Man of the West*, Dell Book #986, 1958, cover by George Gross shows star Gary Cooper.
$3 $15 $50

Burke, John, *Hard Day's Night, A*, Dell Book #D-489, 1964, paperback original, photo cover shows all four of the Beatles.  **$6 $30 $100**

--- *300 Spartans, The*, Signet Book #D-2172, 1962, paperback original, cover by Allison shows star Richard Egan, uncommon. **$10 $35 $100**

Burnett, W. R., *Asphalt Jungle, The*, Pocket Book #6078, third printing 1961, photo cover shows stars of ABC TV series.
$3 $15 $35

Butler, Gerald, *Unafraid, The*, Dell Book #242, 1948, Map Back, cover photo of Burt Lancaster and Joan Fontaine.
$4 $20 $55

Calin, Harold, *Combat: Men, Not Heroes*, Lancer Book #70-060, 1963, paperback original, scarce tie-in with World War II TV series "Combat."
$4 $20 $50

--- *Kings of the Sun*, Lancer Book #70-062, 1963, paperback original, photo

cover shows stars Yul Brynner, George Chakiris, and Shirley Anne Field.
$3 $15 $35

Cameron, Lou, *None But the Brave*, Gold Medal Book #k1511, 1965, paperback original, World War II film, cover shows star Frank Sinatra.
$4 $20 $60

Carpozi Jr., George, *Brigitte Bardot Story, The*, Belmont Book #L504, 1961, paperback original, cover photo shows Bardot, many photos inside.
$10 $35 $100

--- *Clark Gable*, Pyramid Book #R-620, 1962, paperback original, photo cover shows Clark gable, 32 pages of photos.
$10 $25 $75

--- *Marilyn Monroe: Her Own Story*, Belmont Book #L-508, 1961, paperback original. **$10 $45 $125**

Carr, Allan, *Grease: The Cinenovel*, Fotonovel Publications, 1978, first edition thus, photo cover shows stars John Travolta and Olivia Newton-John, all color photos from the film with captions.
$6 $15 $40

Carse, Robert, *Morgan the Pirate*, Dell First Edition #B214, 1961, paperback original, cover by George Gross shows star Steve Reeves.
$3 $18 $40

	G	VG	F			G	VG	F

Cassidy, Bruce, *Rock a Cradle Empty,* Ace Book #51938, 1970, paperback original, photo cover shows star Robert Young, tie-in with "Marcus Welby, MD" TV series. **$3 $12 $25**

Castle, Frank, *Hawaiian Eye,* Dell First Edition #K112, 1962, paperback original, cover by Harry Bennett, 1960s crime TV series.  **$4 $20 $50**

Chandler, Raymond, *Blue Dahlia, The,* Popular Library #043539, 1976, first edition thus, cover shows poster from the film with stars Alan Ladd, Veronica Lake, and William Bendix. **$5 $20 $75**

Charteris, Leslie, *Lady On a Train,* Bonded Book, no number, 1945, paperback original, digest-size, tie-in with Deanna Durbin film. **$12 $75 $145**

Chase, Borden, *Red River,* Bantam Book #205, 1948, tie-in with John Wayne film. **$3 $20 $60**

Christina, Frank and Teresa, *Billy Jack,* Avon Book #N458, 1973, paperback original, photo cover shows star Tom Laughlin, script with introduction by Laughlin, counter-culture film with photos. **$3 $15 $40**

Cleary, Beverly, *Leave It to Beaver,* Berkley Medallion Book #G-406, 1960, paperback original, photo cover shows star Jerry Mathers as "The Beaver." **$5 $20 $60**

Clement, Harry, *Slaughter,* Curtis Book #07263, 1972, paperback original, cover art shows football star/actor Jim Brown; pseudonym of Henry Clement Stubbs, aka Hal Clement. **$3 $15 $40**

Clement, Henry, *By Dawn's Early Light,* Popular Library #00326, 1975, paperback original, photo cover shows star Peter Falk, #4 in series based on "Columbo" TV show; pseudonym of Henry Clement Stubbs. **$4 $20 $50**

Clifford, Francis, *Naked Runner, The,* Signet Book #P3112, 1967, first paperback printing, photo cover shows star Frank Sinatra. **$3 $15 $50**

Cobb, Humphrey, *Paths of Glory,* Dell Book #D-209, 1957, tie-in with Kirk Douglas film. **$5 $25 $75**

Collodi, Carlo, *Walt Disney Tells the Story of Pinocchio,* Whitman Book #556, 1939, paperback original, tie-in with Walt Disney film, illustrated. **$350 $1,000 $2,000**

Cooper, Morton, *Munsters, The,* Avon Book #G1237, 1964, paperback original, photo cover of cast, scarce. **$15 $75 $125**

Crichton, Kyle, *Marx Brothers, The,* Popular Library #410, 1952, cover art shows all five Marx Brothers. **$4 $25 $65**

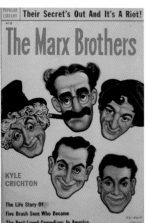

	G	VG	F

Daniels, Norman, *Rat Patrol, The,* Paperback Library #53-387, 1966, paperback original, #1 in series of six novels (five written by David King) in this World War II TV series.
$4 $18 $35

Danne, Max Hallan, *Premature Burial,* Lancer Book #71-313, 1962, paperback original, photo cover shows star Ray Milland; Danne did the screenplay of this Roger Corman horror film based on Edgar Allen Poe story.
$4 $20 $75

David, Peter, *Rocketeer, The,* Bantam Book #29322, 1991, paperback original, cover by Dave Stevens, tie-in with Disney retro film with photos. $3 $15 $40

Davis, J. Madison, *Dead Line,* ibook #49798, 2004, paperback original, first novel based on TV series "Law & Order," photo cover shows stars Elisabeth Rohm, Fred Thompson, Sam Waterston, Jerry Orbach, S. Epatha Merkerson, Jesse L. Martin. 🎞 $3 $10 $25

De Christoforo, Ron, *Grease,* Pocket Book #82235, 1978, paperback original, photo cover shows stars John Travolta and Olivia Newton-John, novelization of script, photos inside.
$4 $15 $40

Demaris, Ovid, *Machine-Gun McCain,* Gold Medal Book #r2230, 1970, film based on his novel Candyleg.
$4 $20 $50

Deming, Richard, *Case of the Courteous Killer, The,* Pocket Book #1198, 1958, paperback original, book #2 of three in "Dragnet" TV series, photo cover shows star Jack Webb.
$5 $20 $75

--- *Case of the Crime King, The,* Pocket Book #1214, 1959, paperback original, book #3 in the "Dragnet" TV series tie-ins, photo cover shows star Jack Webb. 🎞 $6 $30 $90

Devlin, Dean and Emmerich, Roland, *Stargate,* Signet Book #AE8410, 1994, paperback original, novelization of SF film starring Kurt Russell and James Spader. $3 $14 $35

Dick, Philip K., *Blade Runner,* Del Rey Books, #30129, 1982, cover art shows star Harrison Ford from cult film, original title: *Do Androids Dream of Electric Sheep?* 🎞 $5 $25 $75

Dickens, Charles, *Oliver Twist,* Pocket Book #519, 1948, photo cover.
$10 $30 $100

Disch, Thomas M., *Prisoner, The,* Ace Book #67900, 1969, paperback original, photo cover shows star Patrick McGoohan as "Number 6."
$15 $50 $125

Dolinsky, Meyer, *Hot Rod Gang Rumble,* Avon Book #783, 1957, paperback original, JD and racing film, cover shows photo from film. 🎞 $10 $30 $90

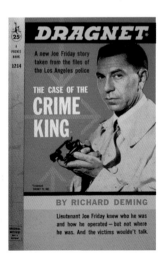

	G	VG	F		G	VG	F

Effinger, George Alec, *Man the Fugitive,* Award Book #AN1373, 1974, paperback original, photo cover shows stars of the CBS TV series "Planet of the Apes"; this is book #1 of at least three books by Effinger, each book:

| | $3 | $14 | $30 |

Ellison, Harlan, *City on the Edge of Forever, The,* Bantam Book #11345, 1978, first edition thus, Star Trek photonovel #1, color photos with captions.

| | $10 | $25 | $85 |

Elman, Richard, *Taxi Driver,* Bantam Book #T2681, third printing 1976, cover art shows stars Robert DeNiro and Jodie Foster. 📷

| | $5 | $25 | $90 |

Emerson, Ru, *Empty Throne, The,* Boulevard Book #00200, 1996, paperback original, photo cover shows star Lucy Lawless as Xena Warrior Princess; Emerson wrote at least three Xena novels, each book:

| | $3 | $14 | $30 |

Fairman, Paul W., *City Under the Sea,* Pyramid Book #R1162, 1965, cover by John Schoenherr, tie-in with "Voyage to the Bottom of the Sea" TV series.

| | $4 | $20 | $55 |

--- *That Girl,* Popular Library #02588, 1971, paperback original, photo cover shows star Marlo Thomas. 📷

| | $4 | $20 | $50 |

--- *World Grabbers, The,* Monarch Book #471, 1964, paperback original, cover by Ralph Brillhart, novel based on "One Step Beyond" TV series. 📷

| | $3 | $15 | $50 |

Fink, Harry Julian, *Major Dundee,* Gold Medal Book #k1519, 1966, paperback original, photo cover shows star Charleton Heston.

| | $4 | $15 | $50 |

Fleischman, A. S., *Blood Alley,* Gold Medal Book #499, 1955, paperback original, cover by Bayre Phillips shows stars John Wayne and Lauren Bacall. 📷

| | $8 | $30 | $100 |

Fleming, Ian, *Chitty Chitty Bang Bang,* Signet Book #T-3705, 1968, first edition thus, tie-in with Dick van Dyke film.

| | $3 | $15 | $40 |

--- *Goldfinger,* Signet Book #D2052, 19th printing 1962, tie-in with Sean Connery James Bond film. 📷

| | $2 | $14 | $32 |

--- *Thunderball,* Signet Book #P2734, 1965, cover by Robert McGinnis.

| | $3 | $18 | $50 |

Fonda, Peter; Hopper, Dennis; and Southern, Terry, Easy Rider, Signet Book #Y4206, 1970, first book edition, cover shows Peter Fonda, script with photos, key counter-culture film.

| | $10 | $30 | $100 |

Was He Saint Or Devil—This Man Who Called
Himself Sri Ahandi?

THE WORLD GRABBERS

A Dramatic, Suspenseful Novel Inspired By The Popular TV Program:
ONE STEP BEYOND

Paul W. Fairman

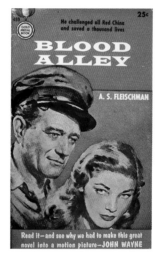

25¢

He challenged all Red China
and saved a thousand lives

BLOOD ALLEY

A. S. FLEISCHMAN

Read it—and see why we had to make this great
novel into a motion picture—JOHN WAYNE

A SIGNET BOOK COMPLETE AND UNABRIDGED

D2052

Ian Fleming

A JAMES BOND THRILLER

Goldfinger

NOW A GREAT MOTION PICTURE

Starring
Sean Connery
as James Bond
and
introducing
Honor Blackman
as Pussy Galore.

A BANTAM GIANT 35¢

Every Book Complete

C. S. FORESTER

Captain Horatio Hornblower

GREGORY PECK
as
"CAPTAIN HORATIO HORNBLOWER"
A WARNER BROS. PRODUCTION
CO-STARRING
VIRGINIA MAYO
Color by TECHNICOLOR

They were the last of the West's
legendary lawless breed—savage men who
lived to kill . . . and killed to live!

The Wild Bunch

Starring William Holden, Robert Ryan, Ernest Borgnine
A major motion picture from Warner Bros.—Seven Arts.   Brian Fox

NOW A SENSATIONAL ABC-TV HIT SERIES!
TV'S TROUBLETRACKING TRIO TAKES
A VIOLENT VACATION IN A PLAYGROUND OF
INTERNATIONAL INTRIGUE!

Charlie's Angels

#3 ANGELS ON A STRING

Created by
IVAN GOFF and BEN ROBERTS
Based on the script by ED LAKSO
Adapted by MAX FRANKLIN

Ballantine Novel 25691/$1.50

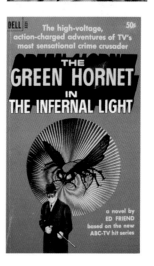

DELL

50¢

The high-voltage,
action-charged adventures of TV's
most sensational crime crusader

THE GREEN HORNET IN THE INFERNAL LIGHT

a novel by
ED FRIEND
based on the new
ABC-TV hit series

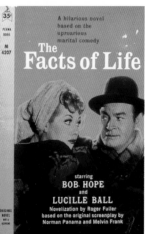

35¢

PERMA
BOOKS

M
4207

A hilarious novel
based on the
uproarious
marital comedy

The Facts of Life

starring
BOB HOPE
and
LUCILLE BALL

Novelization by Roger Fuller
based on the original screenplay by
Norman Panama and Melvin Frank

ORIGINAL
NOVEL

F1410

An original novel based on the ABC-TV
series starring Diana Rigg and Patrick
Macnee as Emma Peel and John Steed

#1

THE AVENGERS

"The Floating Game"

JOHN GARFORTH

| | G | VG | F | | G | VG | F |

Forester, C. S., *Captain Horatio Hornblower*, Bantam Book #A912, 1951, cover by Hy Rubin shows star Gregory Peck, contains three novels. 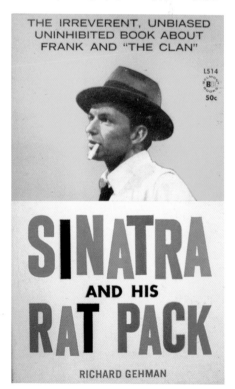 **$4 $15 $35**

Fox, Brian, *Wild Bunch, The*, Award Book #A464X, 1969, paperback original, photo cover shows stars William Holden, Robert Ryan, and Ernest Borgnine; pseudonym of W. T. Ballard. **$6 $30 $75**

Franklin, Max, *Angels on a String*, Ballantine Book #25691, 1977, paperback original, photo cover shows stars of "Charlie's Angels" TV series Kate Jackson, Farrah Fawcett-Majors, and Jaclyn Smith, book #3, novelization of script. **$4 $16 $45**

Frazee, Steve, *Alamo, The*, Avon Book #T-446, 1960, paperback original, photo cover shows stars John Wayne, Richard Widmark, and Lawrence Harvey. **$3 $15 $60**

Friend, Ed, *Alvarez Kelly*, Gold Medal Book #k1732, 1966, paperback original, cover art shows stars William Holden and Richard Widmark. **$3 $15 $40**

--- *Infernal Light, The*, Dell Book #3231, 1966, paperback original, photo cover shows the Green Hornet, based on the TV series. **$10 $35 $100**

Fuller, Roger, *Burke's Law*, Pocket Book #50030, 1964, paperback original, photo cover shows star Gene Barry. **$2 $14 $40**

--- *Facts of Life, The*, Perma Book #M4207, 1960, paperback original, photos cover shows stars Bob Hope and Lucille Ball. **$4 $20 $45**

Fuller, Sam, *Naked Kiss, The*, Belmont Book #L92-596, 1964, paperback original. **$10 $25 $80**

Garforth, John, *Floating Game, The*, Berkley Book #F1410, 1967, paperback original, #1 in the Avengers series, photo cover shows stars Patrick McNee as John Steed and Diana Rigg as Mrs. Peel. **$5 $18 $35**

Garth, Will, *Dr. Cyclops*, Centaur Press #013, 1976, first paperback edition of scarce hardcover, novelization of 1940s horror film. **$8 $30 $85**

Gehman, Richard, *Bogart*, Gold Medal Book #d1572, 1965, paperback original, biography with many photos, cover photo of Humphrey Bogart. **$6 $25 $90**

--- *Sinatra and His Rat Pack*, Belmont Book #L514, 1961, paperback original, photo cover shows Frank Sinatra. **$10 $25 $100**

Gems, Jonathan, *Mars Attacks!*, Signet Book #AE9256, 1996, paperback original, film based on the 1962 SF card series. **$3 $16 $40**

George, Peter, *Dr. Strangelove Or: How I Learned to Stop Worrying and Love the Bomb*, Bantam Book #F-2679, 1964, paperback original, tie-in with the Peter Sellers, George C. Scott film. **$10 $35 $100**

Gibson, William, *Cobweb, The*, Bantam Book #F1337, 1955, in dust jacket, photo cover shows stars Richard Widmark, Lauren Bacall, Charles Boyer, Gloria Graham, rare. **$25 $75 $150**

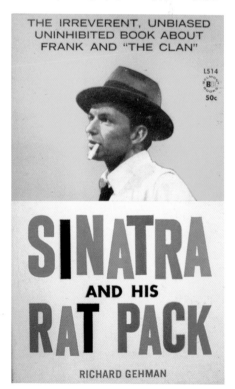

THE IRREVERENT, UNBIASED UNINHIBITED BOOK ABOUT FRANK AND "THE CLAN"

L514

SINATRA AND HIS RAT PACK

RICHARD GEHMAN

	G	VG	F

Goldman, James, *They Might Be Giants,* Lancer Book #74-740, 1970, paperback original, film script, photo cover shows stars George C. Scott and Joanne Woodward in Sherlock Holmes film, scarce.   **$20 $75 $150**

Goodis, David, *Nightfall,* Lion Library #LB131, 1956, back cover photo show stars Aldo Ray and Ann Bancroft.   **$18 $65 $125**

Greene, Graham, *3rd Man, The,* Bantam Book #797, second printing 1950, cover photo shows stars Joseph Cotton and Valli.   **$3 $20 $60**

Gregory, James, *Elvis Presley Story, The,* Hillman Book #130, 1960, paperback original, edited anthology with 32 pages of photos.   **$15 $40 $125**

Grossbach, Robert, *Cheap Detective, The,* Warner Book #89-557, 1978, paperback original, tie-in with Neil Simon film, cover art shows star Peter Falk.    **$3 $12 $30**

Grove, Walt, *Wings of Eagles, The,* Gold Medal Book #649, 1957, paperback original, cover by Barye Phillips shows stars John Wayne, Dan Dailey, and Maureen O'Hara.   **$6 $20 $80**

Haggard, H. Rider, *King Solomon's Mines,* Dell Book #433, 1950, Map Back, photo cover shows stars Deborah Kerr and Stewart Granger.    **$5 $20 $40**

Hamilton, Laurell K., *Star Trek the Next Generation: Nightshade,* Pocket Book #79566, 1992, paperback original, #24 in STNG series.   **$5   15 $50**

Hand, Elizabeth, *Catwoman,* Del Rey Book #47652, 2004, paperback original, photo cover shows star Halle Berry, recent but already collectible.    **$2 $10 $25**

Hardwick, Michael and Mollie, *Private Life of Sherlock Holmes, The,* Bantam Book #55877, 1971, first U. S. edition, cover by Robert McGinnis, tie-in with Billy Wilder Sherlock Holmes film.   **$10 $35 $90**

Hartman, Dane, *Duel For Cannons,* Warner Book #90-793, 1981, paperback original, cover art shows Clint Eastwood on all books, #1 in series of at least 12 books that continue the Dirty Harry story from the films, each: **$4 $20 $55**

Hayes, Joseph, *Desperate Hours, The,* Perma Book #M3007, third printing 1955, classic noir film, photo cover shows stars Humphrey Bogart and Fredric March.   **$5 $18 $45**

Hays, Lee, *Once Upon a Time In America,* Signet Book #AE2839, 1984, paperback original, tie-in with Sergio Leone gangster film starring Robert DeNiro, based on Harry Gray's The Hoods.   **$4 $18 $45**

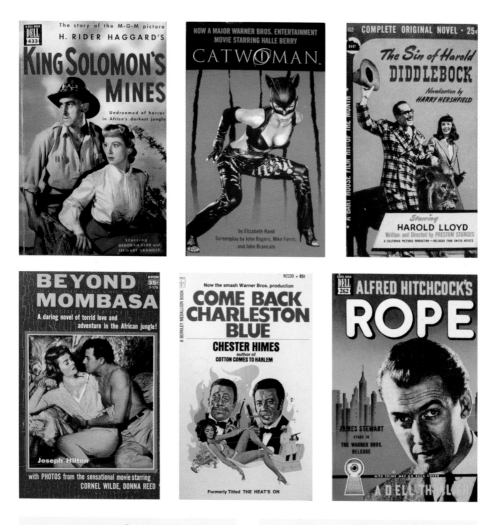

	G	VG	F		G	VG	F

Henrick, Richard P., *Crimson Tide*, Avon Book #78323, 1995, paperback original, photo cover shows stars Denzel Washington and Gene Hackman.
$3 $12 $30

Hershfield, Harry, *Sin of Harold Diddlebock, The*, Bart House #102, 1946, photo cover from film; pseudonym of Walter B. Gibson. 📷
$12 $50 $125

Hiken, Nat, *Sergeant Bilko*, Ballantine Book #229, 1957, paperback original, photo cover of Phil Silvers, two cover versions, each book:
$5 $20 $60

Hilton, Joseph, *Beyond Mombasa*, Avon Book #T-178, 1957, paperback original, photo cover shows stars Cornel Wilde and Donna Reed in steamy embrace. 📷
$4 $20 $45

--- *Cry Baby Killer*, Avon Book #T-230, 1958, paperback original, JD film about a teen-age killer.
$8 $40 $100

Himes, Chester, *Come Back Charleston Blue*, Berkley Book #N2239, 1972, original title *The Heat's On*, cover shows stars Godfrey Cambridge and Raymond St. Jacques. 📷
$8 $20 $65

	G	VG	F

Hine, Al, *Bewitched,* Dell Book #0551, 1965, paperback original, 1960s TV classic.   **$5**   **$20**   **$50**

Hitchcock, Alfred, *Rope,* Dell Book #262, 1948, Map Back, photo cover shows star James Stewart. 🎬 **$8**   **$35**   **$100**

Howard, Vechel, *Last Sunset, The,* Gold Medal Book #s1121, second printing 1961, photo cover shows stars Rock Hudson, Kirk Douglas, Dorothy Malone; pseudonym of Howard Rigsby.
$3   **$20**   **$65**

Huffaker, Clair, *Cowboy,* Gold Medal Book #736, 1958, paperback original, novelization of screenplay, photo cover shows star Glenn Ford. 🎬
$4   **$20**   **$55**

--- *Flaming Star,* Crest Book #S421, 1960, tie-in with Elvis Presley film, no photos.   **$5**   **$25**   **$90**

--- *Posse From Hell,* Crest Book #222, 1958, paperback original, western, tie-in with Audie Murphy film.
$3   **$20**   **$50**

--- *Rio Conchos,* Gold Medal Book #s1459, 1964, movie poster cover, tie-in with Richard Boone and Stuart Whitman film.   **$4**   **$18**   **$35**

--- *Seven Ways From Sundown,* Crest Book #398, 1960, paperback original, tie-in with Audie Murphy and Barry Sullivan film.   **$4**   **$20**   **$50**

--- *War Wagon, The,* Gold Medal Book

#d1807, 1967, western film, cover art shows stars John Wayne and Kirk Douglas.   **$5**   **$20**   **$60**

Huggins, Roy, *77 Sunset Strip,* Dell First Edition #A176, 1959, first book edition, cover by Robert McGinnis, crime TV series.   **$5**   **$20**   **$60**

Hugo, Victor, *Hunchback of Notre Dame, The,* Avon Book #T-190, 1957, photos cover shows stars Gina Lollobrigida and Anthony Quinn. 🎬
$5   **$20**   **$70**

Huie, William Bradford, *Outsider, The,* Signet Book #D2091, 1962, true story of Native American Iwo Jima Marine hero Ira Hayes, photo cover shows star Tony Curtis.   **$4**   **$15**   **$50**

Inge, William, *Bus Stop,* Bantam Book #1518, 1956, photo cover shows star Marilyn Monroe. **$10**   **$40**   **$100**

James, Stuart, *Stranglers of Bombay, The,* Monarch Book #MM601, 1960, paperback original, photo cover, scarce.
$20   **$45**   **$135**

Jenkins, Will F., *Dallas,* Gold Medal Book #126, 1950, paperback original, cover art shows stars Gary Cooper and Ruth Roman. 🎬   **$6**   **$40**   **$100**

Johnston, William, *Captain Nice,* Tempo Book #T-155, 1967, paperback original, photo cover shows star Charles Nelson Rielly, TV series spoofed super heroes.
$3   **$15**   **$30**

	G	VG	F			G	VG	F

--- *Get Smart*, Tempo Book #T-103, 1965, paperback original, photo cover shows Don Adams from "Get Smart" TV spy spoof series. 🎬 **$4** **$15** **$40**

--- *Invaders, The*, Tempo Book #12267, 1973, paperback original, photo cover shows Richie, Potsie, and Fonzie of "Happy Days" TV series, book #3.
$4 **$15** **$35**

--- *Klute*, Paperback Library #64-639, 1971, paperback original, photo cover shows star Jane Fonda.
$3 **$15** **$40**

Kaminsky, Stuart, *Clint Eastwood*, Signet Book #W6159, 1974, paperback original, cover art shows Clint Eastwood, actor biography with photos, mystery author's first book. **$6** **$30** **$75**

Kane, Henry, *Peter Gunn*, Dell First Edition #B155, 1960, paperback original, photo cover shows star Craig Stevens, private eye TV series. **$4** **$20** **$75**

Karmel, Alex, *Something Wild*, Belmont Book #212, 1960, cover art shows star Carroll Baker. 🎬 **$6** **$30** **$75**

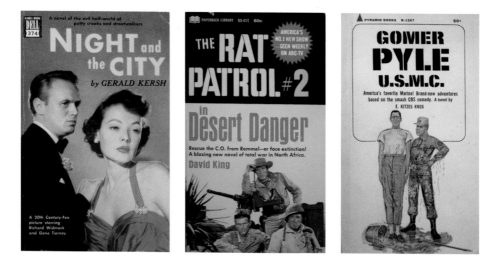

	G	VG	F

Kaufman, Michael T., *Mean Streets,* Award Book #AQ1256, 1974, paperback original, tie-in with Martin Scorsese cult crime film. **$10 $30 $100**

Kerouac, Jack, *Subterraneans, The,* Avon Book #T-390, reprint 1959, tie-in with Beat film. **$5 $35 $90**

Kersh, Gerald, *Night and the City,* Dell Book #374, 1950, Map Back, noir film, photo cover shows stars Richard Widmark and Gene Tierney.  **$4 $20 $65**

King, David, *Desert Danger,* Paperback Library #53-411, 1967, paperback original, photo cover shows stars of TV series "The Rat Patrol," this is #2 of at least six books, all but #1 written by King (#1 was written by Norman Daniels), each:  **$5 $20 $40**

King, Stephen, *Green Mile, The,* Pocket Book #04178, no date, fifth printing 1999, film tie-in edition, photo cover shows star Tom Hanks.
$3 $14 $30

Knight, David, *Dragnet Case No. 561,* Pocket Book #1120, 1956, paperback original, photo cover shows star Jack Webb, book #1 in series of three (also see Richard Deming); pseudonym of Richard S. Prather.
$4 $25 $55

Knox, E. Kitzes, *Gomer Pyle U.S.M.C.,* Pyramid Book #R-1267, 1965, paperback original, cover by Darrell Greene shows stars Jim Nabors and Frank Sutton.
$10 $40 $100

Krepps, Robert, *Boys' Night Out,* Gold Medal Book #s1211, 1961, paperback original, cover photo of stars Kim Novak, James Garner, Tony Randall.
$3 $15 $50

--- *El Cid,* Gold Medal Book #d1169, 1961, paperback original, cover photo of stars Sophia Loren and Charleton Heston.    **$4 $20 $50**

--- *Taras Bulba,* Gold Medal Book #s1253, 1962, paperback original, cover art shows stars Yul Brynner and Tony Curtis.   **$3 $16 $45**

L'Amour, Louis, *Heller With a Gun,* Gold Meal Book #955, second printing 1960, photo cover shows stars Anthony Quinn and Sophia Loren (as a blonde).
$8 $40 $100

--- *Hondo,* Gold Medal Book #347, 1953, paperback original, back cover shows star John Wayne. **$20 $70 $200**

--- *Tall Stranger, The,* Gold Medal Book #700, 1957, paperback original.
$10 $70 $155

Landon, Christopher, *Hot Sands of Hell, The,* Zenith Book #ZB-43, 1960, World War II war film.    **$3 $15 $35**

	G	VG	F		G	VG	F

Lane, Sheldon, *For Bond Lovers Only,* Dell Book #2672, 1966, photo cover shows Ursula Andress, includes Ian Fleming, Sean Connery, Raymond Chandler, Len Deighton, photos inside of Bond women. 📷 **$5 $25 $55**

Laumer, Keith, *Invaders, The,* Pyramid Book #R-1664, 1967, paperback original, photo cover shows star Roy Thinnes, SF TV series. **$3 $12 $30**

Lay Jr., Beiren and Bartlett, Sy, *Twelve O'Clock High,* Bantam Book #743, 1949, cover by Hy Rubin shows film star Gregory Peck. 📷 **$3 $20 $50**

Leasor, James, *Where the Spies Are,* Signet Book #P2839, 1966, cover art shows star David Niven, a James Bond spy spoof. **$3 $20 $40**

Lee, C. Y., *Flower Drum Song, The,* Dell Book #F-175, second printing 1961, cover by Victor Kalin, Rogers & Hammerstein musical film. 📷 **$3 $15 $40**

Lee, Elsie, *Blood Red Oscar, The,* Lancer Book #71-312, 1962, paperback original, photo cover. **$10 $30 $100**

--- *Muscle Beach Party,* Lancer Book #70-073, 1964, paperback original, photo cover. **$15 $40 $135**

Lee, Linda, *Bruce Lee: The Man Only I Knew,* Warner Book #76774, 1975, paperback original, photo cover shows Bruce Lee, many photos. **$10 $20 $65**

Lehman, Ernest, *Sweet Smell of Success,* Signet Book #S1413, 1957, brutal noir, photo cover shows stars Tony Curtis and Burt Lancaster. 📷 **$4 $20 $65**

Leiber, Fritz, *Burn Witch Burn,* Berkley Book #F621, 1962, photo cover, horror movie tie-in, original title *Conjure Wife.* 📷 **$10 $30 $75**

Leinster, Murray, *Land of the Giants,* Pyramid Book #X1846, 1968, paperback original, science fiction TV series; pseudonym of Will F. Jenkins. **$3 $15 $40**

Le May, Alan, *Unforgiven, The,* Crest Book #S244, 1959, western film, photo cover shows stars Burt Lancaster, Audrey Hepburn. 📷 **$4 $20 $50**

Leslie, Peter, *Finger in the Sky Affair, The,* Ace Book #51706, 1966, paperback original, photo cover, #23 in the Man From U.N.C.L.E. TV series. **$10 $35 $100**

Lewis, Herschell G., *Color Me Blood Red,* Novel Book #7N-729, 1964, paperback original, photo cover, horror film tie-in; pseudonym of Herschell Gordon Lewis, also see Blood Feast by L. E. Murphy. **$40 $120 $225**

--- *Two Thousand Maniacs,* Novel Book #7N-719, 1964, paperback original, horror film tie-in and rarest of his three books. **$55 $150 $250**

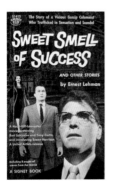

	G	VG	F		G	VG	F

Lewis, Sinclair, *Elmer Gantry*, Dell Book #S10, 1960, cover art shows star Burt Lancaster.   **$2**   **$14**   **$35**

Lipsky, Eleazar, *Kiss of Death, The*, Penguin Book #642, second printing 1947, movie tie-in with film stills, scarce.
   $40   **$85**   **$250**

Loomis, Noel, *Have Gun Will Travel*, Dell First Edition #A156, 1960, paperback original, cover by Robert Stanley shows star Richard Boone. 📷
   $4   **$20**   **$60**

--- *Johnny Concho*, Gold Medal Book #s587, 1956, paperback original, photo cover of star Frank Sinatra. 📷
   $10   **$35**   **$90**

Lovelace, Delos W., *King Kong*, Bantam Book #F-3093, 1965, novelization of the Edgar Wallace and Merian C. Cooper film. 📷   **$8**   **$30**   **$100**

--- *King Kong*, Ace Book #44470, 1976, cover by Frank Frazetta, reprints above

novelization for film remake.
   $5   **$20**   **$75**

Lucas, George, *Star Wars*, Ballantine Book #26061, 1976, paperback original, cover by Ralph McQuarie, ghost-written by Alan Dean Foster, predates the first Star Wars film.   **$12**   **$35**   **$125**

Lyon, Winston, *Batman vs the Fearsome Foursome*, Signet Book #D2995, 1966, paperback original, photo cover shows stars Adam West as Batman and Burt Ward as Robin, tie-in with 1960s film.
   $10   **$30**   **$80**

--- *Batman vs 3 Villains of Doom*, Signet Book #D2940, 1966, paperback original, photo cover shows star Adam West as Batman, tie-in with "Batman" TV series. 📷   **$6**   **$25**   **$75**

MacLean, Alistair, *Guns of Navarone, The*, Perma Book #M4089, 1961, photo cover shows stars Gregory Peck, David Niven, and Anthony Quinn.
   $3   **$15**   **$35**

  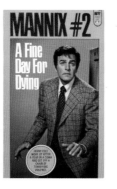 

	G	VG	F		G	VG	F

Malis, Jody Cameron, *Dark Shadows Cookbook, The,* Ace Book #13810, 1970, paperback original, anthology of recipes, tie-in with TV series.
$12 $50 $135

Marshall, Edison, *Viking, The,* Dell Book #F67, second printing 1958, cover by George Gross shows star Kirk Douglas. **$4 $20 $60**

Marshall, S. L. A., *Pork Chop Hill,* Perma Book #M4115, 1958, Korean War film, photo cover shows star Gregory Peck.
$5 $15 $40

Martin, Pete, *Will Acting Spoil Marilyn Monroe?,* Cardinal Book #C-248, 1957, photo cover of Marilyn Monroe, includes 43 inside photos. **$12 $45 $120**

Marx, Groucho, *Groucho and Me,* Dell Book #F-112, 1960, photo cover of Groucho, autobiography.
$4 $15 $50

Matheson, Richard, *Omega Man, The,* Berkley Book #S2041, 1971, first printing this title, movie edition of his novel *I Am Legend,* cover art shows star Charleton Heston. **$5 $20 $65**

--- *Somewhere in Time,* Ballantine Book #28900, 1980, photo cover shows star Christopher Reeve, retitle of his novel, *Bid Time Return.* **$10 $30 $85**

McCargo, J. T., *Fine Day For Dying, A,* Belmont Book #50823, 1975, paperback original, photo cover shows Mannix star Michael Conners, author is Peter Rabe. **$4 $20 $60**

McCulley, Johnston, *Mark of Zorro, The,* Dell Book #D-204, 1957, cover by Victor Kalin, tie-in with the TV series.
$5 $25 $70

Miksch, W. F., *Addams Family Strikes Back, The,* Pyramid Book #R-1257, 1965, paperback original, cover photo shows stars, very scarce. **$25 $75 $175**

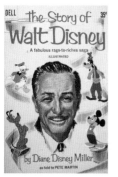 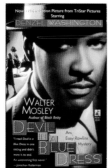 

	G	VG	F		G	VG	F

Millard, Joe, *For a Few Dollars More,* Award Book #A236F, 1967, paperback original, cover art shows star Clint Eastwood.  **$9 $25 $90**

--- *Good, the Bad, the Ugly, The,* Award Book #A274X, 1967, paperback original, cover art shows star Clint Eastwood. **$6 $30 $100**

Miller, Diane Disney, *Story of Walt Disney, The,* Dell Book #D266, 1959, cover by Dempster shows Disney surrounded by his creations, inside photos. **$6 $25 $65**

Millus, John, *Wind and the Lion, The,* Award Book #AQ1468, 1975, paperback original, tie-in with Sean Connery and Candice Bergen film. **$3 $12 $30**

Mosley, Walter, *Devil In a Blue Dress,* Pocket Book #51142, 11th paperback printing 1995, photo cover shows star Denzel Washington. **$3 $14 $35**

Mulford, Clarence, *Hopalong Cassidy, Dell,* no number, 1947, photo cover, digest-size. **$20 $85 $175**

Murphy, Audie, *To Hell and Back,* Perma Book #M-4029, eighth printing 1955, World War II's most decorated hero, his true story made into film, photo cover shows Audie Murphy. **$3 $15 $40**

Murphy, L. E., *Blood Feast,* Novel Book #7N-710, 1963, paperback original, horror film tie-in; pseudonym of Herschell Gordon Lewis. **$40 $100 $225**

Neutzel, Charles, *Queen of Blood,* Greenleaf Classics #GC-206, 1966, paperback original, includes photos from the film. **$75 $150 $350**

O'Neill, James, *Molly Maguires, The,* Gold Medal Book #r1268, 1969, paperback original, cover art shows stars Sean Connery, Richard Harris, Samantha Eggar. **$3 $14 $40**

Oram, John, *Stone-Cold Dead in the Market Affair, The,* Ace Book #51705, 1966, paperback original, photo cover, #22 in the Man From U.N.C.L.E. series. **$10 $40 $100**

Owen, Dean, *End of the World,* Ace Book #D-548, 1962, paperback original, atomic war film and novel, photo cover shows star Ray Milland. **$5 $20 $65**

--- *Konga,* Monarch Book #MM604, 1960, paperback original. **$15 $40 $125**

--- *Reptilicus,* Monarch Book #MM605, 1961, paperback original, photo cover of dinosaur. **$15 $55 $135**

	G	VG	F		G	VG	F

Packer, Eleanor, *Private Lives of the Movie Stars,* LA Bantam #17, 1940, paperback original, rare. **$65 $150 $255**

Payne, Robert, *Barbarian and the Geisha, The,* Signet Book #S1513, 1958, paperback original, cover by Barye Phillips shows stars John Wayne, Eiko Ando. 🎥 **$3 $20 $50**

Pearl, Jack, *Our Man Flint,* Pocket Book #50243, 1965, paperback original, photo cover shows star James Coburn. **$3 $15 $40**

Pearlman, Gilbert, *Young Frankenstein,* Ballantine Book, no number, 1975, paperback original, special book club edition, cover shows film poster with stars Gene Wilder, Peter Boyle. 🎥 **$3 $16 $35**

Petrov, David Michael, *Making of Superman the Movie, The,* Warner Book #82-565, 1978, paperback original, photo cover shows star Christopher Reeve as Superman, inside photos. **$3 $18 $40**

Queen, Ellery, *Study In Terror, A,* Lancer Book #73-469, 1966, paperback original, Sherlock Holmes vs Jack the Ripper film, ghost-written by Paul W. Fairman. **$12 $40 $100**

Racina, Thom, *Sweet Revenge,* Berkley Book #3559X, 1977, paperback original, novel based on the "Baretta" TV series, photo cover shows star Robert Blake. **$4 $20 $65**

Rattigan, Terrence, *Separate Tables,* Signet Book #S1609, 1959, first paperback printing, photo cover shows stars Rita Heyworth, Deborah Kerr, David Niven, and Burt Lancaster, with photos inside. **$3 $14 $35**

Rice, Jeff, *Night Strangler, The,* Pocket Book #78352, 1974, paperback original, novel based on the Richard Matheson screenplay of the TV horror crime series, this is the second book in the series. **$8 $30 $100**

Richards, Tad, *Blazing Saddles,* Warner Book #76-536, 1974, paperback original, novel of the Mel Brooks film, photos inside. 🎥 **$4 $20 $50**

Robertson, Frank, *Rawhide,* Signet Book #S1910, 1961, paperback original, cover shows Clint Eastwood for first time as Rowdy Yates. **$10 $25 $75**

Rock, Phillip, *Dirty Harry,* Bantam Book #S7329, 1971, paperback original, tie-in with film, photo cover shows star Clint Eastwood. **$5 $30 $100**

--- *tick...tick...tick,* Popular Library #08117, 1970, paperback original, racial-oriented film about a black sheriff in Southern town, photo cover shows stars Jim Brown and George Kennedy. **$3 $15 $35**

Ross, Leonard Q., *Dark Corner, The,* Century Mystery #31, 1945, digest-size, cover by Malcolm Smith shows stars Lucille Ball, Clifton Webb. 🎥 **$20 $75 $180**

	G	VG	F		G	VG	F

Rovin, Jeff, *H. P. Lovecraft's Re-Animator,* Pocket Book #63723, 1987, paperback original, Rovin novelizes Lovecraft's story, photo cover from film.

	$4	$15	$45

Ryan, Kevin, *Van Helsing,* Pocket Star Book #93540, 2004, paperback original, photo cover shows star Hugh Jackman.

	$2	$10	$20

Ryan, Patrick, *How I Won the War,* Ballantine Book #U6110, 1967, photo cover shows film's star and Beatle John Lennon.

	$6	$30	$75

Sabatini, Rafael, *Fortunes of Captain Blood, The,* Popular Library #241, 1950, cover by Rudolph Belarski, mentions the Louis Hayward film on the cover. 📷

	$4	$15	$50

Saunders, David, *M Squad,* Belmont Book #91-254, 1962, paperback original, photo cover shows star Lee Marvin; pseudonym of Dan Sontup.

	$4	$15	$40

Schulman, Arnold, *Hole In the Head, A,* Gold Medal Book #891, 1959, paperback original, photo cover shows stars Frank Sinatra and Carolyn Jones.

	$4	$20	$50

Semple Jr., Lorenzo, *King Kong,* Ace Book #44472, 1977, paperback original, cover art by Frank Frazetta. 📷

	$5	$20	$75

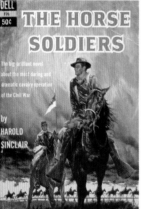

	G	VG	F

Serling, Rod, *New Stories From the Twilight Zone,* Bantam Book #A2412, 1962, first book edition, photo cover shows Rod Serling, collection.
| | $3 | $14 | $35 |

Sharkey, Jack, *Addams Family, The,* Pyramid Book #R-1229, 1965, paperback original, photo cover, the first of two tie-in paperbacks for the popular TV series.  $12 $35 $100

Shaw, Sam, *Marilyn Monroe As the Girl,* Ballantine Book #108, 1955, paperback original, photo cover shows Marilyn Monroe from the film *The Seven Year Itch.* $60 $125 $320

Shulman, Irving, *Amboy Dukes, The,* Avon Book #169, reprint 1949, JD novel and film tie-in with the film *City Across the River.* $4 $15 $40

Sinclair, Harold, *Horse Soldiers, The,* Dell Book #F-76, 1959, cover art by Robert McGinnis shows star John Wayne. $5 $20 $65

Slesar, Henry, *20 Million Miles to Earth,* Amazing Stories SF novel, no number, 1957, paperback original, digest-size, photo cover, author's first book, scarce. $50 $200 $600

Sneider, Vern, *Teahouse of the August Moon, The,* Signet Book #S1348, 1956, cover art by Stanley Zuckerberg, tie-in with Marlon Brando film. $5 $20 $50

Southern, Terry, *Magic Christian, The,* Bantam Book #S5432, third printing 1970, movie edition, photo cover shows stars Peter Sellers, Ringo Starr, and Raquel Welch. $4 $30 $100

Spearman, Frank H., *Whispering Smith,* Popular Library #185, 1949, cover mentions film starring Alan Ladd. $4 $15 $45

Spillane, Mickey, *I, the Jury,* Signet Book #699, 36th printing 1954, back cover shows photos from the film with Biff Elliot as Mike Hammer. $4 $14 $35

--- *I, the Jury,* Signet Book #AE1396, 1981, photo cover shows star Armand Assante as Mike Hammer. $5 $12 $28

Stark, Richard, *Split, The,* Gold Medal Book #d1997, 1966, first edition thus, original title *The Seventh,* cover art by Robert McGinnis, mentions the film; pseudonym of Donald Westlake. $8 $30 $75

Steinbeck, John, *Pearl, The,* Bantam Book #131, 1947, with film photos. $5 $15 $50

--- *Red Pony, The,* Bantam Book #402, 1948, photo cover shows stars Robert Mitchum, Myrna Loy. $6 $20 $65

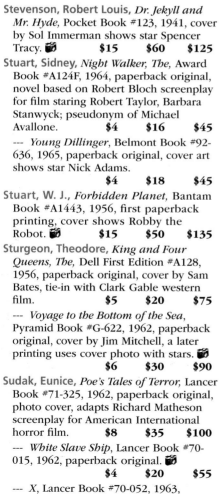

	G	VG	F		G	VG	F

Stevenson, Robert Louis, *Dr. Jekyll and Mr. Hyde*, Pocket Book #123, 1941, cover by Sol Immerman shows star Spencer Tracy. 📷 **$15 $60 $125**

Stuart, Sidney, *Night Walker, The*, Award Book #A124F, 1964, paperback original, novel based on Robert Bloch screenplay for film staring Robert Taylor, Barbara Stanwyck; pseudonym of Michael Avallone. **$4 $16 $45**

--- *Young Dillinger*, Belmont Book #92-636, 1965, paperback original, cover art shows star Nick Adams.
$4 $18 $45

Stuart, W. J., *Forbidden Planet*, Bantam Book #A1443, 1956, first paperback printing, cover shows Robby the Robot. 📷 **$15 $50 $135**

Sturgeon, Theodore, *King and Four Queens, The*, Dell First Edition #A128, 1956, paperback original, cover by Sam Bates, tie-in with Clark Gable western film. **$5 $20 $75**

--- *Voyage to the Bottom of the Sea*, Pyramid Book #G-622, 1962, paperback original, cover by Jim Mitchell, a later printing uses cover photo with stars. 📷
$6 $30 $90

Sudak, Eunice, *Poe's Tales of Terror*, Lancer Book #71-325, 1962, paperback original, photo cover, adapts Richard Matheson screenplay for American International horror film. **$8 $35 $100**

--- *White Slave Ship*, Lancer Book #70-015, 1962, paperback original. 📷
$4 $20 $55

--- *X*, Lancer Book #70-052, 1963, paperback original, photo cover shows

star Ray Milland, Roger Corman film. 📷
$10 $40 $100

Taylor, Rosemary, *Chicken Every Sunday*, Pocket Book #321, 1945, in dust jacket.
$20 $50 $120

Telfair, Richard, *Sundance*, Gold Medal Book #999, 1960, paperback original, based on the CBS TV western series; pseudonym of Richard Jessup.
$3 $15 $40

--- *Target For Tonight*, Dell First Edition #K111, 1962, paperback original, cover by Bob Abbett, tie-in to "Danger Man" TV series (Secret Agent) with star Patrick McGoohan. **$3 $15 $50**

Terry, William, *Hannie Caulder*, Pinnacle Book #P094N, 1974, first U. S. edition, tie-in with film, photo cover of star Raquel Welch. **$5 $20 $50**

Tevis, Walter, *Hustler, The*, Dell Book #3940, 1964, photo cover show stars Paul Newman, Jackie Gleason.
$5 $30 $75

Thom, Robert, *Wild in the Streets*, Pyramid Book #X1798, 1968, paperback original, youth cult film. 📷 **$5 $20 $60**

Thomey, Tedd, *Loves of Errol Flynn, The*, Monarch Book #K58, 1962, paperback original, photo cover of Flynn.
$5 $25 $75

Thompson, Jim, *Ironside*, Popular Library #60-2444, 1967, paperback original, TV, cover photo of Raymond Burr.
$8 $25 $90

--- *Nothing But a Man*, Popular Library #08116, 1970, paperback original, crime film. **$10 $40 $135**

	G	VG	F

--- *Undefeated, The,* Popular Library #60-8104, 1969, paperback original, cover photo shows John Wayne, Rock Hudson. **$10 $30 $90**

Thurman, Steve, *"Mad Dog" Coll,* Monarch Book #MM607, 1961, paperback original, photo cover from film; pseudonym of Frank Castle.  **$8 $30 $100**

Tidyman, Ernest, *High Plains Drifter,* Bantam Book #S7816, 1973, paperback original, cover by Lou Feck shows star Clint Eastwood. **$8 $25 $100**

Tiger, John, *Code Name: Little Ivan,* Popular Library #60-2464, 1969, paperback original, #4 in the Mission Impossible series, photo cover shows star Peter Graves; pseudonym of Walter Wager. **$4 $15 $35**

--- *Mission Impossible,* Popular Library #60-8042, 1967, paperback original, #1 in series, photo cover shows star Martin Landau. **$4 $14 $35**

--- *Wipeout,* Popular Library #60-2180, 1967, paperback original, #4 in I Spy series of seven novels written by Tiger, all but this one have photo covers that show stars Bill Cosby and Robert Culp, each book: **$4 $15 $30**

Turner, Robert, *Scout, The,* Pocket Book #1216, 1958, paperback original, cover by Lou Marchetti, novel based on NBC western TV series "Wagon Train," the inspiration for Star Trek. **$3 $20 $60**

	G	VG	F

Van Arnam, Dave and Archer, Ron, *Lost In Space,* Pyramid Book #X1679, 1967, paperback original, photo cover shows robot, Ron Archer is a pseudonym for Dave Van Arnam. **$5 $20 $60**

Van Hise, Della, *Killing Time,* Pocket Book #554271, 1985, paperback original, cover art by Boris Vellajo shows Spock, tie-in with "Star Trek" TV series, book recalled and pulped because of problems with main characters, scarce. **$15 $40 $100**

Vowell, David H., *Dragnet 1968, Popular Library #60-8045,* 1967, paperback original, second TV series, photos cover shows stars Jack Webb and Harry Morgan. **$4 $20 $45**

Wallace, Lew, *Ben-Hur,* Cardinal Book #GC-75, 1959, photo cover, historical novel made into film with Charlton Heston.  **$5 $18 $60**

Ward, Don, *Gunsmoke,* Ballantine Book #236, 1957, paperback original, cover photo of James Arness, Western TV series. **$6 $35 $100**

--- *Gunsmoke,* Ballantine Book #364K, 1960, photo cover. **$4 $20 $55**

Watkin, Lawrence Edward, *Darby O'Gill and the Little People,* Dell First Edition #A181, 1959, paperback original, a Walt Disney film, introduction by Disney, photo cover. **$4 $20 $50**

	G	VG	F

Wellman, Manly Wade, *Double Life, A,* Century Book #68, 1947, paperback original, cover shows star Ronald Colman. 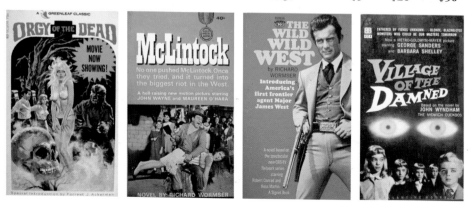 **$12 $60 $145**

Wells, H. G., *War of the Worlds, The,* Pocket Book #947, 1953, photo cover from film. **$5 $20 $65**

Westheimer, David, *Von Ryan's Express,* Signet Book #T2566, fifth printing 1965, cover photo of Frank Sinatra. **$4 $15 $50**

Weverka, Robert, *Easter Story, The,* Bantam Book #Q2411, 1976, paperback original, third book based on "The Waltons" TV series. **$3 $15 $30**

--- *Sting, The,* Bantam Book #08272, 1974, paperback original, cover by Amsel shows stars Paul Newman and Robert Redford. **$3 $15 $40**

Whittington, Harry, *Doomsday Affair, The,* Ace Book #G-560, 1965, paperback original, photo cover, #2 in the Man From U.N.C.L.E. series. **$10 $30 $85**

--- *Fall of the Roman Empire, The,* Gold Medal Book #d1385, 1964, paperback original, photo cover. **$10 $20 $75**

Wilder, Billy and Diamond, I.A.L., *Some Like It Hot,* Signet Book #S-1656, 1959, paperback original, cover photo shows stars Marilyn Monroe, Jack Lemmon, Tony Curtis, photos inside. **$25 $75 $175**

Willeford, Charles, *Cockfighter,* Avon Book #20495, 1974, first edition thus of revised text, photo cover shows star Warren Oates, scarce. **$25 $75 $150**

Williams, Tennessee, *Cat on a Hot Tin Roof,* Signet Book #S1590, 1958, cover photo shows stars Elizabeth Taylor, Paul Newman. **$10 $20 $90**

--- *Streetcar Named Desire, A,* Signet Book #917, 1951, cover by Thomas Hart Benton, tie-in to the film, back cover photo of Vivien Leigh as Blanche DuBois. **$8 $25 $90**

--- *Suddenly Last Summer,* Signet Book #S1757, 1960, photo cover of Elizabeth Taylor in her prime. **$6 $20 $60**

--- *Sweet Bird of Youth,* Signet Book #D2095, 1962, photo cover shows stars Paul Newman, Geraldine Page. **$4 $15 $50**

Wood Jr., Ed, *Orgy of the Dead,* Greenleaf Classics #GC-205, 1966, paperback original, horror film, contains photos, scarce in condition. **$90 $250 $650**

Wormser, Richard, *McLintock,* Gold Medal Book #k1350, 1963, paperback original, photo cover shows star John Wayne spanking Maureen O'Hara. **$5 $20 $65**

--- *Wild Wild West, The,* Signet Book #D2836, 1966, paperback original, photo cover shows star Robert Conrad. **$5 $25 $90**

Wyndham, John, *Village of the Damned,* Ballantine Book #453K, second printing 1960, photo cover shows kids from the film. **$5 $20 $50**

SOCIAL ISSUES:
Sex, Drugs, Juvenile Delinquents and Much More

For many readers and collectors this chapter will be the most interesting and important section of this book. It features paperbacks sensitive to issues of political correctness and offers images of some of the most outrageous and exploitative cover art, titles, and content. You never see books like these anymore, for good or ill.

What I call "social issues" takes in a broad area. It reflects a time of social change in America that was written about in many of the paperbacks from

A SHAMEFUL PATH LED HER THERE—SCARLET SECRETS KEPT HER THERE

35¢

(HOUSE OF FURY)

REFORM SCHOOL GIRL

FELICE SWADOS

Diversey Romance Novel

1

COMPLETE AND UNABRIDGED

the 1940s through the 1970s, and was featured on the covers of the books. The issues examined in these books include sexual issues of all kinds, also promiscuous sex and experimentation, lesbianism, and various other areas of sexual expression in keeping with the sexual revolution. Needless to say, many of these books were very popular with the predominantly male paperback readers during those years – and today.

Also included here are paperbacks on other collectible sub-genres such as juvenile delinquency (gangs, cellar clubs, rumbles), drug use, the Beats (1950s beatnik culture), and racial topics (including interracial relationships). There was also an entire genre of Southern rural sexy women books, mainly due to the success of Erskine Caldwell's *Tobacco Road*. These culminated in the ever popular and endlessly numerous books that feature "bad girls" in the cover art. You'll recognize these women: They're the ones with low-cut blouses, tight skirts, come-on looks, and the ever-present cigarette in hand. These covers, often called "good-girl art" or "pin-up" art, were popular with readers in their heyday and are just as popular today. In some cases the cover art is the only thing that sells these books, some of which are exploitative and often politically incorrect by today's standards. However, books in the social issues category should be looked at by us today as time capsules of their era, and their cover art as postcards from the past, images from the world the way it once was, with all its good and ill aspects.

And there were serious ill aspects. Racially insensitive titles were few and far between, but they did exist, part of the warts of the times. Thus we have books with "insensitive" titles or cover art offensive to Hispanics, Mexicans in particular, using terms such as "wetback." There are also books offensive to African-Americans, such as *Nigger Heaven*, and Asians, notably *12 Chinks and a Woman*. That some of these books, such as the two mentioned, actually told stories that were somewhat sympathetic to the plight of immigrants and blacks, was of little recompense to the many offended by them.

There are also books about gay males and lesbians that exploited their sexual preferences and showed doomed lives with punishment as the only result of their "sin." Lesbian novels abounded, but many were written by men for the fantasy titillation of other men. With the advent of lesbian novelists in the 1950s, such as Marijane Meaker (who wrote as Vin Packer and Ann Aldrich), Ann Bannon, and Valerie Taylor, sensitive and truthful books about these female relationships were published. Mass market gay male literature was much less common and relegated to the shadows until the 1960s, but here also authors like Victor J. Banis did much pioneer work. All of these books are important relics of our collective culture, encompassing the literary and publishing history of our nation and its people.

The astonishing number of books with "girl," "sin," or "virgin" in the title was a coded come-on to male readers that there might be some sex in the book. In those days readers were obsessed with finding and reading "the good parts" in a hot bestseller like *Peyton Place*. Sexy and "sleaze" books proclaimed they were made up only of the good parts! Actually, even the sexiest books in those days, ones with the most overtly sexual cover art or titles, always promised more than they delivered.

This leads us to two hot areas of paperback collecting today, the sexy digests of the 1950s and the soft-core "sleaze" paperbacks of the 1960s. It was a time when sex was taboo and writing about it with too much realism, passion, or vivid description could get you sent to prison, so writers used innuendo and euphemism to tell their stories. For instance, breasts might be described as "golden mounds" and the sex act was called "heated passion" or "untamed lust" – and that's about as far as it could go regardless of the book title, cover art, or what the blurbs said. Nothing of an explicit nature was ever written in these books during that era (nor could it have been by law – and in those days you could be arrested and go to jail for such offenses), so writers and publishers were very careful. However, while the sex in these books looks tame in hindsight today, at the time it was considered very sexy by readers.

The cover art, while often sleazy (hence the term "sleaze"), never displayed full nudity. In fact, you can see more on any public beach these days than was ever shown in the cover art on these books from the 1950s and 1960s. While many of the books appeared to be overtly sexual and explicit, they were not. However, the cover art gave that impression – it could be stark, harsh, passionate, sexy, and sometimes brutal. Some of it was just crude, in image, title, or the rendering of the images, and there was also violence. It all worked to give many of these paperbacks the overall appearance of being sleazy – or, more accurately, soft-core adult books.

With the 1960s came social change, and paperbacks reflected that change. This social change included the Vietnam War, hippie movement, rock music, women's movement, sexual revolution, civil rights movement, gay movement, and their diversity and sundry sub-cultures were reflected in these books.

The little-known secret today is that many famous and popular writers wrote in this genre for quick money. Most wrote a bit too quickly and were ashamed of their work or denied it because of the topics. They didn't want it known that they wrote these books. Other authors were proud of their work or at least did quality work as the professionals they were. This was, after all, throw-away literature of the lowest variety, and none of the authors were ever paid much, usually only a few hundred dollars per book. Some authors described the writing process here as nothing more than "creative typing." They did it to put food on the table or extra cash in their pockets. They wrote under pseudonyms or house names. Today many people would be surprised to learn the names of the big-name authors who were behind some bylines. They include Harlan Ellison (Paul Merchant), Lawrence Block (Sheldon Lord), Evan Hunter (Dean Hudson), Robert Silverberg (Don Elliott, L. T. Woodward), Donald Westlake (Alan Marshall), Marion Zimmer Bradley, and many others.

These books also feature some of the most incredible cover art ever seen in its time. With titles and topics that are just outrageous and amazing, these paperbacks have it all for many collectors. They exist as great fun, are sometimes campy, often naïve, but always fascinating.

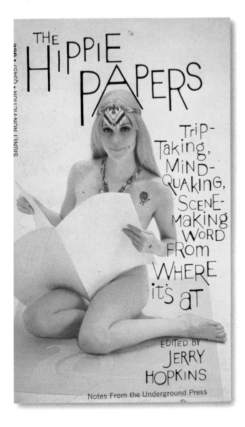

	G	VG	F

Albert, Sim, *Vice Girl,* Berkley Book #G-244, 1959, paperback original, photo cover shows bad-girl with cigarette, "Doris always made sex pay." — **$5 $25 $65**

--- *Woman-Crazy Doctor,* Croydon Book #73, 1954, paperback original, cover by Lou Marchetti, digest-size. **$14 $65 $120**

Aldrich, Ann, *Carol in a Thousand Cities,* Gold Medal Book #d1009, 1960, first book edition, photo cover, lesbian anthology; pseudonym of Marijane Meaker. **$10 $60 $150**

--- *Take a Lesbian to Lunch,* MacFadden Book #125-118, 1971, paperback original, lesbian. **$90 $200 $500**

--- *We Too Must Love,* Gold Medal Book #s727, 1958, paperback original, cover by John Floherty, lesbian. **$15 $65 $125**

--- *We Too Won't Last,* Gold Medal Book #k1313, 1963, paperback original, lesbian. **$12 $50 $125**

--- *We Walk Alone,* Gold Medal Book #509, 1955, paperback original, lesbian anthology. **$10 $40 $120**

Alexander, Marsha, *Sexual Paradise of LSD, The,* Brandon House #1067, 1967, paperback original, mixes sex and drugs. **$15 $65 $155**

Algren, Nelson, *Jungle, The,* Avon Book #T-324, 1959, cover by Darcy, JD novel. **$5 $20 $50**

--- *Man With the Golden Arm, The,* Cardinal Book #C-31, 1951, in dust jacket with needle cover art, drug book. **$25 $100 $200**

--- *Never Come Morning,* Avon Book #185, 1948, JD novel, you'd never know it by the cover art, but this is a novel about the Chicago slums. **$5 $25 $65**

Allison, Clyde, *Have Nude Will Travel,* Berkley Book #Y705, 1962, paperback original, cover by Victor Kalin; pseudonym of William Knoles. **$10 $25 $90**

--- *Lustful Ones, The,* Nightstand Book #1525, 1960, paperback original. **$10 $35 $100**

--- *Million Dollar Mistress,* Midwood Book #64, 1960, paperback original, cover by Paul Rader. **$10 $35 $120**

Amory, Richard, *Listen, the Loon Sings,* Greenleaf Classic #GC284, 1968, paperback original, cover by Robert Bonfils, gay male novel, #3 in Loon Song trilogy; pseudonym of Richard Love. **$15 $70 $160**

--- *Song of Aaron,* Greenleaf Classic #GC222, 1967, paperback original, cover by Robert Bonfils, #2 in Loon Song trilogy, gay male novel. **$12 $60 $150**

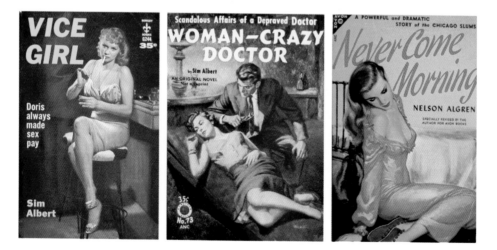

	G	VG	F		G	VG	F

--- *Song of the Loon*, Greenleaf Classic #GC213, 1966, paperback original, cover by Robert Bonfils, gay pastoral novel, #1 in the Loon Song trilogy, landmark gay male literature, first positive gay novel in paperback, before Stonewall. 📷 **$22 $60 $160**

Anderson, Edward, *Hungry Men,* Lion Book #8, 1949, the first Lion Book. **$10 $30 $100**

--- *Thieves Like Us,* Berkley Book #G-130, 1958, JD book, "Teen-age killers on the loose." 📷 **$6 $20 $80**

Anderson, George B., *Sit-In, The,* Ace Book #76835, 1970, paperback original, cover by George Gross, cop killer on radical campus novel. **$5 $20 $75**

Anonymous, *Beatles Up to Date, The,* Lancer Book #72-746, 1964, paperback original, photo cover of the Beatles, full of photos. 📷 **$15 $40 $100**

--- *Bold Stories,* Kirby Publishing Co., #1, March 1950, digest-size, anthology with color comics inside, scarce. **$90 $300 $750**

--- *Bold Stories,* Kirby Publishing Co., #2, May 1950, digest-size, anthology with color comics inside, scarce. **$90 $300 $750**

--- *Bold Stories,* Kirby Publishing Co., #3, July 1950, digest-size, anthology with color comics inside, rare. **$125 $350 $900**

--- *Candid Tales,* Kirby Publishing Co., #1, April 1950, digest-size, anthology with color comics inside, scarce. **$50 $250 $600**

--- *Candid Tales,* Kirby Publishing Co., #2, June 1950, digest-size, anthology with color comics inside, cover art shows Sherlock Holmes parody, rare. 📷 **$75 $300 $800**

--- *Confessions of Love,* Artful Book #1, April 1950, cover by Matt Baker, digest-size, anthology with color comics inside, scarce. 📷 **$25 $75 $250**

--- *Confessions of Love,* Artful Book #2, July 1950, cover by Matt Baker, digest-size, anthology with color comics inside, scarce. **$35 $100 $300**

--- *Honeymoon Romance,* Artful Book #1, April 1950, cover by Matt Baker, digest-size, anthology with color comics inside, scarce. 📷 **$25 $120 $300**

--- *Honeymoon Romance,* Artful Book #2, July 1950, cover by Matt Baker, digest-size, anthology with color comics inside, scarce. **$35 $100 $300**

--- *Juvenile Jungle,* Berkley Book #G-86, 1957, first book edition, JD anthology with James M. Farrell, Nelson Algren, Hal Ellson. **$5 $30 $80**

--- *Love Toy, The,* Novel Library #21, 1949, sexy cover. **$10 $25 $80**

	G	VG	F

--- *Marriage and Sex*, Gold Medal Book, no number (#100), 1949, paperback original. **$8** **$30** **$100**

--- *Taboo*, Novel Book #7N-730, 1964, paperback original, includes Harlan Ellison. **$40** **$100** **$300**

Antholz, Peyson, *All Shook Up*, Ace Book #D-306, 1958, paperback original, JD novel. **$10** **$40** **$120**

Anton, Cal, *Private Life of a Strip-Tease Girl, The*, Beacon Book #B266, 1959, paperback original, burlesque novel. 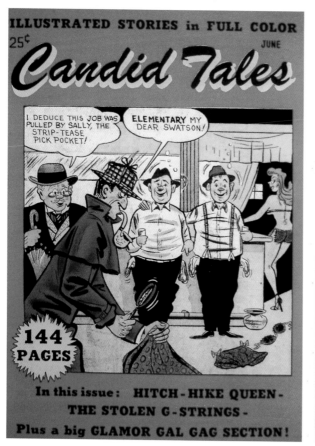 **$5** **$18** **$50**

Appel, Benjamin, *Alley Kids*, Lion Library #LB116, 1956, JD novel, cover by Samson Pollen and Carlos de Mema, reprints Lion #95 with new title and cover art. **$5** **$20** **$45**

--- *Hell's Kitchen*, Lion Book #95, 1952,

	G	VG	F

JD collection.  **$8** **$26** **$75**

--- *Teen-Age Mobster*, Avon Book #T-162, 1957, JD novel. **$6** **$30** **$60**

Appel, H. M., *Illicit Desires*, Quarter Book #54, 1949, classic sexy beach pin-up cover art by George Gross.  **$12** **$50** **$125**

Armory, Richard, *Fruit of the Loon*, Greenleaf Classic #GC307, 1968, paperback original, gay male novel, satire of the Loon Song trilogy; pseudonym of George Davies. **$15** **$50** **$100**

Arnold, Elliott, *Everybody Slept Here*, Signet Book #735, 1949, cover by James Avati. **$3** **$15** **$50**

Arthur, William, *Marriage Later*, Century Book #106, paperback original. **$4** **$25** **$65**

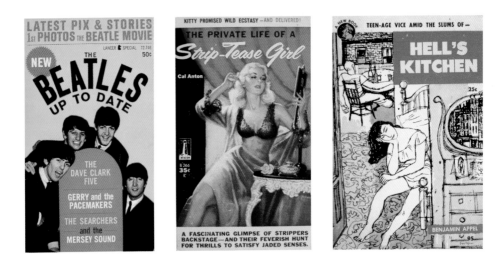

	G	VG	F

Aswell, James, *Young and Hungry-Hearted, The,* Signet Book #1166, 1955, cover by James Avati, novel of young lovers in Lousiana. 📷 **$5** **$20** **$60**

Atlee, Philip, *Naked Year, The,* Lion Book #188, 1954, cover by Samson Pollen. **$6** **$30** **$75**

Attaway, William, *Blood on the Forge,* Popular Library #191, 1953, black-related. 📷 **$3** **$16** **$45**

--- *Tough Kid,* Lion Book #86, 1952, cover by Robert Maguire, sexy woman JD. 📷 **$5** **$30** **$85**

Austin, William A., *Commit the Sins,* Newsstand Library #U165, 1961, paperback original, jazz-sleaze novel. **$5** **$25** **$65**

Avallone, Mike, *Little Black Book, The,* Midwood Book #Y135, 1961, paperback original, cover by Paul Rader, sleaze novel by mystery author. 📷 **$10** **$35** **$100**

Ayers, Ruby M., *Little Sinner, The,* Avon Romance Novel Monthly #1, 1949, sexy, digest-size. **$25** **$50** **$135**

	G	VG	F		G	VG	F

Balmer, Jon, *Fever Hot!,* Exotic Novel #19, 1951, paperback original, digest-size, sexy cover art. **$18** **$100** **$200**

Banis, Victor J., *Why Not, The,* Greenleaf Classic #GC209, 1966, paperback original, his first gay novel under his own name, first Greenleaf gay novel, creator of the Man From C.A.M.P. gay series. **$15** **$35** **$125**

Bannon, Ann, *Beebo Brinker,* Gold Medal Book #d1224, 1962, paperback original, cover by Robert McGinnis, lesbian novel. **$20** **$100** **$250**

--- *Journey to a Woman,* Gold Medal

Book #s997, 1960, paperback original, photo cover. **$15** **$75** **$175**

--- *Odd Girl Out,* Gold Medal Book #s653, 1957, paperback original, cover by Barye Phillips, her first book. 📷 **$20** **$75** **$200**

--- *Woman in the Shadows,* Gold Medal Book #s919, 1959, paperback original, photo cover, lesbian. **$15** **$55** **$130**

Beauchamp, Loren, *Love Nest,* Midwood Book #7, 1958, paperback original, cover by Rudy Nappi, first regular issue Midwood; pseudonym of Robert Silverberg. **$10** **$35** **$100**

	G	VG	F

--- *Sin on Wheels*, Midwood Book #70, 1961, paperback original, sexy cover by Paul Rader. 📷 **$10** **$40** **$120**

Bellmore, Don, *Leopard Lust,* Nightstand Book #NB1864, 1967, paperback original, cover by Robert Bonfils. 📷 **$12** **$35** **$125**

Bennett, Alan, *Cellar Club Girl,* Croydon Book #40, 1953, paperback original, cover by Lou Marchetti, digest-size. **$20** **$75** **$165**

--- *Savage Delinquents*, Bedside Book #BB824, 1959, paperback original, 50 cents cover price, tall format, illustrated cover, JD novel. **$15** **$35** **$90**

--- *Savage Delinquents*, Bedside Book #BB824, 1959, paperback original, "Special BB edition" 60 cents cover price, short format, photo cover shows Betty Page. **$40** **$90** **$200**

--- *Tenement Girl*, Croydon Book #94, 1955, cover by Lou Marchetti, digest-size, JD novel, reprints *Cellar Club Girl* with new title and number. 📷 **$18** **$65** **$145**

Bennett, Fletcher, *Naked Streets,* Playtime Book #606, 1962, paperback original, sleaze novel, fake cop pressures prostitutes for sex and money. **$6** **$20** **$50**

Benton, Ralph, *Psychedelic Sex,* Viceroy Book #VP283, 1968, paperback original, cover by Hughes, hippie sex cult sleaze novel, inside credits L. B. Wright as author. 📷 **$12** **$50** **$100**

Bernard, William, *Jailbait,* Popular Library #392, 1951, cover by Rudolph Belarski, woman JD. 📷 **$10** **$30** **$80**

Berryman, Opal Leigh, *Make It on Temple Street,* Newstand Library #U168, 1961, paperback original, prostitution and drugs sleaze novel, cover by Robert Bonfils. 📷 **$8** **$30** **$90**

Bessie, Oscar, *Bonnie,* Domino Book #72-960, 1965, paperback original, cover photo shows black leather-clad vixen, JD novel about a "girl of the bike gangs." 📷 **$5** **$20** **$60**

Bingham, Carson, *Gang Girls, The,* Monarch Book #372, 1963, paperback original, JD novel, story of the Panther Debs, a female Brooklyn street gang; pseudonym of Bruce Cassidy. **$8** **$25** **$75**

--- *Run Tough, Run Hard*, Monarch Book #487, 1964, paperback original, cover by Ray Johnson, JD novel. 📷 **$5** **$20** **$65**

Blake, Roger, *Commie Sex Trap,* Boudoir Book #1040, 1963, paperback original, photo cover, sleaze novel, GI plays spy to get sex. **$8** **$30** **$75**

Bligh, Norman, *Bad Sue,* Quarter Book #79, 1950, paperback original, digest-size, pin-up style cover art. **$12** **$65** **$135**

	G	VG	F		G	VG	F

--- *Bed-Time Angel*, Ecstasy Novel, no number (#9), 1951, paperback original, digest-size, sexy cover art makes it look like a man's hands are upon a woman's breasts, but it is her own hands. 🎁

| | **$18** | **$90** | **$175** |

--- *Born to Be Bad*, Quarter Book #84, 1951, paperback original, digest-size, pin-up style cover art.

| | **$12** | **$60** | **$140** |

Bodenheim, Maxwell, *60 Seconds,* Novel Library #38, 1950, author was a self-styled Bohemian who wrote spicy novels that are great reads.

| | **$5** | **$25** | **$75** |

--- *Abortive Hussy, The*, Avon Book #146, 1947.

| | **$5** | **$20** | **$60** |

--- *Duke Herring*, Checker Book #6, 1949, cover by Bill Wenzel, sexy gangster novel. 🎁

| | **$10** | **$30** | **$100** |

--- *Naked on Roller Skates*, Novel Library #46, 1950. 🎁

| | **$12** | **$55** | **$145** |

--- *Naked on Roller Skates*, Diversey Novel #2, 1949, sexy, digest-size.

| | **$50** | **$150** | **$325** |

--- *New York Madness*, Avon Book Dividend #3, 1951, digest-size, sexy cover art. 🎁

| | **$15** | **$90** | **$175** |

	G	VG	F		G	VG	F

--- *Ninth Avenue,* Avon Book #352, 1951, racial novel, sexy cover art.
| | **$4** | **$20** | **$55** |

--- *Replenishing Jessica,* Avon Book #191, 1949, sexy cover art.
| | **$5** | **$30** | **$100** |

--- *Virtuous Girl,* Avon Book #168, 1948, sexy cover art. **$5 $20 $75**

Bogar, Jeff, *Confessions of a Chinatown Moll,* Uni-Book #69, 1953, digest-size, sexy cover, "behind the bamboo screen into plush harems, hashish...."
| | **$18** | **$60** | **$160** |

--- *Hill Billy in High Heels,* Uni-Book #65, 1953, paperback original, digest-size, great title. **$15 $75 $150**

Bosworth, Jim, *Speed Demon,* Ace Book #D-267, 1958, paperback original, cover shows racing cars. **$5 $18 $50**

Bowen, Robert Sidney, *Hot Rod Fury,* Monarch Book #374, 1963, paperback original, JD kids and fast cars.
| | **$4** | **$16** | **$45** |

Boyd, Frank, *Flesh Peddlers, The,* Monarch Book #133, 1959, paperback original, cover by Robert Maguire; pseudonym of Frank Kane. **$10 $50 $120**

Bradley, Matt, *Balzac '64,* Jade Book #205 and #206, 1963, paperback original, cover by Robert Caples, two-book set in slipcase, uncommon, as a set:
| | **$20** | **$50** | **$100** |

Branch, Florenz, *Whipping Room, The,* Intimate Novel #24, 1952, paperback

original, digest-size, whipping cover; pseudonym of Florence Stonebraker.
| | **$15** | **$75** | **$135** |

Briffault, Robert, *Carlotta,* Avon Monthly Novel #13, 1949, sexy, digest.
| | **$15** | **$60** | **$125** |

--- *Europa,* Avon Book #272, 1950, brutal bondage/whipping cover art, variant cover art later used on Seven Footprints to Satan, Avon #T-115.
| | **$12** | **$40** | **$125** |

Britain, Sloane N., *Needle, The,* Beacon Book #B237, 1959, paperback original, drug-lesbian sleaze novel.
| | **$20** | **$100** | **$200** |

Brock, Lilyan, *Queer Patterns,* Avon Bedside #3, 1951, digest-size, lesbian novel. **$24 $120 $255**

--- *Queer Patterns,* Eton Book #E-121, 1952, cover by Rudy Nappi, lesbian novel. **$10 $45 $100**

Brown, Eleanore, *Innocent Madame,* Lion Book #73, 1951. **$5 $18 $75**

Brown, Wenzell, *Cry Kill,* Gold Medal Book #s897, 1959, paperback original, cover by James Meese.
| | **$6** | **$30** | **$90** |

--- *Gang Girl,* Avon Book #560, 1954, paperback original, JD novel, cover by CAF. **$6 $20 $75**

--- *Girls on the Rampage,* Gold Medal Book #s1160, 1961, paperback original, woman JD novel. **$6 $25 $80**

	G	VG	F

--- *Hoods Ride In, The*, Pyramid Book #G-439, 1959, paperback original, cover by Harry Schaare, JD novel.
$6 $30 $100

--- *Monkey on My Back*, Popular Library #549, 1954, cover by Owen Kampen, drug novel. $10 $50 $150

--- *Prison Girl*, Pyramid Book #G-345, 1958, cover by Robert Maguire. 📷
$6 $20 $65

--- *Run, Chico Run*, Gold Medal Book #292, 1953, paperback original, cover by Barye Philips, JD novel.
$8 $30 $90

	G	VG	F

--- *Teen-age Mafia*, Gold Medal Book #s917, 1959, paperback original, cover by Barye Philips, JD novel.
$10 $25 $90

--- *Teen-age Terror*, Gold Medal Book #s734, 1958, paperback original, cover by James Meese, JD novel. 📷
$10 $30 $100

--- *Wicked Streets, The*, Gold Medal Book #640, 1957, paperback original, cover by Barye Phillips. $6 $30 $75

Browne, Eleanore, *Immodest Maidens, The,* Novel Library #26, 1949, love cult novel. 📷 $5 $28 $75

	G	VG	F		G	VG	F

Brush, Katherine, *Little Sins,* Avon Monthly Novel #12, 1949, sexy, digest.
$20 $65 $150

Bull, Lois, *Broadway Virgin,* Diversey Novel #1, 1949, digest-size.
$30 $90 $175

--- *Broadway Virgin,* Novel Library #23, 1949, sexy cover. $5 $25 $80

--- *Gold Diggers,* Novel Library #14, 1949, sexy cover. 📷 $5 $25 $75

--- *Illicit Honeymoon,* Magazine Village #6, 1948, digest-size, sexy cover. 📷
$18 $55 $155

Bunyan, Paul, *I Peddle Jazz,* Saber Book #SA-16, 1960, paperback original, mixes jazz with sleaze. 📷
$10 $30 $90

Burroughs, William, *Junkie,* Ace Book #K202, 1964, drugs novel, reprints Ace #D-15 under author's real name.
$15 $30 $100

Caldwell, Erskine, *God's Little Acre,* Signet Book #581, 39th printing 1952, cover by James Avati. 📷 $2 $16 $35

--- *Swell-Looking Girl, A,* Signet Book #818, 1950, cover by James Avati. 📷
$3 $15 $50

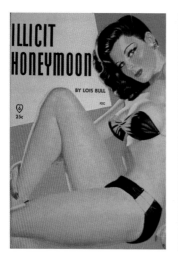

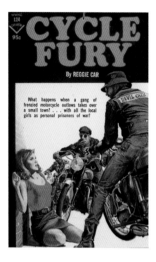

	G	VG	F			G	VG	F

--- *Tragic Ground*, Penguin Book #661, 1948, cover by Robert Jonas uses popular keyhole effect. **$3** **$12** **$35**

Caldwell, Jay Thomas, *Me an' You*, Lion Book #220, 1954, paperback original, black boxer novel, "A two-fisted Negro challenges the white world." 📷 **$8** **$35** **$100**

Calvano, Tony, *Acid Orgy*, Companion Book #523, 1967, paperback original, hippie sex, drugs novel. **$20** **$100** **$175**

Car, Reggie, *Cycle Fury*, Chevron Publications #124, 1967, paperback original, motorcycle gang sleaze novel. 📷 **$8** **$30** **$100**

Caren, Ellen, *Mirabelle Woman of Passion!*, Novel Library #22, 1949. **$5** **$25** **$75**

Carpenter, Jay, *Youngest Harlot, The*, Newstand Library #U130, 1960, paperback original, JD sleaze novel. **$5** **$20** **$50**

Carpozi Jr., George, *Let's Twist*, Pyramid Book #PR-41, 1962, paperback original, early 1960s rock-dance craze, with photos. **$10** **$25** **$65**

	G	VG	F

Carter, Jesse Lee, *Hot Chocolate,* Bronze Book #2, 1952, paperback original, photo cover, digest-size, black-related novel, one of only two Bronze Books, "Men couldn't resist Tami – and Tami couldn't resist!" **$55 $175 $500**

Cassidy, George, *Farm Girl,* Midwood Book #49, 1960, paperback original, cover by Paul Rader, sleaze novel of rural romance. 🎥 **$6 $25 $90**

Cassill, R. V., *Dormitory Women,* Lion Book #216, 1954, paperback original, sex on campus with lesbianism, scarce in condition. **$20 $50 $145**

Castro, Joe, *Satan Was My Pimp,* Playtime Book #660, 1964, paperback original, cover by Robert Bonfils, small town woman and lesbians. **$12 $60 $150**

--- *Young Hoods, The,* Beacon Book #B245, 1959, paperback original, cover by Frank Uppwall. 🎥 **$5 $30 $85**

Champion, D. L., *Run the Wild River,* Lion Book #117, 1952, paperback original, cover by Mort Kunsler, Mexicans terrorized as they enter the United States. **$5 $20 $75**

Chessman, Robert, *Park Jungle, The,* Chariot Book #CB132, 1962, paperback original, JD novel; pseudonym of Hyman Lindsay. 🎥 **$6 $30 $100**

Christian, Paula, *Another Kind of Love,* Crest Book #S-487, 1961, paperback original, lesbian, as "Paul Christian." **$8 $30 $90**

--- *Love is Where You Find It,* Avon Book #G-1091, 1961, paperback original, lesbian. **$9 $40 $100**

--- *This Side of Love,* Avon Book #G-1163, 1963, paperback original, lesbian. **$8 $35 $100**

Christopher, Ben, *Strange Embrace,* Beacon Book #B487F, 1962, paperback original; pseudonym of Lawrence Block. **$8 $55 $120**

Ciraci, Norma, *Detour,* Perma Book #P192, 1952, early lesbian novel. 🎥 **$6 $25 $80**

Clad, Noel, *White Barrier,* Avon Book #676, 1955, paperback original, interracial novel set in Paris after World War II. 🎥 **$6 $25 $75**

Clare, Mary, *White Man's Slave,* Leisure Library #24, 1953, cover by Reginald Heade. **$20 $80 $200**

Clark, Dorine B., *Bachelor Girl,* Intimate Novel #54, 1954, paperback original, digest-size, lesbian novel. **$14 $75 $150**

--- *Gutter Star,* Intimate Novel #52, 1954, paperback original, cover by Frank Uppwall, digest-size, lesbian novel. 🎥 **$15 $60 $175**

	G	VG	F		G	VG	F

Clarke, Donald Henderson, *Millie,* Avon
Bedside Novel #7, 1952, digest-size, sexy.
$20 $75 $155

--- *Millie's Daughter,* Avon Monthly
Novel #16, 1949, digest-size.
$20 $70 $135

--- *Regenerate Lover, The,* Avon Monthly
Novel #3, 1948, digest-size.
$25 $75 $155

--- *Regenerate Lover, The,* Novel Library
#8, 1948, sexy cover art.
$6 $30 $80

Clarke, John, *Lolita Lovers, The,* Monarch
Book #250, 1962, paperback original, JD
novel; pseudonym of Dan Sontup.
$5 $25 $75

Clay, Matthew, *Slum Doctor,* Bedside

Book #817, 1959, paperback original. 🎨
$8 $30 $80

Clayford, James, *Private Life of a Street
Girl, The,* Ecstasy Books, no number
(#4), paperback original, digest-size,
cover by George Gross.
$16 $60 $150

Clifton, Bud, *D For Delinquent,* Ace Book
#D-270, 1958, paperback original, JD
novel.   **$10 $50 $135**

--- *Power Gods, The,* Pyramid Book #G-
410, 1959, paperback original, cover by
Lou Marchetti, JD novel.
$10 $40 $100

Collins, Hunt, *Proposition, The,* Pyramid
Book #151, 1955; pseudonym of Evan
Hunter.   **$9 $40 $120**

	G	VG	F

Collison, Wilson, *Blonde Baby*, Broadway Novel Monthly #8, 1950, digest-size.
$20 $100 $175

--- *Diary of Death*, Novel Library #30, 1949, sexy cover art.
$5 $20 $75

--- *Dishonorable Darling*, Novel Library #32, 1949. **$5 $20 $75**

--- *One Night With Nancy*, Diversey Love Book Monthly #2, 1948, digest-size.
$20 $100 $175

--- *One Night With Nancy*, Avon Monthly Novel #19, 1951, digest-size, sexy cover art. **$20 $70 $160**

--- *One Night With Nancy*, Novel Library #20, 1949, sexy cover.
$6 $30 $85

Colson, Frederick, *Devil is Gay, The*, Brandon House #933, 1965; pseudonym of Richard E. Geis.
$12 $40 $100

Colton, James, *Lost on Twilight Road*, National Library #NLB-100, 1964, paperback original, gay theme; pseudonym of mystery author Joseph Hansen, his first book.
$35 $125 $300

--- *Strange Marriage*, Paperback Library #54-371, 1966, gay theme, reprints hardcover. **$20 $75 $155**

Cooper, Courtney Riley, *Teen-Age Vice*,

Pyramid Book #G252, 1957, reprint, typical bad-boy/bad-girl JD cover art.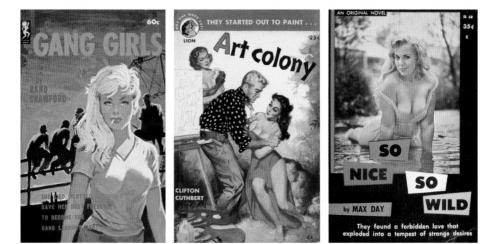
$4 $30 $75

Cooper, Morton, *Delinquent!*, Avon Book #T-247, 1958, paperback original, JD novel. **$5 $20 $85**

Cox, William R., *Hell to Pay*, Signet Book #1555, 1958, paperback original, JD vs the Mob. **$20 $35 $100**

Craig, Jonathan, *Frenzy*, Lancer Book #70-013, 1962, reprints *Junkie!*, drug novel.
$5 $30 $80

--- *Junkie!*, Falcon Book #36, 1952, paperback original, digest-size, "the life and loves of a drug addict!", scarce.
$90 $325 $650

Craigin, Elisabeth, *Either is Love*, Lion Book #74, 1951, lesbian novel.
$5 $30 $90

Crane, Clarkson, *Frisco Gal*, Novel Library #17, 1949, sexy cover art.
$5 $30 $75

Crawford, Brad, *Gang Girls*, Playtime Book #626, 1963, paperback original, JD sleaze novel. **$5 $25 $75**

Culver, Kathryn, *Sleepy Time Honey*, Rainbow Book #110, 1951, digest-size, gorgeous cover art.
$16 $75 $175

Curran, Dale, *Dupree Blues*, Berkley Book #348, 1955, photo cover, a jazz-noir novel of night club life. **$8 $30 $80**

	G	VG	F

	G	VG	F

Cuthbert, Clifton, *Art Colony,* Lion Book #58, 1951, "They started out to paint...."  **$5 $18 $60**

--- *Joy Street,* Lion Book #54, 1951. **$5 $25 $75**

Daly, Hamlin, *Case of the Canceled Redhead,* Falcon Book #25, 1952, paperback original, digest-size; pseudonym of E. Hoffman Price. **$18 $90 $200**

Davids, William, *Bad Girls Club,* Croydon Book #71, 1954, cover by Lou Marchetti, digest-size, JD novel. **$25 $100 $160**

Day, Max, *So Nice So Wild,* Stanley Library #SK68, 1959, paperback original, sexy photo cover; pseudonym of Bruce Cassidy. **$6 $20 $75**

Dean, Anthony, *Invaders, The,* After Hours Book #AH-138, 1966, paperback original, classic fetish cover art by Gene Bilbrew, sleaze novel, female invaders terrorize males. **$10 $30 $90**

Dean, Douglas, *Man Divided,* Gold Medal Book #407, 1954, paperback original, cover by Barye Phillips, "the twilight world of homosexuality." **$15 $25 $80**

De Bekker, Jay, *Gutter Gang,* Beacon #B108, 1954, paperback original, JD novel, cover by Walter Popp, "they came from filthy slums – where even their dreams were dirty!" **$8 $30 $85**

DeKobra, Maurice, *Bachelor's Widow,* Ace Book #S-85, 1954, first U. S. edition. **$6 $20 $65**

--- *Bedroom Eyes,* Diversey Love Book Monthly #1, 1948, cover by Peter Driben, digest-size. **$20 $110 $225**

--- *Bedroom Eyes,* Avon Bedside Novel #4, 1951, cover by Peter Driben, digest-size. **$20 $120 $255**

--- *Bedroom Eyes,* Novel Library #18, 1949, sexy pin-up cover by Peter Driben. **$6 $35 $90**

--- *Love Clinic, The,* Novel Library #28, 1949. **$15 $20 $75**

--- *Street of Painted Lips, The,* Novel Library #9, 1949, sexy cover art. **$5 $25 $75**

--- *Venus on Wheels,* Novel Library #25, 1949, sexy cover art. **$6 $30 $85**

--- *Venus on Wheels,* Broadway Novel Monthly #2, 1950, digest-size. **$22 $100 $200**

Demby, William, *Act of Outrage,* Lion Library #LL20, 1955, cover by Erickson, interracial. **$3 $20 $50**

Demetre, Margaret K., *Creole Desire,* Chariot Book #CB148, 1960, paperback original, sex and politics in small Southern town novel. **$5 $20 $55**

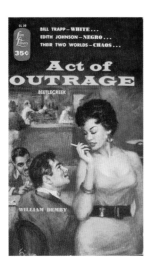

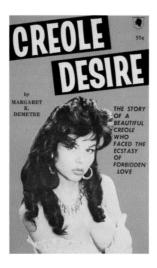

	G	VG	F		G	VG	F

DeMexico, N. R., *Marijuana Girl,* Uni-Book #19, 1951, paperback original, digest-size, photo cover, JD and drugs novel. 📷 **$35 $175 $425**

--- *Marijuana Girl,* Stallion Book #204, 1954, scarce reprint, photo cover, digest-size, JD and drugs. **$30 $120 $260**

--- *Marijuana Girl,* Beacon Book #B328, 1960, reprints Uni-Book digest, drugs. **$40 $100 $300**

--- *Marijuana Girl,* Softcover Library #S75124, 1969, reprint, same cover art used on Beacon edition, JD and drugs novel. 📷 **$18 $75 $135**

de Meyer, John, *Bailey's Daughters,* Lion Book #102, 1952. **$5 $20 $45**

Denton, John, *Chain Gang Love Slave,* Intimate Edition #708, 1962, paperback original, sleaze novel about lust in a women's prison. **$4 $20 $65**

Dern, Peggy, *Help Yourself to Love,* Avon Romance Novel Monthly #3, 1950, digest-size. **$16 $65 $125**

De Roo, Edward, *Fires of Youth, The,* Ace Book #S-105, 1955, paperback original, JD novel. **$14 $50 $125**

--- *Fires of Youth, The,* Ace Book #D-338, 1959, reprints Ace #S-105, JD novel. **$6 $25 $75**

--- *Go, Man, Go!,* Ace Book #D-406, 1959, paperback original, JD novel. **$15 $75 $175**

--- *Little Caesars, The,* Ace Book #D-486, 1961, paperback original, JD novel. 📷 **$15 $50 $120**

--- *Rumble At the Housing Project,* Ace Book #D-417, 1960, paperback original, JD novel. 📷 **$15 $75 $175**

--- *Young Wolves, The,* Ace Book #D-343, 1959, paperback original, JD novel. **$14 $50 $120**

Dexter, John, *Narco Nympho,* Leisure Book #1197, 1967, sleaze and drugs. **$35 $125 $350**

--- *No Adam For Eve,* Evening Reader #1241, 1966, paperback original, lesbian sleaze novel, written by Marion Zimmer Bradley. **$65 $225 $650**

Donner, James, *Women in Trouble,* Monarch Book #MB501, 1959, paperback original, cover by Robert Maguire, abortion novel. **$6 $20 $70**

Drago, Sinclair, *Women to Love,* Novel Library #16, 1949, sexy. **$5 $20 $75**

Drake, H. B., *Slave Ship,* Beacon Book #B217, 1959. **$6 $25 $90**

Dupperault, Doug, *Gang Mistress,* Croydon Book #34, 1953, paperback original, cover by Safran, digest-size, JD. **$30 $100 $225**

--- *Trailer-Camp Girl,* Stallion Book #211, 1954, digest-size, uncommon. **$14 $75 $140**

--- *Wayward Girl,* Croydon Book #84, 1954, cover by Bernard Safran, digest-size, reprints *Gang Mistress* with new title and cover art. **$15 $75 $160**

Du Soe, Robert, C., *Devil Thumbs a Ride, The,* Avon Book #208, 1949, Satan cover by Ann Cantor. **$8 $35 $100**

DuVal, Arlene, *Side Street,* After Hours Book #AH142, 1966, paperback original, cover by Bill Ward. **$12 $30 $100**

	G	VG	F

Easton, Lawrence, *Driven Flesh, The*, Ace Book #S-119, 1955, paperback original.
    $5   **$20**   **$80**

Edd, Karl, *Tenement Kid, The*, Newsstand Library #U122, 1959, paperback original, JD sleaze novel. 📷
    $5   **$20**   **$60**

Ehrlich, Max, *High Side, The*, Gold Medal Book #r2207, 1970, paperback original, cover by Frank Frazetta, outlaw biker novel. 📷 **$12** **$40** **$120**

Eisner, Simon, *Naked Storm, The*, Lion Book #109, 1952, paperback original; pseudonym of C. M. Kornbluth.
    $8   **$40**   **$100**

Eliat, Helene, *Arena of Love*, Lion Book #53, 1951, "The strange story of a sadistic love."   **$5**   **$30**   **$90**

Elliott, Don, *Convention Girl*, Nightstand Book #NB1547, 1961, paperback original, sleaze novel; pseudonym of Robert Silverberg. **$5** **$20** **$65**

--- *Gang Girl*, Nightstand Book #1504, 1959, paperback original, women fighting cover art, JD sleaze novel. 📷
    $12   **$80**   **$200**

--- *Hot Rod Sinners*, Bedside Book #1222, 1962, paperback original, back cover says she was a "hot rod woman" and "gang witch." **$9** **$45** **$110**

--- *Party Girl*, Nightstand Book #NB1509, 1960, paperback original, sleaze novel. 📷 **$5** **$25** **$75**

--- *Sin on Wheels*, Nightstand Book #NB1516, 1960, paperback original, cover by McCauley. **$5** **$25** **$75**

Ellis, Joan, *Campus Jungle*, Midwood Book #32-554, 1965, cover by Paul Rader; pseudonym of Julie Ellis.
    $5   **$20**   **$55**

--- *Gang Girl*, Midwood Book #32-424, 1964, paperback original, cover by Paul Rader, classic JD cover art. 📷
    $12   **$40**   **$120**

Ellison, Harlan, *Deadly Streets, The*, Ace Book #D-312, 1958, first book edition, classic JD novel, his first book. 📷
    $60   **$200**   **$500**

--- *Gentleman Junkie*, Regency Book #RB-102, 1961, first book edition, JD and drugs, cover by Leo and Diane Dillon.
    $35   **$125**   **$275**

--- *Glass Teat, The*, Ace Book #29350, 1970, first book edition, cover by Leo and Diane Dillon, essays about television. **$15** **$30** **$90**

--- *Juvies, The*, Ace Book #D-513, 1961, first book edition, JD novel. 📷
    $50   **$150**   **$400**

--- *Memos From Purgatory*, Regency Book #RB-106, 1961, paperback original, JD, cover by Leo and Diane Dillon.
    $35   **$175**   **$425**

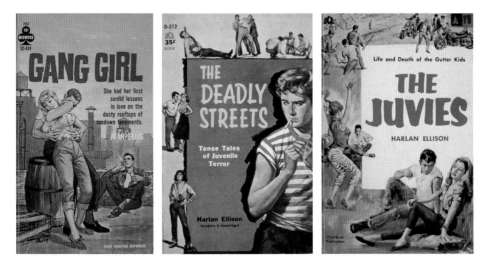

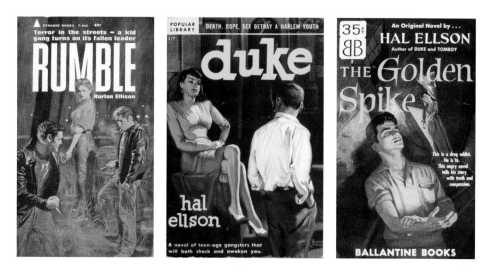

	G	VG	F		G	VG	F

--- *Memos From Purgatory*, Powell Book #OO-154, 1969, reprints Regency book with Ellison on cover.
$14 **$60** **$125**

--- *Rockabilly*, Gold Medal Book #1161, 1961, paperback original, cover by Mitchell Hooks, rock and roll JD novel.
$45 **$100** **$275**

--- *Rumble*, Pyramid Book #G-352, 1958, paperback original, cover by Rudy de Reyna, JD, Ellison's first novel, originally to have been a Lion Book.
$65 **$200** **$500**

--- *Rumble*, Pyramid Books #F-866, 1963, reprint, new cover by Earl E. Mayan. 📷
$25 **$100** **$160**

--- *Spider Kiss*, Ace Book #77793, 1982, cover by Barlcay Shaw, reissue of *Rockabilly* with new title, recalled, corrected edition has color photo of author on the back. **$10** **$30** **$90**

Ellson, Hal, *Duke*, Popular Library #219, 1950, cover by Rudolph Belarski, black JD, "death, dope, sex betray a Harlem youth." 📷 **$5** **$30** **$100**

--- *Golden Spike, The*, Ballantine Book #2, 1952, paperback original, cover by Robert Maguire, novel about a 16-year-old JD and drug addict. 📷
$10 **$45** **$130**

--- *Jailbait Street*, Monarch Book #137, 1963, paperback original, cover by Ray Johnson, JD novel.
$10 **$40** **$100**

--- *Nest of Fear, The*, Ace Book #D-522, 1961, paperback original, JD novel.
$5 **$20** **$60**

--- *Rock*, Ballantine Book #103, 1955, paperback original, black JD novel.
$5 **$30** **$100**

--- *Tomboy*, Bantam Book #945, 1951, cover by Robert Maguire, JD novel, Maguire's first paperback cover. 📷
$8 **$25** **$85**

--- *Tomboy*, Bantam Book #H3973, 1967, cover by James Bama, reprint with new cover art. 📷 **$4** **$20** **$45**

--- *Torment of the Kids, The*, Regency Book #RB-108, 1961, paperback original.
$12 **$70** **$150**

Ellson, R. N., *Sex-Happy Hippie*, Candid Reader #CA954, 1968, cover by Robert Bonfils, cover shows Frank Zappa and others; pseudonym of SF writer Ray F. Nelson. **$15** **$60** **$150**

Emerson, Jill, *I Am Curious (Thirty)*, Berkley Book #Z1818, 1970, paperback original; pseudonym of Lawrence Block.
$35 **$90** **$200**

--- *Sensuous*, Berkley Book #Z-2113, 1972, paperback original.
$30 **$100** **$200**

--- *Threesome*, Berkley Book #Z1870, 1970, paperback original, erotica.
$40 **$100** **$200**

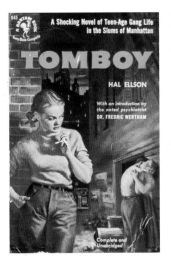

	G	VG	F		G	VG	F

Emery, Carol, *Queer Affair,* Beacon Book #B135, 1957, paperback original, lesbian novel. 📷 **$10 $35 $120**

Evans, Lesley, *Strange Are the Ways of Love,* Crest Book #S-336, 1959, paperback original, cover by Barye Phillips, lesbian novel, written by Lawrence Block, his first book.
$30 $100 $220

Evens, Hodge, *Her Candle Burns Hot,* Rainbow Book #109, 1951, paperback original, digest-size; pseudonym of Dudley Owen McGaughy, aka Dean Owen. 📷 **$35 $135 $275**

--- *Whip-Hand!,* Falcon Book #40, 1952, paperback original, digest-size, scarce.
$40 $150 $350

Everett, Kathleen, *Carnival Piece,* Private Edition #PE-473, 1969, paperback original, written by Ed Wood Jr.
$45 $135 $220

Fairbank, Walton, *Houseboy,* Pyramid Book #216, 1956, interracial novel.
$6 $20 $65

Fante, John, *Ask the Dust,* Bantam Book #1194, 1954, cover by Harry Schaare. 📷
$30 $100 $250

Farrere, Claude, *Black Opium,* Berkley Book #G-120, 1958, cover by Robert Maguire, short format, key drug novel. 📷
$30 $125 $275

--- *Black Opium,* Berkley Book #Y572, 1961, cover by Robert Maguire, in tall format. **$20 $65 $150**

Farris, John, *Harrison High,* Dell Book #F-90, 1959, cover by Robert Maguire, novel.
$3 $20 $50

Felsen, Henry Gregor, *Crash Club,* Bantam Book #A2076, 1960, JD novel about kids in fast cars. **$4 $20 $75**

--- *Hot Rod,* Bantam Book #923, 1951, JDs and fast cars novel. 📷
$6 $35 $100

--- *Road Rocket,* Bantam Book #2315, 1962, JD and racing.
$5 $30 $75

--- *Street Rod,* Bantam Book #1437, 1956, JD and racing, uncommon.
$20 $60 $135

Fisher, Louis, *Wild Party!,* Novel Book #5011, 1960, paperback original, cover by Bill Ward. 📷 **$14 $75 $135**

Fitzpatrick, Thomas K., *Blood Circus, The,* Gold Medal Book #d1921, 1968, paperback original, motorcycle gang.
$5 $25 $75

Flanagan, Roy, *Luther,* Lion Book #114, 1952, interracial. 📷
$6 $25 $90

--- *Whipping, The,* Bantam Book #817, 1950, cover by Harry Schaare, Ku Klux Klan-racial. **$8 $25 $90**

Flora, Fletcher, *Lysistrata,* Zenith Book #ZB-16, 1959, cover by Rudy Nappi, sex war. **$4 $20 $65**

--- *Strange Sisters,* Lion Book #215, 1954, paperback original, lesbian novel.
$10 $50 $130

Ford, Robert B., *Emerald Bikini, The,* Saber Book #SA-43, 1963, paperback original, cover by Bill Edwards, sleaze novel. 📷 **$5 $20 $75**

Frame, Bart, *Co-Ed Sinners,* Croydon Book #48, 1953, paperback original, cover by Bernard Safran, digest-size.
$12 $40 $100

France, Hector, *Musk, Hashish and Blood,* Avon Book #415, 1952, drug-related, evocative title. **$10 $40 $130**

Fredericks, Diana, *Diana,* Berkley Book #G-11, 1955, photo cover, lesbian novel.
$10 $25 $100

--- *Diana,* Berkley Book #G-50, second printing 1957, new photo cover.
$10 $20 $85

Freeman, Gillian, *Leather Boys, The,* Ballantine Book #U5065, 1967, U.K. Mods/delinquents. **$4 $20 $65**

Gallagher, Richard F., *Women Without Morals,* Avon Book #G1100, 1962, first book edition, ultimate bad-girl true stories. 📷 **$6 $30 $90**

Gardner, Miriam, *Strange Women, The,* Monarch Book #249, 1962, paperback original, cover by Tom Miller, lesbian novel, written by Marion Zimmer Bradley. **$50 $120 $350**

--- *Twilight Lovers,* Monarch Book #418, 1964, paperback original, lesbian novel.
$20 $75 $150

Garland, Rodney, *Heart in Exile, The,* Lion Library #LL76, 1956, first paperback printing, gay interest; pseudonym of Adam Hegedus. **$5 $20 $70**

	G	VG	F

--- *Troubled Midnight, The*, Lion Library #LL128, 1956, first paperback printing, cover by Charles Copeland, gay interest.
$5 **$20** **$65**

Garth, John, *Hill Man*, Pyramid Book #112, 1954, paperback original, cover by Julian Paul; pseudonym of Janice Holt Giles. 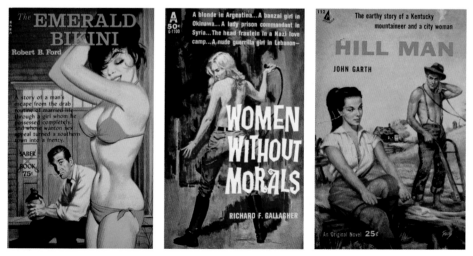 **$40** **$100** **$350**

Gerstine, Jack, *Play it Cool*, Ace Book #D-337, 1959, paperback original, JD novel, "wild days and nights of a young hood."
$14 **$50** **$125**

Gill, Elisabeth, *Wayward Nymph*, Zenith Book #ZB-27, 1959, a "bad girl in town."
$5 **$25** **$55**

Gold, Herbert, *Room Clerk*, Signet Book #1185, 1955, cover by Stanley Zuckerberg, skid row and racial.
$3 **$15** **$50**

Golightly, Bonnie, *Beat Girl*, Avon Book #T-310, 1959, paperback original, Beat novel. **$8** **$50** **$100**

Gonzalez, Babs, *I Paid My Dues*, Expubidence Publishing Corp., no number, 1967, paperback original, photo cover of author, self-published autobiography of jazz man's life and art.
$15 **$50** **$125**

Gonzalez, John, *End of a J.D.*, Gold Medal Book #s1064, 1960, paperback original, cover by Mitchell Hooks, JD novel.
$7 **$30** **$90**

Gordon, Ian, *Harlem Is My Heaven*,

	G	VG	F

Berkley Book #G-78, 1957, novel of racist white man and his relationship with a black woman passing for white.
$8 **$30** **$100**

Gordon, Luther, *Pay For My Kiss!*, Exotic Novel #1, 1949, paperback original, digest-size, cover by Fred Claude Rodewald. **$15** **$75** **$150**

Gould, Lawrence, *Your Most Intimate Problems*, Avon Book, no number, 1949, paperback original, digest-size.
$20 **$75** **$250**

Graham, Carroll and Garrett, *Fleshpots of Malibu*, Broadway Novel Monthly #7, 1950, sexy, digest-size.
$35 **$100** **$225**

Grant, Richard, *Eurasian Girl*, Uni-Book #30, 1952, cover by Warren King, digest-size, white slavery novel.
$18 **$70** **$185**

Grey, Harry, *Call Me Duke*, Graphic Book #G-215, 1956, cover by Samson Pollen, crime author's JD classic.
$4 **$22** **$65**

Grey, Stella, *Abnormals Anonymous*, National Library Book #NLB-106, 1964, paperback original, early gender-bender cover art. **$20** **$65** **$175**

Gropper, Milton Herbert, *Ladies of the Evening*, Broadway Novel Monthly #3, 1950, sexy, digest-size.
$22 **$100** **$155**

	G	VG	F

--- *Three Loose Ladies*, Broadway Novel Monthly #6, 1950, sexy, digest-size. **$25** **$90** **$155**

Guild, Leo, *Seduction*, Avon Special, no number (#1), 1951, digest-size, sexy cover art. 🎭 **$22** **$125** **$255**

Gwinn, William, *Jazz Bum*, Lion Book #225, 1954, paperback original, jazz novel. 🎭 **$10** **$25** **$100**

--- *Way With Women, A*, Lion Book #209, 1954, paperback original, "story of a Jazz bum." 🎭 **$5** **$30** **$90**

Hahn, Emily, *Affair*, Lion Book #57, 1951, abortion novel. **$5** **$20** **$70**

Hale, Laura, *Lovers Don't Sleep*, Exotic Novels #20, 1951, paperback original, digest-size. **$20** **$85** **$200**

Hales, Carol, *Such Is My Beloved*, Berkley Book #G-95, 1958, photo cover, lesbian novel. **$6** **$30** **$100**

Haley, Fred, *Satan Was a Lesbian*, PEC Giant #G-1103, 1966, paperback original, lesbian sleaze. **$20** **$75** **$175**

Hamblett, Charles and Deverson, Jane, *Generation X*, Gold Medal Book #d1582, 1964, paperback original, photo cover, JD. **$5** **$25** **$55**

Hanley, Jack, *Stag Stripper*, Berkley Book #G-171, 1958, photo cover. 🎭 **$5** **$25** **$75**

	G	VG	F

--- *Star Lust*, Avon Book Dividend #2, 1951, digest-size, sexy cover. **$15** **$75** **$165**

--- *Strip Street*, Berkley Book #G-261, 1959, sexy photo cover. **$5** **$20** **$65**

--- *Tent-Show Bride*, Intimate Novel #30, 1953, paperback original, photo cover, digest-size, carnival novel. **$15** **$70** **$135**

--- *Tomcat in Tights*, Avon Monthly Novel #21, 1951, digest-size. **$18** **$85** **$175**

Hanline, M. A., *Man Who Drove Girls Wild, The,* Avon Monthly Novel #14, 1949, digest-size. **$20** **$90** **$175**

	G	VG	F

Harragan, Steve, *Queer Sisters,* Uni-Book #43, 1952, paperback original, digest-size, cover by Bernard Safran, crime and lesbian novel. 📷 **$20** **$100** **$250**

--- *Queer Sisters, The,* Stallion Book #206, 1954, digest-size, reprints Uni-Book #43 with the same cover art by Bernard Safran. **$15** **$75** **$165**

--- *Smuggled Sin*, Stallion Book #215, 1954, reprints Uni-Book, new photo cover shows woman with liquor bottles. **$15** **$75** **$150**

Harris, Amy, *Horizontal Secretary,* Midwood Book #F-248, 1963, paperback original, "she did her best work after five." 📷 **$6** **$25** **$70**

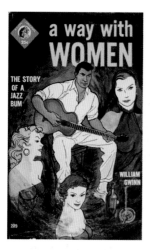

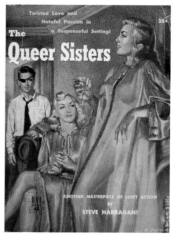

	G	VG	F

Harris, Sara, *Wayward Ones, The,* Signet Book #1146, 1954, "life in a girls' reformatory" by a social worker. 📷
| | $5 | $20 | $60 |

Harrison, Jim, *Wolf,* Manor Book #12164, 1973, first paperback printing, photo cover, counter-culture novel, scarce.
| | $40 | $75 | $125 |

Harrison, Whit, *Any Woman He Wanted,* Beacon Book #B392, 1961, paperback original; pseudonym of Harry Whittington. $10 $30 $100

--- *Man Crazy,* Zenith Book #ZB-35, 1960, aka Girl on Parole.
| | $8 | $40 | $100 |

--- *Native Girl,* Star Novels #761, 1956, digest-size. $10 $55 $125

--- *Rapture Alley,* Carnival Book #918, 1953, paperback original, cover by Rudolph Belarski, digest-size.
| | $25 | $120 | $300 |

--- *Sailor's Weekend,* Venus Book #153, 1952, paperback original, digest-size, cover by Herb Tauss. 📷
| | $25 | $90 | $175 |

--- *Shanty Road,* Original Novels #742, 1952, paperback original digest-size.
| | $12 | $55 | $150 |

--- *Strip the Town Naked,* Beacon Book #350, 1960, paperback original.
| | $14 | $50 | $125 |

--- *Woman Possessed, A,* Beacon Book #B416Y, 1961, paperback original, cover by Robert Maguire. $12 $40 $100

Harvey, Gene, *Leg Artist,* Red Circle Book #3, 1949, pre-Lion Books imprint, sexy leg art cover. 📷 $10 $40 $120

Harvin, Emily, *Madwoman?,* Avon Book #276, 1951, needle cover art, horror story set in a mental hospital for women. 📷
| | $6 | $30 | $80 |

Hastings, March, *Her Private Hell,* Midwood Book #F-271, 1963, paperback original, cover by Paul Rader, lesbian novel. $45 $90 $225

--- *Three Women,* Beacon Book #B190, 1958, paperback original, lesbian novel, "an intimate picture of women in love – with each other!" 📷
| | $10 | $35 | $90 |

Hatter, Amos, *No Time For Sleep,* Venus Book #126, 1951, paperback original, digest-size. $15 $60 $135

Haunt, Tom, *Hot-Rod Babe,* Gaslight Book #GL-124, 1964, paperback original, fast women and fast cars sleaze novel.
| | $6 | $30 | $65 |

Henderson, George Wylie, *Jule: Alabama Boy in Harlem,* Avon Book #400, 1952, black-related. $6 $20 $80

Henderson, James Leal, *Whirlpool,* Popular Library #399, 1952, cover by Harry Barton, racial novel, "she was for sale to the highest bidder." 📷
| | $5 | $20 | $65 |

	G	VG	F

Henry, Joan, *Women in Prison,* Perma Book #239, 1953, cover by James Meese, the woman in prison sub-genre often includes lesbian situations as implied by this cover. 📷   **$5 $20 $80**

Herold, Walt, *Filmtown Stud Writer,* Dragon Edition #DE-124, 1966, paperback original, sleaze novel about Hollywood writer. 📷
$6 $25 $75

Hilton, Joseph, *Angels in the Gutter,* Gold Medal Book #475, 1955, paperback original, photo cover of JD females in police lineup.   **$10 $35 $100**

	G	VG	F

Hitt, Orrie, *As Bad As They Come,* Midwood Book #23, 1959, paperback original, cover by Paul Rader, stunning bad-girl cover art. 📷
$6 $25 $85

--- *Carnival Girl,* Beacon Book #B238, 1959, paperback original, photo cover, carnival sleaze novel.
$5 $30 $100

--- *Carnival Sin* with *Playpet,* Vest Pocket Book #VP101 & 102, 1962, photo covers, two small 2x3-inch paperbacks in slipcase, uncommon, set: 📷
$20 $75 $165

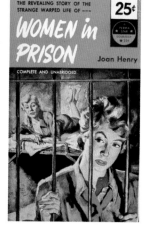

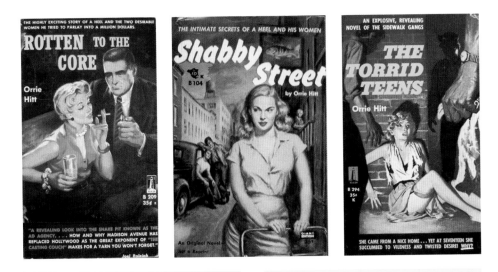

	G	VG	F

--- *Girl of the Streets*, Midwood Book #12, 1959, paperback original, sexy street-girl cover art. **$8 $50 $100**

--- *Ex-Virgin*, Beacon Book #267, 1959, paperback original, brutal cover by Al Rossi. **$20 $45 $125**

--- *Hot Cargo*, Beacon Book #BB203, 1958, paperback original, "gun running and wenching." **$5 $30 $75**

--- *Lady Is a Lush, The*, Beacon Book #B342, 1960, paperback original, novel about an alcoholic wild woman. 📷 **$6 $30 $100**

--- *Married Mistress*, Midwood Book #115, 1962. **$5 $25 $65**

--- *Nudist Camp*, Beacon Book #BB137, 1957, paperback original, cover by Bernard Safran. **$5 $25 $65**

--- *Pushover*, Beacon Book #BB139, 1957, cover by Geygan, classic keyhole peeper cover art. **$5 $20 $55**

--- *Rotten to the Core*, Beacon Book #B209, 1958, paperback original. 📷 **$5 $20 $60**

--- *Shabby Street*, Beacon Book #B104, 1954, paperback original, cover by Walter Popp. 📷 **$6 $30 $75**

--- *Sheba*, Beacon Book #B211, 1959, paperback original, cover by Rudy Nappi. **$5 $20 $65**

--- *She Got What She Wanted*, Beacon Book #B195, 1958, cover by Al Rossi. **$5 $20 $55**

--- *Torrid Teens, The*, Beacon Book #B294, 1960, paperback original, JD novel with brutal rape cover art. 📷 **$7 $50 $120**

--- *Widow, The*, Beacon Book #B222, 1959, paperback original, cover by Al Rossi. **$5 $20 $55**

--- *Wild Oats*, Beacon Book #B-169, 1958, paperback original. **$5 $20 $60**

Hodapp, William, *Crazy Mixed-Up Kids*, Berkley Book #G-12, 1955, first book edition, JD-drugs anthology, needle cover by Gardner Leaver. **$6 $30 $100**

Holland, Dell, *Hellhole of Sin*, Bedside Book #BB1223, 1962, paperback original, drunk nude woman among liquor bottles on table. 📷 **$12 $45 $120**

Holland, Ken, *Strange Young Wife, The*, Beacon Book #662X, 1963, paperback original; pseudonym of Harry Whittington. **$12 $40 $100**

Holland, Marty, *Blonde Baggage*, Novel Library #45, 1950, cover art showing woman in a suitcase is silly but cute. 📷 **$6 $35 $125**

--- *Darling of Paris, The*, Avon Monthly Novel #15, 1949, paperback original, digest-size, photo cover. **$20 $70 $155**

--- *Fast Woman*, Diversey Novel #4, 1949, digest-size, sexy. **$20 $90 $145**

	G	VG	F			G	VG	F

--- *Her Private Passions,* Avon Monthly Novel #2, 1947, digest-size.

     $20   **$90**   **$165**

--- *Her Private Passions,* Avon Book Dividend #5, 1949, digest-size, photo cover.   **$15**   **$60**   **$135**

Holliday, Don, *Chain Gang,* Ember Library #EL-307, 1966, paperback original, sleaze novel with women on a chain gang cover art.   **$5**   **$25**   **$75**

Holmes, Clellon, *Go,* Ace Book #D-238, 1957, JD novel.   **$20**   **$40**   **$120**

Hoover, P. A., *Scowtown Woman,* Ace Book #D-428, 1960, paperback original.

     $10   **$25**   **$75**

--- *Woman Called Trouble, A,* Ace Book #D-290, 1958, paperback original.

     $6   **$20**   **$65**

Hopkins, Jerry, *Hippie Papers, The,* Signet Book #Q-3457, 1968, paperback original, photo cover, counter culture anthology. 📷 **$10**   **$35**   **$100**

Horn, Alan, *Taste of H, A,* Private Edition #PE-384, 1966, paperback original, heroin-drug sleaze novel. 📷

     $15   **$75**   **$175**

House, Brant, *Violent Ones, The,* Ace Book #D-323, 1958, first book edition, cover shows JD girl gang and rumble, JD anthology with Evan Hunter, Gil Brewer, Hal Ellson.   **$7**   **$30**   **$90**

Howard, James, *I Like It Tough,* Popular Library Eagle Book #EB46, 1955, paperback original, drug ring and white

slavery.   **$4**   **$20**   **$60**

--- *I'll Get You Yet,* Popular Library Eagle Book #EB30, 1954, paperback original, woman sold into prostitution by the Mob.   **$4**   **$20**   **$65**

Hudson, Jan, *Gang Girls,* Boudior Book #1024, 1963, paperback original, lesbian JD sleaze novel, scarce; pseudonym of George H. Smith. **$50**   **$125**   **$275**

--- *Satan's Daughter,* Epic Book #113, 1961, paperback original, cover by Doug Weaver, lesbian sadism and masochism (S&M) novel. 📷 **$15**   **$75**   **$155**

--- *Sex and Savagery of Hell's Angels, The,* Greenleaf Classic #GC21, 1966, paperback original, cover by Robert Bonfils.   **$15**   **$65**   **$145**

Hulburd, David, *H is For Heroin,* Popular Library #495, 1953, cover by Rafael DeSoto, drug novel.

     $14   **$60**   **$140**

Hunter, Evan, *Blackboard Jungle, The,* Cardinal Book #C-187, 1955, reprint, cover by Clark Hulings, classic JD high school novel. 📷 **$2**   **$20**   **$55**

--- *Jungle Kids, The,* Pocket Book #1226, 1956, paperback original, cover by Tom Dunn, JD.   **$10**   **$35**   **$120**

Hye, Celie, *I Made My Bed,* Beacon Book #B188, 1958, paperback original, drug and JD novel, photo cover.

     $5   **$20**   **$85**

233
Holland, Marty—Jackson, Shirley

	G	VG	F		G	VG	F

Hytes, Jason, *Perfumed,* with *Pampered* by Kimberey Kemp, Midwood Book #S-277, 1963, paperback original, contains Frank Frazetta plates inside.
$20 $75 $200

--- *Over-Exposed,* Midwood Book #F-207, 1962, paperback original, cover by Paul Rader. 📷 **$8 $35 $100**

Ives, Morgan, *Knives of Desire,* Evening Reader #1240, 1966, paperback original, lesbian sleaze, written by Marion Zimmer Bradley. **$55 $200 $475**

--- *Spare Her Heaven,* Monarch Book #335, 1963, paperback original, cover by

Harry Schaare, lesbian novel, written by Marion Zimmer Bradley.
$30 $100 $200

Jackson, Delmar, *Night is My Undoing, The,* Popular Library #599, JD novel.
$5 $20 $50

Jackson, Ralph, *Violent Night,* Ace Book #S-137, 1954, paperback original, male bondage cover art. 📷
$5 $25 $75

Jackson, Shirley, *Road Through the Wall, The,* Lion Book #36, 1950, cover by Harvey Kidder. 📷
$8 $30 $100

	G	VG	F		G	VG	F

Jakes, John, *G.I. Girls*, Monarch Book #339, 1963, paperback original, cover by Ray Johnson.   **$15 $60 $150**

James, Don, *Girls and Gangs*, Monarch Book #MB534, 1963, paperback original.   **$5 $20 $75**

Jason, Stuart, *Black Emperor*, Lancer Book #75-165, 1971, paperback original, cover by Frank Frazetta, scarce.   **$10 $40 $90**

Jay, Victor, *Affairs of Gloria, The*, Brandon House #906, 1964, paperback original, cover by Fred Fixler, novel, some lesbian content; pseudonym of Victor J. Banis, his first book.   **$20 $45 $135**

Jensen, V. N., *Love of the Dead*, Viceroy Book #VP-310, 1968, paperback original, written by Ed Wood Jr.   **$25 $90 $155**

Jerome, E. D., *Love Hungry*, Croydon Book #12, 1949, cover by L. B. Cole, digest-size, sexy novel.   **$10 $35 $120**

Joesten, Joachim, *Dope, Inc.*, Avon Book #A-538, 1953, paperback original, drug novel, photo cover. 📷   **$14 $50 $125**

--- *Vice, Inc.*, Ace Book #S-58, 1954, paperback original, exposé of white slave trade.   **$6 $25 $75**

Jordan, Gail, *Unleashed Woman*, Uni-Book #28, 1952, digest-size.   **$10 $40 $100**

Jordan, Valerie, *I Am a Teen-Age Dope Addict*, Monarch Book #MB526, 1962, paperback original, drug book, photo cover with hypodermic needle. 📷   **$16 $60 $150**

Kapelner, Alan, *Lonely Boy Blues*, Lion Library #LB92, 1956, cover by Art Sussman, jazz.   **$5 $30 $90**

Karney, Jack, *Some Like It Tough*, Monarch Book #116, 1959, paperback original, JD-waterfront novel.   **$5 $25 $90**

--- *Yield to the Night*, Monarch Book #157, 1960, paperback original, JD novel.   **$6 $20 $75**

Kaufman, Leonard, *Juvenile Delinquents*, Avon Book #433, 1952, JD novel.   **$5 $30 $65**

--- *Juvenile Delinquents*, Avon Book #T-105, 1955, new cover art, JD novel.   **$4 $20 $45**

Kaye, Phillip B., *Taffy*, Avon Book #377, 1951, black JD novel, set in Harlem with stereotype cover art. 📷   **$20 $45 $140**

Keating, E. P., *Good Time Man, A*, Novel Library #13, 1949.   **$5 $20 $75**

Kemp, Kimberly, *Labor of Love, A*, Midwood Book #32-411, 1964, paperback original, cover by Paul Rader, lesbian novel; pseudonym of Gilbert Fox. 📷   **$5 $30 $90**

	G	VG	F		G	VG	F

Kendricks, James, *Adulterers, The,* Monarch Book #158, 1960, paperback original; pseudonym of Gardner F. Fox. **$3 $15 $50**

--- *Beyond Our Pleasure,* Monarch Book #392, 1963, paperback original. **$3 $20 $55**

--- *Wicked, Wicked Women, The,* Monarch Book #MA304, 1961, paperback original, women fighting cover art. **$8 $30 $120**

Kennedy, Mark, *Boy Gang,* Perma Book #M-3006, 1955, JD novel of black gang in Chicago. **$9 $30 $90**

Kent, Nial, *Divided Path, The,* Pyramid Book #32, 1951, gay interest. **$15 $75 $150**

Kerouac, Jack, *Big Sur,* Bantam Book #S2642, 1963, cover by Mitchell Hooks. **$7 $25 $70**

--- *Dharma Bums, The,* Signet Book #D-1718, 1959, cover by Barye Philips, Beat novel. **$6 $45 $100**

--- *Desolation Angels,* Bantam Book #3153, 1966. **$4 $25 $75**

--- *Maggie Cassidy,* Avon Book #G-1035, 1959, paperback original, Beat novel. **$4 $40 $140**

--- *On the Road,* Signet Book #D-1619, 1958, first paperback printing of the Beat classic, cover by Barye Philips. **$10 $40 $140**

--- *Subterraneans, The,* Avon Book #T-302, 1959, Beat novel. **$7 $35 $80**

--- *Subterraneans, The,* Avon Book #T-340, 1959, Beat novel. **$5 $25 $65**

--- *Tristesa,* Avon Book #T-429, 1960, paperback original, cover by Freeman Elliott, Beat novel. **$6 $45 $120**

King, Dave, *Run, Lez, Run,* PEC Book #FL10, 1967, paperback original, lesbian novel, wild cover art. **$10 $40 $100**

Knapp, Dexter, *Gang Girls,* Classic Library #37, 1968, paperback original, JD sleaze novel, inside credits author as Barbara Hoffman. **$8 $30 $100**

Koontz, Dean and Gerda, *Aphrodisiac Girl,* Oval Book #OB-531, 1973, reissue of *Bounce Girl,* adult sex novel by horror author and wife. **$200 $600 $1,200**

--- *Bounce Girl,* Cameo Book #8069, 1972, paperback original. **$250 $750 $1,500**

--- *Hippie Handbook, The,* Aware Books, circa 1970, digest-size, rare. **$225 $700 $1,500**

--- *Pig Society, The,* Aware Books #9501, circa 1970, digest-size, rare. **$225 $750 $1,500**

	G	VG	F

Kramer, George, *School For Girls,* Beacon Book #BB202, 1959. 📷
$5 $16 $50

Kramer, Karl, *Kiss Me Quick,* Monarch Book #121, 1959, cover by Robert Maguire. $4 $20 $75

Lamber, Ruth, *Crafty Dames,* Unique Book #UB127, 1967, paperback original, cover by Bill Ward. 📷 $8 $30 $80

Laurence, Scott, *Georgia Hotel,* Pyramid Book #68, 1952, paperback original, cover by Victor Olson.
$4 $20 $60

Laurence, Will, *Go Girls, The,* Monarch Book #330, 1963, paperback original, cover by Ray Johnson, women looking for kicks. $5 $30 $80

Lawrence, Ann, *Gin Wedding,* Intimate Novel #8, 1951, paperback original, digest-size, photo cover. 📷
$14 $55 $110

Lawrence, Gil, *Woman Racket, The,* Pyramid Book #G-468, 1959, paperback original, cover by Tom Miller, novel about an abortion mill. 📷
$3 $20 $50

LeBlanc, Maurice, *Wanton Venus,* Novel Library #5, 1948, sexy.
$5 $20 $70

Lee, William, *Junkie,* Ace Book #D-15, 1953, paperback original, drug book; pseudonym of William Burroughs, his first book, Ace Double backed with *Narcotics Agent* by Maurice Hellbrant. 📷
$250 $650 $1,500

Leech, Jack, *Satan's Daughters,* Europa Book #1104, 1963, paperback original, cover by Bill Edwards folds out, inside credits John Trimble as author, sleaze novel. $8 $32 $85

Lewis, Bobbie, *Call Girl,* Saber Books, Saber Reader #1, 1967, sexy streetwalker cover art. 📷 $10 $45 $120

Lewis, Jack, *Blood Money,* Headline Book #108, 1960, paperback original, cover by Doug Weaver, sleaze novel, Nazi cult. 📷
$8 $30 $80

Lewton, Val, *No Bed of Her Own,* Avon Monthly Novel #22, 1950, digest-size, sexy cover. $20 $75 $165

--- *No Bed of Her Own,* Novel Library #39, 1950, sexy cover art.
$5 $25 $80

Lief, Max, *Wild Parties,* Novel Library #40, 1950, sexy cover art.
$6 $35 $90

Lindsay, Perry, *Buy My Love!,* Exotic Novel, no number, 1949, paperback original, cover by Fred Claude Rodewald, digest-size, sexy cover art. 📷
$15 $90 $175

Linkletter, Eve, *B-Girl Decoy,* Fabian Book #Z-146, 1961, paperback original, "party-girl" sleaze. 📷 $5 $25 $75

	G	VG	F			G	VG	F

Lipman, Clayre and Michel, *House of Evil,* Lion Book #231, 1954, paperback original. $6 $20 $80

Liston, Jack, *Man Bait,* Dell First Edition #B158, 1960, paperback original, cover by Robert Maguire.  $4 $20 $75

Lobaugh, Elma K., *Devil's Loneliness, The,* Avon Monthly Novel #11, 1949, photo cover, digest-size. $18 $75 $135

Longstreet, Stephen, *Crystal Girl, The,* Novel Library #34, 1950, sexy cover art. $5 $20 $75

Loomis, Rae, *Luisita,* Ace Book #S-70,

1954, paperback original, cover by Robert Maguire shows woman with whip beating a man. 🎁 $5 $30 $75

Lord, Sheldon, *Born to Be Bad,* Midwood Book #14, 1959, paperback original, cover by Paul Rader, bad-girl title tells the tale of her profession, written by Lawrence Block. 🎁 $12 $70 $135

--- *Girl Called Honey, A,* Midwood Book #41, 1960, paperback original, cover by Paul Rader, written by Lawrence Block and Donald Westlake. 🎁 $25 $75 $150

	G	VG	F		G	VG	F

--- *Pads Are For Passion*, Beacon Book #B387, 1961, paperback original, verified by Lawrence Block as his.
$10 **$40** **$120**

--- *Sex Shuffle, The*, Beacon Book #B757X, 1964, paperback original, verified by Lawrence Block as his.
$10 **$35** **$100**

--- *Strange Kind of Love, A*, Midwood Book #9, 1959, paperback original, cover by Rudy Nappi, written by Lawrence Block. **$14** **$60** **$125**

Lorenz, Frederick, *Night Never Ends,* Lion Book #193, 1954, paperback original, cover by Clark Hulings.
$5 **$20** **$60**

--- *Party Every Night, A*, Lion Library #LL63, 1956, paperback original, cover by Robert Schulz. **$5** **$20** **$60**

Lucas, Curtis, *Angel,* Lion Book #162, 1953, paperback original, interracial.
$6 **$30** **$85**

--- *Lila*, Lion Library #LB14, 1955, 1955, paperback original. **$4** **$24** **$65**

--- *So Low, So Lonely*, Lion Book #91, 1952, paperback original, racial.
$5 **$25** **$75**

--- *Third Ward, Newark*, Lion Book #80, 1952, racial. **$6** **$30** **$85**

Lucas, Mark, *Sex Racket,* Saber Tropic #928, 1966, paperback original.
$5 **$18** **$55**

Lynn, Jack, *Wild Woman,* Novel Book #5034, 1961, paperback original, a Tokey Wedge sex and macho private eye novel "dedicated to any guy who knows his capacity – in both women in liquor – and then says 'to hell with it!'"
$10 **$35** **$100**

Malaponte, Marco, *Her High-School Lover,* Beacon Book #B615F, 1963, paperback original; pseudonym of Peter Rabe.
$9 **$50** **$100**

--- *New Man in the House*, Beacon Book #639F, 1963, paperback original.
$10 **$40** **$100**

Malley, Louis, *Tiger in the Streets,* Ace Book #D-251, 1957, paperback original, cover by Vern Tossey, JD novel of Spanish Harlem.
$10 **$35** **$100**

Manners, Dorine, *Sin Street,* Pyramid Book #21, 1950, classic cover art of streetwalker held in huge green hand.
$10 **$50** **$135**

Manners, William, *Big Lure, The,* Lion Book #165, 1953, paperback original, boxing novel. **$5** **$20** **$75**

--- *Wharf Girl*, Lion Book #219, 1954, paperback original. **$5** **$25** **$75**

Manning, Jane, *Reefer Girl,* Cameo Book #330, 1953, paperback original, digest-size, cover by Rudy Nappi, JD and drugs.
$75 **$200** **$550**

	G	VG	F

--- *Young Sinners*, Venus Book #183, 1956, digest-size, cover by Rudolph Belarski, JD and drugs, reprints *Reefer Girl* with new title and cover art.
$35 **$100** **$275**

Marchal, Lucie, *Mesh, The*, Bantam Book #862, 1951, lesbian novel.
$3 **$20** **$55**

Margulies, Leo, *Back Alley Jungle*, Crest Book #419, 1960, paperback original, cover by James Meese, JD anthology.
$4 **$25** **$80**

--- *Young and Deadly*, Crest Book #S272, 1959, paperback original, JD anthology.
$5 **$30** **$100**

Marion, Frances, *Passions of Linda Lane, The*, Diversey Novel #3, 1949, photo cover, digest-size. **$18** **$90** **$155**

Marshall, Alan, *All My Lovers*, Midwood Book #15, 1959, paperback original, first Alan Marshall sleaze novel, written by Donald Westlake. **$15** **$65** **$145**

--- *All the Girls Were Willing*, Midwood Book #28, 1960, paperback original, written by Donald Westlake.
$12 **$40** **$125**

--- *Man Hungry*, Midwood Book #20, 1959, paperback original, cover by Paul Rader, written by Donald Westlake.
$12 **$40** **$120**

--- *Sally*, Midwood Book #22, 1959, paperback original, cover by Paul Rader, lesbian novel, written by Donald Westlake. **$10** **$40** **$135**

--- *Sin Prowl*, Evening Reader #708, 1964, paperback original, may be by Donald Westlake. **$12** **$50** **$100**

--- *So Willing*, Midwood Book #48, 1960, paperback original, written by Donald Westlake and Lawrence Block.
$30 **$50** **$135**

--- *Strange Kind of Love, A*, Midwood Book #9, 1959, paperback original, cover by Rudy Nappi, lesbian novel, written by Lawrence Block. **$14** **$45** **$155**

--- *Virgin's Summer*, Midwood Book #36, 1960, paperback original, cover by Paul Rader, written by Donald Westlake.
$12 **$40** **$120**

Martin, Don, *Blonde Menace*, Red Circle Book #4, 1949, classic title and cover art of this pre-Lion Book.
$6 **$35** **$100**

Martin, George Victor, *Lady Said Yes, The*, Novel Library #35, 1950, photo cover, sexy. **$5** **$20** **$65**

Mason, Gregory and Carroll, Richard, *Border Woman*, Lion Book #59, 1951, cover by Harry Schaare.
$6 **$20** **$80**

Mason, Richard, *World of Suzie Wong, The*, Signet Book #D1552, 1958, cover by James Avati, predates film, Asian woman cover art. **$5** **$20** **$50**

	G	VG	F		G	VG	F

McCollum, R. R., *Passion Has Red Lips,* Rainbow Book #108, 1951, paperback original, digest-size, sexy cover art. 📖 **$20 $100 $225**

McKay, Claude, *Home to Harlem,* Avon Book #376, 1951, cover by Ray Johnson, black-related. **$8 $50 $125**

Mende, Robert, *Tough Kid From Brooklyn,* Avon Book #382, 1951, JD novel, aka *Spit and the Stars.* **$3 $20 $60**

Merchant, Paul, *Sex Gang,* Nightstand Book #1503, 1959, paperback original, short stories with one being JD; pseudonym of Harlan Ellison. **$200 $750 $1,500**

--- *Sex Gang,* Nightstand Book #1503-R, second printing 1959, similar cover to first. 📖 **$90 $200 $400**

--- *Sex Gang,* Reed Nightstand Book #3003, third printing 1973, reworked cover art, scarce. **$100 $300 $650**

Mertes, Jack, *Bobby Sox Sinners,* Newsstand Library #516, 1960, paperback original, sex and drugs sleaze novel. **$5 $20 $65**

Michaels, Bart, *Teen Temptress,* Domino Book #72-743, 1964, paperback original, JD novel about a bad-girl she-wolf. **$5 $25 $65**

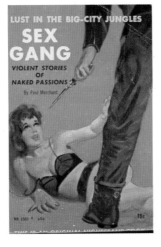

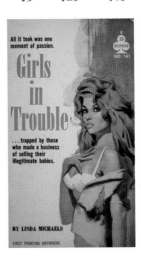

	G	VG	F

Michaels, Linda, *Girls in Trouble,* Midwood Book #161, 1962, paperback original, cover by Paul Rader; pseudonym of Julie Ellis.

| | $6 | $30 | $75 |

Milburn, George, *All Over Town,* Zenith Book #ZB-2, 1958, "small town girls with big city notions – and hell to pay over the difference...." **$5 $20 $55**

--- *Hoboes and Harlots,* Lion Book #202, 1954, paperback original.

| | $5 | $25 | $65 |

--- *Sin People,* Lion Book #159, 1953.

| | $6 | $30 | $90 |

Miller, Carlton, *Incest Street,* Narcissus Book #N-187, 1970, paperback original, adult novel written by SF writer Avram Davidson. **$200 $600 $1,500**

Miller, Nolan, *Why I Am So Beat,* Ace Book #D-398, 1959, JD novel.

| | $10 | $30 | $100 |

Mirbeau, Octave, *Torture Garden,* Lancer Book #74-840, 1965, cover by Frank Frazetta, erotic S&M.

| | $10 | $35 | $90 |

Moon, Bucklin, *Darker Brother, The,* Bantam Book #737, 1949, racial.

| | $4 | $20 | $65 |

Moore, Frances S., *Love Should Be Laughter,* Avon Romance Novel Monthly #2, 1949, digest-size, sexy novel.

| | $15 | $90 | $165 |

	G	VG	F

Moore, Margaret Witte, *Abortion, Murder Or Mercy?,* Gold Medal Book #s1215, 1962, paperback original, early non-fiction about abortion, scarce.

| | $8 | $25 | $90 |

Moravia, Alberto, *Fancy Dress Party, The,* Signet Book #1122, 1954, cover by James Avati.  **$3 $20 $45**

Moreau, Emil, *Suburbia Confidential,* Triumph Book #TNC-305, 1967, paperback original, written by Ed Wood Jr. **$35 $75 $145**

Morgan, Claire, *Price of Salt, The,* Bantam Book #1148, 1953, lesbian novel; pseudonym of Patricia Highsmith, scarce in condition. **$30 $100 $250**

Morgan, Helen, *Killer Dyke,* Exotik Book #W-3, 1964, paperback original, cover by Doug Weaver, lesbian/murder mystery.

| | $10 | $30 | $85 |

Moroso, John A., *Passionate Fool,* Red Circle Book #2, 1949, sexy novel.

| | $15 | $40 | $120 |

Motley, Willard, *Knock on Any Door,* Signet Double Book #802AB, 1950, cover by James Avati, "Live fast, die young, and leave a good-looking corpse."

| | $4 | $20 | $55 |

Myers, Harriet Kathryn, *Small Town Nurse,* Ace D-543, 1962, paperback original, nurse romance; pseudonym of Harry Whittington. **$5 $20 $65**

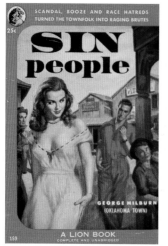

	G	VG	F		G	VG	F

Nichols, Jason, *One, Two, Three*, Viceroy Book #VP-311, 1968, paperback original; pseudonym of Ed Wood Jr.
$35 **$75** **$145**

--- *Sex Museum*, Viceroy Book #VP-299, 1968, paperback original.
$40 **$100** **$200**

Nickerson, Kate, *Boy-Chaser*, Carnival Book #937, 1953, paperback original, digest-size. **$12** **$45** **$120**

Nixon, Henry Lewis, *Confessions of a Psychiatrist*, Beacon Book #B-120, 1954, "every patient his plaything." 📷
$6 **$30** **$80**

Novak, Robert, *B-Girl*, Ace Book #S-174, 1956, paperback original.
$5 **$20** **$60**

O'Farrell, William, *Wetback*, Dell First Edition #A120, 1956, paperback original, cover by Mitchell Hooks, racial novel about border issues. 📷
$5 **$20** **$60**

Offord, Carl, *Naked Fear, The*, Ace Book #S-54, 1954, paperback original, racial topics. **$10** **$25** **$90**

O'Hara, John, *Stories of Venial Sin*, Avon Special, no number (#8), 1951, digest-size. **$15** **$50** **$125**

	G	VG	F

Oliver, A. E., *Motel Girl* with *Strange Sin* by D.W. Craig, Vest Pocket Book #VP103 & 104, 1962, paperback original, photo covers, two 2x3-inch sleaze paperbacks in slipcase, uncommon.
$20   **$75**   **$150**

Packer, Vin, *Spring Fire*, Gold Medal Book #222, 1952, paperback original, cover by Barye Phillips, lesbian novel; pseudonym of Marijane Meaker, her first book. 📷
$12   **$60**   **$165**

--- *Thrill Kids, The*, Gold Medal Book #510, 1955, paperback original, cover by James Meese, JD crime novel.
$10   **$35**   **$110**

--- *Young and Violent, The*, Gold Medal Book #581, 1956, paperback original, cover by James Meese, JD crime novel. 📷   **$18**   **$65**   **$125**

Park, Jordan, *Half*, Lion Book #135, 1953, paperback original; pseudonym of C. M. Kornbluth.   **$15**   **$40**   **125**

--- *Sorority House*, Lion Library #LL97, 1956, paperback original, cover by Clark Hulings, lesbian novel.
$15   **$35**   **$90**

--- *Valerie*, Lion Book #176, 1953, paperback original, cover by Robert Maguire.   **$15**   **$40**   **$125**

Parkhurst, Helen, *Undertow*, Monarch Book #494, 1965, photo cover, true story of a JD boy.   **$5**   **$25**   **$85**

Peters, Royal, *Body or Soul*, Red Circle Book #5, 1949, cover by Anderson, sexy novel. 📷   **$10**   **$35**   **$100**

Pettit, Charles, *Son of the Grand Eunuch, The*, Avon Book #197, 1949. 📷
$6   **$30**   **$75**

Philips, Tom, *Sorority Girls, The*, Monarch Book #273, 1962, paperback original, cover by Rafael DeSoto. 📷
$5   **$30**   **$75**

Price, Don, *Tom's Temptations*, Broadway Novel Monthly #4, 1950, sexy cover art, digest-size.   **$25**   **$90**   **$175**

Pritchard, Janet, *Country Club Cheat*, Uni-Book #68, 1953, digest-size.
$12   **$45**   **$120**

--- *Warped Women*, Uni-Book #9, 1951, paperback original, digest-size, photo cover shows one woman whipping another, lesbian novel.   **$18**   **$75**   **$140**

Pruett, Herbert O., *Abnormal Ones, The*, Beacon Book #B771X, 1964, paperback original, lesbian novel. 📷
$6   **$35**   **$90**

Putnam, J. Wesley, *Playthings of Desire*, Novel Library #15, 1949, sexy cover art.
$5   **$30**   **$80**

Quandt, Albert L., *Baby Peddler*, Original Novel #728, 1953, paperback original, digest-size, JD novel, women in trouble-white slavery novel. 📷
$15   **$70**   **$145**

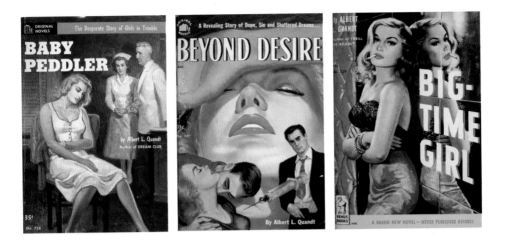

	G	VG	F		G	VG	F

--- *Baby Sitter*, Original Novel #720, 1952, paperback original, cover by Ray Pease, digest-size, JD novel.
$14 **$75** **$150**

--- *Beyond Desire*, Original Novel #707, 1952, paperback original, digest-size, JD and drugs novel, hypodermic needle cover art, reprinted as *Dream Club*.
$25 **$155** **$325**

--- *Big-Time Girl*, Venus Book #129, 1951, paperback original, digest-size.
$15 **$45** **$115**

--- *Boy Crazy*, Original Novel #735, 1952, cover by Herb Tauss, digest-size, reprints *Zip-Gun Angels* with new title and number but same cover art, JD novel.
$20 **$80** **$145**

--- *Cellar Club*, Original Novels #703, 1952, paperback original, digest-size, JD novel.
$20 **$125** **$300**

--- *Crime Boss*, Original Novel #711, 1952, paperback original, digest-size, sexy crime novel. **$15** **$60** **$165**

--- *Dream Club*, Original Novel #726, reprint 1952, digest-size, reprints *Beyond Desire* with new title but the same cover art, hypodermic needle cover, JD and drugs novel. **$20** **$100** **$180**

--- *Gang Moll*, Original Novels #709, 1952, digest-size.
$20 **$90** **$240**

--- *Social Club*, Carnival Book #930, 1954, cover by Robert Schulz, JD and crime, digest-size. **$16** **$80** **$155**

--- *Social Club*, Carnival Book #947, 1954, cover by Robert Schulz, JD, digest-size. **$14** **$70** **$150**

--- *Street Girl*, Quarter Book #91, 1951, paperback original, digest-size, JD-streetwalker novel.
$12 **$45** **$125**

--- *Zip-Gun Angels*, Original Novels #721, 1952, paperback original, cover by Herb Tauss, digest-size, classic JD novel and cover art, reprinted as *Boy Crazy*.
$30 **$150** **$375**

Rand, Lou, *Gay Detective, The*, Saber Book #SA-18, 1961, paperback original, first gay sleuth. **$15** **$75** **$175**

Randolph, Greg, *Rock Me Baby!*, Intimate Edition #707, 1962, paperback original, JD and rock and roll sleaze.
$7 **$25** **$75**

--- *Village Girl*, Intimate Novel #42, 1953, paperback original, cover by Frank Uppwall, digest-size.
$10 **$40** **$125**

Reed, Mark, *Lay Down and Die*, Falcon Book #26, 1952, paperback original, digest-size; pseudonym of Norman Daniels. **$35** **$120** **$250**

--- *Scarlet Bride, The*, Falcon Book #22, 1952, digest-size. **$35** **$120** **$210**

--- *Sins of the Flesh*, Falcon Book #32, 1952, cover by George Gross, digest-size.
$30 **$100** **$225**

--- *Street of Dark Desires*, Rainbow Book #107, 1951, paperback original, digest-size.  **$35** **$135** **$225**

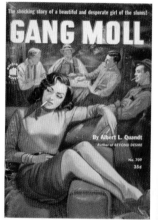

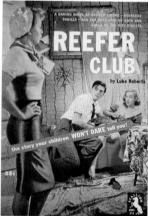

	G	VG	F		G	VG	F

Reltid, Edward, *Amorous Interne, The,* Diversey Novels #6, 1949, sexy, digest-size. **$16 $80 $155**

Rifkin, Leo and Norman, Tony, *Gang Girl,* Uni-Book #74, 1953, photo cover shows woman smoking a joint, female JD and drugs, digest-size. **$45 $165 $350**

Roan, Tom, *Slave Girl,* Falcon Book #31, 1952, paperback original, digest-size. **$20 $100 $220**

Roberts, Colette, *Millions For Love,* Novel Library #31, 1949, sexy. **$5 $20 $75**

Roberts, Luke, *Harlem Doctor,* Uni-Book #75, 1953, paperback original digest-size, black-related novel, uncommon. **$20 $85 $175**

--- *Harlem Model,* Bronze Book #1, 1952, paperback original, photo cover of black couple, black-related, digest-size, "she was tall, tan, torrid – and too hot to handle!" 📷 **$75 $175 $300**

--- *Reefer Club,* Uni-Book #49, 1953, paperback original, cover by Warren King, drugs, digest-size. 📷 **$100 $300 $700**

--- *Reefer Club,* Stallion Book #213, 1954, digest-size, JD and drugs novel, new photo cover used from Basement Gang by David Williams, reprints Uni-Book #49. 📷 **$35 $155 $400**

Roeburt, John, *They Who Sin,* Avon Book #T-321, 1959, paperback original, cover by Darcy, JD and crime novel. **$5 $25 $75**

Ronns, Edward, *Gang Rumble,* Avon Book #T-262, 1958, paperback original, JD novel; pseudonym of Edward S. Aarons. 📷 **$5 $30 $75**

Rothman, Nathan, *Virgie, Goodbye,* Avon Monthly Novel #8, 1948, digest-size, sexy. **$15 $75 $155**

--- *Virgie, Goodbye,* Avon Special, no number (#9), 1951, digest-size. **$12 $65 $120**

Sarlat, Noah, *America's Cities of Sin,* Lion Book #71, 1951, anthology about U. S. cities full of "prostitution…dope… torso murders…." 📷 **$5 $20 $75**

--- *America's Cities of Sin,* Lion Book #97, 1952, reprints Lion #71 with new number and same cover art. **$5 $15 $50**

--- *Sintown U. S.A.,* Lion Book #106, 1952. 📷 **$6 $20 $75**

Saxon, Vin, *Ape Rape,* Rapture Book #202, 1964, sleaze novel; pseudonym of Ron Haydock. **$25 $75 $175**

--- *Pagan Lesbians,* PEC Book #N137, 1966, paperback original, lesbian sleaze novel. 📷 **$15 $90 $175**

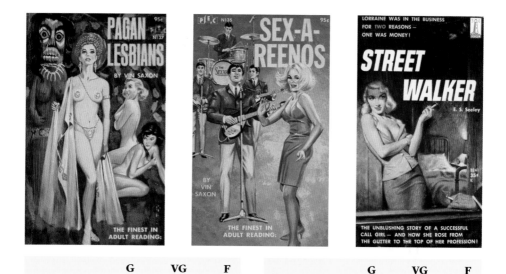

	G	VG	F

--- *Sex-A-Reenos*, PEC Book #N135, 1966, paperback original, sleaze and rock and roll stars. 🎥   **$20**   **$100**   **$200**

Schultz, Alan, *Lady For Love*, Novel Library #42, 1950, sexy cover.   **$5**   **$30**   **$75**

Scott, Anthony, *Carnival of Love*, Red Circle Book #13, 1949; pseudonym of Brett Halliday.   **$10**   **$40**   **$100**

--- *Ladies of Chance*, Novel Library #27, 1949, cover shows naked woman with playing cards and empty liquor bottle.   **$5**   **$28**   **$75**

--- *Web of Sin*, Ecstasy Book #12, 1951, paperback original, digest-size.   **$20**   **$75**   **$175**

Scott, Warwick, *Cockpit*, Lion Book #140, 1953, paperback original, cars, drugs, and women.   **$5**   **$25**   **$80**

Seeley, E. S., *Street Walker*, Beacon Book #B241, 1959, paperback original. 🎥   **$5**   **$18**   **$60**

Semple, Gordon, *Crusher's Girl*, Intimate Novel #40, 1953, paperback original, digest-size.   **$12**   **$50**   **$125**

--- *Shameless Sue*, Croydon Book #21, 1952, paperback original, cover by Lou Marchetti, digest-size.   **$10**   **$35**   **$85**

Shallit, Joseph, *Juvenile Hoods*, Avon Book #T-170, 1957, JD novel.   **$5**   **$25**   **$70**

	G	VG	F

Shaw, Andrew, *$20 Lust*, Nightstand Book #1546, 1961, paperback original, sleaze crime novel, house name used by Lawrence Block. 🎥   **$12**   **$40**   **$120**

--- *Adulterers, The*, Nightstand Book #NB1511, 1960, paperback original, written by Lawrence Block.   **$12**   **$35**   **$100**

--- *Campus Tramp*, Nightstand Book #NB1505, 1959, paperback original, the first Andrew Shaw sleaze novel, written by Lawrence Block. 🎥   **$15**   **$45**   **$125**

--- *Gutter Girl*, Bedside Book #BB1224, 1962, paperback original, bondage and knife cover art, may be Lawrence Block.   **$20**   **$60**   **$125**

--- *High School Sex Club*, Nightstand Book #NB1517, 1960, paperback original, JD sleaze novel, written by Lawrence Block.   **$15**   **$40**   **$120**

--- *Hot Rod Rogues*, Ember Library #EB-375, 1967, paperback original, JD sleaze.   **$12**   **$90**   **$175**

--- *Hush-Hush Town*, Ember Library #EL-336, 1966, paperback original.   **$8**   **$45**   **$125**

Shaw, Wilene, *Out For Kicks*, Ace Book #D-378, 1959, paperback original, JD novel. 🎥   **$8**   **$40**   **$100**

Shelley, Peter, *Soft Shoulders*, Lion Book #15, 1950, cover by Harry Schaare.   **$5**   **$25**   **$90**

	G	VG	F

Shepherd, Billy, *True Story of the Beatles, The,* Bantam Book #HZ2850, 1964, paperback original, photo cover shows the Beatles. **$10 $25 $90**

Sherman, Joan, *Bodies on Fire,* Exotic Novel, no number (#12), 1951, paperback original, digest-size. **$15 $75 $190**

Shulman, Irving, *Amboy Dukes, The,* Avon Book #169, 1948, cover by Ann Cantor, JD novel. **$4 $20 $60**

--- *Amboy Dukes, The,* Avon Book #169, reprint 1949, with new cover art showing zoot-suit kid with debutante cover art, JD novel. **$4 $20 $50**

	G	VG	F

Simmons, Herbert, *Corner Boy,* MacFadden Book #198, 1968, JD, drugs, race. **$5 $20 $65**

Simms, Campbell E., *Cuties,* Avon Book, no number, 1945, paperback original digest-size, sexy cartoons, rare. **$20 $100 $255**

Simon, John, *Sign of the Fool,* Ace Book #76350, 1971, paperback original, cover by Gene Szafran, hippies. **$10 $40 $100**

Sloan, William, *Tear Gas and Hungry Dogs,* Midwood Tower Book #X312, 1963, race riot novel. 📷 **$5 $25 $75**

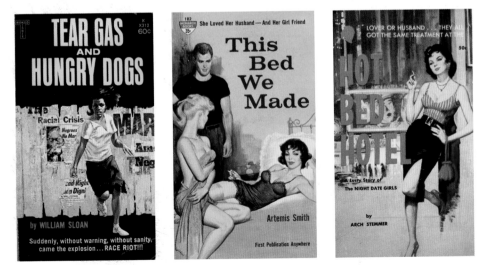

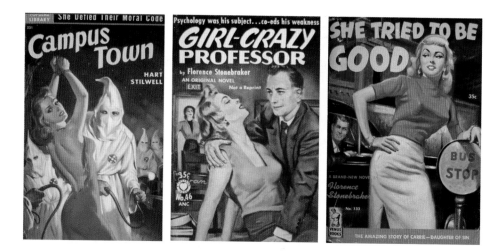

	G	VG	F

Smith, Artemis, *Odd Girl,* Beacon Book #B230, 1959, paperback original, lesbian novel. **$5 $40 $125**

--- *Third Sex, The,* Beacon Book #B268, 1959, paperback original, lesbian novel. **$8 $55 $160**

--- *This Bed We Made,* Monarch Book #182, 1961, paperback original, cover by Rafael DeSoto, lesbian novel "she loved her husband – and her girlfriend." 📷 **$5 $30 $75**

Smith, George H., *Bayou Babe,* Novel Book #5010, 1960, paperback original, Bill Ward's first adult cover. **$35 $100 $150**

--- *Swamp Bred,* Newsstand Library

	G	VG	F

#U131, 1960, paperback original, cover by Robert Bonfils. **$5 $20 $75**

Smith, Rob E., *Devil's Harvest,* Saber Book #SA161, 1969, paperback original, cover by Bill Edwards, sleaze novel with amazing devil cover art. **$18 $100 $200**

Sparkia, Roy Bernard, *Boss Man,* Lion Book #211, 1954, paperback original, plight of migrant farm workers. **$5 $30 $80**

Spenser, Fredric, *Cleo,* Cameo Book #327, 1952, paperback original, digest-size. **$12 $45 $100**

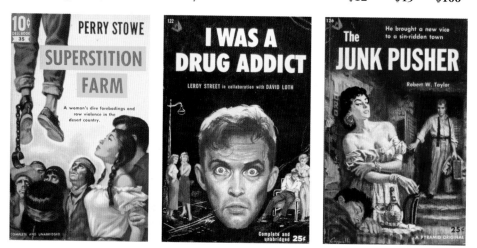

	G	VG	F			G	VG	F

Stemmer, Arch, *Hot Bed Hotel*, Chariot Book #CB-170, 1961, paperback original, streetwalker cover art, "lover or husband…they all got the same treatment at the Hot Bed Hotel." $5 $25 $70

Stevens, Greg, *Swap Academy, The*, PEC Giant #G-1201, 1970, adult sex novel, SF writer Glen Cook's first book. $25 $100 $150

Stilwell, Hart, *Campus Town*, Popular Library #331, 1951, cover by Earle Bergey, Ku Klux Klan in a college town. $25 $60 $175

Stone, Thomas, *Help Wanted – Male*, Novel Library #41, 1950; pseudonym of Florence Stonebraker. $5 $20 $75

Stonebraker, Florence, *Girl-Crazy Professor*, Croydon Book #46, 1953, paperback original, cover by Bernard Safran, digest-size. $12 $45 $100

--- *Shameless Play-Girl*, Croydon Book #55, 1953, paperback original, digest-size. $10 $40 $100

--- *She Tried to Be Good*, Venus Book #133, 1951, paperback original, cover by Rudy Nappi, digest-size. $16 $70 $155

Storm, Elliot, *Hot Date*, Red Circle Book #7, 1949, sexy cover on this early pre-Lion book. $8 $35 $100

	G	VG	F		G	VG	F

Stowe, Perry, *Superstition Farm*, Dell Ten-Cent Book #35, 1950, cover by Robert Stanley. 📷 $8 $35 $100

Street, Leory, and Loth, David, *I Was a Drug Addict*, Pyramid Book #122, 1954, drug novel. 📷 $10 $65 $160

Swados, Felice, *House of Fury*, Avon Book #298, 1951, JD novel, reprints *Reform School Girl* with new title and cover art. $12 $65 $145

--- *House of Fury*, Berkley Book #G-240, 1959, cover by Robert Maguire, reprints *Reform School Girl*. $8 $40 $100

--- *Reform School Girl*, Diversey Romance Novel #1, 1948, one-shot, JD novel, photo cover, digest-size, one of the high spots of JD books and all digest editions, with rare biography page intact 50 percent more. 📷 $300 $750 $2,200

Swenson, Peggy, *Beat Nymph*, Brandon House #932, 1965, paperback original; pseudonym of Richard E. Geis. $12 $35 $100

Taylor, Robert W., *Junk Pusher, The*, Pyramid Book #126, 1954, paperback original, cover by Frank Cozzarelli, drug book. 📷 $20 $75 $175

Taylor, Valerie, *Girls in 3-B, The*, Crest Book #S290, 1959, paperback original, lesbian novel. $6 $35 $90

--- *Return to Lesbos*, Midwood Book #F-329, 1963, paperback original, lesbian. $45 $125 $250

--- *Stranger on Lesbos*, Crest Book #S-355, 1960, paperback original. $12 $45 $100

--- *Whisper Their Love*, Crest Book #187, 1957, paperback original, lesbian, her first book. $25 $100 $200

Thayer, Tiffany, *Call Her Savage*, Avon Book, no number (#14), 1942, with Globe endpapers. $25 $45 $125

Thompson, Hunter S., *Hell's Angels*, Ballantine Book #U7087, 1967, paperback original, photo cover, expands magazine article. $15 $50 $150

Thompson, John B., *Half-Caste*, Beacon Book #B224, 1959, paperback original, interracial novel. 📷 $5 $20 $80

Torres, Treska, *Women's Barracks*, Gold Medal Book #132, 1950, paperback original, French woman at war/lesbian novel. $15 $50 $150

Tracy, Don, *How Sleeps the Beast*, Lion Book #45, 1950, cover by Ray Pease, interracial. 📷 $15 $40 $120

Tralins, Bob, *Jazzman in Nudetown*, Gaslight Book #101, 1964, classic sleaze title mixes sex with jazz and murder. 📷 $10 $35 $90

	G	VG	F		G	VG	F

Treat, Roger, *Joy Ride!*, Rainbow Book #119, 1952, paperback original, cover by George Gross, digest-size.

$20 $75 $175

Trent, Timothy, *All Dames Are Dynamite*, Novel Library #29, 1949, sexy cover.

$5 $22 $80

--- *Night Boat*, Broadway Novel Monthly #5, 1950, sexy, digest-size.

$25 $120 $225

Trevor, Elleston, *Tiger Street*, Lion Book #207, 1954, paperback original, JDs in slums. $5 $25 $85

Tully, Jim, *Road Show*, Pyramid Book #92, 1953, cover by Julian Paul, carnival novel. $5 $28 $80

Tyre, Nedra, *Reformatory Girls*, Ace Book #F-151, 1962, cover by Ray Johnson, lesbian novel. $6 $30 $80

Vane, Roland, *Vice Rackets of Soho*, Archer Book #35, 1951, cover by Reginald Heade shows hypodermic needle cover art, drugs. $15 $65 $175

--- *White Slave Racket*, Leisure Library #8, 1952, cover by Reginald Heade, digest-size, white slavery novel.

$25 $100 $250

	G	VG	F

Van Vechten, Carl, *Nigger Heaven,* Avon Book #314, 1951, in spite of the use of the derogatory word in the title, this is a key black-related mass market paperback. 📷 **$20 $65 $175**

Vast, Jack, *Wrong Kind of Love,* National Library Book #NLB-108, 1967, paperback original, early gay novel.
$7 $40 $100

Verel, Shirley, *Dark Side of Venus, The,* Bantam Book #F-2434, 1962, first U. S. edition, lesbian interest.
$6 $25 $65

Wade, David, *She Walks By Night,* Rainbow Book #116, 1952, paperback original, sexy, digest-size, prowling streetwalker; pseudonym of Norman Daniels.
$18 $125 $220

--- *Walk the Evil Street,* Rainbow Book #111, 1952, paperback original, digest-size. 📷 **$15 $100 $200**

Wall, Evans, *Swamp Girl,* Pyramid Book #39, 1951, cover by Julian Paul, woman whipping woman cover art, a lesser-valued variant edition replaces "raped" with "ravished" on back cover. 📷
$15 $60 $150

Walsh, Paul E., *KKK,* Avon Book #742, 1956, paperback original, Ku Klux Klan exposé, racial issues.
$6 $20 $65

Watkins, Glen, *Reckless Virgin,* Croydon

	G	VG	F

Book #13, 1949, cover by L. B. Cole.
$5 $20 $75

--- *Tavern Girl,* Pyramid Book #17, 1950, sexy cover art. **$10 $25 $90**

Weatherall, Ernie, *Rock 'N Roll Gal,* Beacon Book #B-131, 1957, paperback original, cover by Owen Kampen, JD and rock and roll music novel.
$15 $75 $160

--- *Rock N' Roll Gal,* Beacon Book #B-379, 1961, reprint, same cover as #B-131. 📷
$10 $35 $100

Weatherby, Max, *Long Desire, The,* Zenith Book #ZB-11, 1959, jail bait novel.
$3 $20 $50

Webber, Daniel, *Swapper's Convention,* Narcissus Book #N-186, 1970, paperback original, adult sex novel written by Dean Koontz, scarce. **$300 $1,000 $1,500**

Weigel, Arthur, *Infidelity,* Broadway Novel Monthly #1, 1950, digest-size, sexy cover art. **$15 $90 $175**

--- *Infidelity,* Novel Library #24, 1949, sexy, risqué cover. **$5 $25 $75**

Weiner, Willard, *Four Boys, a Girl and a Gun,* Avon Book #292, 1951, JD gangs in slums novel. **$5 $25 $80**

Weirauch, Anna Elisabet, *Of Love Forbidden,* Crest Book #S392, reprint 1960, lesbian novel translated by Whittaker Chambers.
$5 $20 $65

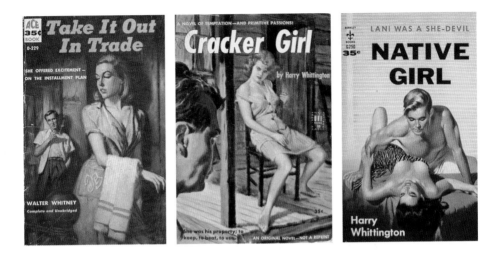

	G	**VG**	**F**

Weiss, Joe, *Gang Girl*, Beacon Book #B155, 1957, paperback original, JD novel with bondage cover art. 📷
$6 $35 $100

--- *Girls Out of Hell*, Falcon Book #28, 1952, paperback original, digest-size, cover art by George Gross, classic bad-girl JD novel. 📷 $25 $150 $265

Weiss, Martin L., *Hate Alley*, Ace Book #D-214, 1957, paperback original, JD novel. 📷 $10 $40 $120

Welles, Kermit, *See No Evil*, Original Novels #710, 1952, paperback original, digest-size. $18 $90 $175

Wells, John Warren, *Women Who Swing Both Ways*, Lancer Book #37002, 1971, paperback original, lesbian novel, dedicated to "Jill Emerson," written by Lawrence Block. $25 $90 $175

West, Ben, *Loves of a Girl Wrestler*, Uni-Book #32, 1952, cover by Ed Cham, digest-size, "a tigress in the ring – a temptress in the boudoir!"
$12 $45 $125

West, Edwin, *Campus Doll*, Monarch Book #189, 1961, paperback original, cover by Tom Miller; pseudonym of Donald Westlake. $12 $50 $130

--- *Strange Affair*, Monarch Book #232, 1962, paperback original, cover by Harry Schaare, lesbian romance.
$15 $50 $150

	G	**VG**	**F**

--- *Young and Innocent*, Monarch Book #165, 1960, paperback original, cover by Robert Maguire. $22 $50 $140

West, Token, *Why Get Married?*, Red Circle Book #12, 1949. $10 $50 $125

Westermier, David L., *Sexecutives, The*, Private Edition #PE-457, 1969, paperback original, cover by Paul Rader, written by Ed Wood Jr. $40 $100 $250

White, Daniel, *Southern Daughter*, Avon Book #547, 1953, paperback original; pseudonym of Day Keene.
$5 $30 $90

White, William Chapman, *Pale Blonde of Sands Street, The*, Popular Library Eagle Book #EB8, 1954. 📷
$2 $18 $40

Whitney, Hallam, *Backwoods Shack*, Carnival Book #931, 1953, paperback original, digest-size; pseudonym of Harry Whitney. $20 $100 $225

--- *Sinners Club*, Carnival Book #923, 1953, cover by Rudolph Belarski, digest-size. $35 $125 $275

--- *Wild Seed*, Ace Book #S-153, 1956, paperback original.
$8 $40 $115

Whitney, Walter, *Take it Out in Trade*, Ace Book #D-229, 1957, paperback original, cover by Verne Tossey, a novel of "transplanted hillbillies and the women who fleece them." 📷
$6 $30 $75

	G	VG	F			G	VG	F

Whittington, Harry, *69 Babylon Park,* Avon Book #F-146, 1962, paperback original, cover by Ray Johnson.
$6   **$30**   **$90**

--- *Across That River,* Ace Book #D-201, 1956, paperback original, Ace Double backed with *Saturday Mountain* by Nathaniel E. Jones. **$8** **$45** **$120**

--- *Backwoods Shack,* Lancer Book Double #72-631, 1962, combined with *Spotlight on Sin* by Doug Dupperault, cover by Weston. **$5** **$25** **$75**

--- *Backwoods Tramp,* Gold Medal Book #889, 1959, paperback original, cover by Barye Philips. **$10** **$50** **$110**

--- *Cracker Girl,* Uni-Book #58, 1953, paperback original, digest-size, "a novel of temptation – and primitive passions!" 📖 **$25** **$120** **$250**

--- *Cracker Girl,* Stallion Book #216, 1954, digest-size, reprints Uni-Book #58 with new cover art. **$20** **$90** **$200**

--- *Native Girl,* Berkley Book #G-250, 1959, "Lani was a she-devil." 📖
$10   **$35**   **$100**

--- *Shack Road Girl,* Berkley Diamond #D2004, 1959, cover by Robert McGinnis, scarce. **$6** **$45** **$150**

--- *Strictly For the Boys,* Stanley Library #SL-72, paperback original, sexy girl photo cover. **$8** **$30** **$80**

--- *Vengeful Sinner,* Croydon Book #35, 1953, paperback original, digest-size. 📖
$25   **$125**   **$255**

--- *Woman on the Place, A,* Ace Book #S-143, 1956, paperback original.
$12   **$40**   **$120**

Wilder, Robert, *Wait For Tomorrow,* Bantam Book #A1181, 1953, cover by James Avati. 📖 **$7** **$30** **$75**

Wilhelm, Gale, *No Letters For the Dead,* Lion Book #52, 1951, cover by Ray Pease, "She sold herself for her lover's sake." **$5** **$20** **$70**

--- *No Nice Girl,* Pyramid Book #G440, 1959, cover by James Bentley, reprints Lion #52 with yet another title.
$4   **$20**   **$40**

--- *Paula,* Lion Library #LB115, 1956, cover by Morgan Kane, reprints Lion #52 with new title and cover art.
$4   **$18**   **$45**

--- *Strange Path, The,* Lion Book #121, 1953, lesbian novel. 📖
$15   **$50**   **$135**

--- *Strange Path, The,* Berkley Book #G-111, 1958, cover by Robert Maguire, lesbian novel. **$8** **$35** **$100**

--- *We Too Are Drifting,* Lion Book #70, 1951, lesbian novel. 📖
$10   **$50**   **$155**

Willeford, Charles, *Black Mass of Brother Springer, The,* Black Lizard Book #390975, 1989, first edition thus, cover by Kirwan, interracial novel, reprints *Honey Gal* with new title. 📖
$10   **$40**   **$120**

	G	VG	F

--- *Cockfighter*, Chicago Paperback House, #B-120, 1962, paperback original.
$20 **$80** **$250**

--- *High Priest of California*, Royal Books Giant #20, 1953, paperback original, cover by Walter Popp, thick digest-size, Willeford's first novel, teamed up with *Full Moon* by Talbot Mundy, cover shows woman whipping another woman. 📷
$55 **$225** **$800**

--- *High Priest of California* and *Wild Wives*, Beacon Book #130, 1956, paperback original on Wild Wives. 📷
$50 **$250** **$600**

--- *Honey Gal*, Beacon Book #B160,

	G	VG	F

1958, paperback original, cover by Walter Popp, interracial. 📷
$100 **$450** **$1,000**

--- *Lust Is a Woman*, Beacon Book #B175, 1958, paperback original, cover by Micarelli, interracial novel. 📷
$75 **$400** **$900**

--- *Lust Is a Woman*, Softcover Library #B1081S, reprint 1967, photo cover, scarce. **$75** **$100** **$300**

--- *No Experience Necessary*, Newsstand Library #U182, 1962, paperback original, cover by Robert Bonfils, toughest of the three Willeford by this publisher.
$60 **$150** **$400**

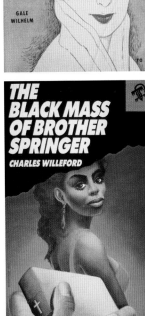

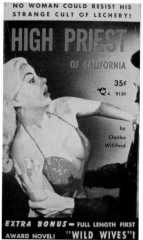
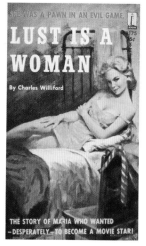

	G	VG	F

--- *Pick-Up*, Beacon Book #109, 1955, paperback original.
| | $50 | $200 | $450 |

--- *Pick-Up*, Beacon Book #B1060, reprint 1967, scarce.
| | $15 | $50 | $100 |

--- *Understudy For Love*, Newsstand Library #U170, 1961, paperback original, cover by Robert Bonfils.
| | $40 | $165 | $375 |

--- *Woman Chaser, The*, Newsstand Library #U137, 1960, paperback original, cover by Robert Bonfils.
| | $20 | $100 | $265 |

Williams, Charles, *Uncle Sagamore and His Girls*, Gold Medal Book #s908, 1959, paperback original, hillbilly novel.
| | $6 | $40 | $140 |

Williams, David, *Basement Gang*, Intimate Novel #32, 1953, paperback original, digest-size, photo cover later reused on *Reefer Club* by Luke Roberts, JD and drugs novel.
| | $18 | $125 | $250 |

Williams, James, *Never to Belong*, Fabian Book #Z-135, 1960, paperback original, interracial sleaze novel.
| | $5 | $30 | $100 |

Williams, John A., *Angry Ones, The*, Ace Book #D-420, 1960, paperback original, interracial, his first book. 📷
| | $12 | $50 | $200 |

	G	VG	F

	G	VG	F

Williams, J. X., *ESP Orgy,* Adult Book #AB419, 1968 paperback original, cover by Robert Bonfils, sleaze that mixes drugs and sex with the 1960s.
$25 $100 $255

--- *Odd Girl Out,* Ember Library #EL344, 1966, paperback original.
$6 $40 $90

--- *Parisian Passions,* Sundown Reader #611, 1966, house name used this time by Ed Wood Jr. $55 $150 $300

Williams, Roswell, *Women Without Love?,* Novel Library #10, 1949, sexy risqué cover art. $5 $20 $75

Wilson, Dana, *Uneasy Virtue,* Avon Monthly Novel #5, 1948, digest-size.
$25 $75 $175

--- *Uneasy Virtue,* Novel Library #12, 1949, sexy cover art.
$5 $20 $75

Wilstach, John, *Love For Sale,* Diversey Novels #5, 1949, digest-size.
$22 $100 $225

Wolfe, Byron, *Lust At the Waterfront,* Saber Book #SA-80, 1964, paperback original. 📷 $5 $20 $60

Wolfson, P. J., *Flesh Barons, The,* Lion Library #LL4, 1954, abortion novel, aka *Is My Flesh of Brass?* 📷
$4 $20 $65

Wood, Clement, *Desire,* Berkley Book #G-160, 1958, photo cover shows two women in lesbian situation, collection of stories, some lesbian-related.
$10 $30 $75

Wood Jr., Ed, *Black Lace Drag,* Raven Book #713, 1963, paperback original, his first book. 📷 $50 $225 $500

--- *Bye Bye Broadie,* Pendulum Pictorial Reader #PP-001, 1968, paperback original, purports to be possible movie tie-in, but the film is unknown or was never made. $30 $125 $250

--- *Death of a Transvestite,* Cougar Book #821, 1967, paperback original, transvestite hitman, sequel to *Black Lace Drag.* $35 $120 $300

--- *Drag Trade,* Triumph Book #TNC-106, 1967, paperback original.
$35 $150 $275

--- *Gay Underworld, The,* Viceroy Book #VP-292, 1968, paperback original.
$35 $125 $250

--- *It Takes One to Know One,* Imperial #786, 1967, paperback original.
$20 $100 $225

--- *Purple Thighs,* Private Edition #PE-474, 1969. $25 $155 $350

--- *Raped in the Grass,* Pendulum Pictorial Reader #PP-002, 1968, paperback original. $35 $150 $250

--- *Sex Shrouds and Caskets,* Viceroy Book #VP-291, 1968, paperback original.
$22 $85 $175

--- *Side-Show Siren,* Sundown Reader #618, 1966, paperback original.
$30 $125 $300

	G	VG	F

--- *Toni – Black Tigress*, Private Edition #PE-474, 1969, paperback original.

	$50	$200	$375

--- *Watts...After*, Pad Library #578, 1967, paperback original, race riot.

	$25	$100	$225

--- *Watts...The Difference*, Pad Library #564, 1966, Los Angeles race riot.

	$30	$100	$250

--- *Young, Black and Gay*, PEC French Line #FL38, 1968, paperback original.

	$40	$125	$200

Woodford, Jack, *3 Gorgeous Hussies*, Novel Library #1, 1948, sexy cover, Woodford's novels were considered sexy and risqué for the era, collected today because of sexy pin-up covers.

	$8	$25	$75

--- *Abortive Hussy, The*, Avon Book Dividend #1, 1950, digest-size.

	$16	$75	$155

--- *Abortive Hussy, The*, Avon Book #146, 1947. 📷

	$5	$20	$60

--- *Dangerous Love*, Broadway Novel Monthly #9, 1950, sexy, digest-size.

	$25	$100	$175

--- *Ecstasy Girl*, Avon Monthly Novel #20, 1951, digest-size.

	$22	$85	$165

--- *Ecstasy Girl*, Novel Library #2, 1948, sexy cover art.

	$6	$25	$75

--- *Free Lovers*, Avon Special, no number (#6), 1951, digest-size. 📷

	$22	$125	$250

--- *Free Lovers*, Novel Library #3, 1948, scarce variant with white background 20 percent more.

	$5	$20	$75

--- *Grounds For Divorce*, Avon Book Dividend #4, 1950, digest-size.

	$25	$80	$155

--- *Grounds For Divorce*, Novel Library #7, 1948, sexy cover.

	$5	$20	$65

--- *Hard-boiled Virgin, The*, Avon Bedside Novel #2, 1951, digest-size.

	$22	$75	$165

--- *Her First Sin!*, Exotic, no number #4, 1949, paperback original, digest-size.

	$20	$55	$150

--- *Male and Female*, Avon Bedside Novel #5, 1951, digest-size.

	$20	$90	$165

--- *Male and Female*, Novel Library #36, 1950, sexy cover.

	$5	$28	$85

--- *Passionate Princess, The*, Avon Bedside Novel #6, 1951, digest-size.

	$22	$100	$200

--- *Passionate Princess, The*, Novel Library #4, 1948, sexy cover.

	$6	$25	$85

--- *Peeping Tom*, Avon Special no number (#3), 1951, digest-size, similar cover art to NL #6 but toned down.

	$25	$110	$220

--- *Peeping Tom*, Novel Library #6, 1948, lingerie pin-up cover art. 📷

	$15	$60	$125

--- *Rites of Love, The*, Avon Bedside Novel #1, 1950, digest-size.

	$22	$80	$175

--- *Teach Me to Love*, Avon Book Dividend #6, 1950.

	$16	$75	$155

--- *Teach Me to Love*, Novel Library #44, 1950. 📷

	$6	$25	$85

--- *Three Gorgeous Hussies*, Avon Special, no number (#5), 1951, digest-size.

	$16	$85	$135

--- *Untamed Darling*, Broadway Novel Monthly #10, 1950, sexy, digest-size.

	$15	$90	$200

--- *Untamed Darling*, Avon Book #297, 1951, "two men and one wild girl."

	$6	$30	$75

Wright, Richard, *Black Boy*, Signet Book #841, 1951, cover by James Avati, racial. 📷

	$5	$25	$75

--- *Native Son*, Signet Book #S794, 1950, cover by James Avati.

	$4	$20	$70

--- *Uncle Tom's Children*, Signet Book #647, 1949, cover by James Avati, a novel of racial discrimination and horror. 📷

	$5	$25	$70

Zinberg, Len, *Strange Desires*, Avon Monthly Novel #6, 1948, digest-size, photo cover, the true name of mystery writer Ed Lacy.

	$15	$65	$135

Zola, Emile, *Shame*, Ace Book #S-76, 1954, first U. S. edition, sexy cover art.

	$5	$20	$60

--- *Venus of the Counting House*, Avon Book #236, 1950, sexy novel about Paris life. 📷

	$5	$20	$50

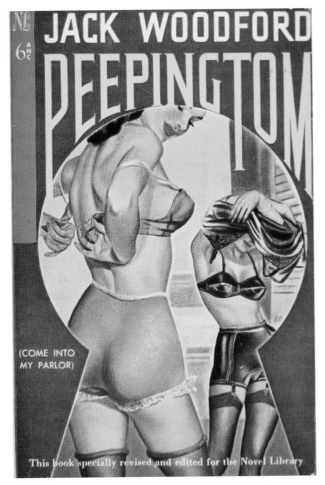

MISCELLANEOUS:
Literary, Historical, War, Romance, Puzzle Books, Joke Books, Others

This final category includes a group of popular sub-genres, a proverbial smorgasbord of what is left in the realm of key collectible paperbacks. This is a diverse category that includes romance and gothics, historical novels and war books, literary novels, bestsellers, items of paperback publishing history, cookbooks, satires, joke books, game books, puzzle books, cartoon and comic book paperbacks, how-to books, and then some.

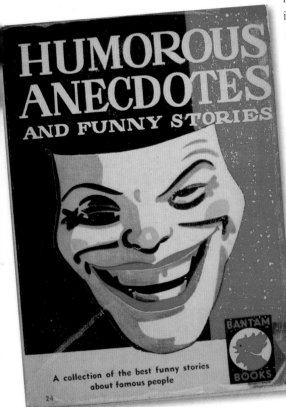

A collection of the best funny stories about famous people

24

Literary

Many of the great literary novelists, stylists, and experimenters of our time had books reprinted in paperback, and some of these have become quite collectible. Giants such as Ernest Hemingway, John Steinbeck, William Faulkner, Turman Capote, F. Scott Fitzgerald, D. H. Lawrence, Sinclair Lewis, William Saroyan, Thornton Wilder and others had significant editions of their work appear in paperback. Some of the most important and key books are listed in this section. These include dust jacketed editions and Armed Service Editions of classic literary novels and books such as William Faulkner's *A Rose For Emily* in the Armed Service Edition, which is a true first edition and scarce.

Historical and War

Historical and war paperbacks, both fiction and non-fiction, are perennially popular with readers in inexpensive paperback editions, and some books and authors have wide followings. The novels of C. S. Forester, most notably his Horatio Hornblower books, are one example. Books about famous battles or wars, about pirates or famous outlaws are also much sought after by readers and collectors. Some of these books are difficult to find and are in high demand, so their values reflect that.

Edison Marshall, F. Van Wyck Mason, Rafael Sabatini, Vardis Fisher, Frank Slaughter, Kenneth Roberts, Mika Waltari, and Frank Yerby were some of the popular historical novelists from the era of the 1930s to the 1960s. Marshall was a popular historical novelist whose paperbacks often had outstanding cover art. Meanwhile, war books, both fiction and non-fiction, are also perennially popular. Here there is great interest in books on the Civil War, World War II, Vietnam, the Napoleonic Era, and ancient Rome and Greece.

Romance

What we think of as the romance genre today began with the mass-market paperbacks from Dell Books in the 1940s. These early Dell Map Back romances even had their own heart-shape logo to differentiate romance titles from Dell's other fiction categories, such as westerns and mysteries.

Beginning in the 1950s, and then into the 1960s and '70s, other publishers like Bantam, Ace, and Ballantine began a steady output of nurse books, romantic gothics, and other out-and-out romance love novels featuring young woman meeting the man of their dreams.

There is an interesting juxtaposition between the art of then and now. In the earlier vintage era of the 1950s and '60s, and the later romance era of the 1980s and '90s, many of the same artists worked

on the covers but with far different orientations on that cover art. In the old days paperbacks were primarily marketed to men and the cover art reflected that targeting. Today, the book market in general, and the romance genre in particular, is targeted at women. Master artists like Robert Maguire, Robert McGinnis, Walter Popp, and Rudy Nappi all produced magnificent art in the old days, featuring tough guys and dangerous dames, and later produced alluring romantic "bodice rippers" for the covers of modern romance paperbacks. In fact, one author of today, Joanna Lindsey, requires the man to be naked on the covers of her novels – not the woman! This turns the tables on the traditional cover art seen on many romance novels.

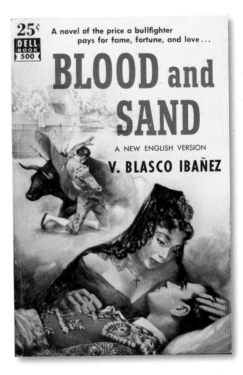

Romance books today are said to be 50 percent of all fiction market sales, so their influence cannot be downplayed; however, while there are thousands of titles, there are not a lot of big money paperbacks in the genre. Those listed here include early classics and originals by popular authors in the genre such as scarce MacFadden paperback originals.

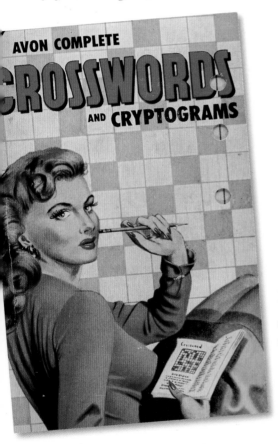

AVON COMPLETE CROSSWORDS AND CRYPTOGRAMS

Joke, Cartoon, Puzzle, and Game Books

Many paperback publishers brought out entertaining and fun books that dealt with jokes, games, puzzles, and other similar topics. Many of these have become scarce and collectible. Some of the most highly valued are the early Dell and Avon crossword puzzle paperbacks. These books in best condition and without any crossword puzzles filled in fetch premium prices, and all are listed here. Truth be told, most of the puzzle books were once fairly common, but many were worked, worn out, and fell apart. Early crossword puzzle books with unworked puzzles are scarce because most of these books were completed by puzzle enthusiasts, and when the books were completed, they were thrown away.

Cartoon books and books that reprint comic book art are also sought after. *Mansion of Evil*, a scarce Gold Medal Book, was one of the first paperbacks to be a color comic book and is valued highly. It began a format in which many comic book superheroes made it to paperback. The Charles Addams paperbacks that collect his macabre New Yorker cartoons are also popular and collectible.

	G	VG	F

Adams, John Paul, *Picture Quiz Book,* Popular Library #223, 1950, paperback original, cover by Alex Schomburg.
     $35 **$75** **$165**

--- *Puzzles For Everybody,* Avon Book #295, 1951, paperback original, the scarce second Avon puzzle book, girly photos inside. 🎁**$90** **$175** **$450**

Addams, Charles, *Addams and Evil,* Pocket Book #50063, 1965, first paperback printing, cover by Charles Addams, cartoons. 🎁
     $4 **$20** **$65**

--- *Black Maria,* Pocket Book #50059, 1964, first paperback printing, cover by Charles Addams, cartoons.
     $5 **$20** **$50**

--- *Drawn and Quartered,* Bantam Book #37, 1946, the first of his cartoon books, predates "The Addams Family" TV series.
     $4 **$30** **$90**

--- *Drawn and Quartered,* Pocket Book #50058, 1964, reprints Bantam #37, cover by Charles Addams, cartoons.
     $4 **$15** **$40**

--- *Homebodies,* Pocket Book #50062, 1965, first paperback printing, cover by Charles Addams, cartoons.
     $4 **$20** **$45**

--- *Monster Rally,* Pocket Book #50061, 1965, first paperback printing, cover by Charles Addams, cartoons.
     $4 **$20** **$45**

--- *Nightcrawlers,* Pocket Book #50060, 1964, first paperback printing, cover by Charles Addams, cartoons.
     $5 **$25** **$50**

Alverson, Chuck, *Wonder Wart-Hog, Captain Crud & Other Super Stuff,* Gold Medal Book #d1781, 1967, first book edition, reprints counter-culture comics that lampoon super heroes, predates *Zap,* Harvey Kurtzman introduction, art by Gilbert Shelton, Vaughan Bode. 🎁
     $1 **$60** **$165**

Anderson, Poul, *Golden Slave, The,* Avon Book #T-388, 1960, paperback original, scarce historical novel by famed SF author. 🎁 **$4** **$20** **$75**

Anonymous, *1000 Facts Worth Knowing,* LA Bantam #10, 1940, text cover, the most common LA Bantam but still rare.
     $35 **$100** **$155**

--- *Avon Book of Modern Short Stories, The,* Avon, no number (#15) 1942, anthology, with Globe endpapers.
     $20 **$50** **$125**

--- *Best Cartoons From Argosy,* Zenith Book #ZB-5, 1958, first book edition. 🎁
     $3 **$16** **$40**

--- *Best From True, The,* Gold Medal Book, no number (#99), 1949, first book edition, photo cover, first Gold Medal Book and only Gold Medal in short format. 🎁 **$12** **$40** **$120**

	G	VG	F			G	VG	F

--- *Challenger Crossword Puzzles*, Readers Choice #34, 1952, paperback original, digest-size. **$60** **$225** **$550**

--- *Crossword Puzzles*, Popular Library #107, 1946, paperback original. **$45** **$155** **$250**

--- *Electric Cook Book, The*, Philadelphia Electric Co., 1959, paperback original, 1950s kitchen cover art makes this book collectible, recipes for "cooking electrically." 📷 **$4** **$15** **$40**

--- *Everybody's Dream Book*, LA Bantam #4, 1940, text cover, rare. **$55** **$150** **$220**

--- *I Was a Nazi Flyer*, Dell Book #21, Map Back, cover by Gerald Gregg, World War II aviation novel. **$10** **$45** **$140**

--- *Man Story*, Gold Medal Book #102, 1950, first book edition, reprints adventure stories from *True* magazine. **$10** **$30** **$90**

--- *Model Railroading*, Bantam Book #A-2, 1950, paperback original, cover by Walter Popp, written by Lionel editors, many photos and drawings of layouts. 📷 **$4** **$20** **$50**

	G	VG	F

--- *Noman*, Tower Book #42-672, 1966, paperback original, comic book in paperback format, T.H.U.N.D.E.R. agents.  **$10** **$40** **$120**

--- *Pony Book of Puzzles*, Pony Book #65, 1946. **$50** **$125** **$225**

--- *Proceed at Your Own Risk*, Quick Reader #146, 1946, jokes, stories and gags, rare. **$35** **$100** **$300**

--- *Smile, Brother, Smile!*, Trophy Book #401, 1946, humor anthology, one of two books in the Trophy series. **$20** **$75** **$225**

--- *Superman*, Signet Book #D-2966, 1966, first book edition, comic book in paperback format, Superman comics, includes origin, scarce in condition. **$10** **$30** **$100**

--- *Terrific Trio, The*, Tower Book #42-687, 1966, paperback original, comic book in paperback format, includes Noman, Dynamo, and Menthor. **$10** **$30** **$100**

Archer, Jules and Sawyer, Maxine, *Sex Life and You*, Red Circle Book #1, 1949, paperback original, text cover, first pre-Lion, scarce. **$10** **$60** **$150**

Arenson, D. J., *Zorro and the Pirate Raiders*, Bantam Book #24670, 1986, paperback original, continues Johnston McCulley's hero, Zorro, recalled for copyright purposes, scarce. **$4** **$20** **$50**

--- *Zorro Rides Again*, Bantam Book #24671, 1986, paperback original, Zorro novel, recalled for copyright purposes, scarce. **$5** **$20** **$55**

Balchin, Nigel, *Small Back Room, The*, Lion Book #31, 1950, cover by Wesley Snyder. **$5** **$18** **$60**

Baldwin, Faith, *Bride From Broadway*, Dell Ten-Cent Book #5, 1950, first book edition, cover by Wesley Snyder, sexy siren cover art captures the feel of the 1930s era in New York City. **$5** **$25** **$65**

Barnett, Lincoln, *Universe and Dr. Einstein, The*, Mentor Book #M71, second printing 1952, cover by Robert Jonas shows Albert Einstein. **$3** **$12** **$35**

Beach, Edward L., *Run Silent, Run Deep*, Perma Book #4061, cover by Clark Hulings, submarine warfare. **$2** **$14** **$30**

--- *Submarine!*, Signet Book #S1043, 1953, submarines in World War II. **$2** **$14** **$35**

Benefield, Harry, *Valiant is the Word For Carrie*, Bantam Book #24, 1946, in dust jacket. **$20** **$45** **$100**

Bengtsson, Fran G., *Long Ships, The*, Signet Book #D1391, 1957, historical novel. **$3** **$20** **$60**

	G	VG	F

	G	VG	F

Beveridge, Elizabeth, *Pocket Book of Home Canning, The,* Pocket Book #217, 1943, rare text dust jacketed edition.
$35   **$100**   **$175**

Bradley, David, *No Place to Hide,* Bantam Book #421, 1949, in dust jacket.
$20   **$70**   **$140**

Brande, Dorothea, *Wake Up and Live,* Pocket Book #2, 1939, only 10,000 copies sold in New York City area.
$55   **$150**   **$350**

Brandon, Michael, *Nonce,* Avon Book #506, 1953, voodoo magic and sex. 🎲
$4   **$20**   **$45**

Brennan, Dan, *Naked Night, The,* Lion Book #197, 1954, paperback original, war novel.   **$5**   **$20**   **$65**

Brewer, Gil, *Appointment in Hell,* Monarch Book #187, 1961, paperback original, cover by Robert Stanley, survivors of a plane crash. 🎲   **$10**   **$65**   **$125**

Brock, Rose, *Longleaf,* Avon Book #10482, 1974, paperback original, gothic romance; pseudonym of Joseph Hansen.
$10   **$45**   **$100**

--- *Tarn House,* Avon Book #5450, 1971, paperback original, gothic romance.
$15   **$50**   **$135**

	G	VG	F		G	VG	F

Brockman, Susan, *Ladies Man,* Bantam Loveswept Book #0648, 1997, paperback original, scarce romance.
$70 $200 $300

Bromfield, Louis, *What Became of Anna Bolton?,* Bantam Book #462, 1948, in dust jacket.   **$35 $90 $175**

Brontë, Emily, *Wuthering Heights,* Pocket Book #7, 1939, only 10,000 copies sold in New York City area.
$40 $150 $290

Brown, Douglas, *Anne Bonny Pirate Queen,* Monarch Book #MA320, 1962, cover by Robert Stanley, historical novel about female pirate; pseudonym of Walter B. Gibson.
$10 $55 $125

Brown, Harry, *Walk in the Sun, A,* Lion Book #76, 1952 war novel.
$5 $15 $55

Brown, Harry C., *Favorite Poems,* LA Bantam Book #8, 1940, paperback original, text cover, rare.
$40 $100 $200

Buchanan, Jack, *Saigon Slaughter,* Jove Book #09107, 1987, paperback original, #7 in the M.I.A. Hunter men's action series, written by Joe Lansdale.
$5 $25 $80

Buck, Pearl, *Good Earth, The,* no number, 1938, the first mass-market paperback, only 2,000 copies distributed in the New York City area on a trial basis, less than a dozen copies known, later reprinted with similar cover art and a number as #11 in the regular Pocket Book series, rare.
$1,500 $6,000 $15,000

--- *Good Earth, The,* Pocket Book #11, 1939, first printing this number, reprints Pocket no number with new number.
$20 $50 $150

Butler, Samuel, *Way of All Flesh, The,* Pocket Book #8, 1939, only 10,000 copies sold in New York City area.
$45 $150 $275

Capote, Truman, *Other Voices Other Rooms,* Signet Book #700, 1949, cover by Robert Jonas, another version of the "keyhole" cover, novel, gay interest.
$3 $25 $75

Capp, Al, *World of Li'l Abner, The,* Ballantine Book #8, 1953, paperback original, cover by Al Capp, cartoons.
$10 $30 $100

Carnegie, Dale, *How to Win Friends and Influence People,* Pocket Book #68, 1940, photo cover, for some reason yet determined the first printing of this book was only distributed in Texas, scarce.
$25 $50 $100

--- *Little Known Facts About Well Known People,* LA Bantam Book #2, 1940, text cover, rare.   **$50 $160 $300**

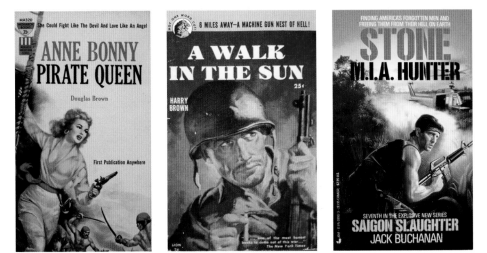

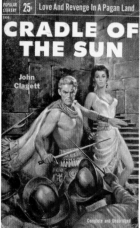

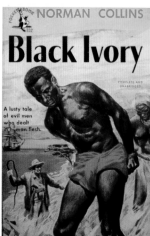

	G	VG	F

Castle, Jayne, *Queen of Hearts,* MacFadden Book #132, circa 1975, paperback original, romance novel; pseudonym of Jayne Bentley. **$10 $40 $100**

--- *Vintage of Surrender,* MacFadden Book #157, 1975, paperback original, romance novel. **$10 $40 $100**

Cavannah and Weir, *Dell Book of Jokes, The,* Dell Book #89, 1945, paperback original, cover by Gerald Gregg, anthology. **$20 $75 $175**

Chambliss, William C., *Boomerang!,* Bantam Book #156, 1948, war novel, Infantry Journal edition in Bantam dust jacket. 📷 **$22 $75 $135**

Clagett, John, *Cradle of the Sun,* Popular Library #566, 1954, historical novel. 📷 **$2 $12 $30**

Clark, Comer, *England Under Hitler,* Ballantine Book #512K, 1961, paperback original, true story of Nazi plans for conquered England in World War II. **$4 $20 $60**

Collins, Norman, *Black Ivory,* Pocket Book #632, 1949, cover by Barye Phillips, historical novel about African slave trade. 📷 **$6 $25 $80**

Corbett, Jim, *Man-Eaters of Kumaon,* Pennant Book #P23, 1953, true adventure, big-game hunter tracks man-eating tigers in India. 📷 **$3 $15 $38**

Cotlow, Lewis, *Amazon Head-Hunters,* Signet Book #S1094, 1954, first paperback printing, cover by James Meese, true adventures among tribes in Amazon, photos. 📷 **$4 $20 $45**

Crane, Aimee, *G.I. Sketch Book, The,* Infantry Journal #S225, 1944, for soldiers overseas, oblong book, soldier art includes future paperback artists John J. Floherty and John McDerrmott. 📷 **$10 $30 $100**

Cuppy, Will, *How to Tell Your Friends From the Apes,* Quick Reader #118, 1944, cover by Axelrod shows caricature of Tarzan author Edgar Rice Burroughs, humor and satire, Tarzan-related. **$8 $30 $75**

Currie, S. M. A., *How to Make Friends Easily,* LA Bantam #5, 1940, paperback original, text cover, rare. **$55 $125 $175**

Cushman, Dan, *Tongking!,* Ace Book #D-49, 1954, paperback original, cover by Rafael DeSoto, pirate novel, Ace Double backed with *Golden Temptress* by Charles Grayson, historical novel. 📷 **$12 $50 $125**

David, Eddie, *Campus Joke Book,* Ace Book #S-171, 1956, paperback original, cover by Pierce. **$5 $20 $60**

Davies, Valentine, *Miracle on 34th Street,* Pocket Book #903, 1952. **$4 $15 $55**

--- *Miracle on 34th Street,* Pocket Book #903, second printing 1959, cover by Frederick Banbery. 📷 **$2 $10 $30**

Davis, Franklin M., *Bamboo Camp #10,* Monarch Book #236, 1962, paperback original, cover by Robert Stanley, Americans soldiers brutalized in Japanese POW camp in World War II. 📷 **$10 $40 $100**

	G	VG	F		G	VG	F

--- *Naked and the Lost, The*, Lion Book #221, 1954, paperback original, military prisoners. **$5** **$25** **$75**

Dean, Robert George, *On Ice*, Bantam Book #148, 1948, Superior reprint in dust jacket. **$25** **$60** **$145**

De Camp, L. Sprague, *Bronze God of Rhodes, The*, Bantam Book #2589, 1963, first paperback printing, scarce historical novel. **$5** **$35** **$70**

--- *Elephant For Aristotle, An*, Curtis Book #09059, no date, circa 1970, first paperback printing, scarce historical novel by SF/F author.  **$10** **$40** **$100**

--- *Golden Wind, The*, Curtis Book #07091, no date, circa 1970, first paperback printing, scarce historical novel. **$5** **$20** **$50**

Dodd, Christina, *Castles in the Air*, Harper Book #08034, 1993, paperback original, cover by Robert Maguire, historical romance, error cover art shows "3-armed lady," the book was recalled and copies destroyed, later reprinted with a new cover by another artist.  **$5** **$25** **$75**

	G	VG	F

Erskine, John, *Private Life of Helen of Troy, The,* Popular Library #147, 1948, cover by Rudolph Belarski, historical novel with famous "nipple" cover art.

$10 $50 $120

Ewing, Frederick R., *I, Libertine,* Ballantine Book #165, 1956, paperback original, cover by Kelly Freas, satire of historical novels; pseudonym of Theodore Sturgeon.

$12 $40 $100

Farr, John, *She Shark,* Ace Book #S-159, 1956, paperback original, modern pirate novel; pseudonym of William Ard.

$5 $25 $65

Faulkner, William, *Intruder in the Dust,* Signet Book #S1253, 1956, murder and racial violence in a Southern town.

$10 $30 $100

--- *Mosquitoes,* Avon Book, no number (#12), 1941, with Globe endpapers.

$45 $175 $425

--- *Rose For Emily, A,* Armed Service Edition #825, no date, circa 1945, paperback original, the hardcover on the cover was made up and does not exist.

$75 $250 $750

Fishbein, M. D., Morris, *Your Questions on Health,* LA Bantam Book #3, 1940 paperback original, text cover, rare.

$55 $150 $250

Fitzgerald, F. Scott, *Diamond As Big As the Ritz and Other Stories, The,* Armed Service Edition #1043, no date, circa 1947, first book edition.

$75 $250 $700

--- *Great Gatsby, The,* Armed Service Edition #862, no date, circa, 1946.

$45 $160 $325

--- *Great Gatsby, The,* Bantam Book #8, 1945, in dust jacket.

$55 $175 $400

--- *Tender Is the Night,* Bantam Book #A867, 1950.

$10 $40 $90

Flaubert, Gustave, *Salambo,* Berkley Book #G-5, 1955, cover by Rudy Nappi, historical novel with sexy cover art.

$10 $35 $120

Forester, C. S., *Beat to Quarters,* Armed Service Edition #Q-18, no date, circa 1944, historical novel.

$10 $35 $100

--- *Commodore Hornblower,* Armed Service Edition #804, 1945, historical novel.

$10 $35 $100

--- *Flying Colours,* Armed Service Edition #F-157, no date, circa 1944, historical novel.

$10 $35 $100

--- *Lord Hornblower,* Armed Service Edition #1187, 1946, vertical format, historical novel.

$12 $45 $100

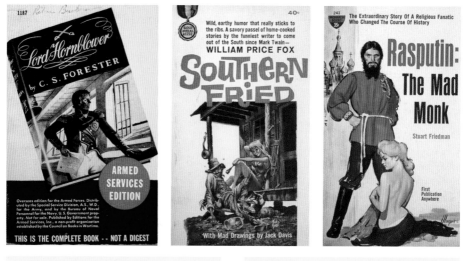

	G	VG	F		G	VG	F

--- *Ship of the Line*, Armed Service Edition #E-133, no date, circa 1944, historical novel. **$10** **$40** **$100**

Fox, William Price, *Southern Fried*, Gold Medal Book #k1232, 1962, paperback original, satire with cover art and inside drawings by Jack Davis. 📷 **$8** **$35** **$100**

Frey, Richard L., *How to Play Canasta*, Novel Library #43, 1950, card game rules. **$3** **$12** **$25**

Friedman, Stuart, *Rasputin: The Mad Monk*, Monarch Book #241, 1962, paperback original, cover by Robert Maguire, historical novel. 📷 **$8** **$35** **$90**

Gibbons, Floyd, *Red Knight of Germany, The*, Bantam Book #A1919, 1959, abridged, true story of World War I ace Baron Von Ricthofen. 📷 **$5** **$15** **$40**

Gibson, Walter B., *Magic Explained*, Perma Book #P-54, 1949, first book edition, simultaneous with Perma hardcover with same number, the paperback is scarce. **$15** **$40** **$100**

Glay, George Albert, *Oath of Seven*, Ace Book #S-102, 1955, paperback original, historical novel about Mau Mau terror in Kenya. 📷 **$5** **$22** **$75**

Goulart, Ron, *An Informal History of the Pulp Magazine*, Ace Book #37070, 1973, cover shows pulp magazine covers,

original title *Cheap Thrills*, collectible reference. **$10** **$25** **$50**

Gregory, Jerome, *Everybody's Book of Jokes and Wisecracks*, LA Bantam #6, 1940, paperback original, anthology of jokes, text cover, rare. **$55** **$155** **$225**

Gruenberg, Sidonie, *Your Child and You*, Gold Medal Book #112, 1950, first book edition, photo cover. 📷 **$3** **$20** **$65**

Hatch, Richard Warren, *Go Down to Glory*, Dell Book #D-114, 1952 in dust jacket. **$100** **$300** **$650**

Heard, Gerald, *Is Another World Watching?*, Bantam Book #1079, 1953, early UFO book. **$3** **$20** **$60**

Hecht, Ben, *Count Bruga*, Avon Book, no number (#11), 1941, with Globe endpapers. **$25** **$75** **$155**

Hemingway, Ernest, *Farewell to Arms, A*, Bantam Book #467, 1949. **$10** **$25** **$65**

--- *Selected Short Stories of Ernest Hemingway*, Armed Service Edition #K-9, no date, circa 1944, first book edition. **$75** **$180** **$450**

--- *Sun Also Rises, The*, Bantam Book #717, 1949, cover by Ken Riley. 📷 **$5** **$15** **$65**

--- *To Have and Have Not*, Armed Service Edition #667, no date, circa 1946. **$15** **$75** **$180**

	G	VG	F		G	VG	F

Henry, O., *Selected Stories of O. Henry*, Armed Service Edition #K-16, no date, circa 1946. **$10** **$40** **$100**

Hibbs, Ben, *Great Stories From the Saturday Evening Post*, Bantam Book #116, 1947, first book edition, cover by Steven Dohamos. 📷 **$3** **$25** **$65**

Higgins, Marguerite, *War in Korea*, Lion Book #82, 1952, cover by Floherty. 📷 **$5** **$20** **$50**

Hilton, James, *Ill Wind*, Avon Book, no number (#4), 1941, in Globe endpapers. **$35** **$75** **$150**

Hinds, Arthur, *Complete Sayings of Jesus, The*, Pocket Book #291, 1945, arranged by Hinds, very scarce. **$15** **$50** **$100**

House, Brant, *Cartoon Annual #2*, Ace Book #S-132, 1955 paperback original. **$5** **$20** **$50**

--- *Little Monsters*, Ace Book #S-145, 1956, paperback original. **$5** **$20** **$55**

Hull, E. M., *Sheik, The*, Dell Book #174, 1947, Map Back, early Dell romance novel. **$2** **$18** **$45**

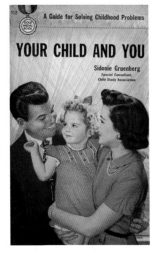

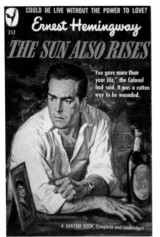

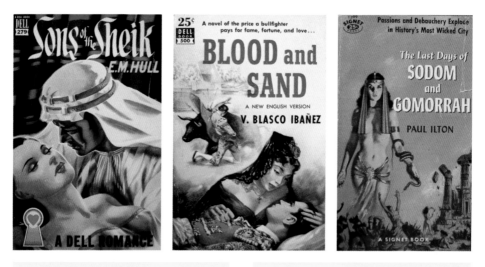

	G	VG	F		G	VG	F

--- *Sons of the Sheik*, Dell Book #279, 1949, Map Back, cover by F. Kenwood Giles, Dell Romance with heart in keyhole logo. 🎲 **$2** **$20** **$50**

Hunt, George P., *Coral Comes High,* Signet Book #1440, 1957, cover by Paul Lehr, with the Marines in the Pacific in World War II. **$4** **$16** **$40**

Ibanez, V. Blasco, *Blood and Sand,* Dell Book #500, 1951, Map Back, cover by Robert Stanley. 🎲 **$3** **$15** **$60**

Ilton, Paul, *Last Days of Sodom and Gomorrah, The,* Signet Book #1399, 1957, cover by Robert Maguire, biblical

historical novel. 🎲
$10 **$30** **$100**

Infantino, Carmine, *Green Lantern and Green Arrow #1,* Paperback Library #64-729, 1972, first book edition, cover by Neal Adams, comic book reprints, contains art by Adams, Gil Kane.
$10 **$45** **$100**

--- *Green Lantern and Green Arrow #2,* Paperback Library #64-755, 1972, first book edition, cover and interiors by Neal Adams, comic book reprints.
$12 **$50** **$120**

Jacobs, Bruce, *Korea's Heroes,* Lion Book

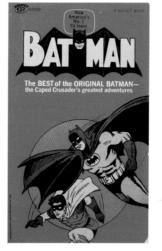

	G	VG	F

#172, 1953, paperback original, the story of the Medal of Honor winners in Korean War. **$6** **$20** **$75**

Kamal, Ahmad, *High Pressure,* Bantam Book #716, 1949, in dust jacket. **$55** **$150** **$225**

Kane, Bob, *Batman,* Signet Book #D-2939, 1966, first book edition, comic reprints. 📷 **$10** **$20** **$50**

--- *Batman vs the Joker,* Signet Book #D-2969, 1966, first book edition, comic reprints, book #3 in series. **$10** **$20** **$60**

--- *Batman vs the Penguin,* Signet Book #D-2970, 1966, first book edition, contains the Penguin and Catwoman comic reprints, book #4 in series. **$12** **$35** **$90**

Keel, John A., *Fickle Finger of Fate, The,* Gold Medal Book #d1719, 1966, paperback original, satire, scarce. 📷 **$10** **$40** **$100**

Kells, Susannah, *Aristocrats, The,* St. Martins Press #91009, 1988, first paperback printing, romance; pseudonym of Bernard Cornwell, uncommon. **$4** **$20** **$45**

--- *Crowning Mercy, A,* Penguin Book #10148, 1987, first paperback printing, cover by Michael Tedesco, historical romance, uncommon. 📷 **$4** **$20** **$50**

	G	VG	F

Kelly, F., and Ryan, C., *MacArthur Man of Action,* Lion Book #67, 1951, his story "from Bataan to Truman." **$5** **$18** **$55**

Kendricks, James, *She Wouldn't Surrender,* Monarch Book #MA301, 1960, paperback original, historical novel about Confederate spy Belle Boyd; pseudonym of Gardner F. Fox. **$5** **$20** **$60**

--- *Sword of Casanova,* Monarch Book #111, 1959, paperback original, historical novel. 📷 **$6** **$20** **$65**

Ketchem, Jack, *Cover,* Warner Book #30245, 1987, paperback original, Vietnam novel; pseudonym of Dallas Mayr. **$10** **$25** **$75**

Key, Alexander, *Wrath and the Wind, The,* Popular Library #608, 1954, historical novel, cover shows slave girl whipping male slave trader. 📷 **$3** **$15** **$40**

Keyhoe, Donald, *Flying Saucers Are Real, The,* Gold Medal Book #107, 1950, paperback original, cover by Frank Tinsley, early UFO book. 📷 **$6** **$30** **$90**

Khayyam, Omar, *Rubaiyat of Omar Khayyam,* Avon Book, no number (#2), 1941, with Globe endpapers. **$20** **$100** **$200**

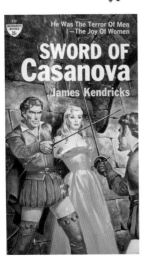

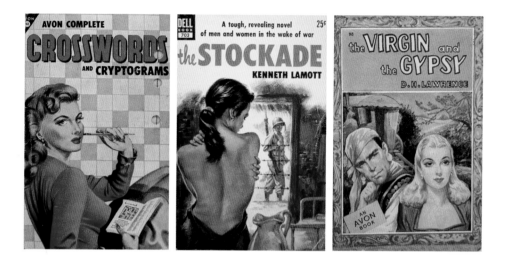

	G	VG	F		G	VG	F

Kinnaird, Clark, *Avon Complete Crosswords and Cryptograms, The,* Avon Book #162, 1948, the second Avon crossword book. 📷 **$125 $350 $750**

Krentz, Jayne Ann, *Maiden of the Morning,* MacFadden Book #249, 1979, paperback original, scarce romance novel; pseudonym of Jayne Bentley. **$20 $75 $200**

--- *Moment Past Midnight, A,* MacFadden Book #224, 1979, paperback original, scarce romance novel. **$20 $60 $175**

--- *Turning Toward Home,* MacFadden Book #192, 1979, paperback original, scarce romance novel. **$25 $75 $200**

Kurtzman, Harvey, *Executive's Comic Book,* MacFadden Book #50-159, 1962, first book edition, reprints Goodman Beaver superhero parody and other strips, Will Elder art. **$10 $40 $125**

--- *Help!,* Gold Medal Book #s1163, 1961, first book edition, photo cover, satire. **$5 $30 $90**

--- *Jungle Book,* Ballantine Book #338K, 1959, paperback original, cover by Jack Davis. **$6 $30 $90**

--- *Mad Reader, The,* Ballantine Book #93, 1954, cartoons from Mad magazine. **$8 $40 $100**

--- *Second Helping!,* Gold Medal Book #s1225, 1962, first book edition, humor. **$5 $15 $60**

Lamott, Kenneth, *Stockade, The,* Dell Book #703, 1953, cover by Griffith Foxley, prisoners on Pacific island during World War II. 📷 **$3 $14 $35**

Lardner, Ring, *Love Nest and Other Stories, The,* Bantam Book #145, 1948, Superior reprint in dust jacket. **$35 $70 $145**

Lawrence, D. H., *Love Among the Haystacks,* Avon Book #248, 1950, collection. **$5 $20 $55**

--- *Virgin and the Gypsy, The,* Avon Book #98, 1946, cover by Paul Stahr. 📷 **$8 $25 $60**

Lawson, Ted W., *Thirty Seconds Over Tokyo,* Bantam Book #S221, sixth printing 1945, text cover, rare. **$20 $50 $125**

Lay, Margaret Rebecca, *Ceylun,* Lion Book #32, 1950, cover by Julian Paul, "She was his untouched wife." **$5 $18 $70**

Lee, Stan, *Amazing Spider-Man, The,* Lancer Book #72-112, 1966, first book edition, cover by Steve Ditko, comic book reprints in the Lancer "Mighty Marvel Collector's Album" series of six books. **$10 $30 $90**

	G	VG	F

	G	VG	F

--- *Fantastic Four, The*, Lancer Book #72-111, 1966, first book edition, cover and interior art by Jack Kirby, comic book reprints. 🎲 **$10 $30 $90**

--- *Fantastic Four Return, The*, Lancer Book #72-169, 1967, first book edition, cover and interior art by Jack Kirby, comic book reprints. **$10 $35 $100**

--- *Here Comes...Daredevil*, Lancer Book #72-170, 1967, first book edition, comic book reprints, art by Bill Everett, Johnny Romita, and Gene Colon. **$10 $30 $90**

--- *Incredible Hulk, The*, Lancer Book #72-124, 1966, first book edition, cover and interior art by Steve Ditko and Jack Kirby, comic book reprints. **$10 $35 $100**

--- *Mighty Thor, The*, Lancer Book #72-125, 1966, first book edition, cover and interior art by Jack Kirby, comic book reprints. **$10 $30 $90**

Lewis, Ellen, *Children's Favorite Stories*, LA Bantam Book #12, 1940, paperback original, edited anthology, rare. **$60 $120 $200**

Lewis, Sinclair, *Babbitt*, Bantam Book #22, 1948, in dust jacket. **$25 $60 $125**

--- *Elmer Gantry*, Avon Book, no number (#1), 1941, the first Avon paperback, with Globe endpapers only. 🎲 **$30 $125 $245**

--- *Ghost Patrol, The*, Avon Book #74, 1946, first book edition, collection. 🎲 **$5 $35 $100**

--- *Kingsblood Royal*, Bantam Book #705, 1949, cover by James Avati, early racial novel, a white man learns he has black blood in his veins and is proud of it. 🎲 **$4 $20 $75**

Libby, Martin, *How to Win and Hold a Husband*, LA Bantam Book #11, 1940, text cover, rare. **$55 $125 $220**

Lindsey, Johanna, *Love Only Once*, Avon Book #89953, 1985, paperback original, cover by Robert McGinnis is a twist on traditional romance art. 🎲 **$3 $14 $40**

Locke, Charles O., *Last Princess, The*, Popular Library #622, 1954, historical novel of the Aztecs. 🎲 **$3 $14 $30**

London, Jack, *Call of the Wind*, Armed Service Edition #K-3, no date, circa 1945. **$6 $40 $100**

--- *Curse of the Snark, The*, Armed Service Edition #H-221, no date, circa 1945. **$10 $50 $120**

--- *Sea Wolf, The*, Armed Service Edition #F-180, no date, circa 1945. **$8 $45 $120**

--- *South Sea Tales*, Lion Book #92, 1952. 🎲 **$6 $35 $100**

--- *White Fang*, Armed Service Edition #G-182, no date, circa 1945. **$5 $30 $75**

	G	VG	F		G	VG	F

Lupoff, Dick and Thompson, Don, *All in Color For a Dime*, Ace Book #01625, no date, circa 1972, first paperback printing, comic book history, photos.
$5 · $20 · $55

MacDonald, John D., *House Guests, The*, Gold Medal Book #m2894, 1973, first and only paperback, mystery writer tells story about family pets.
$10 · $25 · $90

MacIsacc, Fred, *Love On the Run*, LA Bantam Book #18, 1940, text cover, rare.
$50 · $150 · $225

Mailer, Norman, *Barbary Shore*, Signet Book #1019, 1953, cover by Stanley Zuckerberg, postwar stories of people in a seedy Brooklyn, New York boarding house. 📷 $3 · $20 · $75

Mannix, Daniel P., *Those About to Die*, Ballantine Book #275K, 1958, paperback original, Roman gladiators.
$5 · $25 · $50

Marais, Claude, *Saskia*, Lion Book #116, 1952, cover by Geygan, the story of Rembrandt. 📷 $5 · $18 · $60

March, William, *Company K*, Lion Book #111, 1952, cover by Rafael DeSoto, World War II novel. 📷
$5 · $25 · $70

Marshall, Edison, *Caravan to Xanadu*, Dell Book #D157, 1955, cover by George Gross, historical novel.
$2 · $12 · $35

--- *Great Smith*, Dell Book #D102, 1952, cover by Robert Stanley, historical adventure. 📷 $3 · $12 · $40

--- *Love Stories of India*, Dell Book #530 1951, Map Back, romance and adventure.
$3 · $14 · $50

--- *Yankee Pasha*, Dell Book #353 1949, Map Back, cover by Robert Stanley.
$3 · $12 · $50

Mason, Ernst, *Tiberius*, Ballantine Book #361K, 1960, paperback original, biography of debauched Roman emperor; pseudonym of Frederick Pohl.
$6 · $30 · $75

	G	VG	F		G	VG	F

Matheson, Richard, *Beardless Warriors, The,* Bantam Book #F2281, 1961, first paperback printing, World War II novel by horror master. **$9 $45 $120**

Maugham, W. Somerset, *Rain,* Dell Ten-Cent Book #2, 1950, first book edition, cover by Victor Kalin. 📖
$8 $20 $75

McClintock, Marshall, *How to Build and Operate a Model Railroad,* Dell First Edition #D72, 1955, paperback original, photo cover with inside photos of train layouts for hobbyists. **$6 $30 $75**

Millard, Joseph, *Mansion of Evil,* Gold Medal Book #129, 1950, paperback original, done in color comic book format, scarce. **$40 $100 $250**

Miller, Arthur, *Focus,* Popular Library #230, 1950, cover by Rudolph Belarski, sexy cover art belies the seriousness of this brutal but important novel on anti-Semitism. 📖 **$3 $30 $85**

Moore, Robin, *Tales of the Green Berets,*

Signet Book #D3001, 1966, first book edition, cover by Joe Kubert, in comic book format, Green Berets in Vietnam War. **$5 $25 $75**

Moravia, Alberto, *Woman of Rome, The,* Signet Book #S844, 1951, cover by James Avati, Italy in postwar era. 📖
$4 $16 $55

Murray, Ken, *Giant Joke Book,* Ace Book #D-62, 1954, paperback original.
$5 $20 $70

Nathan, Robert, *One More Spring,* Bantam Book #19, 1945, with dust jacket, romance novel. **$15 $45 $100**

O'Hara, John, *Butterfield 8,* Avon Book #94, 1944. **$6 $30 $75**

Olson, Lloyd E., *Skip Bomber,* Ace Book #D-441, 1960, paperback original, B-29 bomber cover art. 📖
$4 $15 $40

Palmer, Diana, *Now and Forever,* MacFadden Book #127, 1979, paperback original, scarce romance novel, her first novel. **$30 $90 $250**

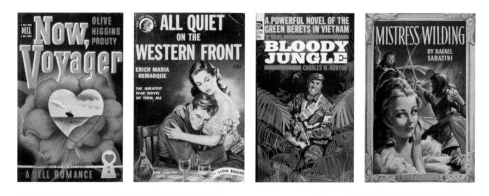

	G	VG	F		G	VG	F

--- *Sweet Enemy*, MacFadden Book #179, 1979, paperback original, scarce romance novel. **$25** **$60** **$135**

Parker, Dorothy, *Enough Rope*, Pocket Book #6, 1939, only 10,000 copies sold in New York City area. 📷 **$40** **$125** **$250**

Parker, Eleanor, *Humorous Anecdotes and Funny Stories*, LA Bantam Book #24, 1940, paperback original, anthology, text cover, rare. **$75** **$150** **$225**

--- *Humorous Anecdotes and Funny Stories*, LA Bantam Book #24, 1940, paperback original, anthology, illustrated cover edition, rare. 📷 **$90** **$300** **$525**

--- *World's Great Love Affairs, The*, LA Bantam Book #12, 1940, paperback original, text cover, rare. **$65** **$200** **$350**

Patherbridge, Margaret, *Pocket Book of Crossword Puzzles, The*, Pocket Book #210, 1943, paperback original. **$20** **$50** **$125**

Payne, Robert, *Blue Negro, The*, Avon Book #373, 1951, first book edition, adventure stories. **$8** **$30** **$90**

Pei, Mario, *Swords For Charlemagne*, Graphic Book #G-208, 1955, cover by Robert Maguire, historical novel. 📷 **$4** **$20** **$50**

Pernikoff, Alexander, *Bushido*, Quick Reader #109, 1943, cover by Axelrod shows World War II terror. 📷 **$7** **$35** **$85**

Petersen, Clarence, *Bantam Story, The*, Bantam Book, no number, 1970, paperback original, no price, giveaway, photo cover, publisher history from 1945 to 1970. **$4** **$20** **$45**

--- *Bantam Story, The*, Bantam Book, no number, second printing 1975, no price, giveaway, updates and expands 1970 edition to 35 years of Bantam paperback publishing. **$4** **$20** **$45**

Prouty, Olive Higgins, *Now, Voyager*, Dell Book #99, no date 1946, Map Back, classic romance novel with Dell heart in keyhole romance logo. 📷 **$5** **$20** **$50**

Rafferty and O'Neill, *Dell Crossword Puzzles*, Dell First Edition #60, 1955, paperback original. **$40** **$110** **$250**

--- *Second Dell Book of Crossword Puzzles*, Dell Book #278, 1949, paperback original. **$130** **$300** **$625**

Remarque, Erich Maria, *All Quiet on the Western Front*, Lion Book #49, 1950, novel of trench warfare in World War I. 📷 **$4** **$14** **$55**

Roberts, Nora, *Irish Thoroughbred*, Silhouette Romance #57081, 1981, paperback original, #81 in Silhouette series, her first novel. **$20** **$90** **$200**

--- *Promise Me Tomorrow*, Pocket Book #47019, 1984, paperback original, scarce romance novel. **$15** **$50** **$150**

Runyon, Charles W., *Bloody Jungle, The*, Ace Book #G-594, 1966, paperback original, cover by G. McConnell, Vietnam novel about the Green Berets. 📷 **$5** **$25** **$65**

	G	VG	F

Sabatini, Rafael, *Captain Blood,* Pocket Book #82, 1940, classic pirate adventure novel. **$5 $25 $100**

--- *Mistress Wilding,* Avon Book #84, 1946, historical novel.  **$5 $25 $85**

--- *Scaramouche,* Bantam Book #5, 1945, cover by Calin. **$4 $18 $55**

Sandburg, Carl, *Selected Poems of Carl Sandburg,* Armed Service Edition #N-6, no date, circa 1946, first edition thus. **$10 $40 $100**

Seagrave, Gordon S., *Burma Surgeon,* Infantry Journal, no number, 1944, Penguin Books imprint published for soldiers in World War II.  **$3 $15 $40**

Siegel, Jerry, *High Camp Super-Heroes,* Belmont Book #B50-695, 1966, paperback original, comic book stories scripted by Siegel, creator of Superman, contains costume heroes Steel Sterling, Fly Man, the Shield, and Web.  **$10 $35 $125**

Shakespeare, William, *Five Great Tragedies,* Pocket Book #3, 1939, only 10,000 copies sold in New York City area. **$55 $175 $350**

--- *Jokes, Gags and Wisecracks,* Dell Book #152, 1947, anthology of jokes and gags. **$25 $90 $165**

Shaplen, Robert, *Love-Making of Max-Robert, The,* Signet Book #789, 1950, cover by James Avati, postwar angst in the Orient.  **$3 $20 $55**

Shay, Frank, *Pirate Wench,* Pyramid Book #G-75, 1953, historical novel about

female pirate Mary Reed.  **$3 $20 $55**

Shea, Vernon, *Strange Desires,* Lion Book #191, 1954, anthology with William Faulkner. **$5 $30 $75**

Silver, Stuart, *Faster Than a Speeding Bullet,* Playboy Press #16760, 1980, paperback original, golden age of radio history and quiz, with Isidore Haiblum.  **$5 $15 $45**

Silverstein, Shel, *Grab Your Socks,* Ballantine Book #163, 1956, paperback original, cover by Shel Silverstein, joke book. **$10 $60 $160**

Slaughter, Frank G., *Fort Everglades,* Perma Book #P155, 1952, historical novel, bondage cover.  **$2 $15 $40**

Smith, H. Allen, *Rude Jokes,* Gold Medal Book # t2347, 1970, paperback original, very scarce. **$10 $25 $65**

Southern, Terry, *Magic Christian, The,* Berkley Book #BG500, 1961, cover by Richard Powers, predates the film, wild satire. **$5 $35 $90**

Stagg, Delano, *Bloody Beaches,* Monarch Book #210, 1961, paperback original, cover by Robert Stanley, World War II novel, "Marines die hard!"; unknown pseudonym.  **$4 $15 $50**

Steinbeck, John, *Cannery Row,* Armed Service Edition #T-5, no date, circa 1944. **$15 $55 $120**

--- *Cannery Row,* Bantam Book #75, 1947, in dust jacket. **$35 $100 $275**

--- *Cup of Gold,* Armed Service Edition #750, no date, circa 1945, pirate novel. **$15 $55 $120**

	G	VG	F			G	VG	F

--- *Cup of Gold*, Popular Library #216, 1950, cover by Rudolph Belarski, pirate novel. **$6** **$35** **$90**

--- *Cup of Gold*, Bantam Book #1184, 1953, cover by Earl Mayan, pirate novel. **$3** **$20** **$50**

--- *Grapes of Wrath, The*, Armed Service Edition #C-90, no date, circa 1945 **$20** **$55** **$150**

--- *Grapes of Wrath, The*, Armed Service Edition #690, no date, circa 1945, reprints ASE #C-90. **$15** **$35** **$85**

--- *Grapes of Wrath, The*, Bantam Book #7, 1945, cover by Bratz. **$5** **$20** **$75**

--- *Long Valley, The*, Armed Service Edition #794, no date, circa 1945. **$32** **$75** **$155**

--- *Pastures of Heaven, The*, Penguin Book #509, 1942. **$30** **$75** **$150**

--- *Pastures of Heaven, The*, Armed Service Edition #703, no date, circa 1945. **$20** **$55** **$120**

--- *Pastures of Heaven, The*, Bantam Book #899, 1951. **$3** **$18** **$55**

	G	VG	F

	G	VG	F

--- *Steinbeck Pocket Book, The*, Pocket Book #243, 1943, first book edition, cover by Leo Manso, collection.
$10 **$30** **$75**

--- *To a God Unknown*, Dell Book #358, 1949, Map Back.
$6 **$30** **$75**

--- *Wayward Bus, The*, Armed Service Edition #1232, no date, circa 1947.
$35 **$100** **$200**

Stevenson, Robert Louis, *Treasure Island*, Quick Reader #130, 1945, cover by Cirkel, abridged, pirate classic, very scarce. **$25** **$85** **$150**

Stolberg, Charles, *Avon Book of Puzzles, The*, Avon Book #27, 1943, first Avon puzzle book. **$60** **$150** **$400**

Stuart, Anne, *Barrett's Hill*, Beagle Book #26585, 1974, paperback original, gothic romance, her first book.
$20 **$50** **$100**

Talbot, Daniel, *Damned The*, Lion Library #LL6, 1954, first book edition, anthology with stories by Jim Thompson, Ernest Hemingway, James Joyce.
$8 **$35** **$80**

Tebbel, John, *Paperback Books, A Pocket History*, Pocket Book, no number, 1964, paperback original, silver text cover, giveaway, publisher history from 1939 to 1964, scarce. **$15** **$50** **$120**

Terrill, Rogers, *Argosy Book of Adventure Stories, The*, Bantam Book #A1158, 1953, first book edition, anthology, contains Robert A. Heinlein. **$3** **$20** **$50**

Toland, John, *Battle: The Story of the Bulge*, Signet Book #T-1862, 1960, cover by Barye Phillips, the World War II battle by a famed historian.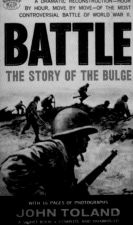
$2 **$16** **$45**

Tracy, Don, *Carolina Corsair*, Cardinal Book #C-228, 1957, cover by James Meese, historical novel about Blackbeard the pirate. 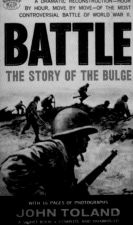 **$2** **$14** **$35**

Van Loon, Hendrik Willem, *Story of Rabelais and Voltaire, The*, LA Bantam Book #20, 1940, text cover, rare.
$65 **$150** **$275**

Vidal, Gore, *Dangerous Voyage*, Signet Book #1003, 1953, first paperback printing, original title *Williwaw*.
$4 **$30** **$75**

Voltaire, *Candide*, Lion Book #107, 1952, a classic gets the sexy cover treatment.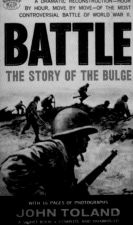
$5 **$20** **$75**

Webster, Miriam, *Avon Webster English Dictionary*, Avon Book #G-1007, 1951, very scarce. **$25** **$100** **$200**

--- *Self-Pronouncing New Webster's Pocket Size Dictionary and Spelling Helper*, Quick Reader #108, 1942.
$10 **$35** **$75**

	G	VG	F		G	VG	F

--- *Self-Pronouncing New Webster's Pocket Size Dictionary and Spelling Helper,* Quick Reader, no number, 1943, same as #108 but says "special edition for service men" on cover, scarce.
$20 **$70** **$155**

Weegee, *Naked Hollywood,* Berkley Book #G-9, 1955, first book edition, photo cover, written with Mel Harris, 150+ photos by ace crime photographer.
$10 **$35** **$100**

Wilcox, Ella Wheeler, *Poems of Passion,* LA Bantam Book #15, 1940, first book edition, text cover, rare.
$60 **$120** **$200**

Wilder, Thornton, *Bridge at San Luis Rey, The,* Pocket Book #9, 1939, only 10,000 copies sold in New York City area.
$50 **$150** **$250**

--- *Heaven is My Destination,* Avon Book #59, 1945. **$8** **$20** **$90**

Wilson, Gahan, *Gahan Wilson's Graveside Manner,* Ace Book #F-331, 1965, first book edition, satire, macabre cartoons. 📷 **$6** **$30** **$75**

Wodehouse, P. G., *Quick Service and Code of the Woosters, The,* Ace Book #D-25, 1953, cover by Norman Saunders.
$5 **$20** **$65**

Wolfe, Thomas, *Web and the Rock, The,* Dell Book #LY-103, 1961, Bill Lyles told me only 640 copies of this edition were ever sold, scarce. **$15** **$30** **$75**

Young, Chic, *Blondie & Dagwood in Footlight Folly,* Dell Books, no number (#1), 1947, paperback original.
$25 **$75** **$175**

THE NAME BEHIND THE BYLINE:
Pseudonyms and House Names

Pseudonyms and house names offer the collector and scholar something different and are always fascinating. Many authors (and even a few artists) in the paperback field often used pen names or pseudonyms, while others wrote under house names. Knowing the difference between these two types of bylines and which name a popular and collectible author wrote under can make a big difference and often be profitable. Hundreds of authors used pen names and house names in the paperback field, and many of them only used these bylines on paperback editions.

Pseudonyms can be used for a variety of reasons. Some authors differentiate this commercial or so-called "popular" work from their more serious work. Others may be writing in an area where they are unknown, so the author (or publisher, or author's agent) may not want to confuse the public by sending out what could be seen as a mixed message. This most often happens when the author is well known in one genre or for a certain type of book or character. The use of a pseudonym can also occur because an author wants to hide his true identity. One author of controversial novels was a college professor who did not want the publicity; another author used a pseudonym to hide money from the sale of those books from the IRS in the 1960s. In many cases an author may have a "day job" in which he does not want his employer to know that he is moonlighting as a writer. Walter Wager wrote hard-boiled Cold War spy novels as John Tiger while he was working at the United Nations. He told me that writing popular spy thrillers under his true name could have caused complications on his job, so he used a pseudonym. The reasons for pseudonyms are endless and endlessly fascinating.

Pseudonyms are names that belong to only one writer or sometimes a two-person collaboration team. House names are something entirely different. You have to be a bit more careful with house names. While a pseudonym belongs to one particular writer (and is the property of that writer), a house name can be used by many writers (and the name is owned by the publisher). Therefore, you have some authors who have written under many house names and many pseudonyms. Under a pseudonym it will always be that particular author. Under a house name it could be that author or other different authors for certain books that appear under that byline. Knowing the difference between the two and the true name behind the byline can mean the difference of a book being worth $1 or $100 or more!

The following is not conclusive; it lists only authors and their pseudonyms (or house names) that are used in this book.

Author Name	Pseudonym
Aarons, Edward S.	Edward Ronns
Adams, Cleve	John Spain
Albert, Marvin	Albert Conroy
Amis, Kingsly	Robert Markham
Ard, William	Ben Kerr, John Farr, Jonas Ward, Thomas Wills, Mike Moran
Avallone, Michael	Sidney Stuart, Vance Stanton
Ballard, W. T.	Neil MacNeil, Brian Fox
Banis, Victor J.	Victor Jay
Beaumont, Charles	Keith Grantland
Beck, Robert	Iceberg Slim
Becker, Stephen	Steven Dodge
Bentley, Jayne	Jayne Castle, Jayne Ann Krentz
Block, Lawrence	Ben Christopher, Jill Emerson, Chip Harrison, some Sheldon Lord, Lesley Evans, completed *Babe in the Woods* as by William Ard, also some Andrew Shaw
Boucher, Anthony	H. H. Holmes
Brackett, Leigh	George Sanders, house name where she wrote at least one book under this byline.
Bradley, Marion Zimmer	Morgan Ives, Miriam Gardner, used house name John Dexter for *No Adam For Eve*
Browne, Howard	John Evans
Brunner, John	Keith Woodcott
Burroughs, William	William Lee
Cassidy, Bruce	Carson Bingham, Max Day
Cormac, Donald	Spider Page
Craig, Georgiana Ann Randolph	Craig Rice, Daphane Sanders
Cornwell, Bernard	Susannah Kells with his wife on three books, two reprinted in U.S. paperbacks as Kells
Crichton, Michael	John Lange
Crossen, Kendall Foster	Richard Foster, M. E. Chaber
Daniels, Norman	Mark Reed, David Wade
Davidson, Avram	Carlton Miller
Davies, George	Richard Armory
De Lint, Charles	Samuel M. Key
Dent, Lester	many books by Kenneth Robeson, a house name
Dresser, Davis	Brett Halliday
Ellis, Julie	Joan Ellis, Linda Michaels
Ellison, Harlan	Paul Merchant

Author Name	Pseudonym
Fairman, Paul W.	ghosted *A Study in Terror* as by Ellery Queen, F. W. Paul house name on two books in Man From STUD series
Fast, Howard	Walter Erikson
Faust, Frederick	Max Brand, Evan Evans
Fearn, John Russell	Vargo Statten, Volstead Gridban (house name, so only some titles)
Fischer, Bruno	Russell Gray
Foster, Alan Dean	ghosted first Star Wars tie-in as by George Lucas
Fox, Gardner F.	James Kendricks
Fox, Gilbert	Kimberly Kemp
Francis, Steven	Hank Janson, but not Gold Star editions, which used Janson as a house name
Gardner, Erle Stanley	A. A. Fair
Garfield, Brian	ghosted Buchanan's Gold as by Jonas Ward (William Ard pseudonym), Bennett Garland
Gault, William Campbell	Will Duke, Roney Scott
Geis, Richard E.	Peggy Swenson, Frederick Colson
Gibson, Walter B.	pseudonyms include Harry Hershfield, Douglas Brown, on most Shadow novels he used house name Maxwell Grant but also see Dennis Lynds
Gifford, Barry	Kent Nelson
Giles, Janice Holt	John Garth
Glidden, Frederick D.	Luke Short
Goines, Donald	Al C. Clark
Goldman, William	Harry Longbaugh
Gottfried, Ted	Ted Mark
Goulart, Ron	Con Steffanson; he also used many other house names
Hano, Arnold	Gil Dodge
Hansen, Joseph	James Colton
Haydock, Ron	Vin Saxon
Hegedus, Adam	Rodney Garland
Highsmith, Patricia	Claire Morgan
Hunt, E. Howard	Gordon Davis, Robert Dietrich
Hunter, Evan	Ed McBain, Hunt Collins, Curt Cannon, Richard Marsten
Jenkins, Will F.	Murray Leinster
Jessup, Richard	Richard Telfair
Kane, Frank	Frank Boyd
Keene, Day	Daniel White, William Richards
Kelton, Elmer	wrote first three of six books under house name Tom Early

Author Name	Pseudonym
King, Stephen	Richard Bachman
Knoles, William	Clyde Allison
Koontz, Dean	Leigh Nichols, Deanna Dwyer, K. R. Dwyer, Owen West, John Hill, used house name of Daniel Webbel
Kornbluth, C. M.	Jordan Park, Simon Eisner, Cyril Judd (with Judith Merrill)
Kuttner, Henry	Lewis Padgett (with his wife, C. L. Moore)
Lake, Joe Barry	Joe Barry
Lange Jr., John Frederick	John Norman
Lansdale, Joe	Ray Slater, Jack Buchanan house name on at least two books
Lewis, Herschell Gordon	L. E. Murphy
Lesser, Milton	Stephen Marlowe
Love, Richard	Richard Amory
Lindsay, Hyman	Robert Chessman
Lynds, Dennis	as Maxwell Grant on all but one of the Belmont Shadow Paperback novels
Mayr, Dallas	Jack Ketchum
McGaughy, Dudley Owen	Dean Owen, Hodge Evens
Meaker, Marijane	Vin Packer, Ann Aldrich, M. E. Kerr
Merrill, Judith	Cyril Judd (with C. M. Kornbluth)
Miller, Bill	half of Wade Miller writer team with Robert Wade
Moorcock, Michael	Edward P. Bradbury
Moore, Brian	Michael Bryan, Bernard Mara
Moore, C. L.	Lewis Padgett (with her husband, Henry Kuttner)
Nelson, Ray F.	R. N. Ellson, Jeffery Lord (house name, only one title)
Neutzel, Charles	David Johnson, Alec Rivere
Newton, William	Spike Morelli
Norton, Mary Alice	Andre Norton, Andrew North
Offutt, Andrew	John Cleve
Oursler, Fulton	Anthony Abbot
Ozaki, Milton K.	Robert O. Saber
Phillips, Judson	Hugh Pentecost
Pohl, Fred	Ernst Mason
Prather, Richard S.	David Knight, Douglas Ring
Price, E. Hoffman	Hamlin Daly
Rabe, Peter	J. T. McCargo house name on two books, Marco Malaponte
Reasoner, James	house name Tom Early, only one book, *The Defiant*, #6 in Sons of Texas series with his wife, Livia
Rigsby, Howard	Vechel Howard

Author Name	Pseudonym
Savage, Jr., Les	Logan Stewart
Sellers, Con	Connie Sellers
Sheldon, Alice	James Tiptree, Jr.
Silverberg, Robert	Robert Randall (with Randall Garrett), Ivar P. Jorgenson, L. T. Woodward, Don Elliott house name, some books as Loren Beauchamp, ghosted *The Cool Man* and *Round the Clock at Volari's* as by W. R. Burnett, Ivar Jorgense, Calvin M. Knox
Smith, George H.	Jan Hudson
Sontup, Dan	David Saunders, John Clarke
Stonebraker, Florence	Thomas Stone, Florenz Branch
Stubbs, Henry Clement	Henry Clement, Harry Clement, Hal Clement
Sturgeon, Theodore	Frederick R. Ewing
Tepper, Sheri S.	E. E. Horlak
Tilton, Alice	Phoebe Atwood Taylor
Trimble, John	Jack Leech
Turtledove, Harry	Eric Iverson for two books in the 1970s
Van Arnam, Dave	Ron Archer
Vance, Jack	John Holbrook Vance, Peter Held
Vidal, Gore	Cameron Kay, Edgar Box
Wade, Robert	half of Wade Miller team with Bill Miller
Wager, Walter	John Tiger
Ward, Arthur Sarsfield	Sax Rohmer
Whittington, Harry	Whit Harrison, Hallam Whitney, Ken Holland, Kathryn Harriet Myers
Willeford, Charles	W. Franklin Sanders as ghost writer
Westlake, Donald	Edwin West, Curt Clark, Richard Stark, Alan Marshall up to 1962
Wollheim, Donald	David Grinnell
Wood, Jr., Ed	Jason Nichols, David L. Westermier, Emil Moreau, Kathleen Everett, J. X. Williams (house name)
Woolrich, Cornell	George Hopley, William Irish
Wyndham, John	John Benyon Harris
Zinberg, Len	Ed Lacy, one book as Ed Lacey

GLOSSARY:
A Collector's Basic Vocabulary

Ace Doubles: early paperback series that began an innovative format containing two books bound back-to-back with a cover for each book.

Advanced Reading Copy (ARC): a pre-publication copy of the book sent out in advance of publication to reviewers or critics, which may contain laid-in information on the book and/or author. It can also be a bound galley, and may have a text cover or the cover of the forthcoming book with "Advanced Reading Copy" noted on the cover.

Anthology: a collection of short stories or articles by various authors.

Back Cover (or B/C): the reverse of the book; the part of the book cover that is bound on the back of the book.

Bookstore Stamp: usually located on the inside front cover or the title page; an ink stamp with the name and address of the second-hand bookstore that sold the book at one time.

Collection: as in a collection of short stories; unlike an anthology, all stories in a collection are always by the same author.

Colophon: special logo of a publisher, usually located on the spine of the book or the bottom of the title page.

Completeist: a type of collector who collects everything in a certain field or genre. A paperback completeist sets his goal of obtaining one copy of every edition of every paperback ever published.

Condition: the particular grade of a book that takes in all the flaws and problems to give an accurate description of the book.

Cropped Cover Art: cover art that has been cut or had a border placed around it. Usually this occurs on reprints where the cover art from the previous printing was reused on another printing but with a portion of it cut out or framed by a border.

Cover: usually refers to the front cover only; this includes all art and text thereon. See "Back Cover."

Cover Illustration: illustration or artwork on the cover of the book. This does not include other items present on the cover, such as text and logo, etc. Photo covers are not referred to as cover illustrations, however, there are covers that mix a photo with artwork.

Digest: about 7.5 by 5.5 inches in size, though size could vary; digests can be perfect bound or stapled. This format, which was a popular paperback format of the 1940s and 1950s, showed the link between paperbacks and magazines. Today it continues in various examples such as *Reader's Digest, Ellery Queen,* and *Analog.*

Dupe: short for duplicate, a term for duplicate copies of a book.

Edges: refers to the three sides of the book where the pages meet and have been trimmed. Edges often were stained yellow, orange, or red on many vintage paperbacks to protect them from insect pests.

Edition: refers to a specific printing and binding of a specific publisher's book.

Fair: a low-end grade that is lower than "good"; a reading copy or filler only, unacceptable for collecting purposes because the condition is so poor. Beware, because books listed under this description may not be complete.

Filler: a lesser grade copy used to fill a hole in a collection or a numbered run of books until a better copy is found.

Fine: highest condition grade of a collectible paperback; like new, no defects.

First Book Edition: more exact term for first edition.

First Edition: first time a book has ever appeared in book form, though it may have appeared in a magazine previously; also known as a "first book edition." A first edition may also be a paperback original (PBO) but not always, and not all first editions in paperback are PBOs.

First Edition Thus: first edition for a particular book, generally under a specific title. At times an author collection will use a different title, or a longer story will be published for the first time in a separate edition all by itself, and is often listed as a first edition thus.

First Paperback Printing: first time a particular book has appeared in paperback. It may have had a previous hardcover or magazine appearance but never a previous paperback edition before this one.

Genre: sub-category of literature or popular fiction. Sometimes it can also refer to popular fiction, as in genre fiction.

Globe Endpapers: for the first 16 early non-numbered Avon Books only, the first printings had what are termed "globe endpapers" where the endpapers, which are connected to the inside front and back covers, have images of globes printed on them.

Good-Girl Art or "GGA": also "pin-up art"; a comic book term for cover art portraying sexy women that often appears on many vintage era paperbacks.

Grading: determining the overall accurate condition of a book.

Highest Book Number: on early paperbacks, one way to ascertain a first printing from a later identical edition is to note the different ads in the back of the book for that publisher's other books in that series, then note what number they are up to in the series. Lower numbers indicate earlier editions.

Hot: can refer to a book or author, where there is very high demand or collector interest and, hence, rising prices.

House Name: pen name given to a book by the publisher and owned by the publisher.

Imprint: separate group, run, or category of books offered by a publisher, which has its own series name, logo, numbering, and similar design.

Key Book: book that has great demand or significance.

Logo: emblematic device used by publishers to identify an imprint or line of books. Also known as a colophon.

Mass-Market Paperback: refers to the method of book distribution rather than a book's size or format. The mass-market distribution system allows for returns that are accepted for credit against future books.

Owner's Plate or Book Plate: adhesive or glued-in label, often with the Latin words "Ex Libris," stating the previous owner's name.

Paperback Original or PBO: edition of an original paperback book that has never before seen publication in any form. This includes no previous paperback printing, no hardcover or digest appearances, and no magazine appearances. A PBO is always a first edition.

Perfect Bound: type of paperback binding where the spine is square, not stapled.

Points: certain aspects of a book's physical structure or description, such as edition, highest book number, globe endpapers, etc. Also any identifying or important aspect of a book that is worth noting for description for sale. Separate from grading or condition. An accumulation of things that describe the book as a unique item or a first edition or PBO.

Pseudonym: also pen name or *nom de plume*; a name that a writer assumes and is published under that is not his true name and is used exclusively by that author.

Rare: generally when less than a dozen copies of a certain edition are known to exist.

Reading Crease: on the cover of the book, parallel to the spine, where the book has been opened and creased from reading.

Reprints: additional editions of a book previously published. A reprint can be in hardcover or paperback, and a book can be reprinted by the original publisher in a new edition, a second printing, and also by another publisher.

Review Copy: copy of the actual published book that has been sent out to reviewers or critics, usually with a review slip or other written matter included.

Review Slip: publisher's laid-in sheet of paper that accompanies a review copy. It gives information on the new book, publication date, and publicity contact person for reviewers and critics.

Run: as in a "publisher's run," referring to all the books published by a certain publisher or all the books in a particular imprint, as in Timescape being an SF imprint of Pocket Books.

Saddle Stitch: type of book binding commonly using staples.

Scarce: a book that may have been seen only a few times during a collector's travels; an edition that hardly ever seems to show up but is not rare.

Scarce in Condition: a book known to be scarce in fine condition only; pristine copies are elusive and hardly ever seen.

Sexy Digests: sexy or pin-up cover art

COULD HE LIVE WITHOUT THE POWER TO LOVE?

Ernest Hemingway

717

THE SUN ALSO RISES

"You gave more than your life," the Colonel had said. It was a rotten way to be wounded.

A BANTAM BOOK, Complete and Unabridged

digest paperbacks of the 1950s.

Sleaze: overall term for sexy paperbacks of the 1960s; commonly refers to soft-core adult paperbacks.

Spine: part of the paperback where the pages are bound.

Spine Roll: curve of the spine of a paperback book due to careless or repeated reading.

Sticker Pull: area where a price sticker has been removed carelessly so that part of the cover or lamination has been pulled off or removed.

"Superior" Reprints: line of paperbacks that were given Bantam dust jackets with better cover art (and sometimes new titles) to be resold to the public.

Uncommon: not scarce, but not common either; an edition not often seen on dealer sales lists, but does show up from time to time.

Want List or Wish List: list of books, usually arranged by author, title, or – most often with vintage paperbacks – by publisher and book number, of books you want to acquire for your collection.

Warp: water damage will cause a book to get wavy or warp.

Water Damage: staining, warping, fading, or pieces of one book cover sticking to another are examples of how moisture or water can harm a paperback.

Worm Hole: small holes in the cover or throughout pages of the book made by tiny egg-laying insects. Insect larva will eat through the book paper, leaving small wavy holes through the pages.

FOREIGN PAPERBACKS

While the scope of this book is concerned only with collectible paperback books published in the United States, a few words should be said about non-U.S. editions published in other countries.

The interest and activity of collecting paperback books today knows no borders or language barriers. In fact, there is a growing international interest in collectible pulp paperbacks of all kinds from all countries. Almost every nation has a cultural history that includes publishers who have printed and sold these books over the last five decades. They were based upon and influenced by the paperback revolution that took place in the United States in 1939 when the first Pocket Books were published and sold to the public.

In many nations of the world, notably but not limited to those in Europe, Central America, and South America, local publishers printed and sold hundreds, if not thousands, of pulp paperbacks. Originally, most of the earliest imprints and editions were translations of American mysteries and other novels. Most of these early 1940s and 1950s books, and even series of books from many nations, either used the cover art from the American paperback or copied it.

From a collector's point of view today, foreign paperbacks are divided into two categories: English language editions and all other non-English language editions.

Many early foreign paperbacks reprinted popular American and British authors who are very collectible. All the giants are here – Raymond Chandler, Dashiell Hammett, Mickey Spillane, Agatha Christie, Ian Fleming, and Arthur Conan Doyle are just a few examples from the mystery genre. These editions in whatever language offer a fascinating look and interpretation of these key collectible authors and books, in their design and cover art.

English language editions are most avidly collected. Obviously, the large collector base in the United States, as well as significant groups of collectors in Canada, Australia, and the United Kingdom, naturally collect books written in their native language. Thus we have, for example, Harlequin Books (the first 500 pre-romance editions) and Studio Pocket books from Canada; Digit, Corgi, Pan, Scion, Curtis-Warren, Spensers, Panther, and many others from England; and Phantom, Star, Cleveland, Horwitz editions, Scientific Thrillers, and American Science Fiction from Australia. All of these books are avidly sought after by collectors in the United States and many nations worldwide.

However, this does not mean that collectors ignore non-English language editions; in fact, quite the opposite is true. English-language readers and collectors frequently search out and cherish many non-English language books and series, especially if they are by authors they collect. Thus we have paperbacks published in Argentina (Rastros); Brazil (Editora Meridiano, Edicoes de Ouro); France (Presses de la Cite,

Serrie Noire, Oscar); Sweden (Jaguar, Meteor, X-Books, Manhattan, Zebra); Denmark (UMC); Italy (Mondadori); Germany (Panther, Krainiach, Rororo); Norway (Ponni-Bok, Norsk Pocketbok, Puma); Portugal (Rififi); and Finland (Lepohetki). There are many other paperback series, imprints, and individual editions that are much sought after and are great fun to collect.

The field of collectible paperbacks has become an international hobby that knows no barriers of borders or language, and the diversity within it is truly amazing. New wonders are being discovered everyday, and it is a wide open area of collecting enjoyment.

RECOMMENDED SPECIALIST BOOK DEALERS

Many of the paperbacks presented in this book will be difficult to obtain without the help of one of the fine book dealers listed below. Many of these men and women specialize in collectible paperbacks. I have dealt with all of them over the course of many years of collecting, and I recommend them all as invaluable sources.

Aladdin Books (John Cannon):
122 W. Commonwealth, Fullerton, CA 92832, phone: 714-738-6115, e-mail: aladdinbooks@earthlink.net

Altair-4 Collectibles (Dan Medart):
328 S. Tustin Ave., Orange, CA 92866, phone: 714-639-5736, e-mail: altair4books@aol.com

Barry R. Levin Books:
720 Santa Monica Blvd., Santa Monica, CA 90401, website: www.raresf.com

Black Ace Books (Rose Idlet):
1658 Griffith Park Blvd., Los Angeles, CA 90026, phone: 323-661-5052, e-mail: roseidlet@aol.com

Black Hill Books (Guy and Jean Smith):
The Wain House, Black Hill, Clunton, Craven Rams, Shropshire, SY7-0JD, U.K., e-mail: blackhillbooks@hotmail.com

Book Castle & Movie World (Steve Edrington):
212 N. San Fernando Blvd., Burbank, CA 91502, phone: 818-845-8586

Brian McMillan Books:
1429 L Ave., Traer, IL 50675, e-mail: brianbks@netins.net

Certo, Nick:
PO Box 10305, Newburgh, NY 12552

Chris Eckhoff Books:
98 Pierrepont St., Brooklyn, NY 11201

Coleman, Bruce:
PO Box 538, Los Angeles, CA 90078, phone: 323-461-4796, e-mail: the57kid6@aol.com.

Cool Books (Tony Jacobs):
2035 Selby Ave., Los Angeles, CA 90025, phone: 310-428-4631, e-mail: ynotact@aol.com

Coven Books:
2036 N. Beachwood Dr. #15, Hollywood, CA 90068, phone: 323-461-4730, e-mail: clovecraft@aol.com

Dannay, Douglas:
36 Margaret Blvd., Merrick, NY 11566, phone: 516-379-1485

Darrell Thede Books:
10818 Floral, Whittier, CA 90606, phone: 562-699-5464

D. C.'s Collectible Book Auctions (David Cochrane):
8025 W. Russell Rd. #2132, Las Vegas, NV 89113, phone: 702-205-9183; e-mail: dcsbooks@peoplepc.com

Derringer Books (Alan Zipkin):
355 Buena Vista East/507W, San Francisco, CA 94117, phone: 415-864-6710

Don Cannon – Books
 PO Box 918, Fullerton, CA 92836, phone: 714-449-1739, e-mail: doncannonbks@earthlink.net

Dreamhaven Books (Greg Ketter):
 912 W. Lake St., Minneapolis, MN 55408, phone: 612-823-6161, e-mail: dream@dreamhavenbooks.com

Edwards, Bruce:
 22319 Delia Ct., Calabasas, CA 91302, phone: 818-591-2699

Faulkner, Brendan:
 PO Box 2925, Danbury, CT 06813, phone: 203-790-8235

Graham Holroyd Books:
 31 Lancer Pl., Webster, NY 14580, e-mail: gholroyd@rochester.rr.com

Green Lion Books (Mark Goodman):
 2402 University Ave. W., St. Paul, MN 55114, phone: 651-644-9070, e-mail: neonjungle22@aim.com

Gryphon Books (Gary Lovisi):
 PO Box 209, Brooklyn, NY 11228, website: www.gryphonbooks.com; e-mail: GryphonBooks@worldnet.att.net

Hackathorn, Art:
 701 Harlan St., Unit E-72, Lakewood, CO 80214, phone: 303-238-8918

Halegua, Richard:
 PO Box 46454, Las Vegas, NV 89114, phone: 702-233-3553, website: www.comic-art.com

Hang Fire Books (William Smith):
 phone: 718-344-8256, e-mail: HangFireBooks@earthlink.net

Heroes & Legends (Myron Cohen Ross):
 18034 Ventura Blvd. #204, Encino, CA 91316, phone: 818-342-2800, e-mail: heroesross@aol.com

James Madison – Bookseller:
 PO Box 20331, Santa Barbera, CA 93120, phone: 805-687-1120, e-mail: sbjamcher@verizon.net

Jeff Page Books:
 30 Manor Rd., St. Catherines, Ontario, L2H-3B5, Canada, phone: 905-646-8268, e-mail: bkscout@cogeco.ca

Kayo Books (Ron Blum):
 814 Post St., San Francisco, CA 94109, phone: 415-749-0554, e-mail: kayo@kayobooks.com

Little Old Bookshop (Brett Brezniak):
 6546 Greenleaf Ave., Whittier, CA 90601, phone: 562-698-1934

Lynn Munroe Books:
 PO Box 1736, Orange, CA 92856, phone: 714-633-3333, e-mail: lumunroe@pacbell.net, website: http://lynnmunroebooks.tripod.com

L. W. Curry Books (Lloyd Currey):
 203 Water St., Elizabethtown, NY, phone: 518-873-6477

Martin Blank Books:
 220 St. Mary's Rd., Winnipeg, Manitoba, R2H-1JB, Canada, e-mail: mblank@mts.net, website: www.booksendsusedbooks.com

Massoglia Books (Marty & Alice Massoglia):
 19801 Vanowen Unit C, Canoga Park, CA 91306, e-mail: martysbooks@pacbell.net

Modern Age Books (Jeff Canja):
 PO Box 325, East Lansing, MI 48826, phone: 517-351-1932

Murder By the Book (Kevin Barbero):
 1645 Warwick Ave., STE 202, Warwick, RI 02889, e-mail: knbooks1@cox.net

Murder One Books (Maxim Jakubowski):
 76-78 Charing Cross Rd., London, WC2H-0BE, U.K., e-mail: murderone.mail@virgin.net

Mystery & Imagination (Malcolm & Christine Bell):
 238 N. Brand Blvd., Glendale, CA 91203, phone: 818-545-0206; e-mail: bookfellows@gowebway.com

Mysterious Bookshop (Otto Penzler):
 58 Warren St., New York, NY 10007, e-mail: info@mysteriousbookshop.com

Old Pueblo Books (Mike Walsh):
 2420 N. Conestoga Ave., Tucson, AZ 85749, phone: 520-760-2745

O'Neill, Terry:
 PO Box 2065, Orange, CA 92859, phone: 714-288-8993, e-mail: terry@nationwidecomics.net

Pattengill, Wally:
 825 Pecos Dr., Waco, TX 76708

Paul Kennedy Books:
 20652 Lassen St., Space 52, Chatsworth, CA 91311, phone: 818-716-9171, e-mail: pkennedybookseller@earthlink.net

Print Matters Used & Rare Books (Bob Riedel):
 42 Washington St., Dansville, NY 14437, phone: 585-335-5332

Second Story Books:
 4914 Fairmont Ave., Bethesda, MD, e-mail: bookguys@secondstorybooks.com

Skyline Books (Rob Warren):
 13 W. 18th St., New York, NY 10011, phone: 212-759-5463, website: skylinebooksnyc.com

Stern, Peter L.:
 55 Temple Pl., Boston, MA 02111, e-mail: psbook@aol.com

Stroud, Terry:
 PO Box 23, Santa Monica, CA 90406, phone: 310-348-7157

Tim Murphy Books:

31 Hewlett Rd., Red Hook, NY 12571, e-mail: timsbks2@citlink.net

Uncle Edgars/Hugos Books (Don Blyly):

2864 Chicago Ave. S., Minneapolis, MN 55407, e-mail: UncleHugo@aol.com

Van Hise, James:

57754 Onaga Tr., Yucca Valley, CA 92284, phone: 760-365-5836, e-mail: jimvanhise@aol.com

Wardzinski, Bob:

12 Rosamund Ave., Merley, Wimbirne, Dorset, BH21-1TE, U.K.

Zardoz Books (Maruice Flanagan):

20 Whitecroft, Dilton Marsh, Westbury, Wiltshire, BA13-4DJ, U.K., website: www.zardozbooks.co.uk

Zimmerli, Andy:

5001 General Branch Ct., Sharpsburg, MD 21782, phone: 301-432-7476

PAPERBACK COLLECTOR SHOWS

The New York Collectible Paperback & Pulp Fiction Expo: Large annual one-day show held in New York City each October, now in its 20th year, presented by Gary Lovisi and GryphonBooks/Paperback Parade magazine, PO Box 209, Brooklyn, NY 11228; for information visit the website: www.gryphonbooks.com.

Paperback Collectors Show and Sale: Large annual one-day show held each year in Los Angeles in March or April; for information contact Tom Lesser at 818-349-3844, tmlesser@aol.com, or Rose Idelt at Black Ace Books at 323-661-5052, roseidlet@aol.com.

Windy City Pulp & Paperback Show: Annual two-day show held in Chicago each March by Doug Ellis, PO Box 45495, Madison, WI 53744; for information visit the website: www.pulpshow.com.

British Paperback Collectors Show: Great one-day show held each year since 1991 in London, usually in November; contact Maurice Flanagan of Zardoz Books for information at his website: www.zardozbooks.com.

OTHER IMPORTANT SHOWS

Pulpcon: Granddaddy of all pulp magazine shows, held annually since the 1970s in Ohio, with many dealers selling collectible paperbacks and other pulp-related items. Contact Rusty Hevlin, PO Box 90424, Dayton, OH 45490, or visit the website at: www.pulpcon.org.

Bouchercon: Annual world mystery convention held at a different city each year; features a varied and well-stocked dealer's room, which also features collectible paperbacks in the mystery genre. Visit the website at: www.bouchercon2008.com.

Worldcon: World Science Fiction Convention held each year in a different city during Labor Day weekend.

San Diego Comic Con: Massive media and comic book illustration event held each July in San Diego, California.

INDEX

ABOUT THE AUTHOR

Gary Lovisi is an MWA Edgar Nominated author for his short fiction as well as the author of many non-fiction articles, interviews, and bibliographies about authors, artists, and collectible paperback books of all kinds. He has been the editor of *Paperback Parade* magazine for over 20 years, the field's leading publication on collectible paperbacks. He is also the sponsor of the Collectible Paperback & Pulp Fiction Expo, an annual book show held in New York City now in its 20th year, which attracts dealers from all over the country. Under his Gryphon Books imprint, he publishes many book-related collector publications. His articles on paperbacks and other collectible books have appeared in *Mystery Scene, Firsts, Illustration, Illustration '05, Crime Time, Shots, Blood N Thunder,* and many other magazines. Find out more at his website: www.gryphonbooks.com.

Photo by Laura Cali

DECIPHER THE DETAILS OF YOUR
COLLECTIBLE BOOKS WITH ACCURACY

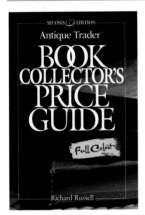

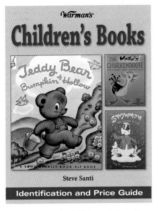

Antique Trader® Book Collector's Price Guide
2nd Edition
by Richard Russell
This full-color edition covers a variety of books, from Americana to science fiction, including 6,000+ updated values, rarity listings, and pseudonym guide.
Softcover • 6 x 9 • 448 pages
1,000 color photos
Item# ATBK2 • $24.99

Warman's® Children's Books
Identification and Price Guide
by Steve Santi
Access updated secondary market pricing, historical details, color photos of covers, collecting tips for favored childhood fables from Golden Books, See Saw Books, Tell-A-Tale books and more.
Softcover • 8¼ x 10⅞ • 256 pages
2,500+ color photos
Item# Z0731 • $24.99

Warman's®
Little Golden Books®
Identification and Price Guide
by Steve Santi
Features secondary market pricing, tips for determining condition of a book, 2,000+ color photos for accurately identifying everything from vintage Little Golden to hip Little Golden Activity books.
Softcover • 8¼ x 10⅞ • 256 pages
2,000 color photos
Item# Z0335 • $24.99

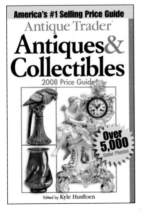

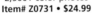

Antique Trader® Vintage Magazines Price Guide
by Richard Russell
and Elaine Russell
Covers magazines of the 1830s to post-WWII, including favorites like the Saturday Evening Post. Features more than 1,000 color photos, plus listings with -categories and updated pricing.
Softcover • 6 x 9 • 304 pages
1,000 color photos
Item# MGZ1 • $19.99

Antique Trader® Antiques & Collectibles 2008 Price Guide
24th Edition
by Kyle Husfloen
Unmatched expert pricing and more than 5,000 spectacular color photos (more than any other price guide), plus facts and identifying figures for 12,000+ listings in this up-to-date price and identification must-have.
Softcover • 6 x 9 • 1,008 pages
5,500 color photos
Item# Z0928 • $19.99